MW01107080

Virginia Woolf, Jean Rhys, and the Aesthetics of Trauma

Virginia Woolf, Jean Rhys, and the Aesthetics of Trauma

Patricia Moran

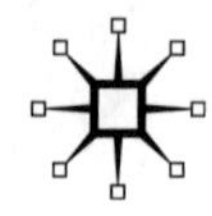

VIRGINIA WOOLF, JEAN RHYS, AND THE AESTHETICS OF TRAUMA

First published in 2007 by
PALGRAVE MACMILLAN™
175 Fifth Avenue, New York, N.Y. 10010 and
Houndmills, Basingstoke, Hampshire, England RG21 6XS.
Companies and representatives throughout the world.

PALGRAVE MACMILLAN is the global academic imprint of the Palgrave Macmillan division of St. Martin's Press, LLC and of Palgrave Macmillan Ltd. Macmillan® is a registered trademark in the United States, United Kingdom and other countries. Palgrave is a registered trademark in the European Union and other countries.

ISBN-10: 1-4039-7482-9
ISBN-13: 978-1-4039-7482-2

Library of Congress Cataloging-in-Publication Data is available at the Library of Congress.

A catalogue record for this book is available from the British Library.

Design by Macmillan India Ltd.

First edition: January 2007

10 9 8 7 6 5 4 3 2 1

Printed in the United States of America.

Contents

Acknowledgments

I would like to acknowledge here the unwavering support and friendship of a number of my colleagues at the University of California, Davis. First and foremost, I thank Joanne Feit Diehl for the almost daily conversations that helped me work through my ideas and interpretations; I could not have written this book without her. Liz Constable, Sandra Gilbert, Michael Hoffman, Kari Lokke, and Alan Williamson all read portions of the manuscript and provided helpful suggestions and advice. I thank David Van Leer for cheering me on and cheering me up; he has been a friend from the very beginning. I owe a special debt to Ray Waddington, whose belief in me has been steadfast. Ray and his wife, Kathie, provided food, encouragement, and conversation and made my family their own; I am deeply grateful for their efforts on my behalf.

I am fortunate to share my interest in Jean Rhys and Virginia Woolf with a lively and supportive community of scholars; I single out for special thanks Eileen Barrett, David Eberly, Jane Garrity, Tamar Heller, Suzette Henke, Mark Hussey, Jane Lilienfeld, Judith Raiskin, and Anne Simpson. Georgia Johnston read the entire manuscript and offered crucial suggestions for improvement. I am also grateful to the members of the University of California Interdisciplinary Psychoanalytic Consortium, where I first presented early versions of some of this work; Jerry Neu, Gabrielle Schwab, and Victor Wolfenstein have been more helpful than they know. To Helene Moglen I am particularly indebted: she has not only read my work with meticulous care; she has been the very model of feminist mentor and colleague.

I wish to thank a number of my former students, whose insight and enthusiasm has helped me bring this work into being. I feel lucky to have worked with Erica Johnson, who has shared my love of Woolf and Rhys. Emily Blair has encouraged me in ways too numerous to mention; her good humor and good sense are deeply appreciated. Cathy Cunningham always had time to help me think through the dark emotional landscapes I examine here. Glenn Keyser and Anjali Williams showed me aspects of Jean Rhys I would never have discovered for myself. Laura Konigsberg and Alice McClean discussed this book over numerous cups of coffee. All have made teaching a joy rather than a job.

I thank the University of California, Davis, for its continuing research support, particularly the award of a Faculty Development Grant in 2001–2002 that made it possible for me to visit the Jean Rhys Collection at the University of Tulsa's McFarlin Library. Then head curator Lori N. Curtis made that time truly enjoyable; I thank her for her hospitality.

Finally, I wish to thank the people who have lived with me as well as with this book. Andrea Cohen and Heidi Riddle have been exemplary models of strength and fortitude. Katherine Karnaky cheerfully made dinner, supervised homework, and chauffeured children, making it possible for me to work. Above all, I must thank my family. David and Patrick daily remind me that there is life outside of work. I dedicate this book to them.

Portions of this book have already appeared in print and have benefitted from the suggestions of many readers. A very early version of chapter 2 appeared as "'The Cat Is out of the Bag and It Is a Tom': Desmond MacCarthy and the Writing of *A Room of One's Own*," in *Essays on Transgressive Reading: Reading Over the Lines*, ed. Georgia Johnston (Edwin Mellen Press, 1997). I thank Wendy Martin for permission to reprint portions of a version of chapter 2 that appeared as "'Cock-a-doodle-dum': Sexology and the Writing of *A Room of One's Own*," which appeared in *Women's Studies: An Interdisciplinary Journal* 30 (2001): 477–498. A shorter version of chapter 3, "The Flaw in the Centre: Writing as Hymenal Rupture in Virginia Woolf's Work," appeared in *Tulsa Studies in Women's Literature* 17, no. 1 (Spring 1998): 101–121; I thank former editor Holly Laird and the University of Tulsa for permission to reprint portions of that essay here. An early draft of chapter 4 appeared as "Gunpowder Plots: Narrative and Sexual Trauma in Virginia Woolf's Work," in *Virginia Woolf Out of Bounds*, ed. Jessica Berman (Pace University Press, 2002).

List of Abbreviations

Jean Rhys

ALMN	*After Leaving Mr. Mackenzie*
GMM	*Good Morning, Midnight*
LJR	*The Letters of Jean Rhys*
Q	*Quartet*
SP	*Smile Please: An Unfinished Autobiography*
VD	*Voyage in the Dark*
WSS	*Wide Sargasso Sea*

Virginia Woolf

BTA	*Between the Acts*
CDB	*The Captain's Death Bed and Other Essays*
D	*The Diary of Virginia Woolf (5 vols.)*
L	*The Letters of Virginia Woolf (6 vols.)*
MD	*Mrs. Dalloway*
O	*Orlando*
P	*The Pargiters: The Novel-Essay Portion of* The Years
R	*A Room of One's Own*
S	"A Sketch of the Past"
TG	*Three Guineas*
TTL	*To the Lighthouse*
W	*The Waves*
W&F	*Women and Fiction: The Manuscript Versions of* A Room of One's Own
W&W	*Women and Writing*
Y	*The Years*
VO	*The Voyage Out*

CHAPTER 1

Experiences as a Body: Virginia Woolf, Jean Rhys, and the Aesthetics of Trauma

"[The adventure of] telling the truth about my own experiences as a body, I do not think I solved. I doubt that any woman has solved it yet."

Virginia Woolf, "Professions for Women"

"These places of possibility within ourselves are dark because they are ancient and hidden; they have survived and grown strong through that darkness. Within these deep places, each one of us holds an incredible reserve of creativity and power, of unexamined and unrecorded emotion and feeling. The woman's place of power within each of us is neither white nor surface; it is dark, it is ancient, and it is deep."

Audre Lorde, "Poetry Is Not a Luxury"

Some years ago, the poet Audre Lorde challenged women to examine the relationship between the erotic and female creativity. By "erotic" Lorde meant much more than genital sexuality; among other things, she defined it as a source of power, "a resource . . . firmly rooted in the power of our unexpressed or unrecognized feeling," "a measure between the beginnings of our sense of self and the chaos of our strongest feelings" ("Uses of the Erotic," 53, 54). The erotic functioned variously, as the "*yes* within ourselves"; as a sensual "lifeforce" informing all levels of our experience; as a well of replenishment and empowerment; as a bridge that allows intersubjective communication (55); and as a lens through which "we scrutinize all aspects of our existence" and "evaluate those aspects honestly in terms of their relative meaning within our lives" (57). Lorde's most compelling image of the erotic gestures to its power to pervade every aspect of female existence: she figures the erotic as akin to the tiny pellet of intense yellow food coloring that was used to color margarine during World War II: "I find the erotic such a kernel within myself. When released from its intense and constrained pellet, it flows through and colors my life with a kind of energy that heightens and sensitizes and strengthens all my experience" (57).[1] Because of its empowering and replenishing aspects, women have "been taught to suspect this resource, vilified, abused and devalued within western society," (53), Lorde wrote; "The erotic has often been . . . used against women. It has been made into the confused, the trivial, the psychotic, the plasticized sensation. For this reason, we have often turned away from the exploration and consideration of the erotic as a source of power and information" (54). Still, Lorde urged women to take up the challenge of accessing the erotic: "[W]e must never close our eyes to the terror, to the chaos which is Black which is creative which is female which is dark which is rejected which is messy which is sinister, smelly, erotic, confused, upsetting" (101).

Lorde's womanifesto of the erotic serves as a useful point of departure for this study of the intersections of modernism, female sexuality, and subjectivity in the work of Virginia Woolf and Jean Rhys. For they, too, discovered the pervasive power of the erotic: over the course of their writing career, both Woolf and Rhys confront those aspects of their individual culture and personal history that had resulted in a degraded sense of female sexuality. In particular, each writer explored the ways in which traumatic childhood sexual experiences informed her relationship to female corporeality and to fiction writing: for Woolf, memories of her half-brothers' inappropriate advances, including a memory of standing on a ledge at age six while a half-brother explored her genitals; for Rhys, a memory of a "mental seduction" by a family friend when she was fourteen. Their narratives about these memories—and the fictions and essays through which they recovered and worked through them—are all the more remarkable in that they appeared at a time when Freud's renunciation of the seduction theory had become the authorizing narrative of the origins of psychoanalysis (a narrative Rhys rejected emphatically and explicitly). As Susan Stanford Friedman has noted, the move from realism to modernism "is symptomatically present in (and partially an effect of) these overlapping displacements of psychoanalysis—from hysteria to dreams, from trauma to desire, from 'seduction' theory to the theory of infantile desire, from female to male subject" ("Hysteria, Dreams, and Modernity" 43). Like the women writers Friedman mentions at the end of her essay,

Woolf and Rhys "haunt the history of male modernism with their insistent return to the scenes of phallocentric repression and oedipal longing, with their persistent construction of (an)other scene of female agency and desire" (64). Their insistence on memory as integral to that agency recalls Sidonie Smith's and Julia Watson's claim that by "citing new, formerly unspeakable stories, narrators become cultural witnesses insisting on memory as agency in its power to intervene in imposed systems of meaning" (14–15).

This study began as an analysis of the ways in which Woolf and Rhys inscribed their anxieties about female embodiment in their very efforts to contest patriarchal devaluations of femininity. As my study developed, however, I found a remarkable correlation between Woolf's and Rhys's narrative descriptions of female sexual experience and the characteristics attributed to traumatic experience by scholars working on survivor testimony. I became interested in the gradual emergence of Woolf's and Rhys's painful memories over the course of their writing careers, as each insistently returned to and rewrote these originary scenes of trauma. Above all, I became interested in the ways in which Woolf and Rhys used narrative form to reproduce and aestheticize the characteristics of traumatic memory. As a number of scholars have pointed out, modernist narrative form, with its emphasis on interiority, memory, psychological verisimilitude, and personal isolation, and its development of fragmented, nonlinear plots, provides an ideal medium for the transcription of traumatic experience. The formal rupture of narrative coherence appealed to Woolf and Rhys, who in turn articulated a gendered aesthetics of trauma. I situate this study, then, within a number of overlapping frames: in addition to scholarship on trauma, my work builds upon and extends the influential critical work on modernist female aesthetics developed by Shari Benstock, Rachel Blau DuPlessis, Susan Stanford Friedman, Bonnie Kime Scott, and others. My study also supports and extends the recent feminist work on women's life-writing, catastrophe, and sexual trauma by such scholars as Suzette A. Henke, Miriam Fuchs, and Janice Doane and Devon Hodges. In the following pages, I summarize each of these conceptual frames and situate Woolf's and Rhys's position within them.

****

Current interest in trauma dates back to the early 1990s, when a number of groundbreaking works appeared: Shoshana Felman and Dori Laub's edited volume *Testimony: Crises of Witnessing in Literature, Psychoanalysis, and History;* Cathy Caruth's edited volume

Trauma: Explorations in Memory, a compilation of two issues of *The American Imago;* and Judith Herman's *Trauma and Recovery: The Aftermath of Violence—From Domestic Abuse to Political Terror,* a study that looked at the commonality of traumatic phenomena within divergent populations, including survivors of war, domestic violence, and incest. The field grew apace, with important work generated in psychology, cognitive science, history, and literature, including that of Jennifer Freyd, Bessel A. van der Kolk, Dominick LaCapra, Daniel Schacter, and others. To be sure, trauma studies has an older line of descent. Although the American Psychiatric Association first included post-traumatic stress disorder as an illness in the *Diagnostic and Statistical Manual of Mental Disorders* (DSM) in 1980, earlier diseases such as hysteria and "shell shock" are clearly the disorder's historical antecedents. In many ways, in fact, Freud's work with hysterical women in the late nineteenth century anticipates contemporary theorists' insistence that the victim recovers from the traumatic memory only when s/he is able to integrate the experience into an "organized, detailed, verbal account, oriented in time and historical content" (Herman 177). In his case history of Dora (1905), Freud identified the formal shortcomings of the hysteric's story—its incompleteness and fragmentation, its chronological confusion, its conscious and unconscious omissions—and similarly argued that the "talking cure" of psychoanalysis enabled the hysteric to repeat, to recognize, and to work through the traumatic event. Freud's model of recovery is, arguably, the basis of the narrative focus of therapeutic treatment for trauma. Indeed, recent scholars of autobiography such as Robert Folkenflik speak of the "writing cure that autobiography offers" (11). James Pennebaker similarly shows that the very attempt to articulate painful memories, particularly in what he terms "expressive writing," is what proves efficacious, leading Suzette A. Henke to question the role of the analyst. "Is he or she truly necessary?" Henke asks. "Might the therapeutic power of psychoanalysis reside more in the experience of 'rememory' and reenactment than in the scene of transference posited by Freud?" (xi). From this perspective, Henke develops the concept of "scriptotherapy," which she defines as "the process of writing out and writing through traumatic experience in the mode of therapeutic reenactment" (xii).

Yet while it is indeed true that Woolf and Rhys engage in the kind of scriptotherapy mapped by Henke, they do not, on the whole, work through traumatic events in their fictions. Instead, Woolf and Rhys develop complex ways of representing trauma and its aftermath: indifferent in large part to "working through" the trauma and developing coherent narratives that integrate traumatic events, these two writers seem far more interested in the ways in which traumatic events impinge upon the working of memory, and the ways in which traumatic memories in turn impinge upon the lives of those afflicted by them. In startling ways, moreover, Woolf and Rhys anticipate what physiology did not discover until some 50 or 60 years after their narratives were published. For, as theoretical models of traumatic memory make clear, traumatic memory differs from what theorists label "narrative memory"; the latter consists of, according to Bessel A. van der Kolk and Onno van der Hart, "mental constructs, which people use to make sense out of experience" (160); ordinary events can typically be integrated into subjective assessment almost automatically, without conscious awareness. Traumatic events, however, cannot: "Existing meaning schemes may be entirely unable to accommodate frightening experiences, which causes the memory of these experiences to be stored differently and not be available under ordinary conditions: it becomes dissociated from conscious awareness and voluntary control" (160).[2] Given the rush of adrenaline that characteristically attends traumatic events, these memories are stored in a different part of the brain—and stored differently. Traumatic events persist as preverbal "body memories" that resist narration: they recur as incomprehensible and intrusive memory fragments that are almost hallucinatory in their intensity. These memories remain "wordless and static" (Herman 175). Indeed, the trauma story is "'prenarrative.' It does not develop or progress in time, and it does not reveal the storyteller's feelings or interpretations of events" (175). Trauma stories instead feature "fragmented components of frozen imagery and sensation" that possess iconic, visual qualities. And while narrative memory is a social act, "traumatic memory is inflexible and invariant. [It] has no social component; it is not addressed to anybody, the patient does not respond to anybody; it is a solitary activity" (van der Kolk and van der Hart 163; see also Culbertson).

Both Woolf and Rhys develop narrative forms that reproduce these characteristics. Obviously their texts are neither preverbal nor prenarrative; however, the use of stream of consciousness techniques, monologues, and first-person narrators enables these writers to move away from conventional linear forms and to mimic instead the gaps, sudden shifts of perspective, and selective personal registers typical of traumatic narrative. As in the models of traumatic memory, highly visual, intrusive fragments of "past time" frequently rupture the narrative "present" and thereby compel characters to reexperience vivid, unwelcome disasters. Hence Septimus Smith, the traumatized war veteran in

Woolf's *Mrs. Dalloway,* finds himself confronted with exploding bombs as he walks down a London street, "as if some horror had come almost to the surface and was about to burst into flames" (15).[3] In some instances, relatively mundane actions provoke the terrifying return of unintegrated memory fragments, as when a man's kiss in Woolf's *The Voyage Out* terrorizes the young female protagonist; her dreams that night become nightmares of entrapment within a damp tunnel or vault: "[S]he found herself trapped . . . alone with a little deformed man who squatted on the floor gibbering, with long nails. His face was pitted and like the face of an animal" (77). Like trauma survivors, characters may try to defend themselves from the onslaughts of traumatic recall by becoming emotionless and robotic. The protagonist of Jean Rhys's *Good Morning, Midnight* deliberately sets out to remake herself into an "automaton" (her term); she creates a schedule for every hour so that she leaves no room for "gaps," her term for the times when her attention wanders and distressing memories return. Many of Woolf's and Rhys's characters resemble trauma victims in the ways in which they suffer from despair, from profound isolation, from the crippling inability to narrate their stories. "To communicate is health," Septimus thinks at one point; yet his suicide is the only effective message he manages to send (and, tellingly, only Clarissa Dalloway "receives" his message).

It is my contention that both Woolf and Rhys arrived at the recognition of the importance of sexual trauma through the writing of a watershed book in which key aspects of these early, repudiated experiences resurfaced. For Woolf, that book was *A Room of One's Own,* where she confronted explicitly the misogynistic claim that women's artistry could never equal that of men's because of their biological inferiority. Despite the book's at times unconscious concurrence with such claims, writing it would prove salutary for Woolf, freeing her critical voice—"I seem able to write criticism fearlessly. Because of a R. Of ones Own I said suddenly to myself last night" (*D*4 25)—and bringing her the unlikely friendship of the suffragette composer Ethel Smyth. This friendship in turn would enable Woolf to develop a female symbolic wherein she confronted her sense that writing for women was an unchaste activity, one associated with the rupture of a virginal hymen or seal of silence—a rupture she associated with her own molestation.[4] Through her friendship with Smyth, Woolf reappropriated the figure of the ruptured hymen, redefining it instead as the emblem of female creativity. Woolf returned to the site of sexual trauma she had abandoned after *The*

Voyage Out in her fiction of the 1930s and 1940s; her last works—*The Years, Three Guineas,* and *Between the Acts*—explore the gaps and lacunae that result from the shame and sexual trauma that attended middle-class female acculturation.

Rhys's accessing of trauma took a somewhat different path. Her most productive period of writing took place in the 1930s, the decade in which she published four of her five novels. Although these novels differ considerably, numerous critics have read them as depicting a composite character, the "Rhys woman," whose passivity, dependency, and self-destruction have drawn much commentary.[5] I read the similarities in these novels through the lens of contemporary work on trauma and memory: Rhys's novels are not "about" trauma; rather, they perform or stage trauma through the manipulation of narrative elements.[6] *Good Morning, Midnight,* Rhys's final novel of the decade and "the last love adventure of a woman who is growing old" (cited in Thomas 27), occupies the same position in Rhys's oeuvre that *A Room of One's Own* occupies in Woolf's: that is, it functions for Rhys as a watershed text, demarcating two distinct phases of her literary production and her understanding of female sexuality.[7] The writing of *Good Morning, Midnight* brought Rhys face-to-face with a need to explore the source of the "doom" that compels her characters to their self-destructive ends. That exploration took Rhys back to her childhood in Dominica and the experience of sexual seduction that had gone out of her memory "like a stone." In the unpublished Black Exercise Book, Rhys challenged the Freudian dismissal of sexual trauma as a hysterical fiction designed to disguise infantile desire; instead, Rhys explores the way in which this mental seduction serves as the origin of her fascination with the plots of erotic domination and romantic thralldom.[8] Significantly, Rhys located her vulnerability to this seduction as having its source in her relationship with her abusive mother. After writing out her memories in the Black Exercise Book, Rhys went on to contextualize the trauma narratives of her early fiction: in what is widely believed to be her masterpiece, *Wide Sargasso Sea,* Rhys shows how Antoinette's masochistic sensibility grows out of her early experiences of maternal repudiation and indifference.

Any study of sexual trauma and recovered memory inevitably conjures up the contemporary controversy of Recovered Memory Syndrome.[9] It is important to keep in mind that the latter refers to memories that have emerged in the process of psychological therapy in a contemporary climate which has developed specialized narrative paradigms for recognizing and understanding childhood sexual abuse. As Marita Sturken points out,

> Recovered memories are not produced in isolation. Rather, they emerge in dialogue with a therapist, or in the context of a therapy group, where testimony falls not on silence but on affirmation. This dynamic draws on the legacy of early second-wave feminism, in which women's consciousness-raising groups allowed women to voice their concerns and struggles in a space where they would not be judged or dismissed. It is also the progeny of the current preoccupation with confession in popular culture, from tabloid journalism to the public testimony of radio and television talk shows. (236)

In their study of incest narratives and their production in relation to historical contexts, cultural politics, and conditions for reception, Janice Doane and Devon Hodges devote a chapter to accounts written in the late nineteenth and early twentieth centuries, "in which women manage to narrate incestuous experiences even before those experiences are given the name *child abuse* or *incest*" (5). "These new interpreters of experience," they explain, "create a space for telling that is almost ghostly, so tenuous is its authority and its claim to be something other than an assault on public morality" (5). Doane and Hodges demonstrate how women have found multiple ways to "tell incest"; they liken incest narratives to fault lines, "where the unsayable disrupts a dominant paradigm for telling" (9). Sexual abuse occupies a similar space in Woolf's and Rhys's fictions and life-writing: simultaneously spectral and disruptive, the unsayable assumes aesthetic properties in its symptomatic narrative effects. Hence the psychoanalytic mechanisms of repression, dissociation, denial, and repetition are key in deciphering the pressure of the unsayable. Significantly, both Woolf and Rhys write in very self-conscious ways about memory and censorship; both use remembering and forgetting as aesthetic tools, deliberately textualizing and drawing attention to the processes of memory retrieval and erasure.[10] Indeed, an admonitory refrain—"What we must remember; what we would forget"—echoes throughout Woolf's last novel, *Between the Acts,* pointing to the fragmentary and censored history of violence against women that undergirds the present day of the novel.

In arguing that sexual trauma is a crucial means of understanding Woolf's and Rhys's particular combinations of content and form—resulting in such formal strategies as noncanonical narrative gaps; rupture and fragmentation of meaning; censored portions; conflations of past and present; undermined chronology; and in Rhys's case, what I term a masochistic aesthetic—I build upon and extend a considerable body of criticism on female aesthetics and modernist women writers.[11] In fact, it was Woolf herself, together with Dorothy Richardson and Gertrude Stein, who initiated this line of inquiry.[12] Woolf's well-known assessment of Dorothy Richardson's achievement—"She has invented, or if she has not invented, developed and applied to her own uses, a sentence which we might call the psychological sentence of the feminine gender. It is of a more elastic fibre than the old, capable of stretching to the extreme, of suspending the frailest particles, of enveloping the vaguest shapes" (*W&W* 191)—remains a succinct and subversive claim that narrative functions as an ideological site and that formal strategies can, therefore, function as acts of contestation and resistance. Woolf seemingly goes on to downplay the radical implications of this claim, stating that Richardson's sentence is a "woman's sentence . . . only in the sense that it is used to describe a woman's mind who is neither proud nor afraid of anything that she may discover in the psychology of her sex" (191). But as Rachel Blau DuPlessis observes, the "woman's sentence" "is Woolf's shorthand term for a writing unafraid of gender as an issue, undeferential to male judgment . . . [It] will thus be constructed in considered indifference to the fact that the writer's vision is seen as peculiar, incompetent, marginal" (33).

Woolf's meditation on the fictional woman writer Mary Carmichael's novel *Life's Adventure* in *A Room of One's Own* has been similarly influential. "Mary is tampering with the expected sequence," the narrator complains of Mary's novel. "First she broke the sentence; now she has broken the sequence. . . . the expected order. Perhaps she had done this unconsciously, merely giving things their natural order, as a woman would, if she wrote like a woman. But the effect was somehow baffling; one could not see a wave heaping itself, a crisis coming around the next corner" (81, 91). In a chapter whose title—"Breaking the Sentence; Breaking the Sequence"—alludes to this passage, DuPlessis explains that "breaking the sentence" "rejects not grammar especially, but rhythm, pace, flow, expression: the structuring of the female voice by the male voice, female tone and manner by male expectations, female writing by male emphasis, female writing by existing conventions of gender—in short, any way in which dominant structures shape muted ones" (32). DuPlessis's chapter title in turn inspired the title of a collection of essays devoted to women's experimental fiction, *Breaking the Sequence*, edited by Ellen G. Friedman and Miriam Fuchs. Here too the passage on Mary Carmichael plays a key role in the editors' delineation of a tradition of women's writing. Calling Mary Carmichael's *Life's Adventure* Woolf's "most prophetic and far-reaching proposal for a new fiction," Friedman and Fuchs, like DuPlessis, identify "breaking the sequence" as a means of voicing the concerns of the marginalized: "To break the sequence is to rupture conventional structures of meaning . . . in order to give presence and voice to what was denied and repressed. The implications of breaking the sequence extend to nearly all of experimental fiction. . . . Woolf provided instruction and strategies for feminine narrative" (15). Kathy Mezei's edited volume *Ambiguous Discourse: Feminist Narratology and British Women Writers* also locates Woolf centrally in its exploration of how women's narrative choices produce female aesthetics. Five out of the twelve essays are devoted to Woolf, a dominance Mezei explains thus: "Because Virginia Woolf wrote so incisively and passionately about the importance of breaking the sentence and the sequence in recognition of writing 'like a woman,' and about the patriarchal hold over women's lives and over the novel form, she rests at the center of this collection" (13).

In addition to playing an important role in identifying narrative conventions as a site of ideological formations, Woolf figures centrally in virtually all critical studies of modernism and female aesthetics.[13] I will highlight here those that intersect most closely with my work. Both Lucio P. Ruotolo and Toni McNaron have written about the dialectic between wholeness and rupture that characterizes Woolf's aesthetic. Ruotolo terms this dialectic the pattern of the "interrupted moment." "A choreography for Woolf's fiction inevitably develops from the rhythm of broken sequence," he writes. "Woolf's own culturally derived disposition to create 'weathertight' castles, art forms that stand above refutation, moves her to collaborate in undercutting her own design. Only when existing structures lose centrality and become, in her idiom, porous and transparent, does nature in some mysterious way inspire experimental ventures" (2, 7). Ruotolo's central thesis, that Woolf became more willing to confront the forces of disorder in constructing her late narrative structures, is persuasive, but he leaves unaddressed the question of female sexuality and its containment and arrogation, a question that preoccupied Woolf in her last works. The "interrupted moment" is, moreover, in essence an expression of traumatic experience. As Toni McNaron points out, Woolf's writings on artistry demonstrate "the profound ambivalence behind [her] reliance on art to provide her with an order unavailable in life":

> Her narrative technique (i.e. "making-up" from moments of sharp recall or impression) could afford her the solace from the nightmarish

> world originating from her personal abuse as well as from the fragmentation of modern life. . . . By insisting on a nonlinear, spontaneous, and psychological approach to writing, she made herself vulnerable to the very scenes and memories her more rational self was attempting to control through artistic composition. (251)

McNaron cites as exemplary the following passage from "A Sketch of the Past": "We are sealed vessels afloat on what it is conventional to call reality; and at some moments, the sealing matter cracks; in floods reality; that is these scenes—for why do they survive undamaged year after year unless they are made of something permanent?" (S 122). McNaron comments:

> [T]hese vessels do not offer reliable protection, and when their glue cracks, a flood occurs which obviously threatens to drown the person inside. This latter conceit of a shell which promises to hold off chaos and danger is strikingly similar to Woolf's view of art itself. That her vessel in this passage is actually permeable and destructable points to a fragility or illusion at the base of her metaphor and its larger analogue, the constructed world of art. (253)

Yet here McNaron overlooks the value Woolf assigns the porous and transparent, a value that enabled her to develop, in her friendship with Ethel Smyth, a way of conceiving of a creative female imaginary, expressed paradigmatically in the ruptured hymenal membrane. Hence while, like McNaron, I view Woolf's aesthetic as formed in relation to trauma—I include the deaths of family members as well as sexual abuse as constitutive of that trauma—like Ruotolo I see Woolf as increasingly willing to confront the forces of disorder and trauma. Indeed, writing served Woolf as a form of "scriptotherapy," enabling her to work through painful memories and experiences. She herself famously described her "shock-receiving capacity" as a welcome sign of a "revelation" that she actualizes in words: "It is only by putting it into words that I make it whole; this wholeness means that it has lost its power to hurt me; it gives me, perhaps because by doing so I take away the pain, a great delight to put the severed parts together" (S 72).[14] In creating this dialectic between wholeness and rupture, Woolf often foregrounds gaps, lacunae, and other spaces of silence. Patricia Ondek Lawrence identifies three types of silences in Woolf's writing: the "'unsaid,' something one might have felt but does not say; the 'unspoken,' something not yet formulated or expressed in voiced words; and the 'unsayable,' something not sayable based on the social taboos of Victorian propriety or something about life that is ineffable" (1). I extend Lawrence's brilliant readings of silences in Woolf's fiction to include the silences that surround or inhabit the trauma of sexual violations.

My work on the web of fiction in *A Room of One's Own* also intersects with a considerable body of feminist work on webs and weaving as tropes for female aesthetics. In a critique of Geoffrey Hartman's "The Voice of the Shuttle: Language from the Point of View of Literature," Patricia Klindienst Joplin objects to the universalizing moves that would erase female specificity from the trope of weaving as storytelling: "For the feminist unwilling to let Philomela become universal before she has been met as female, this is the primary evasion," she charges (30); her essay title claims "The Voice of the Shuttle Is Ours." Similarly, in the aptly titled "Arachnologies: The Woman, the Text, and the Critic," Nancy K. Miller, like Woolf, envisions the web as a material site, "the place of production that marks the spinner's attachment to her web" (288). More broadly, Jane Marcus analogizes the web as a form of feminist practice. Procne's ability to read the story of her sister Philomela's rape in the latter's weaving "is a model for a contemporary socialist feminist criticism. It gives us an aesthetics of political commitment to offer in place of current theories based on psychology or in formalism," Marcus writes (*Art and Anger* 215).[15] Bonnie Kime Scott takes the web as one of her primary conceptual modes in her revisionary history of modernism:

> In my web, as in Woolf's, there is the possibility of agency and selection for the weaver, within the structures of cultural and physical demands. Woolf's figure reminds us of the necessity of multiple attachment, making the creation of pattern and the collection of sustenance possible. Despite the supposed modernist preference for wholeness, she declares the completeness of the textual web an illusion. The cultural systems to which the web is, of necessity, attached includes material, psycho-biographical, historical, and epistemological frames. (*Refiguring Modernism,* vol. 1, xx)

As Scott notes, women's webs are often problematic: Ariadne's weaving leads to her death; Philomela's conveys the story of her sexual violation. Another problem-laden weaver is Penelope, whose ingenuous solution of weaving and unweaving her web to stave off her unwelcome suitors makes her an attractive model of subversive creativity and resistance. Hence Susan Stanford Friedman titles her monumental work on H.D. *Penelope's Web: Gender, Modernity, H.D.'s Fiction:*

> Penelope is a weaver. She too is a trickster, *fabric*/ator, spinner of artifice. She too has a story to tell, woven into a weave of wiles. . . . The loom (womb/tomb) is the scene of motion, constant; the site of production, the place of making, unmaking, and remaking the already narrated. Women's work, the space of women's repetitive time. A web of wiles, a ruse that conceals what it reveals in the discourse of (women's) modernity. (1)

Peggy Kamuf invokes Penelope "to give a name to what is at work in a text like *A Room of One's Own*": "I take Penelope as a shuttling figure in power's household, one whose movement between outside and inside, violence and poetry, the work of history and the unworking of fiction may allow us to frame one or two notions about the place of woman's art" (182). As Rachel Bowlby remarks of Kamuf's Penelope, she is "the Penelope silenced by men, but pursuing her deviously interminable work of deferral by daily undoing, who becomes in effect an early woman writer" (180).

In stark contrast to the central role Woolf has played in the genesis and elaboration of modernist female aesthetics, Rhys remains marginal, although she is an increasingly important figure in postcolonial studies.[16] In pairing her with Woolf, I hope to show how her work on representing memory and psychic states places her at the center of modernist debates about female subjectivity and aesthetics. Rhys's painstaking care for form and style deserves commentary: she often characterizes form as a way of containing or holding the turbulent emotional affect of her work. In a letter, for example, Rhys explains, "I've never got over my longing for clarity, and a smooth firm foundation underneath the sound and fury. I've learnt one generally gets this by cutting, or by very slight shifts and changes" (*LJR* 60). This same dichotomy appears in a passage of *Smile Please,* in which Rhys describes herself as a child looking out at the sea, "sometimes so calm and blue and beautiful but underneath the calm—what? Things like sharks and barracudas are bad enough but who knows. . . . Not think about it! I preferred to see it in the distance, the blue, the treacherous sea" (*SP* 71). Not only does this passage feature the dichotomy between surface and depth that pervades Rhys's work—appearing not only in her style but in certain thematic patterns, such as the need for her protagonists to assume protective masks—it features as well the characteristic repudiation and repression of an unpleasant, perhaps unbearable reality. Rhys's characters live in constant fear of the return of the repressed; for this reason, most of her characters experience their lives as a jumble of the past and the present, in which the present is an almost nonexistent space between the horrors of the past and the fear of the future. Rhys's fictional transcriptions of mental states altered by trauma—transcriptions rooted in her own experience of "unreal" and "trance" states of being (*LJR* 71)—require formal containment in order to buffer and to deaden the otherwise unbearable suffering they record. "Anodyne has always been my favourite word," Rhys observes in one letter describing a "trance day" (71); elsewhere she notes of her habit of attending the cinema, "It is a funny form of . . . I cannot remember the word. Anodyne. Lovely lovely word. Anodyne" (*SP* 130). "Anodyne" is a word immensely evocative of Rhys's prose: her style is in effect anodynic, replete with formal mechanisms for controlling pain or keeping it at bay.[17] As Anne B. Simpson notes, "[I]n the painstaking refinement of her aesthetic, she summoned again and again a vision of the psychic terrain as a wild and frightening place whose borders were uncertain and where time stood still" (2); Simpson points to Rhys's habit of cutting "relentlessly, so that she could convey as much as possible in the fewest words and rely on implication rather than direct statement . . . The quiet that surrounds the words in her fiction often gives them heightened meaning" (17). Like Woolf's would-be writer in *The Voyage Out,* then, Rhys's style enables her to gesture toward silence and the things people don't—or perhaps can't—say.

By examining the process by which Woolf and Rhys accessed traumatic sexual experiences and incorporated them in their narratives, my work intersects with that of several other critics working on women's life-writing and fiction as a medium for traumatic or catastrophic inscription. I have been much influenced by Suzette Henke's formulation of scriptotherapy. As Henke writes, "The act of life-writing serves as its own testimony and, in so doing, carries through the work of reinventing the shattered self as a coherent subject capable of meaningful resistance to received ideologies and of effective agency in the world" (xix). I am also indebted to Miriam Fuch's insightful work on women's narrative approaches to catastrophe: the women in her study use writing as a means of "seeking safer ground and ultimately survival. Consequently they pursue narrative scripts that offer glimpses of reconciliation as well as means of resistance or protest" (4). I have also found Janice Doane and Devon Hodges's analysis of incest narratives in *Telling Incest* enormously useful. Doane and Hodges show how narrative conventions shape not only what can be told but what can be heard, an insight that my work on the dichotomy between private life-writing and public fictions readily supports. Their work on incest survivors' memoirs also makes clear that sexual trauma has long-lasting, damaging effects: "These . . . stories . . . make visible the difficulty of remembering and forgetting . . . With the acknowledgment of lasting trauma in these new tellings also comes an increased understanding and analysis of the limitations of language, and, therefore, of the inevitability of uncertainty, paradox, and reconstruction in giving public expression to private wounds" (8). Although they are speaking of contemporary memoirs here, these words apply equally to Woolf and Rhys, who similarly write of the uncertainty of remembering and the complex desires involved in the act of forgetting.

This study preserves the distinction Woolf and Rhys drew between life-writing intended for self-analysis and fiction produced for a public audience. Woolf's and Rhys's accounts of sexual abuse were private ones, produced as they struggled to define the nature of sexual experience, specifically traumatic experience, in their lives. For both, the point was not to join a community of like-minded sufferers, but to understand the role such experiences had on their approach to corporeality as represented in and through language. Trying to "get it clearer This motif of pain that has gone through all my life," Rhys discovered the source of her "kink" in "the terrible thing . . . the way something in the depths of me said Yes, that is true. Pain humiliation submission that is for me It fitted in with all I knew of life With all Id ever felt It fitted like a hook fit an eye" (cited in Thomas 27, 32; cited in Angier 28). For Woolf, sexual abuse emerged as an important aspect of her disconnection from the female body and corporeal pleasure; her reworking of the ruptured hymen speaks to her need to claim a space for female authority and a female imaginary. This study sets out to examine the arc of each woman's career and the ways in which traumatic sexual experiences inflected those arcs. For in their honest and unflinching depiction of the traumas involved in female sexual experience, both indeed speak to the role of the erotic as "a measure between the beginnings of our sense of self and the chaos of our strongest feelings" (Lorde, "Uses of the Erotic" 54).

****

My study begins with an analysis of *A Room of One's Own*, an essay that powerfully sets out the case for modernist female aesthetics. The first chapter complicates that assessment by juxtaposing Woolf's essay with the sexological literature it originally contested. The *Room* that emerges from such an examination is a vastly more complex document than its canonical status in feminist studies has allowed it to be. In particular, I show how Woolf's essay unconsciously concurs with sexological claims: not only does Woolf persistently image women's writing as watery and diffuse, thus echoing sexologists' claims that women's writing betrays the negative effects of female biology; she also worries that women's books suffer from a mysterious "flaw in the centre," a structural weakness that inscribes the "flaw in the centre" sexologists claimed deformed the female body.

The second chapter builds upon the symptomatic moments I identify in the first chapter, for in the 1930s Woolf began to write explicitly about the conflicts that emerge only sporadically and symptomatically in *A Room of One's Own.* In *Room,* Woolf's imaging of female textuality as inevitably disfigured by rents and tears betrays her unconscious fear that writing for women is an "unchaste" activity that destroys a virginal—hermetically or hymenally sealed—female silence. Through her friendship with the suffragette composer Ethel Smyth, Woolf reassesses the meaning of the ruptured hymen, contesting its patriarchal valuation as a marker of chastity and rewriting it as the threshold of communication between women. This chapter thus explores Woolf's life-writing as a backdrop to her changing assessment of the "flaw in the centre" of the woman writer's fictional web.

After completing *A Room of One's Own,* Woolf planned a revolutionary sequel for which she "collected enough powder to blow up St. Pauls"; yet, in a development that has puzzled many critics, Woolf muted the critique she produced in draft writing such as *The Pargiters.* My third chapter argues that in *The Pargiters, The Years,* and *Between the Acts* Woolf shifts her focus to the ways in which the middle-class woman's acculturation teaches her to censor her physicality, a censorship that typically results not only in female silence about physical experience, but in an atrophied or attenuated relationship to physicality altogether. Woolf's original plan to write "the sexual life of women" becomes instead something we might call the aesthetics of sexual trauma. The middle-class woman in these later works experiences her sexuality within complex and mostly nonverbal codes of shame: in works such as *The Years* and *Between the Acts,* Woolf posits an evolutionary model of traumatic affect, whereby women "inherit" unconscious memory traces—and with those traces a concomitant atrophying of sexual desire and expression.

In my fourth chapter I turn to Rhys's writings on trauma. The writing of *Good Morning, Midnight* at the end of the 1930s brought

Rhys face-to-face with a need to explore the source of the "doom" that compels her characters to their self-destructive ends. The writing of the Black Exercise Book allowed Rhys to recover the memory of her childhood seduction by a family friend, a seduction in which Rhys subordinated the issue of physical contact and insisted instead upon the experience as a "mental seduction." The Black Exercise Book explores the way this "mental seduction" serves as the origin of Rhys's fascination with scenarios of masochistic submission; it also explores how this seduction supersedes even as it recreates and revises the daughter's earlier relationship with an abusive and repudiating mother.

In my last chapter I examine Rhys's fiction within the linked contexts of trauma and masochism. Masochistic submission for the Rhysian character functions as a longing to give up defensive and artificial modes of interaction, "to 'come clean,' as part of an even more general longing to be known, recognized" (Ghent 110).[18] In her later work, moreover, Rhys develops a masochistic aesthetic, one which deploys repetition, suspends and disavows climax, blurs reality and fantasy, and enacts patterns of reversal—an aesthetic that, in dramatizing and exaggerating the relations of submission and dominance, sets up an oppositional site within power hierarchies.

My study concludes with a discussion of how Woolf's and Rhys's narratives and life-writing about sexual trauma provide new sites of locating modernist female aesthetics and new ways of rethinking the retrieval of traumatic memories. What Woolf's and Rhys's texts show is that female modernism takes up female subjectivity at precisely the point that Freud abandoned it, and that women modernists' retrieval and reworking of traumatic stories not only provides motivation for their artistry but enriches considerably our currently impoverished understanding of the uses of and competing claims involved in traumatic memory.

CHAPTER 2

"Cock-a-doodle-dum": Desmond MacCarthy, Sexology, and the Writing of *A Room of One's Own*

"[W]hat is amusing now . . . had to be taken in desperate earnest once. Opinions that one now pastes in a book labeled cock-a-doodle-dum and keeps for reading to select audiences on summer nights once drew tears, I can assure you."

Virginia Woolf, A Room of One's Own

"[A] woman's writing is always feminine; it cannot help being feminine: the only difficulty lies in defining what we mean as feminine."

Virginia Woolf, "Women Novelists"

The most cursory examination of Woolf's discussions of women's fiction reveals her characteristic use of biological figures to delineate "feminine" qualities in writing. In the well-known description of the "woman's sentence," for example, Woolf uses images that evoke a pregnant female body: the "woman's sentence" "is of a more elastic fibre than the old, capable of stretching to the extreme, of suspending the frailest particles, of enveloping the vaguest shapes" (*W&W* 191). More commonly, Woolf falls back on images of fluids and containers to describe women's fictional form. "Energy has been liberated, but into what forms is it to flow?" Woolf asks. Women writers must "try the accepted forms . . . discard the unfit . . . [and] create others which are more fitting"; they must "pour such surplus energy as there may be into new forms without wasting a drop" (67). Often Woolf condemns women's writing as too formless and diffuse: "In the past, the virtue of women's writing often lay in its divine spontaneity . . . It was untaught; it was from the heart. But it was also, and much more often, chattering and garrulous—mere talk spilt over paper and left to dry in pools and blots" (51). A diary entry about Vita Sackville-West's *Passenger to Teheran* similarly finds that "Vita's prose is too fluent. I've been reading it, & it makes my pen run. When I've read a classic, I am curbed &—not castrated: no, the opposite; I cant think of the word at the moment." Woolf goes on to comment that, had she written the book, "I should have run off whole pools of this coloured water" (*D*3 126).

As these pools of colored water suggest, Woolf's images for female writing often point up an anxiety that female corporeality contaminates or impedes artistic achievement. For this reason, *A Room of One's Own* constitutes a crucial turning point in Woolf's thinking about women and fictional form, for in this essay she confronts male sexologists' claims—in particular, those voiced by literary colleagues such as Arnold Bennett and Desmond MacCarthy—that women were biologically incapable of producing great art. *Room*'s narrator, we recall, spends hours in the British Museum; she is aghast at the amount of misogynistic material men have generated about women. The remarkable correspondences between sexological writings and *A Room of One's Own* suggest that Woolf herself had conducted such an investigation. Her account of Judith Shakespeare problematizes the common sexological use of Shakespeare to "prove" women's inferior creativity. *Room,* like many sexological writings, draws distinctions between the writing of poetry and the writing of fiction and speculates about the factors involved in women's early success in writing novels. Finally, *Room,* like sexological accounts, examines how female biology relates to and shapes literary "form."[1] Above all, given Woolf's preoccupation with the damaging effects of censorious men upon women's imaginations, she almost certainly would have found important men's reliance on a sex-based concept of "genius" to dismiss the accomplishments of more talented and productive women writers.

Before turning to that sexological literature, however, I want to examine the genesis of the essay in Woolf's friendship with the literary critic and journalist Desmond MacCarthy. When the narrator pauses to ask her audience, "Are there no men present? Do you promise me that behind that red curtain over there the figure of Sir Chartres Biron is not concealed? We are all women, you assure me?"

(*R* 85), she reminds us that the text in our hands is a book written by a woman for other women. The narrator's mock anxiety functions as an implicit gesture of exclusion and thus as retaliation against the privileged middle-class men who have denied women educational and economic opportunities, exclusions dramatized when the Beadle chases the narrator off the Oxbridge turf and then denies her access to the library in the essay's first chapter. But in fact there were men present and Sir Chartres Biron was hiding behind the curtain during Woolf's writing of *A Room of One's Own:* behind the narrator's manifest insistence upon woman-to-woman communication lurks an uneasy awareness that men are in the audience—men whom Woolf knows, men whom she respects, men whose good opinion matters a great deal indeed. The narrator's stance that "we are all women" is perhaps the essay's most successful fiction, concealing the uneasy tensions and unresolved conflicts that roil beneath the essay's surface charm. Hence *Room* is important not only for its daring articulation of alternative aesthetic models for the production of feminine difference; it also engages Woolf centrally with the questions of self-censorship and silencing that would become hallmarks of her later fiction.

"How visionary censors admonish us"

That Woolf worried obsessively about censorious male auditors is not news: her many discussions of the undermining effect such men have on the woman writer suggest Woolf was painfully aware of her own sensitivity to male disapproval. In a late diary entry, Woolf notes that

> I have been thinking about Censors. How visionary figures admonish us. . . . If I say this So & So will think me sentimental. If that . . . will think me Bourgeois. All books now seem to me surrounded by a circle of invisible censors. Hence their self-consciousness, their restlessness. (*D*5 229)

Woolf's own work demonstrates such self-consciousness and restlessness, as the narrator's naming of Sir Chartres Biron indicates: Sir Chartres Biron had presided over the obscenity trial of Radcliffe Hall's *The Well of Loneliness* in 1928, the year Woolf was writing *Room*. (Hall's book was deemed obscene and censored.) Elsewhere Woolf describes censorious men as the greatest obstacle facing women writers; according to "Professions for Women," they can interrupt or even terminate the woman writer's imaginative engagement with her subject. The chatty intimacy of *A Room of One's Own* thus suggests that an all-woman audience freed Woolf from such writerly constraints: "I get such a sense of tingling & vitality from an evenings talk like that," Woolf reports in her diary after delivering one of the two talks that eventually became *Room*, "one's angularities & obscurities are smoothed & lit" (*D*3 201). Only four years after its publication, however, Woolf recalled *Room*'s audience in a distinctly different light. In a letter to the composer Ethyl Smyth about Smyth's study of women musicians, Woolf urges Smyth to omit personal experiences of discrimination and points to her own practice as an example:

> I didn't write 'A room' without considerable feeling even you will admit; I'm not cool on the subject. And I forced myself to keep my own figure fictitious; legendary. If I had said, Look here am I uneducated, because my brothers used all the family funds which is the fact—Well theyd have said; she has an axe to grind; and no one would have taken me seriously, though I agree I should have had many more of the wrong kind of reader; who will read you and go away and rejoice in the personalities, not because they are lively and easy reading; but because they prove once more how vain, how personal, so they will say, rubbing their hands with glee, women always are; I can hear them as I write. (*L*5 195)

Woolf's use of "they" suggests that she wrote *Room* against a chorus of censorious male voices, a suggestion borne out by her anxiety about her male friends' reaction to the publication of the essay in 1929:

> It is a little ominous that Morgan [E. M. Forster] wont review it. It makes me suspect that there is a shrill feminine tone in it which my intimate friends will dislike. I forecast, then, that I shall get no criticism, except of the evasive jocular kind, from Lytton [Strachey], Roger [Fry] & Morgan; that the press will be kind & talk of its charm, & sprightiness; also I shall be attacked for a feminist & hinted at for a sapphist; Sibyl [Colefax] will ask me to luncheon; I shall get a good many letters from young women. I am afraid it will not be taken seriously. Mrs. Woolf is so accomplished a writer that all she says makes easy reading . . . this very feminine logic...a book to be put in the hands of girls. (*D*3 262)

Woolf's "intimate friends"—Strachey, Fry, and Forster—are men; women's positive reactions do not seem to count. Thus when Woolf worries that "no one would have taken me seriously" or that the essay "will not be taken seriously," she means she worries that *men* will not take her seriously. Women were indeed in the audience, but Woolf clearly cared more about reaching the men who weren't.

Room's origins are complicated.[2] Woolf delivered two talks that form its nucleus—one at Newnham College on October 20, 1928, the other at Girton College a week later. Although no text of either talk survives, they apparently differed. According to a contemporary account by E. E. Phare, the secretary of the Newnham Arts Society, the group that had invited Woolf to speak, the paper Woolf delivered at Newnham was "Women and Fiction." It focused on "domestic architecture" and the masculine bias of "prevailing literary standards." Phare summarized the talk in the college magazine *Thersites*, concluding, "It was a characteristic and delightful lecture and we are most grateful to Mrs. Woolf for coming to us, as well as to Miss Strachey for consenting to preside over the meeting." Her summary has a familiar ring, anticipating the arguments Woolf develops in chapter 4 of *Room*. The talk Woolf delivered at Girton a week later, however, seems to be an early draft of chapter 1. Woolf's diary entry of October 27, 1928, is the only contemporary account of the talk she delivered the day before:

> I am back from speaking at Girton, in floods of rain. Starved but valiant young women—that's my impression. Intelligent, eager, poor; & destined to become schoolmistresses in shoals. I blandly told them to drink wine & have a room of their own. Why should all the splendour, all the luxury of life be lavished on the Julians & the Francises, & none on the Phares & the Thomases? (*D*3 200)

The use of food as a measure of the prosperity of one sex and the poverty of the other in the second talk apparently grew out of a series of meals and dinner parties Woolf attended during the week of the talks. The Woolfs arrived at the Newnham dinner nearly an hour late; according to one attendant, "dinner in Clough Hall, never a repast for gourmets, suffered considerably. Mrs. Woolf also disconcerted us by bringing a husband and so upsetting our seating plan" (Duncan-Jones 14). The next day, Woolf, along with Leonard, Lytton Strachey, and John Maynard Keynes (and possibly E. M. Forster) lunched in the rooms of George "Dadie" Rylands, rooms that "had been decorated by Carrington and overlooked the beautiful Backs of the Cam" (*W&F* xvi). Rylands, a King's fellow, later wrote that he found Woolf's account of the lavish luncheon in *Room* exaggerated:

> [P]artridges *various*? I don't think there could be more than one kind of partridge. And I don't very much like the idea, except that it was very much like college cooking, of a counterpane of sauce with some

> little brown flecks on it. Never mind. And I hope there were *two* wines. I think it unlikely . . . as always with Virginia it is the idealized, the romantic fantasy of what should have been. (Rylands, in J. Noble 175)

When Woolf drove back to Cambridge the following Friday, this time accompanied by Vita Sackville-West, she first called upon her nephew Julian Bell, then in his second year at King's College. Afterwards, she and Vita had dinner with two Girton students at the hotel where the two women were staying. One of the students, Margaret Ellen Thomas, had been responsible for inviting Woolf to speak, but she apparently did not have funds to expend upon dinner: Woolf and Vita paid for themselves. Woolf later reported in her diary that she thought the students "were relieved, not to have to part with quite so many half crowns" (*D*3 204). After dinner, the women toured "the chocolate coloured corridors of Girton, like convent cells" (*D*3 204), a tour that, along with the meals, forms the basis for Woolf's sense of contrast between the "Julians" and the "Thomases."

What emerges from this itinerary is that Woolf's lectures to women students, whom she did not know, came before and after social gatherings with male relatives or with men whom she numbered among her oldest and closest friends. In the diary entry about the hotel meal and Girton tour, in fact, Woolf refers to "Miss Thomas & Miss _____?" (*D*3 204): she cannot remember the name of the other student. While in itself this lapse may not seem significant, it highlights Woolf's sense of distance from the women students who were her hosts. Indeed, what stood out about the talks for the women who recalled them 50 years later was a sense of Woolf's inability to engage with their experiences. M. C. Bradbrook, who stayed on at Girton and eventually became Professor of English, wrote that "we undergraduates enjoyed Mrs. Woolf, but felt that her Cambridge was not ours" (cited by Rosenbaum xviii). Woolf seemed remote and awe-inspiring; U. K. N. Stevenson described her as seeming "absolutely ruthless" (175). The poet Kathleen Raine described Woolf and Sackville-West as goddesses:

> With Virginia Woolf had come her friend Victoria Sackville-West: the two most beautiful women I had ever seen. I saw their beauty and their fame entirely removed from the context of what is usually called "real" life, as if they had descended like goddesses from Olympus, to reascend when at the end of the evening they vanished from our sight. The divine *manna* may belong to certain beings merely by virture of what they are; but *manna* belongs also to certain offices, royal or priestly; and masters in some art were, in those days, invested with the dignity

> of their profession. A "great writer" had about him or about her an inherited glory shed from the greatness of the writers of the past; and about Virginia Woolf this glory hovered. (22)

Women who have published their impressions of Woolf's lectures typically stress their disagreement with her positions. Some of the women felt hurt and embarrassed by what they felt were Woolf's misrepresentations. E. E. Duncan-Jones, who remembered the Woolfs' lateness and Leonard's unexpected appearance as in part responsible for the Newnham dinner's inadequacy, found the publication of *Room* "disquieting": "Her purpose was, of course, to evoke pity for the poverty of the women's colleges: but at the time it made us, her hosts, decidedly uncomfortable" (Duncan-Jones 174–175). Kathleen Raine disagreed not only with Woolf's descriptions of the college's poverty-stricken appearance but with Woolf's thesis that women's writing suffered from such material deprivations:

> [F]rom her famous paper I learned for the first time, and with surprise, that the problems of "a woman writer" were supposed to be different from the problems of a man who writes; that the problem is not one of writing but of living in such a way as to be able to write. . . . I cannot truthfully say that I have ever found that my problems as a writer have been made greater or less by being a woman. The only problem—to write well and to write truly—is the same for either sex. As for time to write, there is always time. (23)

Bradbrook took issue with the style of *A Room of One's Own,* now considered one of the text's most innovative and effective aspects. In "Notes on the Style of Mrs. Woolf," published in the first issue of the Cambridge journal of criticism, *Scrutiny,* Bradbrook excoriated Woolf for her inability to take a position and for resorting instead to "camouflage," camouflage Bradbrook viewed as bad faith, as distasteful, insincere, and artificial feminine wiles:

> [I]t [camouflage] prevents Mrs. Woolf from committing the indelicacy of putting a case or the possibility of her being accused of waving any kind of banner. The arguments are clearly serious and personal and yet they are dramatised and surrounded with all sorts of disguises to avoid an appearance of argument.
>
> . . . the playfulness of *A Room of One's Own* is too laboured. To demand "thinking" from Mrs. Woolf is clearly illegitimate: but such a deliberate repudiation of it and such a smoke screen of feminine charm is surely to be deprecated. (38)

Bradbrook perceptively links the camouflage in *Room* to Woolf's apparent dislike of scholars. Woolf "reserves her heaviest satire" in her novels for Doris Kilman and Charles Tansley, Bradbrook notes, both of whom Woolf depicts as "scholars who have developed the intelligence at the expense of the arts of living" (34). By contrast, Woolf's heroines "live by their social sense," but "[t]heir tact and sensitiveness are preserved in a kind of intellectual vacuum." As evidence, Bradbrook quotes damning phrases from *Mrs. Dalloway* and *To the Lighthouse:*

> Mrs. Dalloway "muddled Armenians and Turks: and to this day, ask her what the Equator was and she did not know." Mrs. Ramsay ponders "A square root? What was that? Her sons knew. She leant on them: on cubes and square roots: that was what they were talking about . . . and the French system of land tenure . . . She let it uphold her, this admirable fabric of the masculine intelligence." Compare the dependence of Mrs. Flanders and even of Lady Bruton. (37–38)

All in all, Bradbrook concludes, "Mrs. Woolf has preserved her extraordinary fineness and delicacy of perception at the cost of some cerebral etiolation" (38).

Raine objected to Woolf's premise that the women's colleges, because of inferior material conditions, were incapable of "lighting the lamp in the spine." She lays particular stress on the women students' sense of special election:

> We were an elect, and of this we were well aware. . . . it was this belief. . . . which has made my own attitude to men in general one of faint intellectual condescension; an attitude of which I only become aware as I remember that all Girtonians believed themselves the mental equals of the best of the men. (18)

Raine also undercuts *Room*'s description of the woman's college as "bare walls raised from bare earth." The lecture took place in Girton's reception-room, she writes, a room hung with imposing "mural panels" of wool embroidery upon ivory satin that depicted "rather heavy foliage and flowers and birds and squirrels for the pleasure of those ladies who were to be educated away from the immemorial and symbolic occupations of Helen, Penelope, Persephone, and Blake's Daughters of Albion" (21). Raine's description of her college room jars with Woolf's account of "chocolate coloured corridors" and "rooms like convent cells":

> [H]ow I loved my College room of my own—two rooms, in fact, a small bedroom and a little sitting-room . . . In the morning, our "gyp"

> brought to each of us a can of hot water, set it in our wash-basin, and covered it with a towel. And we each had a coal-fire (also laid for us daily) and a graceful oval copper kettle, polished on top . . . Each of us had our own desk, writing-chair, arm-chair, and bookshelves, with curtains and covers of fresh clean linen; in many of the rooms still of the original William Morris designs, very old-fashioned it was fashionable to think, in those days when Heal's furniture and the rectilinear style were new. We added, of course, our own touches. (23)

What are we to make of this body of criticism from the original auditors of *A Room of One's Own?* To be sure, all of the writers overlook the fact that *Room* is fiction, not fact; further, the published text inevitably overshadows the writers' memories of the original talks. At the same time, it is impossible to come away from reading the accounts by Raine, Bradbrook, and Phare without concluding, as S. P. Rosenbaum does, that "Woolf may have misjudged her audience" (xvii). These ambitious young women, all of whom went on to distinguished literary and academic careers, may have detected and resented Woolf's dismissive belief, recorded in her diary, that they were "destined to become schoolmistresses in shoals" (*D*3 201). Bradbrook, we recall, went on to connect Woolf's style to her contempt for scholars. None of them shared Woolf's deep sense of academic inadequacy; indeed, the Girton women—Bradbrook, Thomas, and Raine—belonged to an exclusive society modelled upon the Cambridge Conversazione Society, or the Apostles—the elite society to which Woolf's closest male friends and relatives belonged. No wonder these ambitious young women responded to her talks as Queenie Roth, later Leavis, did, as "'crudely'" manifested feminism" (xix). They did not understand the genesis or justification for what Woolf herself would later call her "Victorian manner"; although at some level they understood Woolf was not talking to them, they did not understand that in this case the "surface manner" required their presence as camouflage.

The Victorian Manner of Talking to Men

> *"[T]he Victorian manner is perhaps—I am not sure—a disadvantage in writing. When I read my old* Literary Supplement *articles, I lay the blame for their suavity, their politeness, their sidelong approach, to my tea table training. I see myself, not reviewing a book, but handing plates of buns to shy young men and asking them: do they take cream and sugar? On the other hand, the surface manner allows one, as I have found, to slip in things that would be inaudible if one marched straight up and spoke out loud."*
>
> *Virginia Woolf "A Sketch of the Past"*

Room has another and perhaps in some ways more significant line of descent, one that goes back to Woolf's 1920 quarrel with the journalist Desmond MacCarthy. In order to understand the importance of that quarrel, however, it is necessary to review the long history between the two that preceded their public exchange in the *New Statesman* that year. Woolf had known Desmond MacCarthy since 1905 or 1906; she met him soon after the death of her father and the Stephen siblings' move to Bloomsbury. MacCarthy was one of Thoby Stephen's intimate friends at Cambridge and one of the first regulars at the At Home Thursdays Thoby began to keep in 1905. Like other of Thoby's Cambridge friends—Sydney Saxton-Turner and Lytton Strachey, for example—Desmond MacCarthy was a member of the elite Cambridge intellectual society the Apostles, and, again like Saxton-Turner and Strachey, great things were expected of him. According to Quentin Bell, "MacCarthy seemed even more certain of success than Lytton Strachey":

> [H]e was to be the great English novelist of the twentieth century. His shoulders were ready to accommodate the mantle of Henry James and, hearing him talk—for *he* certainly was not silent—you could not but conclude that he had so charmed and domesticated that intractable creature the English Language that it would do anything for him, give him a force, a range of subtlety that would take him anywhere—into the empyrean if he so wished, and with that, so much native genius and so much good nature. (Bell, 1: 103)

Yet MacCarthy's genius turned out to be his talk, so much so that in an effort to translate his talent to paper, the Woolfs once had Leonard's secretary take down his dinner conversation, only to find the record dull and uninspired (*D*2 120; see also Bell 2: 83). At least two Bloomsbury ventures—the short-lived Novel Club of 1913 and the later Memoir Club—were begun as ways of encouraging MacCarthy to work seriously on a novel. Yet he produced very little fiction, supporting himself instead through literary journalism. Woolf found him a wistful figure:

> His "great Work" (it may be philosophy or biography now, and is certainly to be begun, after a series of long walks, this very spring) only takes shape, I believe, in that hour between tea and dinner, when so many things appear not merely possible but achieved. Comes the daylight and Desmond is contented to begin his article; and plies his pen with a half humourous half melancholy recognition that such is his

> appointed life. Yet it is true, and no one can deny it, that he has the floating elements of something brilliant, beautiful—some book of stories, reflections, studies, scattered about in him, for they show themselves indisputably in his talk. I'm told he wants power; that these fragments never combine into an argument; that the disconnection of talk is kind to them; but in a book they would drift hopelessly apart. Consciousness of this, no doubt, led him in his one finished book to drudge and sweat until his fragments were clamped together in an indissoluble stodge. I can see myself, however, going through his desk one of these days, shaking out unfinished pages from between sheets of blotting paper, and deposits of old bills, and making up a small book of table talk, which shall appear as a proof to the younger generation that Desmond was the most gifted of us all. But why did he never do anything? they will ask. (cited in Bell 2: 81–82)

The "one finished book" Woolf refers to is the appropriately entitled *Remnants* (1918).

Yet despite Woolf's real affection for MacCarthy—"He is the most cooked & saturated of us all. Not an atom remains crude; basted richly over a slow fire—an adorable man, a divine man," she rhapsodizes at one point (*D*3 234–235)—his opinion unfortunately carried immense weight with her, for she found him dismissive, patronizing, and undermining when it came to the subject of women's creativity. In the same diary entry, in fact, she goes on to admit that her affection and enjoyment of his company endured in spite of "his power of taking the spine out of me. Happily we did not get on to that—writing that is to say." Woolf's anxiety about MacCarthy's good opinion steadily increased in the 1920s, a decade in which MacCarthy continued to gain power as a literary critic. As literary editor of the *New Statesman*, a post he assumed in 1920, MacCarthy produced a weekly column on books, writing under the pseudonym "Affable Hawk." In 1928, he became the editor of his own monthly magazine, *Life and Letters*, which he continued to edit through 1933. In the same year that MacCarthy launched *Life and Letters*, he also succeeded Sir Edmund Gosse as the literary columnist of the *Sunday Times*. This inheritance may have carried special resonance for Woolf, for Gosse had been a friend of her father, Sir Leslie Stephen, and was considered "the high priest of the literary establishment, and dispenser of a weekly gospel in the *Sunday Times*" (*D*3 115n4). Woolf's almost automatic reaction of respect is evidenced by her response to his review of the newly recovered diaries of Boswell. "Desmond is being very brilliant," Woolf wrote in her diary, ". . . an odd effect, this disinterment of a mass more of Boswell when one had thought all was known, all settled. And father never knew; & Sir Edmund Gosse is dead" (*D3* 238). MacCarthy's ascension to a literary pantheon of patriarchs is complete.

To some extent, then, Woolf's trepidation about MacCarthy's good opinion is justifiable. As a columnist, he had ample opportunities to comment on women's writing, and in fact he discussed Woolf twice in his *Life and Letters* (August 1928 and December 1929) and reviewed *A Room of One's Own* favorably in the *Sunday Times* on January 26, 1930. Further, his position as editor enabled him to publish Woolf—a mixed blessing indeed, for it also enabled him to critique and reject pieces he found unsuitable. Woolf's diaries demonstrate the oscillations in their relationship—things go well when MacCarthy appreciates Woolf; badly when he doesn't. Woolf basks in his approval:

> Desmond comes in, round as a billiard ball; & this is true of his dear bubbling lazy mind; which has such a glitter & lustre now from mere being at ease in the world that it puts me into a good temper to be with him. He describes, analyses, narrates; does not actually talk. All his blandishments are now active to get articles for "Life & Letters" which comes out in May. I am scarcely flattered to be asked. (*D3* 177–178)

Woolf's obvious enjoyment belies the pose of insouciance she adopts in her concluding line. But as the writing of *A Room of One's Own* shows, MacCarthy's more typical tactic was to criticize the limitations of women's writing; more often than not, Woolf—the better known and clearly more successful writer—was the butt of his attacks.

At this point, we can turn back to the first known quarrel between MacCarthy and Woolf about female creativity, the quarrel conducted in the *New Statesman* in 1920.[3] In September of that year, Arnold Bennett published *Our Women*, in which he argued that "intellectually and creatively man is the superior of woman." The resulting publicity brought it to Woolf's attention. In a diary entry of September 26, 1920, she reports she is "making up a paper upon Women, as a counterblast to Mr. Bennett's adverse views reported in the papers" (*D2* 69). But it was not until MacCarthy reviewed the book favorably in the October 2, 1920, *New Statesman* that Woolf felt compelled to act. MacCarthy agreed with Bennett that "'no amount of education and liberty of action will sensibly alter'" the fact that women's intellectual and creative powers are inferior to those of men; further, Bennett argues—and McCarthy cites him in agreement—that women's "'desire to be dominated is . . . a proof of intellectual inferiority'" (704). Woolf responded with acerbity: how, she demanded, did Affable Hawk account for the increase in both number and skill of women writers from the seventeenth century to the nineteenth?

> When I compare the Duchess of Newcastle with Jane Austen, the matchless Orinda with Emily Bronte, Mrs. Heywood with George Eliot, Aphra Behn with Charlotte Bronte, Jane Grey with Jane Harrison, the advance in intellectual power seems to me not only sensible but immense; the comparison with men not in the least one that inclines me to suicide; and the effects of education and liberty scarcely to be overrated. (*The New Statesman* October 9, 1920, 15)

Had MacCarthy and Bennett genuinely wished to locate a great poetess, Woolf continued, how was it that they had conveniently ignored—or in Bennett's case, dismissed—the legendary accomplishments of Sappho?

Whereas Woolf's first response pointed to the gradual evolution of female excellence, MacCarthy's rebuttal focused the argument much more sharply upon the issue of female genius. In effect he relied upon a common sexological ploy: no woman had ever attained the creative stature of Shakespeare, Beethoven, or Newton and no woman ever would or could, for women were biologically incapable of producing works of genius. This set of beliefs structures MacCarthy's rejoinder to Woolf's materialist arguments. Men of "extraordinary intellectual powers" had been able to overcome the unfavorable conditions Woolf claimed had thwarted creative women, MacCarthy wrote; furthermore, even when women experienced "less unfavorable conditions"—as they did in the fields of literature, music, poetry, and painting—their accomplishments "have hardly attained, with the possible exception of fiction, the highest achievements reached by men." Thus although "a small percentage of women" are equal in abilities to clever men, "they fall short of the few men who are best of all." MacCarthy dismissed Sappho as a fantasm whose reputation was based on mere "fragments" (*The New Statesman,* October 9, 1920, 15–16).

Woolf's rejoinder appeared in the October 16, 1920, *New Statesman;* it is remarkable not only in its anticipation of the arguments of both *A Room of One's Own* and *Three Guineas* but in its now explicit preoccupation with the question of female genius. Pointing to the obstacles still facing women in artistic fields of "less unfavourable" conditions, Woolf writes,

> But, "Affable Hawk" argues, a great creative mind would triumph over obstacles such as these. Can he point to a single one of the great geniuses of history who has sprung from a people stinted of education and held in subjection, as for example the Irish or the Jews? It seems

> to me indisputable that the conditions which make it possible for a Shakespeare to exist are that he shall have had predecessors in his art, shall make one of a group where art is freely discussed and practised, and shall himself have the utmost of freedom of action and experience. Perhaps in Lesbos, but never since, have these conditions been the lot of women. (45–46)

Woolf goes on to attack MacCarthy's use of Isaac Newton as an example of a male genius able to overcome poverty and ignorance. Conceding that Newton "had to encounter about the same amount of opposition that the daughter of a country solicitor encounters who wishes to go to Newnham in the year 1920," Woolf points out that Newton did not face the added discouragement of men like Arnold Bennett, Orlo Williams, or Affable Hawk. Newton, furthermore, possessed the advantage of a tradition, and built upon the work of others: "You will not get a big Newton until you have produced a considerable number of lesser Newtons," Woolf observes.

But male censure is the sore point between the two, and Woolf turns away from her model of artistic Darwinism to address it again:

> [I]t is not education only that is needed. It is that women should have liberty of experience; that they should differ from men without fear and express their difference openly (for I do not agree with "Affable Hawk" that men and women are alike); that all activity of the mind should be so encouraged that there will always be in existence a nucleus of women who think, invent, imagine, and create as freely as men do, and with as little fear of ridicule and condescension. These conditions, in my view of great importance, are impeded by such statement as those of "Affable Hawk" . . . *for a man has still much greater facilities than a woman for making his views known and respected.* (46, emphasis added)

Stung, MacCarthy withdrew from the debate: "If the freedom and education of women is impeded by the expression of my views, I shall argue no longer," he wrote (46).

MacCarthy reneged, however. He repeatedly returned to the topic of female artistry, both in his literary columns and in his sparring conversations with Woolf throughout the 1920s. Woolf reports one such conversation on September 10, 1928, at a time when she was at work on *Room:* "I was amused to find that when Rebecca West says 'men are snobs' she gets an instant rise out of Desmond; so I retorted on him with the condescending phrase about women novelists 'limitations' in Life & Letters" (*D*3 195). That phrase appeared in

MacCarthy's August 1928 review of H. du Coudray's *Another Country:*

> If, like the reporter, you believe that female novelists should only aspire to excellence by courageously acknowledging the limitations of their sex (Jane Austen, and in our own time, Mrs. Virginia Woolf, have demonstrated how gracefully this gesture can be accomplished), Miss du Coudray's first novel may at the outset prove a little disappointing, since here is a writer definitely bent upon the attainment of masculine standards. (*D*3 196n5)

Woolf included not only the anecdote about Rebecca West in *Room* (*R* 35), she included MacCarthy's condescending phrase about women novelists, alluding to it not once but twice (*R* 78, 97). Significantly, although she cites the offending issue of *Life and Letters* in one of *Room*'s only footnotes, Woolf deletes her own name from MacCarthy's parenthetical—a deletion that conceals Woolf's personal affront from most readers, even as it becomes both payback to MacCarthy and an inside joke to Woolf's circle. (MacCarthy was appalled to see his remark quoted in *Room*, and defended himself in the pages of *Life and Letters* by stating his wholehearted admiration of Woolf's work. He went on, however, to applaud again Woolf's recognition of her limitations as a female novelist.)

MacCarthy continued to irk Woolf in the month leading up to her two speaking engagements at the women's colleges. Shortly after the conversation about Rebecca West and the "limitations" of women novelists, Woolf remarks her annoyance with MacCarthy's criticism of her (unspecified) paper's "butterfly lightness"—"How angry I was, how depressed I became," Woolf writes. "Leonard agrees that he has a complex, which leads him to belittle & fondle thus" (*D*3 197). Woolf apparently read "butterfly lightness" as code for feminine froth, for she later challenged Vita Sackville-West's praise of *Room*'s style by stressing the essay's serious purpose and scholarship: "I'm delighted you read my little book, as you call it, dear Mrs. Nick: but although you dont perceive it, there is much reflection and some erudition in it: the butterfly begins by being a loathsome legless grub" (*L*4 101). Sackville-West understood immediately the gendered implications of Woolf's metaphor; she attempted to repair the damage in her BBC broadcast reviewing *Room* by stating that Woolf "enjoys the feminine qualities of, let us say, fantasy and irresponsibility, allied to all the masculine qualities that go with a strong, authoritative brain" (104n2).

MacCarthy made no such concessions. Just days after delivering the second talk at Girton, Woolf wrote that MacCarthy had "destroyed our Saturday walk" (*D*3 203). He is "now mouldy & to me depressing," Woolf complains:

> [H]e is resolute & determined—thats what I find so depressing. He seems to be sure that it is his view that is the right one; ours vagaries, deviations. And if his view is the right one, God knows there is nothing to live for: not a greasy biscuit. And the egotism of men surprises & shocks me even now. Is there a woman of my acquaintance who could sit in my arm chair from 3 to 6.30 without the semblance of a suspicion that I may be busy, or tired, or bored; & so sitting could talk, grumbling & grudging, of her difficulties, worries; then eat chocolates, then read a book, & go at last, apparently self-complacent & wrapped in a kind of blubber of misty self-satisfaction? Not the girls at Newnham or Girton. They are far too spry; far too disciplined. None of that self-confidence is their lot. (203–204)

Woolf goes on to recall how her hosts at Girton seemed relieved when she and Sackville-West paid for their own dinner. Yet if this passage anticipates the connections Woolf will later elaborate in *Room* between poverty and self-assurance—women are spry and self-disciplined, but also starved of food and self-confidence—the vehemence with which Woolf attacks MacCarthy deserves attention. Woolf does not specify the nature of MacCarthy's views, but the context of the entry suggests that they had sparred once again about the nature of women's intellectual and artistic capacities. The charges Woolf brings against MacCarthy—egotism and self-absorption—are in fact the same she had brought against the women students after her return from Girton: "I felt elderly and mature," Woolf wrote in her diary. "And nobody respected me. They were very eager, egotistical, or rather not much impressed by age & repute. Very little reverence or that sort of thing about" (201). Days later, and with MacCarthy as her example, Woolf shifts the charge of egotism from women to men; women are now—*by virtue of their sex*—exempt from the charge.

Woolf's ongoing equation of her "butterfly" or "surface" or "teatable" manner with triviality also surfaces in this entry. For in the same passage as the one attacking MacCarthy's egotism and self-complacency, Woolf records her initial plans for *Room:* "[A] history, say of Newnham or the womens movement, in the same vein [as *Orlando*] . . . I want fun. I want fantasy. I want . . . to give things their caricature value . . . The vein is deep in me—at least sparkling, urgent. But is it not stimulated by applause? over stimulated?" (203). Woolf concludes:

> My notion is that there are offices to be discharged by talent for the relief of genius: meaning that one has the play side; the gift when it is mere gift, unapplied gift; & the gift when it is serious, going to business. And one relieves the other. (203)

"Genius" Woolf defines as the "uncompromising side of me," a more formal mode that garners approval from such trustworthy sources as her sister Vanessa Bell and Bell's fellow painters Roger Fry, Duncan Grant, and Ethel Sands. The "abstract mystical eyeless" mode, moreover, would enable Woolf to correct the vagaries of her playful, talented side. In the same entry Woolf notes that an unnamed reviewer of *Orlando* "says that I have come to a crisis in the matter of style: it is now so fluent & fluid that it runs through the mind like water" (203).[4] Woolf's anxiety about writing in an overly fluent style and her preoccupation with the nature of genius lead, seemingly illogically, to her anger about MacCarthy's self-complacence and dismissiveness.

In fact, Woolf's worry about finding an appropriate outlet for her "gift" and her anger at MacCarthy's dismissiveness are deeply related issues that throw into relief the way in which the cultural, gendered definitions of genius impinged upon and shaped Woolf's thinking about female creativity. For, in order to understand the personal emotion evidenced by the Woolf-MacCarthy exchange—and in order to understand the writing of *A Room of One's Own*—it is necessary to set both exchange and book against the debates about female genius that dominated nineteenth- and early twentieth-century British and European intellectual life, debates that had become increasingly medicalized as scientists and physicians alike relied upon "scientific" evidence to devalue women's intellectual and artistic potential.

Sexology and Female Genius

The term "genius" had been used to devalue British women's artistry as far back as the Renaissance: as Christine Battersby has shown, "The English term . . . was as associated with male sexual and generative powers as the Latin *genius,* which originally meant 'the begetting spirit of the family embodied in the paterfamilias'" (27). Although physicians and other authorities addressed the "problem" of female creativity throughout the eighteenth and nineteenth centuries, the publication of Darwin's *The Descent of Man* in 1871 added "scientific" validation to such arguments and pseudoscientific and pseudomedical articles on female artistry appeared with increasing frequency. Darwin wrote of the 'higher eminence' achieved by males in all activities 'requiring deep thought, reason, or imagination, or merely the uses of the senses and the hands'" (cited in Battersby 118): "If two lists were made of the most eminent men and women in poetry, painting, sculpture, music—comprising composition and performance, history, science, and philosophy, with half a dozen names under each subject, the two lists would not bear comparison," he observed. Women with obvious artistic talent were believed to be "women of the masculine gender."

This rationalization persisted, from Goncourt's often cited maxim "There are no women of genius; the women of genius are men" (e.g., Lombroso in the 1863 *The Man of Genius* and Havelock Ellis in the 1894 *Man and Woman*) to Otto Weininger's claim in 1903 that George Sand, George Eliot, and other gifted women were bisexual or homosexual, evidenced by their "masculine" and "unwomanly" appearances (*Sex and Character* 65–68). Whereas men could be psychically women in Weininger's scheme, however, even "masculine" women could not be psychically men:

> [T]here are women with undoubted traits of genius, but there is no female genius, and there never has been one . . . *and there never can be one* . . . A female genius is a contradiction in terms, for genius is simply intensified, perfectly developed, universally conscious maleness.
>
> The man of genius possesses, like everything else, the complete female in himself; but woman herself is only part of the universe, and the universe can never be the whole; femaleness can never include genius. (189; emphasis in the original)

Sexologists barred women from intellectual achievement because they relied heavily upon age-old binary divisions that assigned mind, intellect, and soul to men while women represented body and matter. Weininger argued that male sexuality is "limited in area and . . . strongly localised," whereas women's sexuality is "diffused over her whole body, so that stimulation may take place almost from any part" (91); he concludes, "To put it bluntly, man possesses sexual organs; her sexual organs possess woman" (92).

Although Woolf certainly knew of Weininger's work—MacCarthy alludes to him in the *New Statesman* debate of 1920—*Room*'s images for the relationship between female body and mind suggest that Woolf had read other sexologists. Havelock Ellis's chapter on "The Artistic Impulse" in *Man and Woman*, for example, stresses the debilitating effects female biology wreaks upon female intellect. Menstruation, or "functional periodicity," is the key to understanding women's basic instability: in a sentence that recalls Professor Von X's hypothetical text "The Mental, Moral, and Physical Inferiority of the Female Sex" (*R* 31), Ellis finds that "[u]nless we bear [menstruation] always in mind we cannot attain to any true knowledge of the physical, mental, or moral life of women" (*Man and Woman* 337). Ellis's images for menstruation depict a fearful feminine biological instability:

> While a man may be said . . . to live on a plane, a woman always lives on the upward or downward side of a curve. (337)
>
> [M]enstruation is a continuous process, and one which permeates the whole of a woman's physical and psychic organism. A woman during her reproductive life is always menstruating . . . just as the moon is always changing. (347)

The connection between the moon and menstruation is, of course, a clichéd one, underlining the way in which Ellis simply adapts cultural stereotypes and recycles them under a veneer of "science." Elsewhere, Ellis argues that women's biological instability exacerbates women's mental instability: "These facts of morbid psychology," he writes, "are very significant; they emphasize the fact that even in the healthiest woman a worm, however harmless and unperceived, gnaws periodically at the roots of life" (347). Containing vague overtones of both Genesis and the Norse myth of Hidhogg, a (female) serpent that gnaws perpetually at the tree of life, this image vividly conveys Ellis's sense that menstruation is a form of secret, hidden blight.

Ellis was especially insistent on the way in which the female body impinged upon female artistry; he held that biological processes prevented women from developing "architectonic form." In this respect, he simply adapted and medicalized arguments against female genius that had appeared earlier in the nineteenth century. Elizabeth Barrett Browning, for example, admitted to making "a religion of genius" and worried that female genius automatically meant "*a woman of the masculine gender*, with her genius very prominent in eccentricity of manner and sentiment" (cited by Battersby, 89). Her anxieties were well-founded: contemporary reviews of her work exclude her from the rank of poet by virtue of sex, arguing that no woman is capable of writing poetry. Thus Sydney Dobell, the Victorian poet and man of letters, somewhat confusingly distinguishes between poetry and poems in a review of *Aurora Leigh:* the work "contains some of the finest poetry written in the century; poetry such as Shakespeare's sister might have written if he had had a twin . . . But it is no poem. No woman can write a poem" (cited in *The Victorian Temper,* 63). Dobell's charge that *Aurora Leigh* is "no poem" apparently means that he believes it is formless, a charge that men would increasingly level against women's writing as the century progressed. In any case, Dobell's use of a hypothetical "Shakespeare's sister" in the context of female writing and genius is provocative: it may well have suggested Woolf's strategy of countering the common masculine complaint that women artists had never achieved the artistry of Shakespeare.[5]

Ellis quotes heavily from such sources in *Man and Woman.* For example, he includes an article by Edmund Gosse about Christina Rossetti that references broader debates about female genius and that anticipates Woolf's narrator in *Room,* who finds it "a perennial puzzle why no woman wrote a word of that extraordinary literature when every other man, it seemed, was capable of song or sonnet" (*R* 43). Gosse writes,

> That Shakespeare should have had no female rival, that the age in which music burdened every bough, and in which poets made their appearances in hundreds, should have produced not a solitary, authentic poetess, even of the fifth rank, this is curious indeed. But it is as rare as curious, for though women have not often taken a very high position on Parnassus, they have seldom thus wholly absented themselves. . . .
>
> It is no new theory that women, in order to succeed in poetry, must be brief, personal, and concentrated. It was recognised by the Greek critics themselves. Into that delicious garland of the poets which was woven by Meleager to be hung outside the gate of the Gardens of the Hesperides he admits but two women from all the centuries of Hellenic song. Sappho is there indeed, because, "though her flowers were few, they were all roses," and almost unseen, a single virginal shoot of the crocus bears the name Erinna. That was all that womanhood gave of durable poetry to the literature of antiquity. A critic, writing five hundred years after her death, speaks of still hearing the swan-note of Errina clear above the jangling chatters of the jays, and of still thinking those three hundred hexameter verses sung by a girl of nineteen as lovely as the loveliest of Homer's. Even at the time of the birth of Christ, Erinna's writings consisted of what could be printed on a page of this magazine. The whole of her extant work, and of Sappho's too, lives on, and of Sappho, at least, enough survives to prove beyond a shadow of a doubt the lofty inspiration of her genius. She is the type of the woman-poet who exists not by reason of the variety or volume of

> her work, but by virtue of its intensity, its individuality, its artistic perfection. ("Christina Rossetti," *Century Magazine*, June 1893)

Gosse not only accords women genius, he puzzles over the complete absence of women poets during the Renaissance, an absence Woolf discusses in *Room* as well as in her response to MacCarthy in 1920:

> According to "Affable Hawk" the fact that no poetess of [Sappho's] genius has appeared from 600 B.C. to the eighteenth century proves that during this time there were no poetesses of potential genius. It follows that the absence of poetesses of moderate merit during that period proves that there were no women writers of potential mediocrity . . . To account for the complete lack not only of good women writers but also of bad women writers I can conceive no reason unless it be that there was some external restraint upon their powers. (*D2* 340)

Thus in *Room* Woolf invents the narrative of Shakespeare's sister, the hypothetical historical account that dramatizes such external restraints.[6]

Woolf may have found Gosse's claim (or claims like it) that women writers succeed only when they are "brief, personal, and concentrated" more unsettling and more difficult to counter, for behind this statement lurks the claims of sexologists that women writers were biologically incapable of developing varied styles or disciplined structures. Ellis seizes upon Gosse's points about form and uses them to discount women's literary achievements and to bolster his own argument that women are biologically incapable of developing form in fiction. His maneuvers are particularly telling when he dismisses the indisputable achievements of nineteenth-century women novelists:

> In fiction women are acknowledged to rank incomparably higher than in any other form of literary art. Thus in England, at all events, in Jane Austen, Charlotte and Emily Brontë, George Eliot, we possess four story-tellers who, in their various ways, are scarcely, for the artistic quality and power of their work (although not for quantity and versatility), behind our best novelists of the male sex. . . . It is only when (as in the work of Flaubert) the novel almost becomes a poem, demanding great architectonic power, severe devotion to style, and complete self-restraint, that women have not come into competition with men. (434–435)

Women's success as novelists is not that noteworthy, Ellis continues, for "fiction in the proper sense makes far less serious artistic demands than poetry, inasmuch as it is simply an idealised version of life, and may claim to follow any of the sinuous curves of life" (435). Women are closer to "social facts," more receptive of detailed social impressions and more tenacious of such impressions:

> In the poorest and least cultured ranks the conversation of women consists largely of rudimentary novelettes in which "says he" and "says she" play the chief parts. Every art . . . has an intellectual and an emotional element: women have done so well in fiction because they are here *organically fitted* to supply both elements. (435–436, emphasis added)

Still, Ellis adds, "[E]ven when we take fiction into account, it cannot be said that women have reached the summits of literature" (436). His reason, not surprisingly, is female biology; women's "quick affectability and exhaustibility" makes sustained creative achievement impossible: "In whatever direction a woman exerts her energies they are all swiftly engaged and no reserve is left" (436). This phrasing suggests that menstruation saps and blights female creativity. Indeed, Ellis condemns women's poetry for qualities that recall his claim that "the blood of women is more watery than that of men . . . in women . . . a certain degree of anaemia may be regarded as physiological" (422). Women's poetry similarly evidences anaemia; it

> has a tendency to be either rather thin or rather diffuse and formless. . . . We have a Sappho and a Christina Rossetti . . . but it is difficult (I will not say impossible) to find women poets who show in any noteworthy degree the qualities of imagination, style, and architectonic power which go to the making of great poetry. (433)

Woolf seems to address this charge explicitly in *Room:* Chloe and Olivia, characters created by the hypothetical novelist Mary Carmichael, share a laboratory, where they engage "in mincing liver . . . a cure for pernicious anaemia" (*R* 87).[7]

Nevertheless, sexological claims about the drawbacks of female biology echo with force in *Room*. Like Ellis, Woolf worries that women's writing is too diffuse, too formless, too fluid—indeed, as we have seen, anxieties about the watery fluency of her own style were attendant at *Room*'s inception. Lady Winchelsea "became diffuse" (*R* 64), while the Duchess of Newcastle's intelligence "poured itself out . . . in torrents . . . which stand congealed in quartos and folios that nobody ever reads" (*R* 65). The word "congealed" is instructive, for it suggests the coagulating properties not of water but of (menstrual?) blood. Even Woolf's image for the undisciplined riot of Margaret Cavendish's work—she likens it to "some giant cucumber [that] had spread itself over all the roses and carnations in the garden and choked them to death" (*R* 65)—evokes a comparison between a waterlogged tasteless vegetable and the distilled and thereby powerful floral essences. Questions about the appropriate form for women's writing recur at the close of this chapter in *Room,* moveover, where Woolf reiterates even as she revises the notion of a correspondence between biological sex and writing. Novels consist of sentences "built . . . into arcades or domes," Woolf observes, a phrase that resonates with Ellis's insistence on "architectonic form." And like Ellis, Woolf elaborates the correspondence between female physicality and literary form:

> And this shape too has been made by men out of their own needs for their own uses. There is no reason to think that the form of the epic or of the poetic play suits a woman any more than the sentence suits her. But all the older forms of literature were hardened and set by the time she became a writer. The novel alone was young enough to be soft in her hands . . . Yet who shall say . . . that even this most pliable of forms is rightly shaped for her use? No doubt we shall find her knocking that into shape for herself when she has the free use of her limbs; and providing some new vehicle, not necessarily in verse, for the poetry in her. For it is the poetry that is still denied outlet. (*R* 80)

Woolf's vision of a time when the woman writer has "free use of her limbs" reminds us of the many times in *Room* that fiction and poetry issue from the female pen "disfigured," "deformed," "cramped," and "twisted" (*R* 52, 64, 72, 73). Even worse, women's novels almost always suffer from a mysterious "flaw in the centre" that rots the work from within (*R* 77), an image that recalls the way in which, for Ellis, menstruation gnaws in secret at the very root of a woman's being.

Nowhere does this preoccupation with the relationship between the female body and fictional form emerge with more clarity than in Woolf's discussion of the importance "physical conditions" will play in the future development of women's writing:

> The book has somehow to be adapted to the body, and at a venture one would say that women's books should be shorter, more concentrated, than those of men, and framed so that they do not need long hours of steady and uninterrupted work. For interruptions there will always be. Again, the nerves that feed the brain would seem to differ in

> men and women, and if you are going to make them work their best and hardest, you must find out what treatment suits them. (*R* 81)

Woolf agrees with Edmund Gosse that women should be brief and concentrated, but her reasons resemble Ellis's. For although Woolf refuses to specify the sources of interruption, given the context of physicality and the body, she almost certainly refers to menstruation. In fact Woolf had made such a connection about her own work when she described her "mind . . . woolgathering away about Women & Fiction, which I am to read at Newnham in May":

> The mind is the most capricious of insects—flitting fluttering. I had thought to write the quickest most brilliant pages in Orlando yesterday—not a drop came, all, forsooth, for the usual physical reasons, which declared themselves today. It is the oddest feeling: as if a finger stopped the flow of the ideas in the brain: it is unsealed, & the blood rushes all over the place. (*D3* 175)

The brain and the uterus become interchangeable, as the figurative fluency of ideas issuing from the brain yields to the literal fluency of blood issuing from the uterus. Woolf gives expression here to common late Victorian beliefs about the body's "economy," expressed succinctly by Henry Maudsley in "Sex in Mind and Education" (1874):

> The energy of a human body being a definite and not inexhaustible quantity, can it bear, without energy, an excessive mental drain as well as the natural physical drain which is so great at that time . . . Nor does it matter greatly by what channel the energy be expended; if it be used in one it is not available for use in another. What Nature spends in one direction, she must economise in another direction.

This notion of the body's economy held true for men as well; Woolf makes mention throughout her life of the way in which her father's work on the *Dictionary of Literary Biography* resulted in nervous illness and mental instability for the two children born to him during that time. For example, Woolf blames her father's writing for the "phantomlike" drift of her brother Adrian's life: "[T]he D.N.B. crushed his life out before he was born. It gave me a twist of the head too. I shouldn't have been so clever, but I should have been more stable, without that contribution to the history of England" (*D2* 277). Writing and reproduction cannot coexist.

The "Androgynous" Mind

The famous call for artistic androgyny in *A Room of One's Own* must also be set in sexological context, as a response to Weininger's famous claim that genius is "simply intensified, perfectly developed, universally conscious maleness," although "the man of genius possesses, like everything else, the complete female in himself" (189). Woolf responds to this claim by going back to an older definition of genius, Coleridge's notion of the "androgynous mind" as "resonant and porous," a mind that "transmits emotion without impediment," one that is "naturally creative, incandescent, and undivided" (98).[8] This older understanding, which she elaborates in a series of sexualized figures, substitutes for the "single-sexed" mind Woolf abhors. "No age can ever have been as stridently self-conscious as our own," she declares (99), and such sex-consciousness creates dead literary texts, "horrid little abortions" (103).

As Ellen Bayuk Rosenman has noted, this section of *A Room of One's Own* is disappointingly conventional, even heterosexist, as Woolf relies upon metaphors of heterosexual intercourse and childbirth to structure the "fertilised" imagination capable of producing living, transcendent works of art. Rosenman attributes this conventional solution to Woolf's acknowledged "profound, if irrational" investment in the social structure (*R* 98); this section of the essay is the site of tension between "the materialist and transcendent threads in Woolf's argument" (Rosenman 110). Again, however, we must consider the sexological arguments that *A Room of One's Own* both contests and assimilates. For despite the various scenes of women together, which the text posits as the source of a new literary tradition—two women friends mincing liver together in the laboratory, mother and daughter walking down a street of shops together—*A Room of One's Own* never goes so far as to posit a "feminine" imagination of "simply intensified, perfectly developed, universally conscious" femaleness. In fact, these scenes of the "androgynous" mind "celebrating its nuptials in darkness" depict female sexuality as *subject* to the male portion of the brain: "If one is a man, still the woman part of the brain must have effect; and a woman also must have intercourse with the man in her" (98). Here, the man experiences only a vague "effect" from the female portion of the brain, while the woman "must have intercourse with the man," a much more coercive arrangement. Even the scene of the "androgynous" writer ends by sounding suspiciously male: "The writer [. . .] once his experience is over, must lie back and let his mind celebrate its nuptials in darkness" (104).[9] Significantly, the doubly fathered text has "two heads," suggesting that Woolf implicitly accedes to the cultural split in which mind is masculine and body is feminine. What Woolf finds "profound, if irrational" may be, once again, the traces of sexological thinking that she is finally unable to contest: the female body needs the corrective of masculine logic.

"Cock-a-doodle-dum" Revisited

As the epigraph at the beginning of this chapter suggests, Woolf had to take sexological arguments in "desperate earnest" to construct a defense of the intrinsic value of female difference and female creativity. That she succeeded brilliantly is proven by the book's enduring popularity as an accessible introduction to feminist literary criticism and women's writing. Her materialist analysis of the conditions necessary for creativity anticipates much of what later feminist criticism elaborates. Ironically, the very germ of the book—the need to defend the possibility of a female "genius"—has almost disappeared from contemporary discussions and analyses of the text.

Writing *A Room of One's Own* would prove to have a salutary effect on Woolf, freeing her critical voice ("I seem able to write criticism fearlessly. Because of a R. of ones Own I said suddenly to myself last night" [*D*4 25]) and energizing her with the vision of a "sequel" (eventually *Three Guineas, The Pargiters,* and *The Years*): "And I'm quivering & itching to write my—whats it to be called?—'Men are like that'—no thats too patently feminist: the sequel then, for which I have collected enough powder to blow up St Pauls" (*D*4 77). In analyzing and rebutting the misogynistic arguments of sexology Woolf faced down some of her worst anxieties about writing as a woman. In effect, Desmond MacCarthy served as Woolf's most personal representative of the censorious Beadle of literature. Woolf thus becomes in her writing of the text the pioneering rebel of her own description:

> It would have needed a very stalwart young woman in 1828 to disregard all those snubs and chidings and promises of prizes. One must have been something of a firebrand to say to oneself, Oh, but they can't buy literature too. Literature is open to everybody. I refuse to allow you, Beadle though you are, to turn me off the grass. Lock up your libraries if you like; but there is no gate, no lock, no bolt that you can set upon the freedom of my mind. (*R* 78–79)

One had to be something of a firebrand in 1928 to state those sentiments, and Woolf's sense of revolution emerges in her imagery: whereas the lamp in the spine lights with a hazy glow, genius consumes all impediments, and Mary Carmichael illuminates the caves of female friendship with a match, the female revolutionary of literature torches misogynistic texts with the fire of her indignation.

Although she would continue to find Desmond MacCarthy's criticism demoralizing—"[I]ts true—a snub—even from Desmond depresses me more than the downright anger of Arnold Bennett—it saps my vitality" (*D4* 43) Woolf complained after MacCarthy "sneered" at her in an essay on the novel in which he described *Mrs. Dalloway* as "a long wool-gathering process."—in general Woolf began to find men's biased dismissals of her strangely invigorating. Hence when James Laver published "Supreme Gift Denied to Women" in the *Evening Standard* (cited in *D3* 256n9), he admitted that no one could "wish to deny the quality of greatness to Virginia Woolf," despite his thesis that "women had failed to reach the front rank in the creative arts." Woolf's distortion of this remark in her diary is telling: "'[N]obody need seek to *qualify* the greatness of Miss Virginia Woolf'—hah! I hope Arnold Bennett sees that" (*D3* 255–256, emphasis added). "Qualifying" Woolf's talent is precisely what men like MacCarthy and Bennett did, as when MacCarthy congratulated Woolf for "courageously acknowledging the limitations of her sex." Woolf's pleasure in sparring with men emerges in a diary entry after Arnold Bennett's death in 1931; Woolf found herself sorry he would no longer irritate her, "for he abused me; & yet I rather wished him to go on abusing me; & me abusing him" (*D4* 16).[10] Apparently, writing *A Room of One's Own* enabled Woolf to deal in part with those censorious male voices she had worried about when she first published the essay and anxiously waited for her friends' reactions.

To his credit, Desmond MacCarthy seems to have gotten Woolf's points. When Woolf initially recorded her misgivings about *Room*'s audience, she imagined her "intimate friends"—all male—as dismissive and patronizing. She imagined their comments: "easy reading . . . this very feminine logic . . . a book to be put in the hands of girls" (*D3* 262). The "girls" of the time did not understand its import, as we have seen. But Desmond MacCarthy did; and his favorable review delighted Woolf, who responded with a letter of thanks:

> It was a great delight to read your article. I never thought you would like that book—and perhaps you didn't: but anyway you managed to write a most charming article, which gave me a great and unexpected

> pleasure. (Apart from that, you must let me collect your articles. This is no joke).
>
> By the way, did you refer to Lawrence? The novelist marked by an initial? He was not in my upper mind; but no doubt in the lower. (*L4* 130)

In his review of the essay, MacCarthy singled out for mention the novelist "Mr. A," "an exceedingly gifted living novelist, clearly recognisable under an initial" (*Sunday Times,* January 26, 1930). MacCarthy did not identify the novelist. But no doubt he understood—even after reading Woolf's disclaimer that she could only have "unconsciously" meant Lawrence—that much of *A Room of One's Own* laments the inability of the woman writer to "put on her body," to write freely as a woman, because of the inevitable interruption and obstruction posed to her work by misogynistic opinions. Women writers are harassed, pulled from the straight, turned off the grass, driven mad. Woolf stresses, moreover, that this damage to women occurs primarily because the male writer needs to protect his privilege and a sense of his own worth in the face of female excellence. MacCarthy, of course, wrote as "Affable Hawk." It seems Woolf reached her audience after all.

But Woolf reached another audience she did not anticipate: *Room*'s publication brought her to the attention of the pioneering woman composer Ethel Smyth. Nearly 72 to Woolf's 48, Smyth seemed at first an unlikely friend: almost entirely deaf, she was egocentric in the extreme, obsessed with her sense of grievance that her music was overlooked. Yet Woolf had long been aware of Smyth, whose autobiographies she admired and whose revolutionary zeal might have impressed her (Smyth had been imprisoned as a suffragette; the composer of the suffragette battle song "The March of the Women," she "conducted the march from her jail cell with a toothbrush" [Marcus, *Virginia Woolf* 51]). "An old woman of seventy one has fallen in love with me. It is at once hideous and horrid and melancholy-sad. It is like being caught by a giant crab," Woolf wrote jokingly to her nephew (*L4* 171). In point of fact, Smyth would prove to be an enormously liberating figure for Woolf, enabling her to express openly her anger at the patriarchal arrogation of female sexuality.[11] This friendship would specifically enable Woolf to recognize and work through a residual anxiety, which emerges only symptomatically and sporadically in *A Room of One's Own,* that writing publicly for women represented a form of impurity or loss of chastity. Woolf's engagement with the oppressive meanings attached to chastity and her reappropriation of the ruptured hymen as the emblem of female creativity are the subjects of the following chapter.

CHAPTER 3

"The Flaw in the Centre": Writing as Hymenal Rupture in Virginia Woolf's Work

In a remarkable letter to Ethel Smyth in 1930, Virginia Woolf locates the source of female creativity in women's "burning centre."

> If only I weren't a writer, perhaps I could thank you and praise you and admire you perfectly simply and expressively and say in one word what I felt about the Concert yesterday. As it is, an image forms in my mind; a quickset briar hedge, innumerably intricate and spiky and thorned; in the centre burns a rose. Miraculously, the rose is you; flushed pink, wearing pearls. The thorn hedge is the music; and I have to break my way through violins, flutes, cymbals, voices to this red burning centre . . . I am enthralled that you, the dominant and superb, should have this tremor and vibration of fire round you—violins flickering, flutes purring; (the image is of a winter hedge)—that you should be able to create this world from your centre. (*L4* 171)

Evocative of Georgia O'Keeffe's paintings or Judy Chicago's dinner plates, the burning rose contests the notion that women's genitals represent lack.[1] Instead, Woolf envisions a female geography of stunning power and presence, and Smyth becomes an erotically charged figure precisely because she is "dominant and superb." Woolf's refashioning of the two stories that undergird this letter—the prince's discovery of Sleeping Beauty inside a castle overgrown with briars and Siegfried's similar discovery of the Valkyrie goddess Brunnhilde inside a flame-encircled castle—grants both women aggressive, even transgressive roles: the woman warrior who defied patriarchal decrees becomes an apt avatar for Smyth, the daughter of a general and a militant feminist. Woolf assumes the role of masculine aggressor, "breaking her way" into Smyth's "centre" and seducing Smyth in turn with her writing: "I wont scratch all the skin off my fingers trying to expound," Woolf continues, " . . . I recur to the rose among the briars, like an old gypsy woman in a damp ditch warming her hands at the fire" (*IA* 172).[2]

Woolf describes the creative woman in terms of centrality and centers throughout her career, but this letter to Smyth marks an important shift in her use of this motif.[3] In the 1920s "centrality" serves Woolf as a standard of aesthetic wholeness and completion—and significantly, women's writing often fails to measure up: if "nothing appears whole and entire, then one heaves a sigh of disappointment . . . This novel has come to grief somewhere" (*R* 76). Woolf complains that women's novels suffer from a mysterious defect, a "flaw in the centre" that destroys their structural integrity: "I thought of all the women's novels that lie scattered, like small pock-marked apples in an orchard, about the secondhand book shops of London. It was the flaw in the centre that had rotted them" (*R* 77). But by 1930 Woolf had come to question her investment in "wholeness," apparently, for her descriptions of female creativity begin to foreground moments of rupture in the "complete" atmosphere of the woman artist. This shift in Woolf's aesthetic marks her recognition and "working through" of a conflict that emerges only sporadically and symptomatically in *A Room of One's Own,* where Woolf's imaging of female textuality as inevitably disfigured by rents and tears betrays her unconscious fear that writing for women is an "unchaste activity" that destroys a virginal (hermetically or hymenally sealed) female silence. From this conflicted and unconscious concurrence with patriarchal constraints on female speech and sexuality, Woolf moves to a valorization of the ruptured membrane, now an "elastic fibre," the site of mediation and exchange and the suspension of many elements at once. In effect, Woolf reconceptualizes the hymen, contesting its patriarchal valuations of chastity and presence—woman as intact and closed and silent container for man—and rewriting it as the threshold of communication between women. Decentering the hymen thus, Woolf reclaims it as the site of female difference.

This reclamation of one of the most symbolic—and in some ways most oppressive—aspects of female corporeality anticipates in striking ways Luce Irigaray's call for a "female imaginary" to redress women's "exile" or "homelessness" in the symbolic order. In a series of compelling images—the notorious "lips," but also the placenta and the mucous membranes—Irigaray has brought attention to the way in which female bodies are obliterated by patriarchal systems of representation. Western "isomorphism," the privileging of metaphors that describe male but not female bodies (e.g., unity, form, the visible), leaves women with images of "women-for-men": symbolically speaking, the female body resembles, reflects, or complements the male body, but in all cases maleness is the norm and female specificity is erased.[4] Irigaray writes that "this morpho-logic does not correspond to the female sex: there is not 'a' sex. The 'no sex' that has been assigned to the woman can mean that she does not have 'a' sex and that her sex is not visible nor identifiable or representable in a definite form." ("Women's Exile" 111). Margaret Whitford summarizes Irigaray's position thus:

> [S]ymbolic systems are subtended by a male imaginary which, despite the denials of Lacanian theorists . . . is intimately connected with the phenomenology of the male body and its self-representation as phallic. The specificity of the female body is missing from these systems of representation, and as a result, women are seen—and forced to see themselves—as defective and "castrated" men. It is a regime of sexual "indifference," in which representation accords no specificity to the female. ("Irigaray's Body Symbolic" 104)

Irigaray attempts to restructure the imaginary by deliberate interventions in the symbolic, through the creation of a set of positive metaphors and myths with which women can identify. Those who charge Irigaray with essentialism overlook the ways in which her work powerfully reclaims aspects of female corporeality that have simply vanished from public (or even private) discussion. It is indisputable, for example, that her image of "lips that speak together" challenges "sexual indifference" and restores female specificity to the speaker(s). At one and the same time, Irigaray exposes the limitations of available phallocentric definitions of female sexuality even as she proposes an active, positive, and self-sufficient alternative: "She has produced a powerful metaphor for women's potentially excessive pleasures to hold up against the confining representations granted them in dominant discourses," remarks Elizabeth Grosz (*Sexual Subversions* 117).

Woolf's metaphorization of the hymen contests "isomorphism" in a manner that closely resembles Irigaray's recent and less well-known theorization of the mucous membranes, and it is here that Irigaray illuminates the political critique implicit in Woolf's imagery. Irigaray envisions the "female sex" as the

> threshold that gives access to the *mucous*. Beyond classical oppositions of love and hate, liquid and ice—a threshold that is always *half-open*.

> The threshold of the *lips,* which are strangers to dichotomy and oppositions. Gathered one against the other but without any possible suture . . . They do not absorb the world into or through themselves . . . They offer a shape of welcome, but do not assimilate, reduce, or swallow up. (*An Ethics of Sexual Difference* 18–19)

Like the hymen, the mucous is a site of mediation and exchange; always open, it challenges the notion that woman is a closed container belonging to man. Furthermore, the mucous cannot be split off from the body and thus resists appropriation by the male imaginary, which Irigaray suggests elsewhere might be "exclusively dependent on organs."[5] Evading binary categories, the mucous refers to both mouth and genitals and refuses definite shape: "It is neither simply solid nor is it fluid. It is not stable in a fixed form; it expands, but not in a shape; its form cannot readily be visualized," Whitford observes ("Irigaray's Body Symbolic" 103). Finally, the mucous images female specificity in a way that includes the maternal body but does not reduce female sexuality to the "maternal feminine"; at the same time, in keeping with Irigaray's tenets for a "female imaginary," it is an image that does not rely for its existence on the repression or symbolic murder of the maternal body. In this respect, it fulfills Irigaray's call for the invention of words and sentences that "translate" the bond between mothers and daughters, "a language that is not a substitute for the experience of *corps-á-corps* as the paternal language seeks to be, but which accompanies that bodily experience, clothing it in words that do not erase the body but speak the body" (Irigaray, "Body Against Body," 18–19).

As we shall see, Woolf's rewriting of the hymen as the site of female creativity and sexual difference exceeds patriarchal constraints in a way reminiscent of Irigaray's use of the mucous. But Woolf's transformation of the hymen also works to illustrate the Italian feminist practice of *affidamento,* or "entrustment," a concept based on Irigaray's theorizing of women's relationships. Teresa de Lauretis defines entrustment as a relationship between women "in which one woman gives her trust or entrusts herself symbolically to another woman, who thus becomes her guide, mentor, or point of reference—in short, the figure of symbolic mediation between her and the world."[6] Significantly, Woolf's valorization of hymenal rupture occurs most vividly—and almost exclusively—in letters written to Ethel Smyth in the 1930s. As Suzanne Raitt points out, Woolf's fascination with "Ethel's exceptional frankness—her unwomanly character, in Virginia's terms" enabled Woolf to confront her conflicts about the female body and sexuality; Raitt speculates that Smyth's frank discussions of her sexuality "perhaps held in their bravado the key to a more authentic feminine honesty" for Woolf. Similarly, Jane Marcus credits Smyth, a militant and angry older woman artist, with helping Woolf "to release all her anger at male aggression . . . [Smyth] taught her how to fight, as earlier she had literally taught Mrs. Pankhurst and the suffragettes how to throw rocks."[7]

Smyth sought out Woolf after the publication of *A Room of One's Own* in 1929, when she saw her own experiences as a pioneering woman composer reflected in Woolf's meditations upon the difficulties that impeded the woman writer. For her part, Woolf perceived in Smyth a source of maternal protection, but an unusual maternal protection composed of courage, artistic drive, and unabashed egotism:

> [W]hat you give me is protection, so far as I am capable of it. I look at you and (being blind to most things except violent impressions) think if Ethel can be so downright and plainspoken and on the spot, I need not fear instant dismemberment by wild horses. Its the child crying for the nurses hand in the dark. You do it by being so uninhibited: so magnificently unself-conscious. This is what people pay £20 a sitting to get from Psycho-analysis—liberation from their own egotism. (*L4* 302–303)

As early as 1921, in a review of Smyth's autobiography and long before she knew Smyth personally, Woolf had remarked Smyth's "extreme courage and extreme candour"; at that time Woolf wrote Lytton Strachey, "I think she shows up triumphantly, through sheer force of honesty" (*L2* 405). This candor and lack of self-consciousness prompted Woolf to question her own bias against self-revelation:

> [F]or months on first knowing you, I said to myself here's one of these talkers. They dont know what feeling is, happily for them. Because everyone I most honour is silent . . . I have trained myself to silence; induced to it also by the terror I have of my own unlimited capacity for feeling. . . . But to my surprise, as time went on, I found that you are perhaps the only person I know who shows feelings and feels. Still I cant imagine talking about my love for people, as you do. Is it training? Is it the perpetual fear I have of the unknown force that lurks just beneath the floor? (*L4* 422)

Smyth's relentless curiosity—her letters often consisted of lists of questions about Woolf's personal life—forced Woolf to confront those lurking and unknown forces that resulted in self-censorship, and eventually Woolf wrote freely to Smyth about her sexual timidity, her suicidal impulses, her bouts of madness, and her development as a writer.[8] In this sense, Smyth licensed a self-interest (Woolf called it egotism) that Woolf had come to abjure as both a personal failing and an aesthetic fault.[9] Woolf came to rely so heavily upon Smyth's directness, in fact, that she once likened her to ozone: "[R]eally I find your atmosphere full of ozone; a necessary element; since in my set they never praise me and never love me, openly; and I admit there are times when silence chills and the other thing fires" (*L*5 2).

Woolf herself recognized that her attraction to Smyth grew out of a need for a maternal surrogate: "[Y]ou are, I believe, one of the kindest of women, one of the best balanced, with that maternal quality which of all others I need and adore," she enthused in one letter (*L4* 188). But Smyth's maternal practice afforded Woolf a very different model of femininity than that promoted by her mother, Julia Stephen. In Woolf's fictional and biographical portraits, the conventional mother undermines the woman artist, urging selflessness and the adoption of a "dishonest" style of flattery and indirection that Woolf labeled the "tea-table manner." Smyth, by contrast, exemplified the "plainspoken" and "downright" and engaged in direct, defiant action and self-promotion; according to Nigel Nicolson and Joanne Trautmann, "Fighting for a performance of her work gave her almost as much pleasure as composing it" (*L4* xv). Whereas the Angel in the House urges the woman writer to remain "pure"—that is, reticent—about female sexuality, Smyth wrote openly, and in her volumes of autobiography publicly, about her sexual liaisons and bodily functions: "[H]ow you love periods, w.c.'s, excrement of all sort," Woolf teased in one letter (*L4* 372). Woolf's favorite image for Smyth—an indomitable and uncastrated wild cat whose wounds refuse to heal, an image that almost always recurs in conjunction with Smyth's battles to get her music played and taken seriously—speaks not to Woolf's perception of Smyth as masculine, I think, but rather to Woolf's perception of Smyth as unmastered by patriarchal conceptions of femininity and undaunted by the conflict such self-assertion incurred.[10] Smyth's egotism remained intact, or uncastrated. The corollary of this reading is, of course, that the conventional mother teaches the woman writer to accept subordination and the patriarchal notion that women are castrated, inferior, inadequate.

Hence I believe Woolf was not far off when she told Smyth that her egotism liberated Woolf's and thereby accomplished what psychoanalysts did for their patients at twenty pounds a sitting. Through her letters to Smyth Woolf effects what Susan Stanford Friedman has called a "writing cure"; that is, Woolf both recognizes and works through her fear that writing for women represents a loss of chastity.[11] In Freud's model of this process, the patient moves from the symptomatic behavior that acts out repressed memories (repetition) to remembrance through the mechanism of the "transference," "new editions," or "reprints" of the symptomatic behavior in which the analyst becomes a substitute for one of the original (typically parental) figures.[12] Freud stresses the "intermediary" nature of the transference, its artificiality, its "provisional character": "We render [the behavior] harmless, and even make use of it, by according it the right to assert itself within certain limits. We admit it into the transference as to a playground, in which it is allowed to let itself go in almost complete freedom."[13] Woolf's letters to Smyth function as this kind of intermediate space or playground, for Woolf did not consider letter-writing "serious" work; she often notes that a letter has been sent without revision, and in her letters to her closest friends she strives for a casual intimacy that inscribes her sense of the recipient's personality: "It is an interesting question—what one tries to do, in writing a letter—partly of course to give back a reflection of the other person" (*L4* 98). In her efforts to respond to Smyth's preoccupations with "periods, w.c.'s, and excrement," Woolf took up the question of how corporeality impinged upon her own writing: in the safety of "entrustment," she examined the way in which the Victorian cult of chastity abrogated female sexuality—and with it female speech.[14]

The Rending and Tearing of Instincts

Urging Smyth, in the 1930s, to write her memoirs Woolf describes female sexuality as primary "truths" omitted from women's autobiographies: "There's never been a womans autobiography," Woolf complains. "Nothing to compare with Rousseau. Chastity and modesty I suppose have been the reasons. Now why shouldn't you be not only the first woman to write an opera, but equally the first to the tell the truths about herself?" (*L6* 453). Another letter goes even further: Woolf explicitly compares the woman writer's revelations of her sexual experiences to rupturing the hymen, as if a virginal female silence alone guarantees a woman's purity. "I'm interested that you cant write about masturbation. That I understand," Woolf begins.

> What puzzles me is how this reticence co-habits with your ability to talk openly magnificently, freely about—say H.B. [Henry Brewster, Smyth's lover]. I couldn't do one or the other. But as so much of life

> is sexual—or so they say—it rather limits autobiography if this is blacked out. It must be, I suspect, for many generations, for women; for its like breaking the hymen—if thats the membrane's name—a painful operation, and I suppose connected with all sorts of subterranean instincts. I still shiver with shame at the memory of my half brother, standing me on a ledge, aged about 6, and so exploring my private parts. Why should I have felt shame then? (459–460)

The sexual is "blacked out" for women because of the need to preserve "chastity and modesty," a process of censorship Woolf claims has been imposed upon women for so many generations that it has become habitual, a kind of instinct. Thus even to speak of the sexual is akin to the loss of a fetishized virginity: to write is to fall. Louise DeSalvo has argued that Woolf's intensified efforts to discover the source of her depression resulted in the recovery of this memory of molestation, recorded not only here but in the contemporaneous "A Sketch of the Past," where Woolf searches unsuccessfully to locate the "word" that could define "so dumb and mixed a feeling" (S 69) as her sense of the impropriety of sexual assault. DeSalvo links Woolf's concern about self-censorship to the repression of this memory.[15] But although Woolf indeed associates hymenal rupture with memories of her molestation, she does not use it as an image of self-censorship—on the contrary, breaking the hymen becomes an explicit image here for self-revelation and for writing about female bodily and sexual experience. In this context, the contrast Woolf draws in her earlier letter—between women's "chastity and modesty" and Rousseau—assumes added meaning: just as Rousseau attributes a portion of his literary creativity to sexual self-satisfaction, so Woolf reappropriates the scene of female sexual dispossession, depicting the woman writer as the breaker of her own hymen, her seal of silence.

This letter contains Woolf's clearest equation of writing with hymenal rupture. Yet once alerted to the existence of this trope, it is possible to discern its symptomatic, deeply censored movement in *A Room of One's Own*, the 1929 text that is Woolf's most celebrated analysis of women and writing.[16] The draft revisions of *Room* tie Woolf's preoccupation with the structural "flaw in the centre" of women's texts to an unspoken, unconscious anxiety that breaking silence for women is a violation of female chastity; over and over again Woolf figures that violation as an agonizing "rending and tearing" at the "root" of the woman writer's "being."[17] In the published version, the fictional web is gender neutral, and only the text's imperfections reveals its human creator: "[W]hen the web is pulled askew, hooked up at the edge, torn in the middle, one remembers that these webs are not spun in mid air by incorporeal creatures, but are the work of suffering human beings, and are attached to grossly material things" (*R* 43–44). But the draft of this passage implicitly connects the tear "in the middle" with the woman writer's body:

> [W]hen the web is pulled askew, hooked up here, or with a great hole in it there, [the centre] then one remembers that these webs are not spun in mid air by incorporeal creatures, but . . . are attached to grossly material things . . . in short the spider is a human being: I was [no doubt] thinking as I [made] this simile of the spiders web, of certain strains & holes that to my mind still slightly disfigure the webs made by women.[18]

Woolf's language repeatedly breaks down the distinctions between woman writer and female body: beginning with an attack on the notion that writers are incorporeal, Woolf ends by suggesting that the woman writer is only too corporeal, too much a victim of that "grossly material thing," the female body. Women writers hence produce texts "disfigured" by "strains" and "holes," an equation that equates the "great hole" in the female web with a hole in the woman writer's sexual/textual center. But although this "great hole" might suggest Woolf's anxious concurrence with then-current sexological formulations that women "lack" penises, it soon becomes clear that the "great hole" speaks to Woolf's internalized belief that breaking silence for women is as traumatic as the rupture of the virgin's hymen.

As Woolf explains to Smyth, the rupture of the hymen is a "painful operation . . . connected to all sorts of subterranean instincts." As Woolf explicitly notes in these later letters, to break silence is akin to breaking the hymen because both acts violate internalized prohibitions against female self-assertion, and in *Room*, where hymenal imagery only emerges in shadowy and fragmentary fashion, the act of breaking "chaste" silence is an act of such defiance and compulsion that it results in stillborn or illicit language and acute mental anguish. Woolf's hypothetical sixteenth-century woman writer suffers from this hymenal proscription. With her desire to write at war with the "impurity" of breaking silence, she is "tortured and pulled asunder by her own contrary instincts" and "lost her health and sanity to a certainty" (*R* 51). The published version mutes the violence attendant at the scene of writing: in the draft this woman remains Judith Shakespeare, and only the irresistible "force of her gift broke through" her father's ban on her writing. This compulsive force causes enormous "pain, with what rending & tearing of instincts . . . <she was> up against something so deep in herself" (*W&F* 82–83). In both the draft and published versions of *Room,* the governing metaphor of writing as childbirth subsumes hymenal imagery: hence Judith Shakespeare's illegitimate pregnancy, a synecdoche in the published version for her stillborn literary creations, drives her to suicide and eternal silence. Yet writing remains a primarily sexual lapse, and the social disgrace pertaining to illicit and unchaste female textuality repeatedly mars women writers' productions: it remains residually in Woolf's images of textual stillbirth and twisted and deformed offspring as well as in the narrator's assertion that "whole flights of words would need to wing their way illegitimately into existence before a woman could say what happens when she goes into a room" (*R* 91).

Woolf's study of the Bible and Christian history during her composition of *Three Guineas* would later enable her to clarify the latent and symptomatic connections *Room* draws between female speech and the loss of chastity.[19] In this later essay, Woolf shows how Saint Paul defines chastity not only as an aspect of female sexuality—"The woman's mind and body shall be reserved for the use of one man and one man only" (*TG* 167)—but as an aspect of female *speech:* "'Let the woman keep silence in the churches,'" Woolf quotes, "'for it is not permitted unto them to speak; but let them be in subjection . . . And if they would learn anything, let them ask their own husbands at home: for it is shameful to speak in the church'" (167).[20] As Woolf points out, the focus of this ban is on the spectacle of speech issuing from the female body: hence Saint Paul requires women to veil themselves when speaking publicly (122). In *A Room of One's Own,* where the connections between chastity and silence remain more muted, Woolf invokes the veil as the "relic of chastity" that conceals, not the female body, but the woman writer's ruptured hymen and loss of chastity.[21] Thus the great nineteenth-century women writers whose writings prove them "victims of inner strife . . . sought effectively to veil themselves by using the name of a man. Thus they did homage to the convention . . . that publicity in women is detestable. Anonymity runs in their blood. The desire to be veiled still possesses them" (*R* 52). In the drafts, where women's writing also suffers from "a radical fault in its structure," the veil of anonymity pays "homage to the profound instinct which lay at the root of womens being" (*W&F* 83, 84). Veiled and concealed, hymenal rupture still disfigures women's writing in the published text, however; like the hole in the spider's web, the "flaw in the centre" destroys all pretense of structural integrity in women's writing:

> She was thinking of something other than the thing itself. Down comes her book upon our heads. There was a flaw in the centre of it. And I thought of all the women's novels that lie scattered, like small pock-marked apples in an orchard . . . It was the flaw in the centre that had rotted them. (*R* 77)

Rotten at the core, women's texts, like Eden apples, betray their creators' unseemly trespass upon the male preserves of literature, their unholy defiance of patriarchal taboos.[22]

Women writers cannot deliver a "whole and entire" literary text in *Room*, then, in part because their work issues from a mind that has been "pulled from the straight," but more importantly because Woolf involuntarily assents to the Pauline proscription: women must remain silent in order that they themselves remain "whole and entire." Thus in the drafts Woolf images the eventuality of delivering a "whole and entire" work of art to "a man carrying a precious jar through a crowded street, <afraid> that it may be broken at any moment,—can scarcely fail to be cracked & damaged in transit" (*W&F* 85). This choice of a conventional image of female virginity to render the fragility of the work of art has the effect of collapsing women themselves into works of art: by this logic, the woman who writes, who tries to create herself as subject, inevitably damages her worth as object. In this context, it is significant that Woolf envisions the profession of writing as an alternative to the "oldest profession": "the shady and amorous" Aphra Behn must write for money after "the death of her husband and some unfortunate adventures of her own" (*R* 67). The sacrifice of her chastity and reputation "earned [women] the right to speak their minds": "Here begins the freedom of the mind," Woolf writes, "or rather the possibility that in the course of time the mind will be free to write what it likes" (*R* 62, 67). Woolf suggests that the freedom of the mind depends upon the sexual freedom of the body, yet in acting upon either freedom, *Room*'s woman writer inevitably becomes damaged goods—and her work reflects that damage.

In fact, in the 1920s Woolf consistently faults women's texts for improperly inscribing their authors' female bodies. She claims, for example, that "in the early [eighteen] forties . . . the connexion between a woman's art and a woman's life was unnaturally close, so that it is impossible for the most austere of critics not sometimes to touch the flesh when his eyes should be fixed upon the page" (*W&W* 137). That unnatural proximity seems to be a result of Woolf's own apprehension that the woman writer's body impinges upon her work and causes defective writing. Writing of Lady Winchelsea and the Duchess of Newcastle in *A Room of One's Own,* Woolf notes that "In both burnt the same passion for poetry and both are deformed and disfigured by the same causes" (*R* 64): the body of the woman and the body of her text become indistinguishable. (The sentence might better read, "In both women burnt the same passion for poetry and *both women's works* are deformed and disfigured by the same causes"). Furthermore, because the language of deformation remains independent of the poetry it ostensibly describes, it inadvertently outlines another possibility: it suggests that the woman writer's female body (internally disfigured by her ruptured hymen?) deforms her literary efforts. This misshapen body gives birth only to misshapen writing. Thus images of deformation undermine the distinctions Woolf draws between the "free life in London" of *Room's* hypothetical sixteenth-century woman writer and the chaste nineteenth-century Charlotte Brontë.[23] Of the former, Woolf writes that the stress of defying sexual codes creates "a strained and morbid imagination," whence issues writing that is "twisted and deformed" (*R* 52). The latter, on the other hand, cannot "get her genius expressed whole and entire" because of her inner, figurative self-divisions: "Her books will be deformed and twisted," Woolf writes (*R* 72–73).

Throughout *A Room of One's Own,* then, the ideal of the "whole and entire" work of art is at variance with Woolf's concomitant definition of the work of art as a precious jar that "can scarcely fail to be cracked & damaged in transit": given *Room's* conviction that writing is akin to a rupture in chastity, women writers seem doomed to producing flawed and damaged work. In the 1930s, however, the conflicted valuation of chastity evinced in *Room* gives way to Woolf's anger about patriarchal culture's arrogation of female sexuality. Woolf now portrays female socialization and the patriarchal emphasis on chastity as the source of women's crippling and deformation. Woolf's diary establishes the moment of this shift as the preparation for the lecture "Professions for Women": Woolf suddenly "conceived an entire new book—a sequel to *A Room of One's Own*—about the sexual life of women: to be called Professions for Women perhaps—Lord how exciting! This sprang out of my paper" (*D*4 6). If a specific project never materialized, "the sexual life of women" did become Woolf's abiding concern in the 1930s; in effect she undertook the very study she had first outlined in *Room* as a worthy project for a student at Girton or Newnham, "[t]hat profoundly interesting subject, the value that men set upon women's chastity and its effect upon their education" (*R* 67).

Although Woolf's analysis of chastity emerges—albeit in fragmentary form—in many writings in the 1930s, I want to highlight some of the specific ways that analysis reshaped her vision of the creative woman.[24] Consider, for example, Woolf's depictions of the successful woman writer as tea-table hostess. In the 1924 "Mr. Bennett and Mrs. Brown," Woolf compares the conscientious writer to a skillful and sensitive society hostess: "Both in life and in literature it is necessary to have some means of bridging the gulf between the hostess and her unknown guest on the one hand, the writer and his unknown reader on the other" (*CDB* 110). At this point, Woolf self-consciously singles out Jane Austen as Shakespeare's equivalent and Woolf's own most honored foremother. But Austen's status for Woolf as the greatest of her literary foremothers is inseparable from Austen's status as a *ladylike* woman writer, one who has perfected the tea-table manner that Woolf herself had mastered as a girl, a manner Woolf portrays elsewhere as the quintessential trait of the Victorian lady. In the essay "Indiscretions," Woolf even likens Austen to the pure woman pouring out tea: "[F]rom the chastest urn into the finest china Jane Austen pours, and as she pours, smiles, charms, appreciates" (*W&W* 73). Austen resembles the Angel in the House who advises the woman writer to charm, to conciliate (60); a pure vessel herself, her art evokes the porcelain fragility Woolf figures as artistic perfection in *Room*'s draft. Unlike other women writers whom Woolf criticizes for overly watery and diffuse female fluidity, Austen's textual fluids remain pure and contained, social fluids suitable for public consumption, and a direct contrast to those produced by the rupture of the woman writer's hymen.[25]

After writing "Professions for Women" in 1931, however, Woolf condemned this kind of conciliatory manner in women's writing. In that essay, the woman writer murders the Angel in the House because the latter's advice of flattery and indirection makes it impossible for the woman writer to say what she really thinks in her review of a man's novel. "'Above all, be pure,'" the Angel admonishes the woman writer, as if speaking the (female) mind inevitably leads to a loss of chastity. Woolf's account of the conciliatory manner in "A Sketch of the Past" visits the same ground, although the shadowy figure of the mother no longer haunts the scene of writing. Acknowledging that "the surface manner allows one . . . to slip in things that would be inaudible if one marched straight up and spoke aloud" (Ethel Smyth's tactic, one imagines), Woolf goes on to criticize her early reviews for their ladylike decorum, the product of "tea-table training":

> When I read my old *Literary Supplement* articles, I lay the blame for their suavity, their politeness, their sidelong approach, to my tea-table training. I see myself, not reviewing a book, but handing plates of buns to shy young men and asking them: do they take cream and sugar? (S 150)

Nowhere is this condemnation of the tea-table manner more marked—or more ambivalent—than in Woolf's disavowal of Jane Austen as her favorite literary woman in a letter to Ethel Smyth. Here Woolf finally admits that she prefers the imperfect and passionate Brontës to Austen's technical perfection:

> JA is not by any means one of my favorites. Id give all she ever wrote for half what the Brontes wrote—if my reason did not compel me to see that she is a magnificent artist. What I shall proceed to find out, from her letters . . . is why she failed to be much better than she was. Something to do with sex, I expect; the letters are full of hints already that she suppressed half of her in her novels—Now why? (*L*5 127)

Austen, mermaid-like, hides the "half of her" that has "something to do with sex," and only Woolf's "reason," the half of Woolf similarly disconnected from "something to do with sex," compels her to recognize Austen's formal and technical prowess, that which renders Austen "a magnificent artist." Yet Woolf is no longer content to celebrate the technical mastery that necessitates the erasure of female corporeality. Austen could have been, should have been, much better. She failed where the Brontës didn't; she failed to inscribe her anger and rage at the repression of female sexuality. The woman writer as hostess no longer obtains. With this shift in mind, then, let us turn to Woolf's reconceptualization, in the 1930s, as of the hymen the site of female exchange and creativity.

"(Its never too late to rend)"

Although Woolf continued to describe the successful work of art in terms of "wholeness" and "completion" in the 1930s, she no longer envisioned the ruptured membrane as a flaw in the woman writer's work.[26] Woolf now depicts the hymen as a mediating membrane, an "elastic fibre" that suspends diverse elements in its capacious folds, a creative element specific to women. A symptomatic marker of Woolf's sense of the disfigurement and anguish of female creativity in *Room*, the hymen now becomes an emblem of communication. The problematic "centre" gives way to a valorization of "centrality," an atmosphere created for and around others by the creative woman.

A scene in *The Waves* illustrates this deliberate linkage of the ruptured hymen to female creativity and communion. Reading Shelley's "The Question" as a virginal schoolgirl, Rhoda imagines herself, like the poet, wandering down a "lush hedge" and gathering the flowers growing therein; she repeatedly stresses her desire for a receptive, empathic audience ("I will give; I will enrich . . . I will bind my flowers in one garland and . . . present them—Oh! to whom?" [*W* 214]). In contrast to the poet, however, Rhoda's offer of flowers develops from a voluptuous creative release Woolf depicts as a fantasy of autoerotic self-defloration:

> There is some check in the flow of my being; a deep stream presses on some obstacle; it jerks; it tugs; some knot in the centre resists. Oh, this is pain, this is anguish! . . . Now my body thaws; I am unsealed, I am incandescent. Now the stream pours in a deep tide fertilising, opening the shut, forcing the tight-folded, flooding free. To whom shall I give all that now flows through me, from my warm, my porous body? I will gather my flowers and present them—Oh! to whom? (*W* 213–214)

Images of rupture and release, fused with other favorite images for female creativity (the "incandescent" work that "consumes all impediments" in *Room;* the woman writer as fisherwoman in "Professions for Women"), underline the complex notion of audience that informs this passage: Rhoda refers to herself both as active "giver" and as porous and receptive. That Rhoda fails in her attempts to communicate with others and eventually commits suicide does not alter the fact that Woolf has begun to use the ruptured hymen as a positive emblem of women's creative powers.

I suggested earlier that Woolf's relationship with the pioneering composer Ethel Smyth provided the impetus for this transformative symbolization of female corporeality. Smyth's unique combination of maternal solicitude and artistic and feminist ambition enabled Woolf to develop an image of female creativity that encompassed the creativity of both the mother and the woman artist. Earlier, in the 1920s, the decade in which Woolf first began to formulate a "female aesthetic," Woolf represents the mother's creativity as far more powerful and far-reaching than that of the (often marginalized) female artist.

For example, in *A Room of One's Own,* the male poet of Woolf's description relies upon female domestic creativity to "fertilise" his literary vision: "He would open the door of drawing-room or nursery . . . and find her among her children perhaps, or with a piece of embroidery on her knee . . . the centre of some different order and system of life" (*R* 90). This scene revisits the famous passage in *To the Lighthouse* in which Mr. Ramsay breaks in upon Mrs. Ramsay's reading to James, only to plunge his "beak of brass" into the "fountain and spray" of her "delicious fecundity" (*TTL* 58–59). The painter Lily Briscoe, by contrast, remains isolated; literally standing at the verge of the lawn, she negotiates her vexed relation to the maternal surrogate by drawing "a line there, in the centre" (*TTL* 310)—a line that speaks to Mrs. Ramsay's, not Lily's, "centrality."

Woolf's work on female creativity in the 1920s thus seems haunted not only by the bad-faith advice of the Angel in the House, but by a deep anxiety that the creative woman competes with the mother who inevitably "wins" by cultural decree.[27] Yet it is also true that Woolf's first attempts at bridging this division occur in this decade. Consider Woolf's well-known discussion of the "woman's sentence," a term Woolf first uses in her review of Dorothy Richardson's *Revolving Lights* in 1923:

> She has invented, or, if she has not invented, developed and applied to her own uses, a sentence which we might call the psychological sentence of the feminine gender. It is of a more elastic fibre than the old, capable of stretching to the extreme, of suspending the frailest particles, of enveloping the vaguest shapes . . . It is a woman's sentence, but only in the sense that it is used to describe a woman's mind by a writer who is neither proud nor afraid of anything that she may discover in the psychology of her sex. (*W&W* 91)

Despite Woolf's disclaimer—a sentence can only be gendered insofar as it describes the psychology of the writer—her images suggest another difference for the formal differences she detects in the "woman's sentence." Woolf's imagery evokes both the hymen and the pregnant body: both are "capable of stretching to the extreme, of suspending the frailest particles, of enveloping the vaguest shapes." This "float" between pregnancy and the hymen is unusual in Woolf's descriptions of creative consciousness, although other descriptions of creative perception similarly figure the creative mind enveloped by a uterine or other transparent membrane: in "Modern Fiction" consciousness is a "luminous halo," the "semi-transparent envelope [that] surround[s] us from the beginning of consciousness to the end." And Woolf explicitly associates consciousness with a kind of preoedipal synaesthesia in "A Sketch of the Past," where she gropes for the words to capture "the feeling, as I describe it sometimes to myself, of lying in a grape and seeing through a film of semi-transparent yellow":

> If I were a painter . . . I should make a picture that was globular; semi-transparent. I should make a picture of curved petals; of shells; of things that were semi-transparent; I should make curved shapes, showing the light through, but not giving a clear outline. Everything would be large and dim; and what was seen would at the same time be heard; sounds would be indistinguishable from sights. (66)

Here Woolf celebrates creation as quintessentially preoedipal, a "globed compacted thing" (*TTL* 286) that remains protected from outside contact by a benign, apparently maternal surround.

As the letter that celebrates Smyth's "burning centre" demonstrates, however, Woolf saw in Smyth a model of the female creative process in which the woman artist's atmosphere *requires* rupture to succeed—and that rupture, tellingly, is the presence of her intimates, other creative women. Woolf's allusions to the Sleeping Beauty story thus feature the moment of violent rupture, the moment of female communication that enables female creativity. In a letter in which Woolf casts herself as the imprisoned and quiescent princess, she tells Smyth, "[A]lready I am spun over with doubts and impaled with thorns. Would you and Vanessa know how to burst through, free and unscathed? I suppose so . . . (a joke—if I had any red ink, I would write my jokes in it, so that even certain musicians—ahem!)" (*LA* 168). Frequently Woolf deliberately moves between images, from creation as pregnancy to the creativity of hymenal communion. Preferring to keep her "atmosphere unbroken," her shell protected, Woolf explains, "If I stay away [from her work in progress] . . . I break the membrane and the fluid escapes—a disgusting image, drawn I think from the memory of Vanessa's miscarriage." Teasingly, she adds, "All the same, I shall come, for a night, and let the membrane break if it will" (185). Finally, despite Woolf's enduring, residual "disgust" with female fluidity, the membrane exists to rupture. "Take away my affections and I should be . . . like the shell of a crab, like a husk . . . I should be nothing but a membrane, a fibre, uncoloured, lifeless, to be thrown away like any other excreta," she told Smyth (202–204); the hymen only exists insofar as it receives the precious life-blood of female communion. Smyth thus compares favorably to the "sun-dried and shell-like" Vernon Lee: "[Y]ou *do* continue, being, thank God, not a finished precious vase, but a porous receptacle that sags slightly, swells slightly, but goes on soaking up the dew, the rain, the shine, and whatever else falls upon the earth" (*L6* 406).

That Smyth understood the import of Woolf's language and responded to it in kind emerges in an astonishing exchange the two conducted concerning an alleged "maidenhead removal" operation (*L5* 223). Smyth writes Woolf that "lots of girls have themselves operated on nowadays so as not to endure tortures on marriage nights. . . . Why not try it now? (Its never too late to rend)." "[W]hat a lark!" Woolf responds. "Shall we go and be done together? Side by side in Bond Street?" (*L5* 223).[28] With her determination to express sexual experiences as openly as possible in her writing, her compassionate curiosity about Woolf's own self-confessed frigidity, and her easy participation in the teasing metaphors Woolf delighted in, Smyth became Woolf's most important sounding board for the creation of a female imaginary, a discourse that reappropriated female sexuality and that celebrated female specificity: the power of women *together* to re-create the world with themselves as central. Smyth's power and vitality created a protective aura in which Woolf no longer feared "dismemberment by wild horses." A figure of "entrustment" or "symbolic mediation," Smyth encouraged Woolf's "putting it into words" by listening to Woolf's stories about herself: because of Smyth's "maternal quality," Woolf wrote, she could "chatter faster and freer" to her than to anyone, certain Smyth's "perspicacity" would "*penetrate* . . . [her] childish chatter" (*L4* 188, my emphasis). And Woolf could then respond in kind: "Next time it shall be the other story—yours" (*L4* 188).

The violent rupture that becomes for Woolf the image of this exchange thus conflates birth with sexual penetration and rewrites the daughter's aching eroticism for a lost maternal protection as the scene of mutual exchange, mutual support, mutual erotic dependence. Each woman enters and exits the other's symbolic "centre," sure of her welcome and hopeful that the example of female creativity contained therein will further her own creative efforts. Of all the important women in Woolf's life—many of whom similarly functioned as maternal surrogates in Woolf's imaginative life—it was Smyth alone whom Woolf described in language identical to the language she used to describe her mother. Woolf's exultation in Smyth's ability to create a world "from her centre" resonates with Woolf's similar celebration of her mother's centrality: "[T]there she was, in the very centre of that great Cathedral space which was childhood"

(S 81); "[s]he was central. I suspect the word 'central' gets closest to the general feeling I had of living so completely in her atmosphere that one never got far enough away from her to see her as a person" (S 83); "[G]eneralised; dispersed . . . the creator of the crowded merry world which spun so gaily in the centre of my childhood . . . she was the centre; it was herself" (S 84).[29] Smyth thrilled Woolf by demonstrating how the woman artist also creates a world from her centre, and how such creation need not require the woman writer to "put down the body she has so often laid down," the fate Woolf had herself assigned to her paradigmatic woman writer Judith Shakespeare. With Smyth's encouragement, Woolf discovered creativity is incarnation, the word made female flesh. Such a discovery is, indeed, the very material of writing.

CHAPTER 4

Gunpowder Plots: Sexuality and Censorship in Woolf's Later Works

When Woolf first conceived of a sequel *to A Room of One's Own* in 1931, she imagined this new work would address "the sexual life of women" *(D4* 6), a subject that struck her as possessing incendiary potential: "I'm quivering and itching to write my—whats it to be called?—'Men are like that?'—no that's too patently feminist: the sequel then, for which I have collected enough powder to blow up St Pauls" *(D4* 77). Yet the various texts that arguably emerged from Woolf's engagement with "the sexual life of women"—"Professions for Women," *The Pargiters* (abandoned and published posthumously), *The Years,* and *Three Guineas*—play down or subordinate women's relationship to their corporeality. Instead, in these texts Woolf shifts her focus to the ways in which the middle-class woman's acculturation teaches her to censor her physicality, a censorship that typically results not only in female silence about physical experience, but in an atrophied or attenuated relationship to physicality altogether. These texts are also marked by increasingly negative assessments of maternity and female heterosexuality; and while Woolf at times condemns the cult of chastity in *The Years* and *Three Guineas,* she herself moves toward a valorization of the single or asexual woman—or the aged woman who Woolf imagines has outlived her sexuality—in her essays and fiction (e.g., Eleanor in *The Years* and Miss La Trobe and Lucy in *Between the Acts*). The revolutionary plots which were to blow up St. Paul's did not materialize.

What happened to the revolutionary fervor with which Woolf opened her last decade of writing? Why did Woolf never inscribe the "sexual life of women"? Or, perhaps more accurately, why did her inscriptions take such an attenuated and fragmentary bent? In tracing Woolf's revisions from *The Pargiters* to *The Years,* critics such as

Charles G. Hoffman, Mitchell A. Leaska, and Grace Radin have suggested that Woolf's aesthetic principles influenced the removal or dilution of didactic and polemical passages on female sexuality.[1] Such deletions would be consistent with Woolf's lifetime conviction that anger and didacticism damaged works of art and betrayed the personal grievances of the author; after all, she wrote a friend, "[A] novel is an impression not an argument" (*L5* 91). Still, another set of aesthetic principles might have governed the surviving traces of Woolf's original plan to examine "the sexual life of women," something we might call the aesthetics of sexual trauma. *The Years* and *Between the Acts* both feature a specific traumatic event which then reverberates throughout the text in question: in *The Years,* six-year-old Rose encounters an exhibitionist on her forbidden trip to and from a toy store, an encounter which haunts her throughout the rest of her life; in *Between the Acts,* thirty-nine-year old Isa reads about the gang rape of a young girl in a newspaper, and this shocking account intrudes upon her thoughts the rest of the novel's day. These scenes of trauma differ from those Woolf depicts in earlier novels: while not as debilitating as shell shock is to Septimus Smith in *Mrs. Dalloway,* for example, these sexual shocks are traumatic enough to alter irrevocably the characters to whom they occur.[2] The effect of traumatic sexual experience, moreover, reaches well beyond the individual woman: in *The Years* and other texts of this period, Woolf posits an evolutionary model of traumatic affect, whereby other female family members seem to "inherit" unconscious memory traces—and with those traces, a concomitant atrophy of sexuality and physicality.

Hence I propose that we read Woolf's "muting" of her critique in a somewhat different light than has hitherto been suggested: since the "sexual life" of English middle-class women meant for Woolf its abrogation and subsequent attenuation, her fictional methods needed to convey the process of repression that turned women's sexual desires into the shameful and guilty emotions she described as "subterranean instincts." As Grace Radin points out, Woolf's reading of Turgenev during her early work on *The Years* functions as a commentary on what Woolf herself was trying to do;[3] significantly, what Woolf admired in Turgenev was his habit of developing complex biographies for his characters, then eliminating most of the details, only allowing the essential aspects of the character to survive in the published version. This process of editing and eliminating meant that "the writer states the essential and lets the reader do the rest," Woolf notes; the reader responds to what is "only a birds eye view of the pinnacle of an iceberg" *(D4* 173). This conception of a submerged narrative foundation, invisible to the reader's eye but demanding the reader's active engagement with what is simultaneously essential and absent, seems particularly useful in considering Woolf's depictions of sexual trauma in her writing in the 1930s; what becomes immediately obvious is that many of Woolf s female characters—not just the traumatized Rose or Isa—exhibit classic symptoms of shame when female sexual experience or desire is at issue. The tangled roots of shame and traumatic sexual experience, then, underpin Woolf's treatment of adult female characters; their invisible presence is key to understanding Woolf's revolutionary project of exploring "the sexual lives of women."

"What is the Word for So Dumb and Mixed a Feeling?"

The explicit connections between traumatic sexual experience and damaged female lives that Woolf drew in the 1930s developed out of her intensive examination of her own sexuality, an examination spurred in large part by her newfound friendship in this decade with Ethel Smyth. Smyth's passionate response and identification with the polemic of *A Room of One's Own* caused her to contact Woolf, and together they delivered talks about the problems facing women artists. [4] It was in a letter to Smyth that Woolf first identified what she would later call the source of her artistic vision, her "shock-receiving capacity": "I have been thinking at a great rate—that is with profuse visibility," she told Smyth. "Do you find that is one of the effects of a shock—that pictures come up and up and up, without bidding or control?" (*L5* 334). And it was at the end of this decade—and during the writing of *Between the Acts*—that Woolf apparently recovered a specific memory of sexual abuse at the hands of her half-brother, a process of recognition and recovery that arguably emerged from her engagement with "the sexual life of women." [5] In the two brief discussions of this experience—one in a letter to Smyth, the other in the autobiographical sketch Woolf left unfinished before her suicide—Woolf connects sexual abuse to female speech and reticence in ways consistent with theoretical writing on trauma. [6] At the same time, she also questions the origins and meaning of the persistent and disabling sense of shame that pervades her memories of this event. In the first of these accounts, the letter to Smyth, Woolf writes,

> I'm interested that you can't write about masturbation. That I understand. What puzzles me is how this reticence co-habits with your ability

> to talk openly magnificently, freely about—say H.B. I couldn't do one or the other. But as so much of life is sexual—or so they say—it rather limits autobiography if this is blacked out. It must be, I suspect, for many generations, for women; for its like breaking the hymen—if thats the membrane's name—a painful operation, and I suppose connected with all sorts of subterranean instincts. I still shiver with shame at the memory of my half-brother, standing me on a ledge, aged about 6, and so exploring my private parts. Why should I have felt shame then? (*L6* 459–460)

For Woolf, to speak about female sexual experience is analogous to the rupturing of the hymen and the loss of one's chastity, as I showed in my last chapter. Here, I wish to focus on Woolf's enduring inability to account for the shame she (re)experiences in recalling this memory: "I still shiver with shame . . .Why should I have felt shame then?" she wonders. At the same time that this unaccountable shame from the past permeates her body, causing a corporeal reaction some 50 years after its originary cause, Woolf enacts the way in which censorship and repression converge at the site of her naming of female sexual experience: "as so much of life is sexual—or *so they say*—it rather limits autobiography if this is blacked out" (emphasis added). Even as Woolf comments on a constraint based upon repression, then, she replays it: an unnamed "they" say life is sexual, whereas Woolf apparently speaks from the assumed standpoint of an asexual woman whose experience has been blacked out.

Woolf was, of course, in the process of writing the autobiographical "A Sketch of the Past," wherein she first describes the scene of her abuse by her half-brother Gerald and her reaction to it in a passage dated April 1939:

> I remember how I hoped that he would stop; how I stiffened and wriggled as his hand approached my private parts. But it did not stop. His hand explored my private parts too. I remember resenting, disliking it—what is the word for so dumb and mixed a feeling? It must have been strong, since I still recall it. This seems to show that a feeling about certain parts of the body; how they must not be touched; how it is wrong to allow them to be touched; must be instinctive. (*S* 69)

Woolf tries to account for an emotion that evades description, a single "word" that somehow could contain so "dumb and mixed a feeling." Her explanation for this evasive feeling, moreover, turns the blame upon herself: it was wrong of her to allow herself to be touched, as if she had choice and control of the matter. And, even more interesting, she moves the question of shame away from a personal reaction to a broader, more generalized, evolutionary inheritance. As in her letter to Smyth, Woolf puzzles over her mute reaction of shame, finally concluding that it derives from what she calls in that letter "subterranean instincts." Woolf links this "instinctive" reaction generally to female silence, as well as to her own lifelong "looking-glass shame," in which the compulsive looking at her own image produced a deep sense of shame and guilt (S 68). She traces her dissociation from corporeal pleasure to these experiences: "[T]his ['inherited dread'] did not prevent me from feeling ecstasies and raptures spontaneously and intensely and without any shame or the least sense of guilt, so long as they were disconnected with my own body" (S 68).

I do not intend to dwell upon the biographical aspects of trauma in Woolf's life, which have been much discussed (e.g., DeSalvo, McNaron). Instead, I wish to draw attention to how Woolf's descriptions correspond to theoretical models of traumatic memory and shame before proceeding to a discussion of how Woolf fashioned a narrative aesthetic in the 1930s that would accommodate sexually traumatic events and that would, simultaneously, extend the affect of traumatic sexual experience into an "inherited dread" and "subterranean instinct" reaching deep into the corporeal experiences of Woolf's fictional middle-class women. To begin with, Woolf's elimination of clear causal connections for her characters' traumatic reactions is consistent with what theorists know about how the mind reacts to traumatic events. Traumatic memory differs from what theorists label "narrative memory": the latter "consists of mental constructs, which people use to make sense out of experience" (van der Kolk and van der Hart 160); ordinary events can typically be integrated into subjective assessment almost automatically, without conscious awareness. Traumatic events, however, cannot:

> [F]rightening or novel experiences may not easily fit into existing cognitive schemes and either may be remembered with particular vividness or may totally resist integration. Under extreme conditions, existing meaning schemes may be entirely unable to accommodate frightening experiences, which causes the memories of these experiences to be stored differently and not be available under ordinary conditions: it becomes dissociated from conscious awareness and voluntary control. (160)[7]

Traumatic events exist in a kind of time lag: they are not experienced fully by the victim at the time of the trauma, yet they recur with startling intensity, with a compulsive force over which the victim is powerless. These memories remain unnarratable: they "lack verbal narrative and context" and instead "are encoded in the form of vivid sensations and images" (Herman, *Trauma and Recovery* 31). Traumatic events *possess* their victims, moreover, forcing them to relive their terrorizing moments of self-dispossession. Roberta Culbertson has written that, instead of normal memory, victims experience a series of "body memories" that accompany the threefold aspects of trauma—the numbness at the time of victimization, the absorption of the perpetrator's message, and the reduction to a survival mode of existence:

> These memories of the body's responses to events are primary, prior to any narrative, and they may well surpass the victim's narrative ability because they pass beyond his knowledge. Memories of these split bits of experience are for this reason intrusive and incomprehensible when they reappear: there is nothing to be done with them. They obey none of the standard rules of discourse: they are the self's discourse with itself and so occupy that channel between the conscious and the unconscious that speaks a body language. They appear at first when the chatter dies down, then more and more forcefully, as if they will come out, will be eliminated by the body. But they are fragments, not something told. (178)

Culbertson enacts the difference between the narrativization of trauma—"something told"—and the fragmented intrusive remnants of actual traumatic memory by embedding within her essay several autobiographical passages about her own childhood sexual abuse. Most of these passages are logical accounts with clear beginnings, middles, and ends; Culbertson inserts these events in time and provides a retrospective meaning for them within the context of the essay and her present life. Several passages, however—jumbles of sensations, colors, emotions—illustrate the difference between *representations* of trauma and their actual felt and fragmentary "reality": traumatic memories do not make sense, can never make sense, for the very reason that they exist in a kind of limbo, the "channel between the conscious and the unconscious that speaks a body language." The victim, in effect, translates that body language into speech and story, reassembling the shards of memory into narrative—much as Freud first described the process in *Studies in Hysteria* [*Standard Edition* 2] in 1895. The story that results is just that, something that can be told to another. In fact, writers on trauma such as Judith Herman, Suzette Henke, Dori Laub, and James Pennebaker stress the necessity for the victim's creating a narrative of the traumatic event, taking fragmented components of frozen imagery and sensation" and reassembling them into "an organized, detailed, verbal account, oriented in time and historical content" (Herman, *Trauma and Recovery* 177). In part, creating a narrative enables the victim to recover the emotional affect: "[T]he patient must reconstruct not only what happened but also what she felt," Herman writes. "The description of emotional states must be as painstakingly detailed as the description of facts" (177). Here, Herman goes back to Freud, for in his Clark lectures on psychoanalysis in 1924 Freud stressed the same point: the hysteric cannot get rid of her symptom just by recounting the traumatic episode which underpinned it; the emotional affect must emerge in order for the symptom to subside and disappear. For Laub, creating a narrative is a way of counteracting the alterity of traumatic memories:

> The traumatic event, although real, took place outside the parameters of "normal" reality, such as causality, sequence, place and time. The trauma is thus an event that has no beginning, no ending, no before, no during and no after. This absence of categories that define it lends it a quality of "otherness," a salience, a timelessness and a ubiquity that puts it outside the range of associatively linked experiences, outside the range of comprehension, of recounting and of mastery. Trauma survivors live not with memories of the past, but with an event that could not and did not proceed through to its completion, has no ending, attained no closure, and therefore, as far as its survivors are concerned, continues into the present and is current in every respect. (69)

Hence Laub argues that the victim must "re-externalize" the event by articulating and transmitting the story to a listener and empathic witness, "and then take it back again, inside" (69). Crucial to Laub's argument is the listener: "The listener . . .is a party to the creation of knowledge . . .The testimony to the trauma thus includes its hearer, who is, so to speak, the blank screen on which the event comes to be inscribed for the first time" (57). According to Laub, then, the story does not exist and cannot be told in the absence of this empathic witness: "[T]he absence of an *addressable other*, an other who can hear the anguish of one's memories and thus affirm and recognize their realness, annihilates the story" (68, emphasis in the original). Suzette Henke has extended this model of testimony to include writing, what she calls "scriptotherapy" (xii); the person who writes of trauma must address another, and indeed, writing may actually accentuate the benefits of disclosure insofar as that writing requires orientation in time, the ordering of events, the creation of a narrative.

These models of the dialectical composition of testimony provide an important tool for distinguishing between Woolf's biographical accounts of sexual abuse and her portrayal of scenes of sexual trauma in *The Years* and *Between the Acts*. As I have shown, Smyth does function as an empathic listener, an "addressable other," in exactly the manner Laub delineates; she was arguably Woolf's most important correspondent and sounding board in the 1930s, someone with whom Woolf discussed, among other things, sexuality, mental illness, and suicide dreams. Woolf's letters to Smyth and her unfinished reminiscences demonstrate both the traumatic content of her memories—the fragmentary, intrusive, corporeal qualities identified by trauma theorists—and Woolf's ability and willingness to embed these memories in narrative, adding, for example, chronology and speculation about possible consequences (e.g., looking-glass shame and her inability to enjoy pleasures connected with the body). But the therapeutic narrative of trauma is not what Woolf creates in *The Years* and *Between the Acts*. Here Woolf focuses on "iconic" scenes of sexual trauma, particularized sets of images and bodily representations that crystallize the experience (Herman, *Trauma and Recovery* 38): these scenes intrude upon and rupture the narrative in a way that mimics traumatic experience and that refuses integration. Hence the reader bears witness in only the most limited way: instead of becoming a conduit for narrative coherence, as in Laub's or Henke's models, in reading about the traumatic event and its aftermath we are forced to experience the traumatic event as it functions for the character—we too encounter intrusive and recurring fragmentary memories that remain static, unexplained, incoherent. Given Woolf's customary anxiety about "the reader on the other side of the page," it seems important to consider what these intrusive, iconic memories accomplish in terms of Woolf's goal of inscribing "the sexual life of women."

In these last two novels, significantly, Woolf relegates traumatic experience to a modality of memory that contrasts with the models of memory she offers as "normative." Woolf develops two models of memory in *The Years:* the first model posits an "I" as a knot at the center of experience, a model Eleanor enacts in "drawing on the blotting-paper, digging little holes from which spokes radiated. Out and out they went; thing followed thing; scene obliterated scene" (*Y* 367). Here the model of memory is additive, broadening out from and glossing a primary sensory self or ego.[8] The second model does not foreground the "knot" but rather examines the interplay between the multiple strata of past memories and the present moment, a model that Woolf typically employs to depict intersubjective relationships.

When North meets Sarah and Maggie after many years, for example, he finds that "At first he scarcely remembered them. The surface sight was strange on top of his memory of them, as he had seen them years ago" (*Y* 346); later in the same episode, he wonders whether there was "always . . . something that came to the surface, inappropriately, unexpectedly, from the depths of people, and made ordinary actions, ordinary words, expressive of the whole being" *(Y* 349*)*. The past lies beneath and glosses the present moment; significantly, the "something" that comes to the surface suggests that "knot" or "center" in the web of Eleanor's drawing, a coherent register of personality.

Rose's traumatic memories, by contrast, exist in the isolated medium of traumatic, "iconic" images that remain solely her own, recalling Culbertson's description of traumatic memory as the "self's discourse with itself" (178). After Rose first sees the exhibitionist, a sight that Woolf presents imagistically and in the more immediate format of free indirect discourse—"[He] sucked his lips in and out. He made a mewing noise. But he did not stretch his hands out at her; they were unbuttoning his clothes" (*Y* 29)—Rose experiences a traumatic nightmare, and then finds herself incapable of narrating the experience: "'I saw . . .' Rose began. She made a great effort to tell her the truth; to tell [Eleanor] about the man at the pillar-box. 'I saw . . . ' she repeated. But here the door opened and Nurse came in" *(Y* 42). Many years later Rose again tries to narrate the trauma and again fails. A chance action recalls her past: "[S]uddenly she saw Eleanor sitting with her account books; and she saw herself go up to her and say, 'Eleanor, I want to go to Lamley's':

> Her past seemed to be *rising above* her present. And for some reason she wanted to talk about her past; to tell them something about herself that she had never told anybody, something hidden. She paused, gazing at the flowers in the middle of the table without seeing them. There was a blue knot in the yellow glaze she noticed. *(Y* 167, emphasis added)

In contrast to North's encounter with Sarah and Maggie, when he feels the present float on top of the past, Rose's past "rises above" the present, dominates it, dominates the knot in the center, returning Rose to the perceptual, traumatic experience of her childhood. The knot Rose sees outside herself, furthermore, suggests the splitting and dissociation typical of traumatic memory: The traumatic event possesses her and dispossesses the self, to use Laub's and Culbertson's language. No wonder, then, in the same passage, when Martin comments, "What awful lives children live!" turning to his sister for affirmation—"Don't they, Rose?"—she answers, "Yes . . .And they can't tell anybody" *(Y* 159).

Rose never does succeed in narrating her traumatic encounter to any other character, a fact that gains significance from Eleanor's apprehension of the therapeutic model of narrative sharing: "sharing things lessens things . . . Give pain, give pleasure an outer body, and by increasing the surface diminish them," she thinks to herself late in the novel (*Y* 352). The movement Woolf charts here is precisely that described by Herman, Laub, Pennebaker, and others: the translation of inner experience to narrative—with its concomitant requirements of chronology, empathic witnessing, the reclamation of emotional affect—results in the attenuation and diminishing of painful memories at best, their management and containment at least. Rose herself seems to understand the necessity of narration: in the chapter in which she finds herself possessed by the traumatic return of the past, she protests to her cousins that "talk" is "the only way we have of knowing each other" (*Y* 171). Yet Rose does not succeed in giving pain a surface life, an outer body, and hence deep in the strata of her memory she seems to retain vivid and fixed images of her traumatic experience. Indeed, Rose's inarticulate immersion in the traumatic memory illustrates Dori Laub's sense of trauma's alterity, its "otherness," its "timelessness and ubiquity"; because such memory exists outside normative narrative and chronological schemes, it "continues into the present and is current in every respect" (69). By extension, her experience remains unintegrated in the book: because she never "works through" the experience, it remains an unchanging moment of stasis within the book's shifting and mutable depictions of the multiple strata of the past. If indeed talk "is the only way we have of knowing each other," Rose remains radically unknown, both to the other characters and to the reader.

"*Why Should I Have Felt Shame Then?*"

I want to return to the question of shame that Woolf poses in conjunction with her own autobiographical account of sexual trauma. For the opening section of *The Years* suggests that sexuality is both foregrounded and denied for the female characters in ways that embed sexual desire and the female body in profound and inexplicable contexts of shame. Hence Rose's traumatic encounter with the exhibitionist—which she keeps to herself initially out of a sense of guilt and shame for defying her sister's instructions that she not go out alone—is only the most overt and explicit version of the shame affect that becomes associated with female sexuality. Interest in shame has gathered momentum in recent decades, fueled by the work of Helen Block Lewis, Leon Wurmser, and Andrew P. Morrison, and by the revival and extension of the affect theorist Silvan Tomkin in the work of Donald L. Nathanson, Gershen Kaufman, and others, including Eve Sedgewick and Adam Frank, whose 1995 edition of *Shame and Its Sisters: A Silvan Tomkins Reader* notably brought shame into the mainstream of literary criticism. As Liz Constable notes in her excellent overview of shame theory, Helen Block Lewis's pathbreaking work clearly delineates two poles of the shame experience, one intrapsychic, the other intersubjective (although the terminology is that of recent relational psychoanalysis, particularly that of Jessica Benjamin).[9] Lewis writes,

> Because the self is the focus of awareness in shame, "identity" imagery is usually evoked. At the same time that this identity imagery is registering as one's own experiences, there is also vivid imagery of the self in the other's eyes. This creates a "doubleness of experience," which is characteristic of shame. Shame is the vicarious experience of the other's negative evaluation. In order for shame to occur, there must be a relationship between the self and the other in which the self cares about the other's evaluation. Fascination with the other and sensitivity to the other's treatment of the self render the self more vulnerable in shame. ("Shame" 107–108)

An actual witness or judge need not be present; Benjamin Kilborne writes that, "Since shame is at bottom shame about the self, felt in interaction with an other, I am ashamed as I imagine I appear to you . . . shame deals not only with appearances (i.e., how I appear to you), but also with *imagined* appearances (i.e., how I *imagine* I appear to you), shame allows me to realize that I am that object that another is looking at and judging" (38). Similarly, the feminist philosopher Sandra Lee Bartky calls shame "the distressed apprehension of the self as inadequate or diminished: it requires if not an actual audience before whom my deficiencies are paraded, then an internalized audience with the capacity to judge me . . .shame requires the recognition that I *am*, in some important sense, as I am seen to be" (86). Wurmser, too, connects the experience of shame to an internal sense of contempt, that the self is exposed as "failing, weak, flawed, and dirty" ("Veiled Companion" 67). The experience of shame is, furthermore, soul-destroying, in part because the self feels radically cut off from the other or from society in general. Lewis calls shame "the 'sleeper' that fuels the irrational guilt whose malignant consequences Freud was the first to describe" ("Shame—the Sleeper" 1). She continues, "The metaphors for shame—'I could have died on the spot'; 'I wanted to sink through the floor' or 'crawl into a hole'—reflect our everyday understanding of shame's momentary lethal impact on the self" (1). Elsewhere she remarks the diminution of self involved in the shaming experience: "The self feels not in control but overwhelmed and paralyzed. The self feels small, helpless, and childish" ("Shame" 111). Andrew P. Morrison, listing the types of shame-related phenomena—for example, contempt, put-down, ridicule—adds "mortification": "its root indicates that shame 'kills'" ("The Eye Turned Inward" 287). He continues, ". . .this speaks eloquently to the importance of shame as a potentially overwhelming negative affect, the source . . . of some suicides of later adulthood that reflects the 'guiltless despair' of unrealized ambitions and goals" (288). Silvan Tomkins eloquently describes the diminishment of and estrangement from self that is at the heart of the shame affect:

> [S]hame is the affect of indignity, of defeat, of transgression, and of alienation. Though terror speaks to life and death and distress makes of the world a vale of tears, yet shame strikes deepest into the heart of man. Shame is felt as an inner torment, a sickness of the soul. It does not matter whether the humiliated one has been shamed by derisive laughter or whether he mocks himself. In either event he feels himself naked, defeated, alienated, lacking in dignity or worth. (*Reader* 133)

Tomkins, the originator of affect theory, links shame affect to curiosity and interest. He notes that shame is experienced more closely, more *as* self, than other affects; it is registered on the face and involves in particular emotional constellations linked to the perceptual register, to seeing and being seen: "Why is shame so close to the experienced self?" he asks. "It is because the self lives in the face, and within the face the self burns brightest in the eyes. Shame turns the attention of the self and others away from other objects to this most visible residence of self, increases its visibility, and thereby generates the torment of self-consciousness" (136). Similarly, Helen Block Lewis writes,

> Shame, which involves more self-consciousness and more self-imaging than guilt, is likely to involve a greater increase in feedback from all perceptual modalities. Shame thus has a special affinity for stirring autonomic reactions, including blushing, sweating, and increased heart

> rate. Shame usually involves more bodily awareness than guilt, as well as visual and verbal imaging of the self from the other's point of view. ("Shame" 108)

As many commentators note—and as many of us know from personal experience—the experience of blushing can lead to an exacerbation of the experience of shame. Tomkins observes, "[W]hen the face blushes, shame is compounded. And so it happens that one is as ashamed of being ashamed as of anything else" (*Reader* 137). Tomkins insists, however, that shame is profoundly ambivalent:

> In shame I wish to continue to look and to be looked at, but I also do not wish to do so. There is some serious impediment to communication which forces consciousness back to the face and the self. Because the self is not altogether willing to renounce the object, excitement may break through and displace shame at any moment, but while shame is dominant it is experienced as an enforced renunciation of the object. (*Reader* 137–138)

He sums up this quandary thus: "Shame-humiliation involves an ambivalent turning of the eyes away from the object toward the face and the self" (137). Indeed, shame often involves averting or covering the face, attempting to hide from the derision of the other. Otto Fenichel writes:

> "I feel ashamed" means "I do not want to be seen." Therefore, persons who feel ashamed hide themselves or at least avert their faces. However, they also close their eyes and refuse to look. This is a kind of magical gesture, arising from the magical belief that anyone who does not look cannot be looked at. (qtd. in Wurmser, "Veiled Companion" 67)

Wurmser, like Tomkins, identifies the eyes and perception as the locus of shame: "[T]he eye is the organ of shame par excellence," he writes (67).

In her extensive work on shame, Helen Block Lewis found consistently that women suffered more from shame—often disguised as depression—than did men. To begin with, in her studies on field dependence, "a cognitive style that catches the self in relation not only to its physical surround but in relation to others," Lewis discovered that women were more field dependent than men ("Shame" 103). Lewis also proved a correlation between field dependence, shame, and later depression (104). Joseph Adamson and Hilary Clark summarize the connections between shame, humiliated fury, and depression thus:

> [S]hame has traditionally shaped the experience of women under patriarchy. Women and others who suffer from inequality in power are particularly prone to the humiliated rage that stems from unacknowledged shame, a rage turned on the self and transformed to guilt because one does not feel entitled to it. Again, as the passive experience of being devalued and disempowered, shame is linked with low self-esteem and depression; it has been established that roughly twice as many women as men suffer from depression. (*Scenes of Shame* 22)

Many women, furthermore, learn to associate shame with femininity and female flesh. As Susan Bordo notes in her extensive work on eating disorders, many women experience their appetites as excessive, as too much. So, too, do women experience their bodies as too much: too much flesh, too much blood, too many possibilities for embarrassment. Women learn that respectability means "not to make spectacles of oneself," not to draw untoward attention, not, in some sense, to be "seen."

Although trauma and shame seem linked in an intuitive way, theorists of trauma and theorists of shame have tended to work in parallel, nonintersecting paths. [10] Recently, however, both theorists of shame and literary critics have begun to turn their attention to the ways in which traumatic experience and shaming may be intertwined. Significantly, Lewis links "humiliated fury"—the rage generated by unacknowledged shame—to sexual and physical abuse. When a trusted other—a member of one's family or a well-known family friend—sexually abuses a child, the child experiences "the profound shame that this betrayal of trust always occasions" ("Shame" 100). The humiliated fury this shame generates is then turned upon the self: "Humiliated fury has very little place to go except back down on the self, when one has been seduced, to become a component of one's humiliation. It is for this reason that the violation of the incest barrier between the powerful adult and the relatively powerless youngster is so damaging" ("Shame" 100). William Martin distinguishes between trauma and shame thus: "Put simply, trauma theory focuses on the proto-experience of an individual and her need to have it conceptualized through language, while shame theory provides a framework explaining often pathological forms of behavior as symptoms of intense shame."[11] The similarities between the two experiences is more than causative, however. As Donald L. Nathanson points out, what made Lewis's 1971 study a landmark analysis of shame was "her meticulous demonstration that guilt is usually well-worded and easily accessible, whereas shame is silent, image dependent, and demanding of sympathetic confirmation before it can be approached in therapy" ("Shame/Pride Axis" 184). In other words, both the traumatic experience and the shame experience are imagistic, bodily based, and speechless, and so painful as to require banishment from consciousness. Both kinds of experience can be processed only dialectically, in the presence of an empathic or sympathetic audience.

With these formulations in mind, let us turn back to *The Years* and its urtext, *The Pargiters.* (In this respect, *The Pargiters* resembles the narratives Turgenev created for his characters and then eliminated.) Shame—specifically shame about female corporeality and sexual desire—is everywhere in these texts. Woolf is particularly astute at grasping the ways in which shame requires a sense of another, a witness, before whom the person so affected feels "caught" in a light beamed upon the person's shortcomings. "Don't be caught looking," Eleanor warns her younger sisters when they peer through the window at an eligible young man: they are in the impossible position of needing to find husbands yet forbidden to exhibit sexual desire or even sexual curiosity (*Y* 19, *P* 18). Eleanor, the maternal surrogate, here functions as the voice of "enforced renunciation" of interest and enjoyment, to use Tomkins's phrasing. In *The Pargiters,* Woolf elaborates upon the sisters' experience of shame:

> Both Delia and Milly blushed with a peculiar shame, when Eleanor said, "Don't be caught looking"—they wanted to look at the young man; they knew it was wrong to look; they were caught looking; they disliked being caught: they were ashamed, indignant, confused-all in one—& the feeling, since it was never exposed, save by a blush or a giggle; wriggled deep down into their minds & sometimes woke them in the middle of the night with curious sensations, unpleasant dreams that seemed to come from one fact—that Abercorn Terrace was besieged on all sides by what may be called street love. (*P* 38)

Sexual desire—curious sensations that immediately transmute into unpleasant dreams—gets entangled in the shame affect and "wriggle[s] deep into their minds," a phrasing that suggests Eve's sexual fall as the result of the serpent's temptation. After all, wanting to know what one is explicitly forbidden to know is the basis of Western culture's most enduring myths of female perfidy—Pandora and her box, Eve and the forbidden fruit, Bluebeard's wife and the bloody chamber, Psyche and her mysterious lover Eros (significantly, three of these stories—those of Pandora, Bluebeard, and Psyche—involve looking at a forbidden sight). What Woolf suggests, moreover, is that sexual curiosity and desire are literally driven underground, significant in light of Woolf's pervasive linking of sexual interest and desire with the word and location of the "subterranean." Similarly, when Rose encounters the exhibitionist, she is worried that her father will be angry at her for having seen what she should not have seen. Her shame and guilt render her speechless:

> The grey face that hung on a string in front of her eyes somehow suggested to her a range of experiences in herself of which she was instinctively afraid; as if, *without being told a word about it, she knew that she was able to feel what it was wrong to feel she* could not say to her sister, even, was that she had seen a sight that puzzled her, and shocked her, and suggested that there were things brooding round her, unspoken of, which roused *curiosity* and physical fear. (*P* 50, my emphasis)

Female sexual curiosity becomes linked to furtive, shameful emotions; throughout these descriptions Woolf's emphasis is on forbidden sight and curiosity, followed by and shrouded in subsequent shame and silence. To use Tomkins's formulations, shame is inextricably linked to the ambivalent desire to look, "an auxiliary to the affect interest-excitement and enjoyment-joy" (Nathanson, "A Timetable for Shame" 20). Shame thus functions as a means of modulating interest in or excitement about an object. As Nathanson observes, "[T]he universal caution 'curiosity killed the cat' seems to indicate a general cultural awareness that the affect interest needs a modulator" (20). That Woolf herself linked her ambivalent "looking-glass shame"—the compulsive and yet shameful specular encounter with her own image—to her experience of sexual molestation further supports the link between forbidden sights and experiences and subsequent shame and silence.

In her third essay in *The Pargiters,* Woolf explicitly links Rose's experience of seeing something that interested her but that she somehow knew was wrong for her to see to Eleanor's caution to Delia and Milly against looking. Considering the constrictions which surrounded these young women in order to protect them (silently) from "street love," Woolf writes, "not only did it restrict their lives, and to some extent poison their minds—lies of all sorts undoubtedly have a crippling and distorting effect, and none the less if the liar feels that his lie is justified—but it also helped to bolster up, to harden, and substantiate a conception of the utmost importance about conduct, not only in the minds of the Pargiter sisters, but in the minds of their brothers" (*P* 52). This "hardening" introduces into the passage an indictment of phallicism, and of patriarchal law which restricts women because men are unrestrained. Woolf continues: "And yet they were all completely uncertain as to what conduct was right; and yet they all had dangling before them, as they grew older, the conviction that some convention was absolutely necessary for them, and not for their brothers. The question of chastity was therefore complicated in the extreme" (*P* 53). Significantly, the word "dangling" will recur in Woolf's final revision of Rose's traumatic nightmare of the exhibitionist, the man at the pillar box:

> Something had swum up on top of the blackness. An oval white shape hung in front of her—dangling, as if it hung from a string. She half opened her eyes and looked at it. It bubbled with grey spots that went in and out. She woke completely. A face was hanging close to her as if it dangled on a bit of string. She shut her eyes; but the face was still there, bubbling in and out, grey, white, purplish and pockmarked. (*Y* 41)

Woolf's layering of sexual imagery is quite dense: she limns not only the face of a man masturbating and reaching climax, but the physical description—the mottled coloring and the rhythmic movement, the enlarging and deflating of the "dangling," elongated oval—evokes a grotesque image of male genitalia. In light of Woolf's own experiences with her half-brothers, it is perhaps not surprising that in the draft version of Rose's trauma the experience results in her mistrust of her brother. "After the adventure in the street," Woolf writes, "Rose changed slightly but decidedly in her feeling for Bobby. Again it is difficult to say how far this change was the result of the shock; how far she felt some fear or dislike for her brother because of his sex" (*P* 54). Woolf's refusal to pin down the exact nature of Rose's "adventure" is consistent with her final version, in which the event affects Rose throughout her life in ways Woolf refuses to narrate.

Woolf's persistent use of the word "subterranean" to describe women's so-called "instincts" must also be contextualized within the forbidden, in particular the taboos placed upon female curiosity and interest in the sexual aspects of self or other. Woolf develops this aspect of shame most fully in her narrative about the Pargiters' cousin Kitty, whose full name—Katharine Persephone Malone (*P* 69)—hints at the abrogation and burial of her sexuality. Even if Kitty had felt attraction for someone, Woolf writes, "she was so much restrained by the conventions of the society in which she lived that her response . . .would have been instantly checked by the knowledge she must conceal it"

(*P* 109). Woolf details the "very strict moral code" that Kitty has learned since she was a little girl, from kicking up her legs to standing at her window at night in her nightgown, "from saying or doing anything which could suggest even remotely that she felt physically or ideally attracted" by men (*P* 109). Hence her kissing the farm boy behind the haystack, although pleasurable, rouses considerable guilt: "[S]he knew that she was committing an appalling crime" (109). The end result is the atrophying of her sexual desire and interest:

> [S]he felt much less, physically, than [young men her age] did—for the physical side of love had been so repressed not only in her, but in her mothers and grandmothers, that it was much weaker, even in a girl of perfect physique like Kitty, than in a young man like Tony Ashton who was physically less perfect, but sexually much better developed, since no restrictions had been placed either on him or on his fathers or grandfathers that were comparable in severity with those that had surrounded Kitty almost since birth. (*P* 109)

Here Woolf introduces the evolutionary concept of sexual restraint, developed after generations of restrictions on middle-class women's sexuality. She reiterates: "Kitty . . . therefore inherited the effects of an education which, if we attribute any importance to education, was bound not merely to teach her a certain code of behaviour, but also to modify the passion itself" (*P* 110). Hence in the Victorian age "the young girl . . .has hardly any passion left":

> Either it has been extinguished by the process of education, or as happened with Kitty, passion still existed but was so much restricted that it was a furtive, ill-grown, secret, subterranean vice, to be concealed in shame, until by some fortunate chance, a man gave the girl a chance, by putting a wedding ring on her finger, to canalise all her passion, for the rest of their lives, solely upon him. (*P* 110)

Woolf links here the wedding ring to the "canalising" of women's passion, a linkage that suggests patriarchal ownership of the hymen and the vagina. The word "subterranean" suggests that by the time passion does become legitimated in marriage, it is too late: passion no longer exists, except in a furtive and somehow shame-filled form. Consider, too, Woolf's use of subterranean passages in *The Voyage Out*, where the traumatic shock of Richard Dalloway's kiss provokes the following nightmare of Rachel's "walking down a long tunnel," that opens into a vault where she finds herself "trapped" in the company of "a deformed man who squatted on the floor gibbering, with long nails. His face was pitted and like the face of an animal" (*VO* 77). This passage anticipates Woolf's memory of sexual assault in "A Sketch of the Past," where Woolf links the assault to her "looking-glass shame" and a dream of seeing "the face of an animal" in a mirror (S 69). Yet the bestial, deformed man's appearance in a nightmarish and constrictive female terrain suggests that femaleness is a deformed and lunatic manifestation of maleness. After all, Woolf characterizes herself at 15 as "a nervous, gibbering, little monkey . . . mopping and mowing, and leaping into dark corners" (116). As she tells Smyth in a letter, moreover, her recurrent "suicide dream" is one of finding herself alone in a drainpipe: "[S]uddenly, I approach madness and that end of a drainpipe with a gibbering old man" (*L4* 298).

Subterranean Instincts

> *"But as so much of life is sexual—or so they say—it rather limits autobiography if this is blacked out. It must be, I suspect, for many generations; for women, for its like breaking the hymen—if thats the membrane's name—a painful operation, and I suppose connected with all sorts of subterranean instincts."*
>
> (L*6:460*)

Woolf's strong belief in a kind of Darwinian process of atrophy in middle-class women's sexuality is striking; she insists again and again on the ways in which generations of acculturation have made women unwittingly connive in their own sexual frigidity and deformation. Given what we now know about the ways in which the children of trauma survivors are themselves affected by the parents' experience, it is necessary to consider Woolf's portrayals of women's "subterranean instincts" as yet another ramification of female sexual disinheritance through forms of sexual assault. Woolf's sense of the "inherited dread" and "subterranean instincts" clustered around female corporeal experience anticipates the current theoretical interest in understanding the way in which trauma extends beyond the individual into the community. In particular, her writing resonates with that of the psychoanalytic theorists Abraham and Torok, whose work focuses on trauma experiences that pass intergenerationally through inherited unconscious "phantoms."

For Abraham and Torok, the basis of psychic life is the principle of "introjection," the way in which we "open and fashion and enrich ourselves, transcend trauma, adjust to internal or external upheaval and change, create forms of coherence in the face of emotional panic and chaos" (14). Introjection is a three-fold process:

1. Something—good or bad—occurs to someone.
2. The person "appropriates" the experience through play, creativity, fantasy, or any number of activities.
3. The person becomes aware of the occurrence and understands "why and how the scope of self has been modified and expanded" (14). The event, in other words, is given a place in the person's emotional existence.

Trouble occurs when something interferes with the process of introjection. Abraham and Torok, like the early Freud and like their countryman Sandor Ferenczi, returned to the early problems in psychoanalysis, "the effects of forgotten painful memories, the nature of traumas, and their role in the development of neurosis" (16). Abraham and Torok examine the "mental landscapes of submerged family secrets" and "the preservation of a shut-up or excluded reality" (18). In particular they analyze the psychological weight of "unwanted, shameful, or untoward reality" and the process by which such reality becomes psychically isolated, split off from "the free circulation of our ideas, emotions, imaginations, creations, responses, initiatives, and contact with other people." This process of confining unbearable experiences to an inaccessible region of the mind is what Torok terms "incorporation" or "preservative repression": "Preservative repression seals off access to part of one's own life in order to shelter from view the traumatic moment of an obliterated event" (18). Abraham and Torok go on to develop a model of the psychic "secret," by which they mean a trauma "whose very occurrence and devastating emotional consequences are entombed and therefore consigned to internal silence, albeit unwittingly, by the sufferers themselves" (99–100). These "secrets," in turn, can become "phantoms," mechanisms by which a family's secrets are transmitted unconsciously and intergenerationally. One family member's unconscious fear or conflict can thus become a legacy, warping and distorting the lives of his or her descendants.

Abraham and Torok's belief in the unconscious transmission of traumatic conflict resonates with Woolf's conviction that forms of "inherited dread" distorted the sexual lives of middle-class women, a conviction she develops most fully in *The Years* and *Between the Acts*. As noted above, Rose's encounter with the exhibitionist remains unintegrated and inarticulate in *The Years*. Yet aspects of that repressed memory do seem to affect, even to enter the subconscious mind, of another member of her family. At the family reunion that closes the novel, Rose's niece Peggy suddenly glimpses "a state of being, in which there was real laughter and happiness, and this fractured world was whole; whole, vast, and free" (*Y* 390). Her problem becomes one of articulation: "But how could she say it?" (390). Her attempt to articulate this sudden vision of coherence, of a moment when "this fractured world was whole" fails miserably. In spite of herself, Peggy's felicitous vision suddenly evokes a vicious personal attack on her brother. Peggy herself recognizes that something has gone horribly awry: "She had got it wrong. She had meant to say something impersonal, but she was being personal" (390). In fact, Peggy's fragmented effort echoes Woolf's description of Rose's traumatic vision of a "face . . . hanging close to her as if it dangled on a bit of string":

> There was the vision still, but she had not grasped it. She had broken off only a little fragment of what she meant to say . . . Yet there it hung before her, the thing she had seen, the thing she had not said. But as she fell back with a jerk against the wall, she felt relieved of some oppression . . .She had not said it, but she had tried to say it. (391)

Peggy tries to protect herself from a counterattack by dissociating herself from the present, by going back to a happy memory of a summer evening when she and her brother North are adolescents with a shared secret. She is afraid of ridicule, ashamed of herself. But all sit in silence until Kitty Lasswade arrives: "They all got up. Peggy got up. Yes, it was over, it was destroyed, she felt. Directly something got together, it broke. She had a feeling of desolation. And then to have to pick up the pieces, and make something new, something different, she thought, and crossed the room" (392).

Why does Peggy's attempt to articulate an impersonal vision of wholeness veer off into an attack on her brother? Why do all sit in silence instead of responding? And why does Peggy feel "relieved of some oppression" because she has attempted, however unsuccessfully, to describe an unnamed and inarticulate "it"? At some level, it seems that Rose's repressed memory has intruded into the novel's "present day." For Peggy's attack on her brother recalls the passage in *The Pargiters* wherein Woolf states that the encounter with the exhibitionist changes Rose's relationship to her brother (there named Bobby, not Martin). As Woolf makes clear, Peggy's memories of her brother are of harmony and a united front toward their parents, making her compulsive attack on him even more illogical. That no one responds—Eleanor, the original intended recipient of Rose's experience is, significantly, one of those present—suggests that Peggy's attempt to say what cannot be said is *itself* important, as if all instinctively understand Eleanor's apprehension that "sharing things lessens things [. . .] Give pain, give pleasure an outer body, and by increasing the surface diminish them" (352).

Peggy's sense of fragmentation, of a rupture of wholeness, reverberates with other such scenes in Woolf's fiction, most notably Mrs. Ramsay's pause on the threshold of the dinner party before bringing it to an end, as well as Lily Briscoe's later memory of Mrs. Ramsay, Charles Tansley, and herself on the beach. "Making of the moment something permanent" (*TTL* 161) is the very essence of Woolf's aesthetic, as she makes clear in her development of the concept of "moments of being" in "A Sketch of the Past." What is distinct about this scene in *The Years* is that the moment expresses disharmony and anger against the brother and that the family witnesses this anger in some kind of silent recognition.

In *The Years,* Woolf succeeds in inscribing the "sexual life of women," not by describing and enumerating the kind of factual material she initially envisioned, but by using her considerable skills in writing novels about silence and the things people don't say—in other words, by capturing the more elusive and more fragmentary corporeal shock of sexual trauma and the kinds of experiences that evade language. Instead of trying to explain women's sexual lives, Woolf represents the traumatic events that dispossess women and that curtail female sexual expression. She thereby succeeds in finding words that can describe "so dumb and mixed a feeling."

Significantly, when Woolf returned to the subject of sexual trauma in *Between the Acts,* her use of the myth of the rape of Philomela as a paradigmatic and originary account of female storytelling situates rape as the foundational moment of women's sexual experience. That account is unspoken yet hauntingly present, pervading *Between the Acts* much as Rose's sight of the exhibitionist haunts other characters' psyches in *The Years.* Thus when Isa attempts to come to her husband's aid by expanding a Shakespeare passage he is reciting, the "first words that came into her head" are not Shakespeare, but a line from Keats's "Ode to a Nightingale": "'Fade far away and quite forget what thou amongst the leaves has never known,'" Isa quotes (*BTA* 54). What Woolf demonstrates is that "what we would forget" is never forgotten; the spectral traces of the traumatic past linger on, haunting us all.

CHAPTER 5

When the Pervert Meets the Hysteric: Jean Rhys's Black Exercise Book

In 1938, Jean Rhys interrupted her composition of *Good Morning, Midnight* to write out an account of a "mental seduction" by a family friend that had occurred when she was 14. Calling the seduction "the thing that formed me that made me as I am" (cited in Thomas 27), Rhys describes the memory as intrusive and compulsive, noting that it was a great relief to set the novel aside and write it out.[1] Rhys notes further that she has been drinking heavily, and that *Good Morning, Midnight* had taken on a compulsive life of its own, with words and sentences echoing over and over again in her head. To her surprise, she awoke one day to find that the novel had vanished out of her mind; instead, it was if she were back in Dominica, reliving her childhood. Rhys began to write out her memories, finding it a relief not to have to torture her material into the form of a novel and finding also that she didn't need to drink as much. Although Rhys claims that she wrote the account for one, possibly two reasons, she never specifies what those reasons are. It becomes clear, however, that whatever reasons Rhys had in mind, her account of this mental seduction is an attempt to understand the compulsive and repetitious nature of what she termed her "doom," a "motif of pain" that has pervaded her life and from which she cannot escape. The resulting narrative is a fascinating, firsthand account of childhood sexual trauma in 1905 and its subsequent far-reaching effects upon one woman's life, as if Dora stepped out of the pages of a male-authored case history to claim her status as subject and her story as her own. Indeed, Rhys consciously and deliberately positions her narrative against that of an unnamed "gent"—almost certainly Freud—whose book on psychoanalysis she leafs through at Sylvia Beach's bookstore in Paris. Yet Rhys's foregrounding of the Mr. Howard narrative in the Black

Exercise Book has obscured another aspect of Rhys's "doom," the brutal punishment she endured at the hands of her mother and the way in which that punishment facilitated Rhys's conviction that "pain humiliation submission yes that is for me" (cited in Thomas 27). Mr. Howard's "mental seduction" of Rhys becomes, then, a moment of crystallization and recognition, one that draws together and simultaneously eroticizes diverse strands of her experience—her mother's violence, her Catholic education, the racial tensions and inequities in Dominica—forming in Rhys the "kink" (her term) that would impel her to develop a distinctly masochistic aesthetic in her fiction.

Rhys's account is particularly interesting given its close correspondence to the phenomenon contemporary researchers have named "recovered memory," the reemergence of memories of childhood sexual abuse after years of dissociative amnesia.[2] Yet, as if anticipating the skepticism of those who question the reliability of such memories, Rhys herself stresses the malleability of her memory. She repeatedly draws attention to her forgetting, noting of the seduction, "What happened was that I forgot it!? It went out of my memory like a stone" (cited in Angier 29; in the notebook the exclamation point and question mark are superimposed upon one another). Similarly, in a passage of her autobiography that seems to refer obliquely to these experiences, Rhys makes the following curious remark: "I shut away at the back of my mind any sexual experiences, for of course some occurred, not knowing that this would cause me to remember them in detail all the rest of my life. I became very good at blotting things out, refusing to think about them" (*SP* 50). At other times Rhys notes her capacity for fugue or trance states when under duress. Hence when abandoned by her first lover, Rhys describes "a complete blank" in which she apparently took a taxi ride, gave away his gift of a Christmas tree, and brought home a full bottle of gin (*SP* 100–101).[3] During the crisis period following her third husband's arrest, Rhys writes a friend that she is experiencing "one of my 'trance' days . . . the unreal feeling which is I suppose kindly Nature's way when complete catastrophe arrives. Anodyne has always been my favourite word" (*LJR* 71).

These passages demonstrate Rhys's prescient understanding of the way in which the mind can split off or dissociate during times of trauma or extreme stress. In fact, her description of blotting out the "mental seduction" by refusing to think about it—a process which she claims simultaneously and paradoxically preserves the events in question—anticipates contemporary findings on the mechanisms by which people *actively* inhibit memory retrieval. As Martin A. Conway notes,

"[I]f a memory . . . associated with something that is familiar . . . is actively avoided every time that familiar object is seen, then the memory becomes repressed and the avoided item is later difficult to remember" (319). Jennifer J. Freyd argues that such motivated forgetting is especially likely when a child is sexually abused by a relative or other caregiver: "[A]mnesia for the abuse is an adaptive response, for amnesia may allow a dependent child to remain attached to—and thus elicit at least some degree of life-sustaining nurturing and protection from—his or her abusive caregiver," she writes (*Betrayal Trauma* 180).[4] In her study of different types of abuse victims, Lenore C. Terr finds that experiences of repeated trauma elicit defense mechanisms such as denial, numbing, self-hypnosis, depersonalization, and dissociation as the victim learns to anticipate the abusive behavior; such mechanisms in turn inhibit memory retrieval (72).[5] Guilt and shame may also become motivations for keeping silent and "blotting out" the events.

As in Woolf's work, then, writing becomes for Rhys the means of confronting sexual trauma and sorting out her own conflicted responses to it; and, again like Woolf, Rhys accepts the vagaries of memory and allows her life-writing to reflect memory's mutability. But while Rhys pursues the question of "what we must remember, what we would forget" with the same sense of urgency as does Woolf, Rhys's accounts, both biographical and fictional, remain resolutely fixed on the individual response to sexual trauma and exploitation.

The Black Exercise Book: An Overview

Rhys wrote this autobiographical account in pencil in a small black exercise book, now part of the Jean Rhys Collection held by the McFarlin Library at the University of Tulsa. The entire narrative takes up about 112 pages of the notebook, and the handwriting ranges from fairly legible at some points to completely illegible at others: significantly, the pages describing the traumatic sexual experience are among the most incoherent, both in terms of grammar and in terms of handwriting. Other factors also make an accurate transcription difficult: Rhys often wrote words above, under, or beside other word choices and added comments in the top and bottom margins of the notebook, and she occasionally carried on sentences up the side margins. Hence a sentence will often contain variants and two lines of thought may continue at the same time. Three times Rhys censors her account: twice she scores over the lines repeatedly, making it impossible to read what she has written underneath; the third suppression is an actual excision, a neatly torn out section of approximately three lines in the middle of the notebook page. These elisions disrupt Rhys's description of the whippings she received from her mother and the description of what Mr. Howard actually did. Despite the difficulties of reading the notebook, Rhys's narrative has a discernable tripartite structure. In the first 50 pages, Rhys describes her childhood in Dominica, including her education at a Catholic convent and her beatings at the hands of her mother. The description of the seduction occupies about 20 pages in the middle, and at this point Rhys claims to write the end of her story with a description of Mr. Howard's easy and respectable death at the age of nearly 80 and her own subsequent amnesia about the experience. Yet this is not the end of the story in the notebook: Rhys goes on to describe her nightmares, her mother's failure to respond to her emotional distress, and her renunciation of her conventional dreams of marriage and motherhood; the account comes to a close in a fragmentary conversation about "hysterical lady novelists" that takes place between Rhys and a "quiet" man she identifies only by the initial L (perhaps her second husband, Leslie, a publishers' agent).

Rhys repeatedly calls attention to her desire to tell her story as accurately as possible at the same time that she dramatizes her inability to do so. In this respect, her narrative bears a strong resemblance to Freud's description of hysterical narratives in his introductory remarks to the case history of Dora. Here Freud enumerates the characteristics of such stories: they suffer from deliberate and accidental omissions, true amnesias, fictional constructs developed to fill in the amnesias, faulty chronology, and fragmentary status. Rhys's narrative similarly suffers from gaps—some deliberate, as I note above—and similarly lacks a clear chronology; but in contrast to Freud's obsession with creating a complete and seamless narrative, Rhys is well aware and completely accepting of her failures in recall: an accomplished practitioner of modernist fiction, she draws attention to and incorporates these lapses of memory in her account.[6] Early on, for example, she wonders what she had done to deserve constant punishment; she comes to no definite conclusion, but suggests that she has either "blotted out" the memory or simply never known what it was she was supposed to have done. She characterizes her memories about the actual seduction as similarly untrustworthy and indeterminate. She finds, for example, that she cannot remember with any precision how long the seduction went on, noting that it could have been months or even weeks, but that perhaps it only seemed that way. She then tries to pin down her memories by determining how many occasions she and Mr. Howard met, counting up to six but concluding that there were more. She also explains that while the seduction went on she felt that she was living in an unpleasant dream, that she felt drugged; and that her family and other people seemed unreal, as if they had become shadows. She notes curiously how the entire episode vanished from her memory for over 30 years. Given the fact that Rhys felt this mental seduction was the source of her "doom," she displays remarkably little rancor toward Mr. Howard, observing that if she herself had only been a more healthy-minded person, the experience would not have affected her. As is common with childhood sexual abuse victims, Rhys blames herself for not figuring out a way to make the seduction stop and for being drawn in: calling herself a fool, she scolds herself because she "lapped it up & asked for more" (cited in Angier 28).[7]

Although the notebook was a private journal, Rhys evidences considerable anxiety about audience and whether or not she will be believed. Her anger at the "gent" whose book on psychoanalysis she picks up at Sylvia Beach's bookstore is directed at his insistence on the fictitious character of the hysteric's story. Recalling not the exact words but the overall meaning, Rhys quotes and attacks the charges that infuriate her: "Women of this type will invariably say that they were seduced when very young by an elderly man. . . . They will relate a detailed story which in *every* case is entirely ficticious [*sic*]" (cited in Thomas 45). Rhys mockingly assumes the voice of the psychoanalytic gent, who reduces his women patients to cases identified only by numbers and whose blanket diagnosis is that they are all crazy. Above all, Rhys reacts furiously to the gent's "laying down the law about the female attitude & reactions to sex," refuting his dismissal and his sure knowledge of his own authority: "No honey I thought It is *not* fictitious in every case. By no means. & Anyhow how do you know" (cited in Thomas 45). Rhys ends her tirade against the psychoanalytic gent with an impossible request, that one man would try to write fairly about women.[8] In doing so, she inadvertently supplies an answer to Freud's famous question—What do women want?—even as she articulates her resentment at Freud's reduction of his women patients to nameless, numbered case histories whose individual stories of sexual seduction he lumps together and dismisses as generic tales disguising the women's own sexual fantasies. Rhys tries to resist the relevance of Freud's dismissal to her own autobiographical efforts by drawing a distinction between the seductions of his patients and her own: whereas Freud is concerned with physical seductions, Rhys herself is concerned with a mental one. Yet Freud's reductive dismissal clearly rankles Rhys, for she returns to her task with a renewed commitment to telling her story as accurately as possible; her admission of the unreliability of her memories thus speaks to her desire to represent trauma in its vagaries and inexactitude.

That Rhys's rebuttal of the psychoanalytic gent specifically and patriarchal authority more generally comes at the opening moment of her testimonial is significant in a number of ways. For one thing, it reminds Rhys that at the time of the seduction she did not tell anyone because, like the "potty cases" dismissed by the psychoanalytic gent, she did not think she would be believed. Freud's dismissal of traumatic narratives as hysterical sexual fantasies thus reenacts the isolation Rhys had experienced as an adolescent even as it reinforces her conviction that when a man's word contradicts a woman's, hers is dismissed. As Rhys makes clear, moreover, Mr. Howard's standing in the community—a respected landowner, an Englishman—makes him particularly invulnerable in comparison to her own status as a colonial, a girl, and a family scapegoat. In fact, his position is so exalted, Rhys writes, that his wife, who Rhys felt certain knew about the relationship, did not interfere or try to stop it; instead, the wife loathed Rhys. In addition to reviving questions of her own authorial credibility, Freud's dismissal of women's stories of trauma may have seemed like yet another violation to Rhys, who had apparently gone to the bookstore for help in understanding her emotional plight. Jeffrey Moussaieff Masson contends that the analyst who is trained to believe that traumatic memories are fantasies "does violence to the inner life of his patient and is in covert conclusion with what made her ill in the first place" (191). He continues, "The silence demanded of the child by the person who violated her (or him) is perpetuated and enforced by the very person to whom she has come for help. Guilt entrenches itself, the uncertainty of one's past deepens, and the sense of who one is is undermined" (192). Rhys's trip to Shakespeare and Company in search of insight into her own troubled past—in search, as it appears, of Freud's help—indeed forces her to confront the patriarchal structures of domination that compelled her silence in the first place.

But Freud's dismissal does not silence Rhys. Instead she returns to her story with renewed commitment, with a vow to be as accurate as possible and not to exaggerate. Rhys sets out her account as baldly as she can: Mr. Howard, an estate owner on another Dominican island and an old family friend, breaks his journey back to England and makes a lengthy visit of some months to Roseau, the

Dominican capital and city of Rhys's birth. Rhys had heard a lot about Mr. Howard and looked forward anxiously to meeting him. At dinner she found herself "captivated" by his including her in his conversation, drawing her out and treating her with deference as if she too were an adult. The next day Mr. Howard asks her to take him out driving to see the town and when they reach the Botanical Gardens he proposes that they rest on a secluded bench. He asks her age and when she tells him 14, he responds by saying that she is "quite old enough to have a lover" (cited in Thomas 29).[9] Rhys then experiences a physical shock so sudden that she felt as if her heart stopped; from her mature perspective, she attributes this shock to her own immaturity and ignorance, noting that her religious and writing "fits" made her younger in mind than her biological age. While she is pondering what she does know about lovers, Mr. Howard reaches inside or unbuttons her dress and fondles her breasts, commenting that she is indeed old enough for a lover. This objectifying gesture—as if Mr. Howard were testing the ripeness of fruit—paralyzes Rhys and she tries to deny that anything is happening to her. Rhys's handwriting is noticeably incoherent at this point in the notebook, and her sentences now become fragmentary as well. Rhys's fragmentary prose conveys her feelings of distress, her autonomic responses to his cold, heavy hand, and her indecision about whether the event is deliberate or not. She also notes a dissociative split in her mind, as she focuses on a tree branch which bends over the bench they are sitting on. The incident ends when they hear voices coming along the road; Mr. Howard calmly removes his hand and they return to Rhys's home, Mr. Howard casually making small talk. Rhys remembers that she herself didn't speak.

Rhys fiercely insists upon her initial resistance to Mr. Howard's seduction, describing her repulsion and fear, and when he asks her to accompany him the next day she tells her mother she won't go without telling her mother why. Her mother, exasperated by Rhys's excuse that she would rather read, tells Rhys that her behavior is rude and Rhys reluctantly complies. On this outing, however, Mr. Howard only buys her her favorite sweets and tells her stories about London and India. Rhys finds herself relenting, won over by his charm and attention, and the next time he asks her to accompany him she readily accepts. When they reach the same bench where the first fondling took place, Mr. Howard asks Rhys if she would like to belong to him and then goes on to frame that belonging as a form of sexual slavery. Rhys provides only a few sketchy details about this ongoing narrative but for the most part it concerns Mr. Howard's ownership and humiliation of Rhys: he will abduct her; she will seldom be allowed to wear clothing; he will force her to wait upon him and his guests while naked; he will tie her hands with ropes of flowers; he will punish her for the slightest infraction; and so on. But the element that most captures her imagination and to which she refers repeatedly is the threat of punishment—"I shall punish you & force you to" (cited in Thomas 31)—and Mr. Howard's insistence upon her free consent. Rhys underscores the surreal, dreamy, hallucinatory quality of this mental seduction, going so far as to describe the serial story as an addictive drug. By the time her mother begins to suspect something is going on between her and Mr. Howard, Rhys is hooked and, anxious to preserve her access to this opiate, she lies to her mother.

Rhys states that little physical contact took place, although her phrasing of that claim is ambiguous: "He didnt touch me again only once" (cited in Thomas 29). Does she mean he didn't touch her again after the first time, or that he did touch her again, but only once more? Sue Thomas has argued that the appearance of this passage, much later in the notebook than the initial description of Mr. Howard's fondling her breasts, suggests that something else did take place, "a possibly violent sexual act, equivocally a rape" (32). It is true that this sentence, in conjunction with several other fragmentary passages, hints at a more violent encounter that takes place after the initial incident of fondling: in this later passage, when her mother asks her why she's been crying, Rhys lies and says she hasn't been. Earlier, however, Rhys wrote that her mother only suspected something long after the seduction had started, and that by then Rhys had become proficient in lying. Whatever has made her cry has clearly come later in the "mental seduction." Other fragments—partially illegible and some literally torn out of the notebook—are both more explicit and more disturbing than Rhys's description of Mr. Howard's fondling and serial narrative. The most dramatic example of censorship, a three-line section of notebook carefully torn out from the middle of the page, begins with a fragment of Mr. Howard's remark that he would simultaneously caress and punish Rhys, then, after the excision, Rhys places the scene near a frangipani tree (92). The frangipani tree gestures back to the branch of the tree Rhys fixed on during Mr. Howard's initial fondling; further, Rhys goes on to link the frangipani tree explicitly to tears and violation: "The frangipani flowers must be carefully picked for if the branch is broken the tree bleeds huge drops of thick white blood drip from it. I am still young enough to know that everything is alive & I turn my eyes away not to see the tree bleed" (cited in Thomas 38).

Thomas argues that this passage "may effect the representation of Rhys's embodied experience of a second touch," an inscription

> made plausible with reference both to a Dominican metaphorical discourse of racial/ethnic "nativeness" and the English tradition of figuring male seduction of women as the picking of flowers. Violence, excessive force, wounds/tears the tree/creole, the white blood figuring catechrestically both semen and a fetishized "pure" European genealogy. The drops and Rhys's tears which prompt her mother's questioning are reminiscent of Meta's warning that the "unclean" Rhys will weep tears of blood. (47)

Thomas also links the violated tree to the trope of metamorphosis in Greek myth, as in, for example, the myth of Daphne's turning into a tree in order to escape sexual violation at Apollo's hands (49).

While Thomas makes a plausible case that the sexual violation may have been more extensive than Rhys either admits or remembers, my own interest remains in the narrative Rhys deliberately chose to fashion.[10] Rhys insists that the seduction she found most damaging was a "mental seduction"; hence it is arguable that her dramatic censoring of the text at the points where she comes closest to describing actual physical contact works to foreground this claim. This refusal to privilege physical contact over mental seduction is significant, for what seems to torment Rhys most about the seduction is that it functioned as a form of *recognition* for her, a psychological confirmation of her own sense of self: "Yes, that's true. Pain humiliation submission—that is for me It fitted in with all I knew of life, with all I'd ever felt It fitted like a hook fit an eye" (cited in Angier 28). When Mr. Howard first tells Rhys she is old enough to have a lover, Rhys ponders what she knows about the subject, deciding that a lover is someone who is strong and hurts you, like the man in the novel *Quo Vadis*. Indeed, throughout the notebook, Rhys consistently equates punishment with love and love with submission to punishment. Mr. Howard's apparent ability to perceive Rhys's own masochistic sensibility, then, is why Rhys feels complicit in her seduction: "I only struggled feebly. What he had seen in me was there all right" (cited in Angier 28).[11]

Many elements in Rhys's experience conform to contemporary theoretical writings on childhood sexual abuse. The initial fondling—the heavy cold hand on her breast, Rhys's denial that anything is happening, her sense of paralysis and speechlessness—suggests a characteristic shutting down: "[W]hile in a constant state of autonomic hyperarousal, [abused children] must also be quiet and immobile, avoiding any physical display of their inner agitation. The result is the peculiar, seething state of 'frozen watchfulness' noted in abused children" (Herman, *Trauma and Recovery* 100). Rhys's inability to tell anyone, her sense of self-blame, and her guilt are also all common reactions. The perceptual alterations Rhys records—her sense of being drugged or hypnotized, her feeling that other people were becoming shadows—suggest states of dissociation and depersonalization typical in such circumstances, and the intrusive nature of the experience and the shock Rhys experiences in fact may account for her long amnesia and for the suddenly spontaneous recovery of the memory more than 30 years later. But Rhys's sense that Mr. Howard recognized her—that he had seen something inside her of which she was already aware—suggests that the encounter with Mr. Howard was a repetition of an earlier trauma.

"I was . . . given a kink that would last the rest of my life"

Why does Rhys equate love with violence, cruelty, and humiliation before she meets Mr. Howard? In the notebook, prior to the encounter with Mr. Howard, Rhys describes years of beatings at the hands of her mother; in fact, Rhys herself connects Mr. Howard's seemingly intuitive understanding of her masochistic sensibility to these childhood beatings. Rhys reports that she endured these beatings in "stubborn silence," until one day she snapped and screamed, saying "God curse you if you touch me I'll kill you. Something that was no" (cited in Thomas 33). Her mother responds by washing her hands of Rhys:

> She gave me such a curious look—a long, sad look.
> Ha, youre growing up then . . . She said 'I've done my best, it's no use. You'll never learn to be like other people.' (cited in Angier 24)

Rhys does not really know why her mother beat her other than to make Rhys more like other people, but elsewhere she reports that she was punished for her voracious reading. Rhys explains, however, that the family servant Meta punished her for reading, telling Rhys that her eyes were going to drop out and stare back at her from the page. Whatever the reason, Rhys writes that her mother perceived "something alien in me which would devour me and make me unhappy & she was trying to root it out at all costs" (cited in Thomas 33; cited in Angier 24). Sue Thomas has interpreted this phrase as a reference to exorcism, as if Rhys were possessed, an interpretation Thomas links to the history of obeah in Dominica. Yet a broader meaning can be attributed to "something alien": Rhys *did* in fact stand out in the family, an extremely fair-haired and fair-skinned child in an otherwise darker-skinned, dark-haired family—her given name, "Gwendolyn," means "white" in Welsh—and she *was* unusually bookish, unusually religious, and unusually identified with blacks. Carole Angier, Rhys's biographer, notes that by the time Rhys was 13 she was considered "the difficult daughter" (22); by the standards of Rhys's mother and her aunt—identical twin sisters who lived together almost all their lives—she did not measure up: "Her behaviour was disapproved of, her thoughts were disapproved of, her feelings (especially her feelings) were disapproved of" (23). In the Black Exercise Notebook Rhys vividly depicts the temperamental differences between her mother and herself: when Rhys tries to describe to her mother how she identifies with the sad and indifferent landscape, for example, her practical mother doses her imaginative daughter with castor oil and Rhys takes to writing poetry instead to work off the worst feelings of sadness. Later, Rhys will think twice about telling her mother about Mr. Howard because she remembers getting dosed with castor oil for her overheated imagination. Twice in the notebook Rhys writes that she is fond of her mother, but the ambivalence is palpable: at the first mention she adds that she also despises her; the second time she ends a passage of her feelings with the blanket abbreviation "etc." The "etc" functions as a kind of shorthand, a breezy gesture in the direction of all the conventional emotions a daughter is supposed to feel for her mother.

Because the Mr. Howard narrative is so compelling, critics who have analyzed the Black Exercise Book have tended to overlook the abusive nature of this mother-daughter relationship; even a critic as sympathetic as Angier suggests that Rhys probably exaggerated the extent of her mother's punishment (24).[12] Yet most records—including Angier's—depict this relationship as extraordinarily vexed and conflict-ridden. Rhys was born nine months after an older sister who died in infancy, and in fact she may have been conceived as a replacement. But, according to Angier, Rhys's mother was unable to overcome her grief: as Angier observes, moreover, the child born to "a mourning mother . . . can be left with a lifelong sense of loss and emptiness, of being wanted by no one and belonging nowhere; of being nothing, not really existing at all" (11). Such an outcome is consistent with Rhys's lifelong sense that she was a "ghost." Furthermore, the birth of another daughter some five years later—a daughter who seemed to be everything Rhys was not—exacerbated the situation; Rhys once said, "My mother didn't like me after Brenda was born" (qtd. in Angier 12). I see no reason to doubt Rhys's claim that her mother beat her severely. The notebook suggests, moreover, that Rhys reacted to her mother's constant beatings in a manner that resembles the reactions of an abused child.[13] In discussing her parents, for example, Rhys writes that, in spite of her mother's beatings, she feared her father, not her mother. Judith Lewis Herman notes that it is common for the abused child to idealize one parent, and that typically the idealized parent is also the abuser: "In her desperate attempts to preserve her faith in her parents, the child victim develops highly idealized images of at least one parent. . . . commonly, the child idealizes the abusive parent and displaces all her rage onto the nonoffending parent" (*Trauma and Recovery* 106). Rhys's strained attempts to show her "fondness" for her conventional, respectable, and pragmatic mother suggest this very kind of splitting. By contrast, Rhys depicts her father—the parent to whom she reacts with fear—as nurturing and responsive to her emotional distress. In one passage, Rhys describes how she spills some tea on his bed and how she stands there too frightened to speak. Her father reacts by holding her and stroking her with great gentleness; Rhys recalls how she longed to tell him about her mother's punishment, the punishment that would give her the "kink" that would last the rest of her life. Yet this passage also suggests her father's relative distance from household life, underlining yet again Rhys's sense of isolation within the family. Again, such a situation is typical of abusive environments: the child feels isolated within the family, for she feels cut off from the other adults in her world who are in a position to save her but do not. Herman writes that "[t]he reasons for this protective failure are in some sense immaterial to the child victim, who experiences it at best as a sign of indifference and at worst as complicit betrayal . . . The child feels that she has been abandoned to her fate" (101).

Rhys follows this description of her father's kindness with a description of her poetry, the poetry that is written in the space of maternal discipline, disapproval, withdrawal, rejection, and the refusal to listen to the daughter. Rhys then includes a list of her favorite words, which tellingly includes pain, shame, sleep, sea, and silence. This progression of words charts a gradual movement from feeling to non-feeling, from experiencing an unpleasant external jolt, through the internalized affect of shame, through three stages of disconnection, ending in what seems like death by drowning within hearing of the incessant rhythm of the waves, a sound that gradually gives way to silence.[14] The rhythmic—

and aesthetic, formally organized—"tug and suck" (Woolf's phrase) of the waves suggests a suicidal withdrawal that in effect returns Rhys to the primal world of infancy and a state of non-differentiation, a state that for Rhys, like Woolf, conflates womb and tomb. When Rhys later shows one of these poems, written at age 11 or 12, to a Frenchman, he is shocked, telling her they are the work of one who is doomed. In the context of the notebook, the word "doom" acquires multiple meanings, for Rhys describes her relationship with Mr. Howard as the source of her "doom." Hence Rhys herself links her mother's punishment with the proposed punishments of Mr. Howard.

Rhys recounts stopping her mother's beating of her twice. The second description—identical in many respects to the first—ends when the mother explicitly pronounces Rhys doomed, a scapegoat fated to wander alone through life:

> She said I've done my best its no use. You'll never be like other people.
> "You'll never learn to behave like other people."
> There you are. There it was
> I'd always suspected it, but now I knew. That went straight as an arrow to the heart, straight as the truth. I saw the long road of isolation & loneliness stretching in front of me as far as the eye could see & further I collapsed cried heartbroken as my worst enemy could wish
> I see now that she was trying to drive out something she saw in me that was alien that would devour me. She was trying to drive it out at all costs—However after this she ceased her efforts (cited in Angier 24, cited in Thomas 33)

The situation Rhys describes here is a complex one. The mother's gaze, rather than affirming the daughter, instead seems to pierce the daughter's boundaries, discovering something evil and possessed at the very core of her being. And when the mother cannot destroy this evil that she perceives, she repudiates the daughter, consigning her to complete isolation, a universe void of human connection. Trauma victims in general feel the loss of "a basic sense of trust"; they feel themselves to be "utterly abandoned, utterly alone, cast out of the human and divine systems of care and protection" (Herman 52). But the abused child is even more vulnerable than the adult victim, for she "must compensate for the failures of adult and care and protection with the only means at her disposal, an immature system of psychological defenses" (*Trauma and Recovery* 96). The result is a splitting of the caretaker into idealized images on the one hand, horrifying reality on the other; the abused child "is unable to form inner representations of a safe, consistent caretaker" and "fragmentation becomes the central principle of personality organization . . . Fragmentation in the inner representations of others prevents the development of a reliable sense of independence within connection" (106–107).[15]

The abused child's search for protection makes him or her highly vulnerable to forming abusive relationships in adolescence and adulthood. For, in addition to experiencing personality fragmentation, the abused child grows up into someone who searches for a relationship in which he or she can be dependent. "[H]aunted by the fear of abandonment," Herman writes, the victim will continue to find attractive those "powerful authority figures who seem to offer the promise of a special caretaking relationship" (111):

> [T]he survivor has great difficulty protecting herself in the context of intimate relationships. Her desperate longing for nurturance and care makes it difficult to establish safe and appropriate boundaries with others. Her tendency to denigrate herself and to idealize those to whom she becomes attached further clouds her judgment. Her empathic attunement to the wishes of others and her automatic, often unconscious habits of obedience also make her vulnerable to anyone in a position of power or authority. Her dissociative defense style makes it difficult for her to form conscious and accurate assessments of danger. And her wish to relive the dangerous situation and make it come out right may lead her into reenactment of the abuse. (111)

Mr. Howard's relationship with Rhys conforms to this description. In fact, the Black Exercise Book develops a number of parallels between the mother and Mr. Howard: both can see within her; both have a sense of her as bad; both of them tell her she needs punishment. But Mr. Howard's seduction effects a series of reversals: Mr. Howard celebrates the depravity he perceives, while her mother repudiates it; Mr. Howard's punishments are literary, imaginative, consensual, while her mother's are literal, brutally physical, nonconsensual; Mr. Howard probes her mind, her mother ignores it or, worse, doses Rhys with castor oil.

Rhys's anguished depiction of her accession to Mr. Howard, that she "lapped up" his serial story and "asked for more," suggests a guilty sense of complicity (cited in Angier 28). As Herman points out,

> Participation in forbidden sexual activity also confirms the abused child's sense of badness. Any gratification that the child is able to glean from the exploitative situation becomes proof in her mind that she instigated and bears full responsibility for the abuse. If she ever

> experienced sexual pleasure, enjoyed the abuser's special attention, bargained for favors, or used the sexual relationship to gain privileges, these sins are adduced as evidence of her innate wickedness. (104)

But Rhys's phrase suggests more than guilty compliance or pleasure. Her sense that she "lapped up" what Mr. Howard had to offer and "asked for more" suggests deep emotional craving, and the kittenish oral metaphor inevitably points back to the primal needs of infancy and mother's milk. Mr. Howard's serial story begins, significantly, with a critique of the way her mother dresses her and his asking Rhys whether she wouldn't rather belong to him; recording her shocked and breathless reaction, Rhys writes that the serial story and the "intoxicating" mental seduction now began (cited in Angier 27). Rhys, I think, misidentifies the moment: the seduction begins when Mr. Howard attacks her mother and offers to take her place, thereby providing the milk of human kindness so conspicuously absent from that relationship.[16] As her word choices suggest, Mr. Howard responds to—feeds—an emotional hunger in Rhys, in contrast to her mother, who perceives in Rhys something "alien" and appetitive, uncontrollable and excessive, a hungry force she needs to "root out" of Rhys before it "devours" her. What Rhys finds "intoxicating" and "irresistible" in Mr. Howard's "mental seduction" seems, pathetically enough, to be encouragement and interest from an authoritative adult: "Mostly he talked about me me me. It was intoxicating . . . irresistible" (cited in Angier 27).

In the wake of Mr. Howard's seduction, Rhys begins to shape her narrative into a story about two daughters, Elsa and Audrey. Elsa experiences a series of terrifying nightmares in which she must follow a man, who looks at her with hate and loathing, into the forest at night. These passages would emerge as Antoinette's serial nightmares in *Wide Sargasso Sea:*

> I have left the house . . . It is still night and I am walking towards the forest I am wearing a long dress and thin slippers, so I walk with difficulty, following the man who is with me and holding up the skirt of my dress. It is white and beautiful and I don't wish to get it soiled. I follow him, sick with fear but I make no effort to save myself; if anyone were to try to save me, I would refuse . . . . He turns and looks at me, his face black with hatred. . . . Now I do not try to hold up my dress, it trails in the dirt, my beautiful dress. (*WSS* 35–36).

In the Black Exercise Book, the soiled dress is not described as white but rather as velvet, but the color white and the texture of the velvet suggest that the nightmare is one of defloration. Indeed, in the Black Exercise Book the nightmare continues with a literal enactment of a sexual fall, as the dreamer stumbles and, unable to get back up, continues to crawl on her hands and knees after the man who looks at her with hate and loathing. Cringing with fear, Elsa reaches a wall where whatever is to happen will happen: "I lie with my face against the earth cringing   waiting—sick mad with terror unable to move cringing waiting" (cited in Thomas 36). At this point, she wakes up screaming and both her younger sister and her mother respond. The mother at first responds with solicitude, at which point Elsa describes, in a first person narration, how she has become little again, a child who implores her mother never to let her go. Very quickly, however, the mother grows angry with the terrified daughter; she insists that the daughter control herself before she upsets her younger sister. This fragmentary story concludes when her mother takes her arms away and leaves her to attend to her younger sister: Elsa realizes that she is alone, that no one can save her. "The thing that formed me   that thing that made me as I am" is not, then, simply Mr. Howard's mental seduction, but rather Mr. Howard's mental seduction *and* the mother's indifference and repudiation.

"A World of Fear and Distrust"

I want to turn now to another aspect of Rhys's writing that develops out of the "mental seduction" that occurs in the space of maternal absence. Rhys's sense that she deserves punishment is a common result of child abuse. Herman writes that the abused child develops "a system of meaning" that will justify the treatment she receives, and "Inevitably the child concludes that her innate badness is the cause." Eventually, "The language of the self becomes a language of abomination" and the victim comes to believe herself "outside the compact of ordinary human relations" (105). A number of psychoanalytic writers have elaborated on the ways in which this sense of innate badness becomes a permanent part of the abused child's personality structure. In a 1932 essay, Sandor Ferenczi analyzed the process by which the abused child comes to internalize a sense of self that is contaminated. He concluded that the abused child, paralyzed with fear at the moment of trauma, comes to identify with and to introject the aggression, guilt, and shame of the menacing person or aggressor (298–299), in effect internalizing the adult's feelings of hatred for him or her (303). Self-blame and self-hatred, in other words, derive from abusive intersubjective relationships and become destructive intrapsychic currents. While Ferenczi writes specifically about childhood sexual abuse, Herman finds the same process at work in a more general conceptualization of child abuse:

> By developing a contaminated, stigmatized personality, the child victim takes the evil of the abuser into herself and thereby preserves her primary attachments to her parents. . . . adult survivors who have escaped from the abusive situation continue to view themselves with contempt and to take upon themselves the shame and guilt of their abusers. The profound sense of inner badness becomes the core around which the abused child's identity is formed, and it persists into adult life. (*Trauma and Recovery* 105)

Rhys's bewilderment over why she was punished so severely suggests this very need to find fault in herself, repeatedly stating that she cannot remember what it was she had done.

The Black Exercise Book demonstrates numerous ways in which Rhys's social and cultural surround supported her mother's sense that she was innately bad; furthermore, these contexts are in part what would have made Mr. Howard's scenarios of erotic domination seem so familiar. The history of slavery and the enduring racial unrest in the Dominican islands, for example, provide an important context for understanding Rhys's recognition of and familiarity with the dynamics of domination and submission.[17] Rhys felt akin to blacks, even at times wished to be black herself, but this sense of kinship was rooted in her perception of blacks as dirty and degraded and subject to punishment. Rhys's anger at the treatment of the slaves is the first evidence of her taking the side of the underdog: "I would feel sick with shame at some of these stories I heard of the slave days   told casually   even proudly   The ferocious punishments   the salt kept ready to rub into the wounds. . . . I became an ardent socialist & champion of the downtrodden" (cited in Raiskin, *WSS* 155–156). At the same time, Rhys adds, "It added to my sadness that couldnt help but realise they didnt really like or trust white people much White cockroaches they called us" (cited in Raiskin, *WSS* 155). In *Smile Please,* Rhys describes how she tried to talk to a black girl she admired: "[S]he turned and looked at me. . . . This was hatred—impersonal, implacable hatred" (*SP* 39). Rhys's fear of blacks, her own deep-rooted sense that they were dangerous, primitive, and animalistic, emerges repeatedly in her writing.

At the same time, as a child and privileged Creole girl, Rhys had caretakers who were black. Veronica Marie Gregg observes that Rhys's Creole identity was "sustained by the simultaneous love and hatred of black people" (67); "The white woman's education—her initiation into conventional standards—is constructed over and against, even as it depends upon, the excluded, sexually promiscuous, not-quite-human blacks" (68). Rhys's description of the vexed relationship she had with her black nursemaid, Meta, is particularly important in this context. In *Smile Please*, Rhys describes Meta as "the terror of my life" who "always seemed to be brooding over some terrible, unforgettable wrong" (22). Her stories "were tinged with fear and horror"; and she especially delighted in telling Rhys about zombies, soucriants and loups-garous (23). She taught Rhys to fear cockroaches by telling her they would fly in at night, biting her mouth and leaving an open wound, for "the bite would never heal" (23), an image of wounding or even castration that suggests taboos placed on female speech and erotic pleasure.[18] Meta was not allowed to slap Rhys but instead shook her violently, while Rhys in turn shouted "Black Devil" at her (24). In *Smile Please* Rhys blames Meta for showing her "a world of fear and distrust" which continued for the rest of her life (*SP* 24), echoing Rhys's sense of what her mother's beatings and Mr. Howard's seduction accomplish in the Black Exercise Book.[19]

This "world of fear and distrust" confirms and amplifies the instability and hostility of what were Rhys's earliest experiences of dependency and care. Rhys's description of Meta resembles what Toni Morrison has described as "[t]he other side of nursing, the opposite of the helping, healing hand . . . the figure of destruction . . . whose inhuman and indifferent impulses pose immediate danger" (*Playing* 84), an alter ego Morrison identifies in white writers' depictions of the African American nanny. But Meta's dislike for and punishment of Rhys in many respects simply reiterates in a different register her mother's fault-finding and repudiation. Like her mother—although for different reasons—Meta objected to Rhys's reading; like her mother, Meta constantly found fault with Rhys and threatened her with future visitations of sorrow.[20] Rhys clearly connected her mother's and Meta's punishments, for when Rhys writes that her mother wanted to "root out" "something alien" in her, she immediately follows that passage with a description of how even having dirty fingernails provokes Meta, who tells Rhys she will be punished by having to weep tears of blood.

The reference to dirty nails is telling, for Rhys writes later in *Smile Please* that she took special care to be slovenly and dirty, especially at the Catholic convent where she refers to herself as an "outcast" (*SP* 14). "I . . . took defiant pride in looking worse every day," Rhys writes: another sign that she is indeed a "bad girl" (*SP* 14).

Rhys's education also furnished her contexts for finding the dynamics of erotic domination familiar and "natural." At the Catholic convent school she attended, Rhys notes coming into contact with numerous stories and representations of martyrdom presented within the rubric of redemptive love. In the early part of the notebook, Rhys writes that Mother St. Anthony read aloud from the lives of the saints during the two-hour thrice-weekly sewing sessions. Rhys mentions in particular Saint Cecilia, Saint Barbara, and Saint Dorothy, all virgins, all of whom were martyred for their faith and their sexuality: Saint Cecilia "was tortured to death for rejecting her pagan bridegroom on the day of her wedding" (Walker 157); Saint Barbara was tortured by her pagan father because he wanted her to renounce Christianity (91); Saint Dorothy resisted perversion at the hands of two women and was beheaded (Attwater and John 108). For Catholics, these deaths reenact the passion of Christ, a version of redemptive love that triumphs through the endurance of torture, blood, ridicule, and suffering. The Baltimore Catechism to this day advises children to "think: how much Our Lord must have loved me to suffer those nails, those thorns, those bleeding wounds, such humiliations, such heartbreak" (Baltimore Catechism, n.p.). As a student at a convent school, moreover, Rhys would have been exposed to the explicit scenes of humiliation and torture memorialized in the Stations of the Cross, 14 depictions of the Passion displayed at regular intervals around a Catholic church: it is customary to observe the Stations of the Cross on Fridays by walking the Stations in order and drawing appropriate lessons in humility and endurance from Christ's example.[21] Prayers urge worshippers to identify with Christ's suffering, even to experience it vicariously: the catechism recommends, for example, that at each station the supplicant begin his or her meditation with the following appeal to the Virgin Mary: "Holy Mother, pierce me through,/ In my heart each wound renew/ of my Savior crucified" (252). Rhys reports in the Black Exercise Book that she became extremely religious during the period just before Mr. Howard's arrival; she longed to convert to Catholicism and become a nun. In *Smile Please* Rhys writes that, in imagining herself as a nun, she specifically wanted to ponder the Five Glorious and the Five Sorrowful Mysteries (*SP* 65). Rhys refers here to the decades of a rosary, the circlet of beads that worshippers use to count and to organize prayers to the Virgin Mary: five groups of ten beads each (ten Hail Marys) linked by a single bead set apart (one Our Father). In reciting the five decades of the rosary, the worshipper ponders one of three sets of Mysteries, the Joyful, the Sorrowful, or the Glorious, which roughly adhere to Christ's childhood, His Passion, and the aftermath of the Crucifixion. Rhys's choice of the Sorrowful and Glorious Mysteries is consistent with her fascination with a redemptive love that triumphs through suffering; significantly, she omits the Joyful Mysteries, which focus on such events as the Annunciation and the Nativity. Erotic domination, not childbirth and motherhood, holds Rhys's interest.

Within this context, the version of a lover Rhys recalls in relation to Mr. Howard's statement that she was old enough to have a lover—a dark man who would hurt her, resembling the man in *Quo Vadis*—seems significant. Although Rhys may have been drawing upon later knowledge to conceptualize her childhood notions of lovers—two cinematic versions of *Quo Vadis* appeared, in 1912 and 1924—she was probably referring to the immensely popular novel by Henryk Sienkiewicz, published in 1896.[22] She was clearly familiar with the novel only two years later, for when she sat the Oxford and Cambridge Higher Certificate in Roman History at the Perse School in England she claimed to remember nothing from lessons, but to have gotten all her information from *Quo Vadis;* the examiners were apparently impressed by her allusions to Nero's emerald eyeglass and to the shell-shaped bath in which Petronius took his own life (Angier 43). Certainly the way in which Rhys phrases her comparison suggests she had read the book at the time of the seduction, for she assumes the narrative stance throughout of trying to capture the temporal immediacy of her reactions at age 14 to Mr. Howard. The plot of *Quo Vadis* reiterates the connection between erotic domination in romance and the Passion of Christ: it is the story of a Ligian princess taken hostage by the Romans who is adopted by Roman Christians; a prominent patrician, Marcus Vinicius—a "wild-maned Roman stallion" (173)—notices her and arranges for her ownership to be transferred to him. Although she is secretly attracted to him—and *Quo Vadis* makes clear that he is attractive as a result of his brutal aggression, his authority, and his power—she defends her chastity and escapes.[23] Love and hate are intertwined for the two male protagonists, Vinicius and his uncle Petronius; and punishment is inextricable from love:

> [T]he torments and humiliations [Vinicius] imagined he would inflict after he found [Ligia] heightened his excitement. He wanted her, yes, but he also wanted her as a broken slave. . . . There were days he dreamed about the whip marks on her delicate white flesh, and then he wanted to heal them with kisses. Once or twice the thought of murder glinted in his mind. He thought he could be happy only if he killed her. (149)

Similarly, when Petronius orders his slave Eunice whipped for refusing to sleep with another man, she asks him to whip her every day rather than make her leave him; when he indeed follows through with the punishment, she responds with renewed devotion:

> He turned directly to the girl. "Have you been whipped?"
>
> She threw herself at his feet just as she had before and pressed her lips mutely to the hem of his toga. "Oh, yes, my lord." Her voice trembled with . . . gratitude and joy. "Oh, yes, indeed, my master!" (120)

Eventually the theme of martyrdom in the service of secular love shifts to the theme of martyrdom in the service of divine love, and the novel focuses on the deaths of the Christians who have been incarcerated at the Colosseum. Nero devises a series of sadistic tortures to amuse the crowds: some Christians are fed to packs of wild dogs, others are fed to lions, some are crucified on burning crosses, and in one particularly gruesome section women are raped to death by large animals. Sienkiewicz describes all of these tortures in excruciating detail.[24] Nero and his evil empress, Poppaea, reserve a special torment for Ligia, who is bound naked to the horns of an aurochs, a form of ox. It is during this torment, significantly, that Marcus Vinicius suddenly finds faith in Christ; he spends the remaining period of her torture—she is, of course, eventually rescued—sitting under his uncle's mantle, chanting "I believe! I believe! I believe!" Amid the carnage of Nero's last days, the pair escapes.

Rhys would later allude to *Quo Vadis* in her short story "Till September Petronella," which portrays a violent sadomasochistic relationship between Julian, a musician, and his mistress: "When they're amorous they're noisy and when they fight it's worse. She goes for him with a pen-knife. Mind you, she only does it because he likes it, but her good nature is a pretence. She's a bitch really" (*Collected Stories* 131). (D. H. Lawrence based his depictions of Halliday and Pussums in *Women in Love* on this couple, the musician Philip Heseltine and Bobby Channing or "Puma"; like Rhys, he too portrayed the pair's relationship as sadomasochistic). The story is narrated by an artist's model, Petronella Grey, who is secretly attracted to Julian, despite the fact that he constantly makes disparaging remarks about her, likening her, for example, to a "devouring spider." He is also an overt misogynist who sits around reading books "about the biological inferiority of women" (129).[25]

Petronella nonetheless feels a strong attraction to him; she recalls how "Once, left alone in a very ornate studio, I went up to a plaster cast—the head of a man, one of those Greek heads—and kissed it, because it was so beautiful. Its mouth felt warm, not cold. It was smiling. When I kissed it the room went dead silent and I was frightened" (131–132); she explicitly connects this memory to Julian: "I love Julian. Julian, I kissed you once, but you didn't know" (132). Rhys draws here on a scene in the first chapter of *Quo Vadis* when the slave girl, Eunice, expresses her love for Petronius by kissing a statue of him in the guise of Hermes: "[W]hen her face was at the level of the statue's head, she . . . threw her arms around the marble neck. Then, pressing her rosy flesh to the pale carved body, she started kissing Petronius' stone lips" (12). The attraction to the brutalizing man who responds coldly and punitively, the man who cannot in a sense see women as people—Petronella remarks her fear of the statue's "blind eyes" (132)—emerges in the common image of kissing unresponsive stone.[26]

"Something in the Depths of Me Said Yes"

Captivity, degradation, humiliation, torture, punishment—these are the prominent features Rhys singles out for mention in her portrait of her childhood prior to meeting Mr. Howard; these features are, significantly, the ones Rhys repeatedly identifies as the most "captivating" and "intoxicating" elements of the latter's "mental seduction." While in many respects Mr. Howard resembles the classic portrait of the child molester—buying Rhys candy, flattering her by treating her as an adult, singling her out for special attention, and so on—the extraordinary effect of his seduction seems to inhere in Rhys's conviction that he intuited her own "badness"—and found it sexual. For underwriting the disciplinary, racial, and educational scenarios of Rhys's childhood are a set of binary structures: white/black (and more specifically, white woman/ black woman); master/slave; good girl/bad girl—and, implicit in her education at a Catholic convent, virgin/ whore. Rhys, the beaten and slovenly bad girl, the humiliated and punished child who feels akin to the degraded blacks of her perception, clearly identifies with the degraded term of each set. Mr. Howard's "serial story" foregrounds and eroticizes the degraded term; in his fantasies of stripping Rhys naked, bedecking her with the jewelry of the black Dominican women, and taking her sexual captive, he makes explicit that he recognizes her for exactly what she thinks she is—a whore.

Rhys would later attribute to this mental seduction the genesis of a female life that stands against the conventional life of the mother. In a story based on the notebook, "Good-bye Marcus, Good-bye Rose," the supposed loss of chastity involved in the seduction makes possible a female life outside the boundaries of the respectable. Here the seducer, Captain Cardew, an "aged but ageless god," explains to a "shocked and fascinated" Phoebe that "love was not kind and gentle, as she had imagined, but violent. Violence, even cruelty, was an essential part of it" (*Collected Stories* 287). Phoebe believes that the captain has somehow intuited her real personality: she "began to wonder how he had been so sure, not only that she'd never tell anybody but that she'd make no effort at all to stop him talking. That could only mean that he'd seen at once that she was not a good girl—who would object—but a wicked one—who would listen. He must know. He knew. It was so" (288–289). Phoebe decides that being a "wicked girl" is more difficult than being a good girl, but she also decides she is up to the challenge. Recalling Mother Sacred Heart's injunction that "Chastity in Thought, Word and Deed was your most precious possession" (289), Phoebe initially feels sorrow about "some vague irreparable loss" but then consoles herself that she now needn't worry about whether she'd get married or not:

> Now she felt very wise, very grown-up, she could forget these childish worries. She could hardly believe that only a few weeks ago she, like all the others, had secretly made lists of her trousseau, decided on the names of her three children. Jack. Marcus. And Rose.
>
> Now good-bye Marcus. Good-bye Rose. The prospect before her might be difficult and uncertain but it was far more exciting. (289–290)

A subversive female agency, in other words, emerges from the masochistic scenario; female power emerges from the fantasy of being controlled and brutalized by another.

Both the Black Exercise Book and *Smile Please* record how the Mr. Howard experience changed the nature of Rhys's reading habits.[27] In the Black Exercise Book Rhys describes how reading *High Wind in Jamaica* reminded her of herself a child, specifically in the passages concerning the little Creole girl, Margaret, who is "beaten in the thoroughgoing West Indian fashion," used as a prostitute, and finally thrown overboard; although Rhys finds it a good book, she condemns the author for rendering Margaret "idiotic" (cited in Thomas 34). This reference, of course, suggests a moment of genesis for *Wide Sargasso Sea* and the character of the West Indian girl who is sexually used and thrown away. But the theme of degraded female sexuality fascinated Rhys after her "mental seduction," and she used reading as a way of escaping into a fantasy world of dominance and submission. Rhys notes that "as soon as I could I lost myself in the immense world of books, and tried to blot out the real world" (*SP* 50); "[F]rom books (fatally) I gradually got most of ideas and beliefs" (50). Two aspects of her reading seem significant in light of her own writing. First, in search of information about sex, Rhys repudiates the pictures of childbirth she discovers in her father's medical books: "I was so horrified that I shut the book, put it back and avoided going into his consulting room again. As to the diagrams, I didn't believe them. Impossible" (49). Instead, given free rein in the local library, she discovers a preference for books about prostitutes: "I liked books about prostitutes, there were a good many then, and vividly recall a novel called *The Sands of Pleasure* written by a man named Filson Young. . . . It was about an Englishman's love affair with an expensive demimondaine in Paris" (50–51). The rejection of maternity, the fascination with the owning or buying of women that crystallizes in the figure of the "demimondaine" or semi-prostitute, and the emphasis on illegitimate or degraded female sexuality will all become prominent themes in Rhys's fiction.

It is unclear in *Smile Please* whether Rhys had discovered her reading preferences before or after Mr. Howard's "mental seduction." The order of events in the chapter "Facts of Life" suggests, however, that the experience with Mr. Howard may have impelled Rhys to "blot out the real world" in reading about women's degradation and commodification. *Smile Please* was published after Rhys's death in 1979; as its subtitle *An Unfinished Autobiography* indicates, she died before its completion. Well into her eighties during its composition and apparently no longer trusting her memory when it came to factual accounts, Rhys conceived of the memoir as a series of vignettes presented in chronological order rather than as a continuous narrative (Athill "Foreword" 4). The vignettes in "Facts of Life" appear in the following order: Rhys, initially ambivalent about learning about sexuality, finally goes into her father's library where she finds the terrifying diagrams about childbirth. The next vignette concerns her dog, Rex, who copulates with another dog during a walk one day; Rhys's obvious dismay incurs the ridicule and laughter of passersby. When she reaches home, in tears, Rhys ask her mother whether the dog will die of a disease but her mother only responds in the negative and then looks at her silently. Rhys remarks:

> After this I shut away at the back of my mind any sexual experiences, for of course some occurred, not knowing that this would cause me to remember them in detail all the rest of my life. I became very good at blotting things out, refusing to think about them.
>
> Gradually this withdrawal became curiosity, fascination. (*SP* 50)

It is after this oblique and puzzling remark that Rhys discusses her reading preferences.

Rhys's matter-of-fact shrugging off of "sexual experiences" "for of course some occurred" is hence framed by a repudiation of maternity on the one side, a fascination with prostitution on the other. Unnamed and unspoken events occupy the moment of "blotting out," yet the extraordinary change in Rhys's reading suggests the process of what Ferenczi terms "traumatic progression or precocity," a process of premature sexual awakening, "a sudden, surprising blossoming, as if by magic, of new faculties following violent shock":

> It is only natural to think of fruit that ripens or becomes sweet prematurely when injured by the beak of a bird, or of the premature ripening of wormy fruit. Shock can cause a part of the person to mature suddenly, not only emotionally, *but intellectually as well.* I remind you of the typical "dream of the wise baby" singled out by me so many years ago, in which a newborn child or infant in its cradle suddenly begins to talk, indeed teaches wisdom to all the family. Fear of the uninhibited and therefore as good as crazy adult turns the child into a psychiatrist, as it were. In order to do so and to protect himself from the dangers coming from people without self-control, he must first know how to identify himself completely with them. It is unbelievable how much we can learn in reality from our wise children, the neurotics. (301)

Yet, while the "sexual experiences" Rhys refuses to name seem to have impelled this precocious interest in a degraded and commodified female sexuality, the chapter poses more questions than it answers. Does Rhys's horror at the childbirth diagrams or her anxiety about sexual disease have a connection to whatever happened with Mr. Howard? Does her mother's silent look refer to Rhys's sense that her mother knew about what went on with Mr. Howard? Why does Rhys omit the episode with Mr. Howard in her "official" memoir, one which contains numerous, essentially verbatim transcriptions of the Black Exercise Book? Is the withdrawal from everyday life and the "curiosity and fascination" that lead to reading about prostitutes a result of the seduction? And finally and perhaps most significantly, what does Rhys mean when she writes that she both blotted events out *and* remembered them in detail—at the same time?[28]

While it seems virtually certain that the "sexual experiences" Rhys mentions refer to Mr. Howard, Rhys's refusal to retell the story of Mr. Howard and her location of her mother in the crucial space between maternity and prostitution is, paradoxically, the most opaque and the most accurate enactment of her case of "mental seduction." The events that went out of her memory "like a stone" lay quietly intact, silent and unmoving, deep within her psyche, only unearthed by Rhys's insistent need to write her stories, stories about the desires and fantasies of women who compulsively seek out degradation and abuse in a desperate search for the caretaking and love they can never find.[29] In a letter to a woman who cannot consciously remember her rape but dreams about it instead, Ferenczi writes,

> I know from other analyses that a part of our being can "die" and while the remaining part of our self may survive the trauma, it awakens with a gap in its memory. Actually it is a gap in the personality, because not only is the memory of the struggle-to-the-death effaced, but all other associatively linked memories disappear . . . perhaps forever. (Qtd in Masson, 147)

It is fitting that Rhys marks the moment of her transformation with a gap.

CHAPTER 6

"A Doormat in a World of Boots": Jean Rhys and the Masochistic Aesthetic

Near the end of Jean Rhys's *Good Morning, Midnight,* the protagonist, Sasha Jansen, very drunk and alone in her room with a gigolo, struggles against his advances, only to find herself pinned beneath him, her dress torn, tears trickling down her face, speechless in the face of his taunts and threats of violence and gang rape ("[I]n Morocco it's much easier. You get four comrades to help you, and then it's very easy. They each take their turn. It's nice like that" [182]). Yet instead of reacting with anger or fear, Sasha somewhat disturbingly proclaims her resurrection as a subject and human being: noting the concrete fact of René's "hard knee between my knees," Sasha submits, thinking, "My mouth hurts, my breasts hurt, because it hurts, when you have been dead, to come alive . . . " (182). Even when Sasha finally rouses herself enough to fend off the gigolo's attack, this disturbing definition of rebirth persists: the novel ends as Sasha welcomes into her bed a traveling salesman who has denigrated her as a "sale vache" or dirty cow, a man to whom she has earlier responded with fear and repulsion, calling him "the ghost of the landing" and "the priest of some obscene, half-understood religion" (35). Hence Sasha's embrace of the traveling salesman is to some extent an assent to his (and others') characterization of her as dirty, sullied, degraded. In fact, it is arguable that Sasha's "rebirth" results in her murder at the hands of this man: the title of the novel alludes to an Emily Dickinson poem in which the speaker turns her back on day (life) and embraces night (death) instead.

Such emotionally and physically violent scenes pervade Rhys's fiction, from the "date rape" that inaugurates Anna's downward spiral into prostitution in *Voyage in the Dark* to the near-death sex play in

Wide Sargasso Sea that impels Rochester to reject Antoinette and eventually to incarcerate her in Thornfield's attic.[1] Yet surprisingly little critical attention has been paid to this pervasive masochism in Rhys's fiction or to its source in traumatic events that have left her protagonists in the grip of a disabling and dehumanizing sense of shame.[2] At the beginning of *Good Morning, Midnight*, for example, Sasha wants only to hide from the world: imaging herself in terms of stagnation and impasse, she attempts to turn herself into an unfeeling automaton, a robot who follows a predetermined "programme" and whose halfhearted acquiescence to a Paris makeover stems from a protective desire to blend in and escape notice by acquiring the appropriate physical and emotional "armour" (her term). In this context, then, by threatening rape the gigolo manages to breach Sasha's protective shield, forcing her from a numbed and insensate state into an explicit recognition of suffering and pain. Given the devastating history Sasha details—her apparent exile from her land of birth, her family's rejection of her, the death of her newborn son, her abandonment by her husband, and numerous humiliations endured at the hands of employers, family members, and lovers—her ability, finally, to feel pain is indeed a moment when she returns from death to life, from unfeeling to feeling. Anita Phillips calls such masochism healing, in that it brings "sensation back to despair" and "an existing state of inarticulate suffering into contact with what is usually considered to be its opposite, an erotic investment" (61, 62). Yet such an equation sidesteps the self-destructive, even suicidal, aspects of Sasha's behavior. Instead, an accurate reading of Rhys's fiction needs to take into account the ways in which masochistic behavior, in Leon Wurmser's words, "is set up to undo, yet also to perpetuate, the traumas that have brought about a searing sense of unlovability—myriad vain efforts to restore love and acceptance" (194).

This chapter argues that masochism functions for the Rhys character as a complex response to psychic trauma; it locates the impulse for masochistic submission in what Emmanuel Ghent has identified as a "deep longing for surrender, a yearning to be known, recognized, 'penetrated'" (134). "Masochistic phenomena," he writes, "have often been traced to deprivation, traumata and developmental interferences suffered in the early preoedipal years" (116): the infant develops a falsely compliant self, but carries into adulthood "a continuing longing to surrender this false self in the hope of a 'new beginning'" (117). Rhys's fiction similarly traces the connection between early environmental failure and the later turn to masochism. In fact, in her repeated return to and reworking of masochism, Rhys increasingly makes the connection between the repudiating mother and the brutalizing lover more explicit: *Wide Sargasso Sea,* her last novel, details the early childhood traumas that predispose Antoinette to masochistic submission.

Yet Rhys does more than simply create portraits of women whose masochism functions as a response to trauma. Her later fictions in particular demonstrate the accuracy of Gilles Deleuze's claim that masochism is essentially formal in its structure and operation. Both *Good Morning, Midnight* and *Wide Sargasso Sea* deploy the formal mechanisms Deleuze identifies as constitutive of perverse desire, thereby creating a masochistic aesthetic that works to dramatize and to expose the operation of power relations.[3] In this way Rhys's later fictions fulfill Luce Irigaray's call for a female mimicry in the realm of discourse, "in which the woman deliberately assumes the feminine style and posture assigned to her . . . in order to uncover the mechanisms by which it exploits her" (*This Sex* 220). Conceding that representations of female masochism seem congruent with "those desires which are assumed to be 'natural' for the female subject," Kaja Silverman argues that "some very unorthodox desires and patterns of identification can be concealed behind what may often be only a masquerade of submission, including ones which are quite incompatible with a subordinate position" (59). Rhys's characters similarly conceal unorthodox desires and patterns of identification behind masquerades of submission; the protagonists of the later fictions in particular dramatize the gulf between an outward conformity and an inner rebellion and insubordination.

A General Overview of Traumatic Patterns in Rhys's Novels

Although the traumas differ from novel to novel, it is useful to consider some general characteristics of Rhys's fiction in relation to trauma theory before turning to specific analyses of the novels in the context of masochism. To begin with, the fates Rhys assigns to her characters are consistent with the profile of the sexual abuse survivor, who often develops a "deviant and debased self-image" and engages in a "masochistic search for punishment" (Herman *Father-Daughter Incest* 30). Rhys's novels similarly depict self-destructive and self-punishing female protagonists who seem caught up in repetitious and compulsive patterns of behavior that point back to traumatic experiences in their various pasts, experiences that remain fragmentary and only partially articulated, and hence, unprocessed. Several of

Rhys's novels—most notably *Voyage in the Dark* and *Good Morning, Midnight*—employ narrative form to mimic the effects of trauma: these novels are not "about" trauma but rather stage the experience of trauma and its aftermath through the manipulation of narrative elements. Mieke Bal has argued that models of traumatic inscriptions can be translated into narrative terms:

> Discussions of whether repression or dissociation accompanies trauma can be brought to bear on the consideration of memory as narrative. In narratological terms, repression results in ellipsis—the omission of important elements in the narrative—whereas dissociation doubles the strand of the narrative series of events by splitting off a sideline. In contrast to ellipsis, this sideline is called paralepsis in narrative theory. In other words, repression interrupts the flow of narrative that shapes memory; dissociation splits off material that cannot then be reincorporated into the main narrative. (ix)

Both repression of connective material and dissociative split-off plot lines and flashbacks occur commonly in all of Rhys's novels. Her characters live in a truncated present: radically cut off from their childhoods, their lands of birth, and their families of origin, painful and half-glimpsed memories of the past haunt them. What Thomas Staley writes of *Quartet*'s Marya holds true for all these women: "There is in Marya a sense of a lost past which has been stolen from her, and it is this sense of loss and being plunged into a fearful and 'shallow world' that allows her to move from one circumstance to another finding protection from the shadows" (40). "Allows" is not quite the right word: these lost pasts and painful absences provoke the kind of compulsive, self-destructive behavior that is the hallmark of the Rhys heroine. Hence traumatic events live on in the protagonists' present lives, in the fragmented narrative chronology, in the protagonists' inability to remember or unwillingness to narrate crucial information, in the disruption of the narrative by memories that pose more questions than they answer, and above all in the haunted, obsessive thought patterns of the protagonists.

In effect, then, Rhys's fictions tell a double story: the events in the narrative present reactivate for the protagonists anterior experiences that then emerge in fragmentary form. This temporal split is characteristic of traumatic memory. Cathy Caruth has remarked that "the impact of the traumatic event lies precisely in its belatedness, in its refusal to be simply located, in its insistent appearance outside the boundaries of any single place or time. . . . trauma is not a simple or single experience of events but . . . events, insofar as they are traumatic, assume their force precisely in their temporal delay" (*Trauma* 9). The splitting of the narrative mirrors the dissociative thinking and patterns of depersonalization that are typical of trauma survivors. David Spiegel, Thurman Hunt, and Harvey E. Dondershine have argued that since trauma inheres in the experience of being objectified and turned into a thing, the survivor is left "with an overwhelming and marginally bearable sense of helplessness, a realization that one's own will and wishes become irrelevant in the course of events" (249). This sense of helplessness, humiliation, and pain can become split off as the survivor reconsolidates her personality:

> Once the self is divided in a powerful way, the experience of unity becomes problematic, since ordinary self-consciousness is no longer synonymous with the entirety of self and personal identity. Rather, it becomes associated with the awareness of some warded-off tragedy, the moment of humiliation and fear, the act of cowardice, the sense of having been degraded. The person comes to feel that there is an inauthentic self which carries on the everyday functions of life but with the sense of numbing, the lack of genuine pleasure in otherwise pleasurable activities. (249)

Rhys's protagonists seems similarly split: they anticipate disaster and find it familiar when it happens. Often her characters "recognize" their "dooms" in ways that anticipate Rhys's own recognition of Mr. Howard's sadomasochistic scenarios as uncannily familiar. When Anna first has sex with Walter Jeffries in *Voyage in the Dark*—an event that Rhys figures as a rape in the original, suppressed version of the novel—she thinks, "Of course you've always known, always remembered, and then you forget so utterly, except that you've always known it. Always—how long is always?" (37); later, after she has been abandoned by Jeffries, Anna says, "I saw that all my life I had known that this was going to happen, and that I'd been afraid for a long time, I'd been afraid for a long time" (96). *After Leaving Mr. Mackenzie*'s Julia suffers from "a feeling of foreboding, of anxiety, as if her heart were being squeezed, [that] never left her" (45). In *Quartet,* when Marya learns that her husband has been incarcerated, leaving her stranded in Paris without a job or any money, she tries to flee her impending fate, which she defines as "a vague and shadowy fear of something cruel and stupid that had caught her and would never let her go. She had always known it was there—hidden under the more or less pleasant surface of things. Always. Ever since she was a child. . . . You could only try to walk very fast and leave it behind you" (33). Sasha in *Good Morning, Midnight* finds herself trapped in numerous literal versions of a recurrent nightmare, wherein she must attend the Exhibition no matter how hard she tries to escape. Remembering a job she lost in a humiliating manner, Sasha recalls her futile search to discover the cashier: "[I]t becomes a nightmare. I walk up stairs, past doors, along passages—all different, all exactly alike" (26). Although she will dream momentarily of "escaping her fate" (37), she eventually concludes, "The passages will never lead anywhere, the doors will always be shut" (31). As she later tells a man she meets, "I don't believe things change much really; you only think they do. It seems to me that things repeat themselves over and over again" (66).

The numbed affect of the protagonists speaks to the process of dissociation. Rhys's protagonists often perceive themselves as ghosts or zombies, a motif familiar to Rhys from her Caribbean background.[4] This kind of depersonalization is consistent with the profile of trauma survivors. According to the DSM IV, "Diminished responsiveness to the external world, referred to as 'psychic numbing' or 'emotional anesthesia,' usually begins soon after the traumatic event": the person loses interest in meaningful activities, suffers from a sense of estrangement from other people, and feels incapable of emotion, especially emotions having to do with intimacy and sexuality (464). In depersonalization "individuals experience disturbances in the reality of self so that they report feeling as if they were 'dead,' 'a robot,' or 'unreal'" (Putnum 119). Rhys's characters typically perceive themselves as the living dead after they have been abandoned or otherwise stranded or humiliated. Antoinette becomes the ghost who haunts Thornfield Hall, while Marya similarly imagines herself to be "a grey ghost walking in a vague shadowy world" (46). When Julia tries to explain the story of her life to George Horsfield in *After Leaving Mr. Mackenzie,* she does so in a way that underlines her own distance from it: "She spoke as if she were trying to recall a book she had read or a story she had heard and Mr. Horsfield felt irritated by her vagueness, 'because,' he thought, 'your life is your life, and you must be pretty definite about it. Or if it's a story you are making up, you ought to at least have it pat'" (50). Later, back in London after a ten-year absence, Julia imagines "the ghost of herself coming out of the fog to meet her . . . It drifted up to her and passed her in the fog. And she had the feeling that . . . it looked at her coldly, without recognizing her" (68). In *Voyage in the Dark,* when Anna fails to persuade Walter to take her back—"[I]f I never see you again I'll die. I'm dying now really, and I'm too young to die," she imagines telling him (97)—she gives up. "I didn't care any more," she says:

> It was like letting go and falling back into water and seeing yourself grinning up through the water, your face like a mask, and seeing the bubbles coming up as if you were trying to speak from under the water. And how do you know what it's like to try to speak from under water when you're drowned? (98)

Her image of herself as a drowned but still-animate person recurs: later, at the cinema, listening to the piano music and trying to distract herself, a line from Coleridge's "Kubla Khan" drifts into her mind: "Never again, never, not ever, never. Through caverns measureless to man down to a sunless sea . . . " (107; ellipsis in the original).[5] Anna's musings suggest her profound sense of entombment, her sense of herself as the living dead. Her drift into prostitution follows immediately upon her claim that "I didn't want to talk to anybody. I felt too much like a ghost" (114). Once she is "dead," she no longer cares what happens to her.

Sasha in *Good Morning, Midnight* is Rhys's most developed portrayal of depersonalization. Sasha arrives in Paris determined not to feel: "I'm a bit of an automaton, but sane, surely—dry, cold and sane. Now I have forgotten about dark streets, dark rivers, the pain, the struggle and the drowning . . . " (10; ellipsis in the original). Sasha admits that some memory remains—"[T]here always remains something. Yes, there always remains something . . . " (10; ellipsis in the original)—but she deliberately struggles against remembering what has happened to her by creating "programmes" for herself. "Planning it all out" at the beginning of one "sombre dimanche" ("Gloomy Sunday"), Sasha mentally ticks off a list: "Eating. A movie. Eating again. One drink. A long walk back to the hotel. Bed. Luminal. Sleep. Just sleep—no dreams" (17). The staccato pacing of the prose marks her desire to overcome emotional affect, to turn herself into an automaton. Sasha also constructs a programme to manage her everyday interaction—such as it is—with other people: "At four o'clock next afternoon I am in a cinema on the Champs Elysées, according to programme. Laughing heartily in all the right places" (16); discussing the necessity of programmes, Sasha warns herself against emotion: "Above all, no crying in public, no crying at all if I can help it" (15). Every aspect of her life becomes associated with this kind of automatic response: "I have been here five days. I have decided on a place to eat in at midday, a place to eat in at night, a place to have my drink in after dinner. I have arranged my little life" (9). Sasha makes clear, furthermore, that the purpose of the programme is to defend against the onslaught of memory: "The thing is to have a programme, not to leave anything to chance—no gaps. No trailing around aimlessly with cheap gramophone records starting up in your head, no 'Here this happened, here that happened'" (15). This mechanistic plan, a substitute for any generative or optimistic hope for the future, will enable Sasha to sleepwalk through the rest of her life: "What about the programme for this afternoon? That's the thing—to have a plan and stick to it. First one thing and then another, and it'll all be over before you know where you are" (52).

Sasha's fear of the "gaps" through which memory seeps in spite of her best attempts is well-founded: she has returned to Paris—the site of her greatest happiness and most profound loss—after a long absence, and the city's streets, cafes, and above all its music bring her lost youth flooding back to her. These material reminders evoke sensory-based memories, a process common in the intrusive and disruptive return of traumatic experiences. Distinguishing between traumatic (non)memories and narrative memories, Susan J. Brison writes that the former "are 'articulated' . . . in a way less dependent on linguistic and other symbolic representations and more dependent on sensory representations, than are narrative memories . . . they are more tied to the body than are narrative memories. Indeed, traumatic memory can be viewed as a kind of somatic memory" (42). Roberta Culbertson calls this kind of traumatic memory "embodied."[6] The first page of the novel points to the power of embodied or somatic triggers: when Sasha hears a recording of Billie Holiday's blues song "Gloomy Sunday" she dissolves into tears: "It was something I remembered," she tells the couple sitting next to her at the bar.[7] Although the narrative elides the actual event, the words of this haunting song create a context of desolation, unbearable loss, and suicidal despair.[8] In fact, it is this involuntary and unwelcome reminder that spurs Sasha into becoming an automaton and into designing a programme that will seal the gaps through which memories come unbidden and unwanted. But because she is in the physical environment of her past she finds herself remembering in spite of herself. Music in particular enables memory's return: "I walk along, remembering this, remembering that, trying to find a cheap place to eat—not so easy round here. The gramophone record is going strong in my head: 'Here this happened, here that happened. . . .'" (17; ellipsis in the original). Walking through the streets she hears the strains of *L'Arlésienne* and is immediately engulfed in a humiliating memory of a time she was starving to death and got picked up by a man: "The orchestra was playing *L'Arlésienne,* I remember so well. I've just got to hear that music now, any time, and I'm back in the Cafe Buffalo, sitting by that man" (87). This flashback in particular exemplifies the way in which dissociative memories alter Sasha's sense of herself along dimensions of age, a common mark of depersonalization syndrome (Putnum 119), for Sasha is surprised when she returns from her reverie in the present day: "Walking to the music of *L'Arlésienne*. . . . I feel for the pockets of the check coat, and I am surprised when I touch the fur of the one I am wearing" (91; ellipsis in the original).

Depersonalization and its accompanying characteristics of dissociative recall are not the only ways in which trauma alters narrative chronology. Sasha shares with the protagonists of the earlier novels, particularly Anna of *Voyage in the Dark,* the peculiar sense of time that is characteristic of survivors.[9] As Ernst Van Alphen writes, "Narrative frameworks allow for an experience of (life) histories as continuous unities," but for survivors, "this illusion of continuity and unity . . . has become fundamentally unrecognizable": "The most elementary narrative framework, which consists of the continuum of past, present, and future, ha[s] disintegrated" (35). Brison notes that "[t]rauma undoes the self by breaking the ongoing narrative, severing the connections among remembered past, lived present, and anticipated future" (41). She adds that the "disappearance of the past and the foreshortening of the future are common symptoms of those who have survived traumas of various kinds" (43). For Rhys's characters, the past is a painful set of disjointed and intrusive memories that erupt into the present, while the future does not exist, or if it does exist, it exists as a set of meaningless repetitions. In a stunning summary of the way in which trauma alters the sense of her life as a cohesive continuum, Sasha thinks: "You are walking along a road peacefully. You trip. You fall into blackness. That's the past—or perhaps the future. And you know that there is no past, no future, there is only this blackness, changing faintly, slowly, but always the same" (*GMM* 144). At the end of her longest flashback, one in which Sasha finally provides the background to her marriage and pregnancy, she gets to the point where her infant son died and the narrative again becomes fragmentary: "This happened and that happened. . . . And then the days came when I was alone" (142; ellipsis in the original). Her attempt to describe the end of her marriage evokes narrative chronology only to render it generic and meaningless: "[I]t was after that that I began to go to pieces. Not all at once, of course. First this happened, and then that happened" (143). Her vision of the rest of her life is one in which everything dissolves into a meaningless mass of identical hotels, streets, and rooms, where she marches along to the outlines of her programme:

> Eat. Drink. Walk. March. Back to the hotel. To the Hotel of Arrival, the Hotel of Departure, the Hotel of the Future, the Hotel of Martinique and the Universe. . . . Back to the hotel without a name in the street without a name. You press the button and the door opens. This is the Hotel Without-a-Name in the Street Without-a-Name, and the clients have no names, no faces. You go up the stairs. Always the same stairs, always the same room. (144–145; ellipsis in the original)

"[T]here is always tomorrow," Sasha concludes (145), but it is clear that she expects little of tomorrow except more of the same. Indeed, she adds, "[W]hen I have had a couple of drinks I shan't know whether it's yesterday, today or tomorrow" (145).

Voyage in the Dark similarly depicts a protagonist who has lost all sense of continuity in her life history as a result of traumatic events. In the opening two lines of the novel, Anna describes the change in her domicile—from an unnamed but identifiable West Indian island to England—in a way that dramatizes the breach in her sense of continuity: "It was as if a curtain had fallen, hiding everything I had ever known. It was almost like being born again" (7).[10] In this new rebirth, however, the 18-year-old Anna has no parents and no protection, since her stepmother has cheated her and then cast her off. Anna finds, moreover, that she cannot fit the disparate pieces of her life together: "The colours were different, the smells different, the feeling things gave you right down inside yourself was different. Not just the difference between heat, cold; light, darkness; purple, grey. But a difference in the way I was frightened and the way I was happy" (7). The rupture in her psyche is so extreme, in fact, that Anna finds it hard to reconcile the two parts of her existence: "Sometimes it was as if I were back there and as if England were a dream. At other times England was the real thing and out there was the dream, but I could never fit them together" (8). "If England is beautiful, [my island's] not beautiful. It's some other world" (52), she tells Walter in one of the rare moments in a Rhys novel when the heroine tries to share her sense of psychic pain. Yet her attempts to communicate only underscore her sense of the unreality of her own life: "But when I began to talk about the flowers out there I got the feeling of a dream, of two things that

I couldn't fit together, and it was as if I were making up the names" (78). As her fragmented memories of Dominica continue to puncture the narrative present of the novel, it becomes clear that Anna has suffered a number of serious emotional blows—the death of both parents, the contempt and dismissiveness of her stepmother, the loss of her island, and with it her remaining family, including the maternal and nurturing black servant, Francine, from whom Anna was already separated by her sense that the latter hated her for being white. But these emotional blows cannot be integrated into the narrative present: they remain split off in the fragmentary and incoherent memories relegated to flashbacks.

The ending of *Voyage in the Dark* dramatizes the ways in which repeated traumas have destroyed Anna's sense of narrative chronology, of a discernable past, present, and future. In a delirium from the botched abortion, Anna is finally able to bring the two disparate parts of her experience, Dominica and England, together, but now they are indistinguishable from one another: past and present run together. The charwoman's remark about Anna's hemorrhaging—"It ought to be stopped" (185)—becomes mixed up in Anna's fevered mind as a reference to Carnival in Dominica ("[I]t ought to be stopped somebody said it's not a decent and respectable way to go on it ought to be stopped" [184]), her own memory of trying to stop Walter's rape ("Stop stop stop—I thought you'd say that he said" [186]), and her recent abortion itself ("Stop," I said. "You must stop" [177]). Similarly, her memory of a fall from a horse in Dominica becomes mixed up with her first encounter with Walter (her figurative "fall") as well as her sense of nausea and dizziness: "I thought I'm going to fall nothing can save me now but still I clung desperately with my knees feeling very sick" (187). The original ending is actually more effective than the published version in showing how much of her experience Anna has had to delete from her conscious narration: in her delirium Anna narrates the deaths of her parents, Walter's rape, and her own sense of death as a release, a return to the waves and the sea: "It was so still so still and lovely like just before you go to sleep and it stopped and there was the ray of light along the floor like the last thrust of remembering before everything is blotted out and blackness comes . . . " ("Part IV (Original Version)" 389; ellipsis in the original). In dying, Walter's rape—the "last thrust of remembering"—is finally blotted out for good. In the published version, urged to "give the girl a chance" by her publishers, Rhys eliminated most of this detail: instead, hearing in the doctor's pronouncement that "'She'll be all right . . . Ready to start all over again in no time'"

(187; my ellipsis) echoes of Walter's cousin Vincent's advice that she should "start fresh"(172), Anna envisions a future in which, like Sasha, she survives only to suffer again and again and again:

> When their voices stopped the ray of light came in again under the door like the last thrust of remembering before everything is blotted out. I lay and watched it and thought about starting all over again. And about being new and fresh. And about mornings, and misty days, when anything might happen. And about starting all over again, all over again. . . . (188; ellipsis in the original)

Forcing Anna to remain alive to start all over again seems worse than having her die; as Heather Ingman remarks, "[I]n view of the contrast built up in the novel between cold, hypocritical England and the warmth of Anna's memories of her West Indian island, the thought that she dies surrounded by these memories rather than surviving to suffer again makes the original ending paradoxically the more optimistic" (114).

Romantic Thralldom, Erotic Domination, and Masochistic Compulsion

A demeaning relationship with a dominating or even brutalizing man forms a prominent part of the Rhysian character's "doom." Rachel Blau DuPlessis has described this kind of erotic domination as "romantic thralldom":

> Romantic thralldom is an all-encompassing, totally defining love between apparent unequals. The lover has the power of conferring self-worth and purpose upon the loved one. Such love is possessive, and while those enthralled feel it completes and even transforms them, dependency rules. The eroticism of romantic love, born of this unequal relationship, may depend for its satisfaction upon dominance and submission. . . . such thralldom has the high price of obliteration and paralysis. (67)[11]

This definition aptly describes the kind of relationship that prevails in Rhys's novels and many of her short stories. But Rhys's are darker portraits of erotic domination than the relationships DuPlessis points to, for Rhys shades her portrayals with the elements of degradation and humiliation characteristic of masochism. As in relationships of romantic thralldom, masochism involves a complex need for recognition from an idealized, powerful other. That need is paradoxical in nature, for as Jessica Benjamin explains, "The fantasy of erotic domination embodies both the desire for independence and the desire for recognition. . . . [it] is a paradox in which the individual tries to achieve freedom through slavery, release through submission to control" (*Bonds of Love* 52). The pain of violation serves a number of important psychic needs. To begin with, physical pain can substitute for "the psychic pain of loss and abandonment" (61). Pain can also function as a low-level narcotic and can induce a trance-like state; it "blots out high-level thinking, along with complex and symbolic self-awareness" (Baumeister 72). One reason it does so is that it forces the masochist to focus on bodily sensation; as Anita Phillips observes, "[T]he ordeal involved in sexual submission cannot help but produce a sense of focus in the body, and this is important to combat the malaise that can result from an imaginative dispersal over an undefined terrain" (139). She argues that masochistic practices force "definition" and "location" (139). Pat Califia speaks of the masochistic experience as a "healing process": "A good scene doesn't end with orgasm—it ends with catharsis," she writes (134). She cites one woman's cathartic response: "The bubble of my self, the prison of my mind, exploded, expanded . . . I was hurtling forward on deep, sobbing currents of my breath, waves unleashed from the bottom of the sea. Then long throbbing seconds of liberation and silence and obliteration" (qtd. in Baumeister 73). Baumeister comments, "The image of silence and obliteration at the bottom of the sea captures the escape from self and world that seems to form the heart of the masochistic experience" (73). Phillips calls the masochistic experience a form of "renewal, a recharging of batteries" (62): "[M]asochism protects you from your engulfing fear of the entire universe by encouraging one part of it to invade you and ravish you" (63).

Of course, Baumeister, Califia, and Phillips are speaking of deliberate and consensual masochism, whereas Rhys's protagonists seem drawn into masochistic relationships as a form of repetition compulsion and inarticulated psychic need. Yet her protagonists' responses often resemble those described by consensual participants, and in fact, evidence suggests that traumatic events in childhood can point the adult to masochistic forms of erotic behavior, something that is significant in light of the Rhysian protagonist's haunted past.[12] Jessica Benjamin points to the psychoanalytic consensus that masochism is a way of managing psychic pain, early object loss, and the experience of fragmentation; she describes how "narcissistic dilemmas . . . are 'solved' by the infliction of pain administered by an idealized authority" (*Bonds of Love* 261n9). Emmanuel Ghent distinguishes between the psychic concept of "surrender," "a quality of liberation and expansion of the self as a corollary to the letting down of defensive barriers," and masochistic submission, which he argues is a distortion of the desire for surrender; submission "often represents the miscarriage of a wish to dismantle [the] false self" (108, 134). Robert J. Stoller refers to traumatic childhood events as "grains" that can gradually evolve into the perversions (*Pain and Pleasure* 43); elsewhere he calls the individualized sexual script that produces arousal a "micro-dot," a highly compressed and encoded system of information that, if decoded, could produce a history of the person's psychic life. Significantly, he views infantile sexual traumas and the rage and hatred they produce as central to the development of the "micro-dot": "[I]t is hostility—the desire, overt or hidden, to harm another person—that generates and enhances sexual excitement. . . . The exact details of the script underlying the excitement are meant to reproduce and repair the precise traumas and frustrations—debasements—of childhood" (*Sexual Excitement* 6, 13).

Stoller's idea of the "micro-dot" parallels Ethel Specter Person's contention that sexual behavior is closely linked to identity, and mediated not only by gender but by what she terms the "sex print," an "unchangeable and unique" pattern of sexual behavior that is as personal as a fingerprint. The sex print is "an individual's erotic signature," the "individualized script that elicits erotic desire" (620). It is experienced as "sexual preference," as "deep rooted and deriving from one's nature. To the degree that an individual utilizes sexuality (for pleasure, for adaptation, as the resolution of unconscious conflict) . . . one's sexual 'nature' will be experienced as more or less central to personality" (620). If we can speak of a writer's work as possessing a sex print or micro-dot, Rhys's corpus is one of female sexuality organized by and played out in masochistic scripts. Insofar as her fictions inscribe traumatic loss, the masochistic scenarios speak to deep dependency needs and the fear of loss and abandonment—anticipating, in fact, the biographical pattern Rhys will later identify in the Black Exercise Notebook, whereby the masochistic relationship substitutes the domineering and humiliating man for the punitive, rejecting mother. Yet as Rhys's career progressed, she moved from depicting masochistic characters to embodying masochism and trauma within literary form itself: portraits of romantic thralldom and erotic domination give way to a masochistic aesthetic, one that deploys repetition, suspends and disavows climax, blurs reality and fantasy, and enacts patterns of reversal—an aesthetic that, in dramatizing and exaggerating the relations of submission and dominance, sets up an oppositional site within power hierarchies.

Quartet, Rhys's first novel, is her most explicit exploration of the development, progress, and end of a sadomasochistic relationship. Marya and Stephan, newly married, are in Paris for Stephan's business, a rather shady operation involving the exchange of what seems to be stolen goods. When he is arrested and imprisoned, Marya is destitute and falls ill, at which point she is picked up by the Heidlers, a couple very much at the center of the Montparnasse world (he is an art dealer, she is a painter). They take her in, and it becomes clear that they have done so because Heidler is interested in Marya while his wife, Lois, is interested in hanging on to Heidler at whatever cost. The ménage à trois drags on, with Lois growing ever more malicious and spiteful, until finally Marya moves to a hotel that caters to kept women such as herself. She becomes more and more obsessed with Heidler, but her increasing acquiescence to her degrading circumstances seems to have an obverse effect on him, and he begins to withdraw. When Stephan is released from prison, however, Heidler again grows possessive, demanding that Marya choose between them; she retorts that she will stay with Stephan the short time he has been allowed before he is expelled from the country. Heidler makes good on his threat and breaks off the affair. In the meantime, Stephan learns about Heidler and, in the penultimate scene, knocks Marya down and leaves her, saying "Voila pour toi" ("That's for you") (185). The novel ends as Stephan allows himself to be picked up by another demimondaine. "Encore une grue" ("Again a whore"), he thinks (186).

What makes *Quartet* such a compelling fiction is its explicit and detailed presentation of the psychodynamics of masochism, a presentation Rhys focalizes through Marya. Initially, Marya does not seem particularly masochistic. To be sure, she exhibits a dependent and child-like passivity when Stephan meets her in the opening chapters; she has drifted into a monotonous, nomadic life as a chorus girl that she conducts "very mechanically and listlessly": "A vague procession of towns all exactly alike, a vague procession of men also exactly alike" (16). She drifts into marriage with Stephan in part because he seems to know her: "[S]he felt strangely peaceful when she was with him, as if life were not such an extraordinary muddle after all, as if he were telling her: 'Now then, look here, I know all about you. I know you far better than you know yourself. I know why you aren't happy. I can make you happy.'" (17). Marya responds to his air of certainty: Stephan seems "definite," with a "clean-cut" and "hard" mind, "disconcertingly and disquietingly sceptical" (17). He promises, furthermore, to indulge Marya, to spoil her like a child: "He told her . . . that if she were happy and petted she would become charming. Happy, petted, charming–these are magical words. And the man knew what he was talking about, Marya could see that" (18). Despite her qualms about Stephan's shady business dealings, her fear of some "vague, dimly-apprehended catastrophe," Marya responds positively to his indulgence of her: "Stephan was secretive and a liar, but he was a very gentle and expert lover. She was the petted, cherished child, the desired mistress, the worshipped, perfumed goddess. She was all these things to Stephan—or so he made her believe. Marya hadn't known that a man could be as nice as all that to a woman—so gentle in little ways" (22). Given Marya's sense of herself as wandering through a landscape peopled with ghosts, Stephan's nurturing response to Marya in effect conjures her into existence; as she later tells Lois, "Stephan's a—vivid sort of person. . . . He made me come alive" (60).

Hence when disaster strikes, Marya finds herself back in the "vague and shadowy" world that Stephan's recognition, clarity, and indulgence had banished (33). It is at this point that she becomes vulnerable to the machinations of the Heidlers. Marya intuits that something is not quite straightforward about their dealings with her, but she is gradually drawn into their schemes as they in turn awaken her masochistic desires. Significantly, when Lois tries to persuade Marya to join the household and then to satisfy Heidler sexually, Marya begins to long for a kind of pleasure she images as pain. She feels a "strange excitement" (47) connected to living with them: "[S]he began to wonder why the idea of living with the Heidlers filled her with such extraordinary dismay. After all, she told herself, it might be fun" (49). Similarly, after Heidler propositions her, Marya experiences a fierce "longing for joy, for any joy, for any pleasure" like a "mad thing in her heart. It was sharp like pain and she clenched her teeth. It was like some splendid caged animal roused and fighting to get out. It was an unborn child jumping, leaping, kicking at her side" (74). Rhys links this mixture of pain and pleasure to the "gay, metallic music of the merry-go-rounds" (47).[13] These grating, mechanistic pleasure machines substitute repetitive circles for meaningful movement; the piston-like motion of the merry-go-round suggests sexual activity even as it exchanges artificial thrills and pulsations for sexual gratification. Later Marya will stop to watch a little girl going round:

> There was a merry-go-round . . . where the tram stopped. Children were being hoisted on to the backs of the gaily painted wooden

> horses. Then the music started to clank: "Je vous aime." And the horses pranced around, pawing the air in a mettlesome way.
>
> Marya stayed there for a long time watching a little frail, blonde girl who careered past, holding tightly on to the neck of her steed, her face tense and strained with delight. The merry-go-round made her feel more normal, less like a grey ghost walking in a vague, shadowy world. (57)

The merry-go-round becomes an emblem of a sterile sexuality that is obsessive and mechanical, played out to the "clanking" and insincere strains of "Je vous aime" ("I love you"). That Marya—who, blond and frail herself in appearance, clearly identifies with the little girl on the horse—feels more normal and less spectral in watching this scene suggests that the little girl's "tense and strained delight" has called up her own association of pleasure and pain: the sounds have pierced her self-enclosure. And Lois will eventually mock Marya in a manner that clarifies the image of the merry-go-round: "'Let's go to Luna-park after dinner . . . We'll put Mado [Marya] on the joy wheel, and watch her being banged about a bit. Well, she ought to amuse us sometimes; she ought to sing for her supper; that's what she's here for, isn't it?" (85).

Marya is well aware of the cruelty involved in the Heidlers' invitation; after Lois's first attempt at persuasion "[a] sentence she had read somewhere floated fantastically into her mind: 'It's so nice to think that the little thing enjoys it too,' said the lady, watching her cat playing with a mouse'" (62). Similarly, when she first meets the Heidlers, her reaction is unequivocal: Heidler has a "wooden" face and Marya sees in his eyes "a curious underlying expression of obtuseness—even of brutality" (11). But after she finds herself destitute, she looks to Heidler "with appeal": "[S]he felt passionately grateful to him. She was sure that he knew she was ill and near to tears. He was a rock of a man with his big shoulders and his quiet voice" (43). The "thought of Heidler" stands between Stephan's prison and her: "He was big and calm and comforting. He said 'Don't worry. I love you, d'you see?' And one hadn't worried. At least, not so much" (110). Again Marya responds to someone who is definite and certain, and, again she responds to a man who treats her as if she were a child. Here the dual images of Marya as both child and caged animal emerge in a degraded manner. Many scenes depict Heidler soothing and calming Marya as if Heidler were parent instead of lover: until he comes into the bedroom, for example, Marya "was in a frenzy of senseless fright. Fright of a child shut up in a dark room. Fright of an animal caught in a trap" (90). "What is it? What is it, then?" he asks, " . . . There, there, there!" (90). Later, after a humiliating fight, Marya appeals to Heidler in "a little voice like a child" and he again responds by holding her: "She was quivering and abject in his arms, like some unfortunate dog abasing itself before its master" (131).

Marya responds to Heidler in part because he, like Stephan, accepts her dependency. But whereas Stephan overlooks Marya's prior sexual experiences, Heidler relishes reminding Marya of her degradation. When he first tells Marya that he is attracted to her, for example, he does so in terms that make clear his sense of his control and her sexually degraded subordination: "I knew that I could have you by putting my hand out. . . . I've been watching you; I watched you tonight and now I know that somebody else will get you if I don't. You're that sort. . . . I've every right to take advantage" (72). Marya responds at first with anger, but his touch on her arm results in submission: "When he touched her she felt warm and secure, then weak and so desolate that tears came into her eyes" (72–73). Heidler's insulting phrase—"You're that sort"—functions as a moment of recognition: Marya realizes she *is* "that sort." Rhys hints that Heidler has intuited Marya's "sex print"; later, when they consummate their affair, Marya feels like a lost child who has been found: "I was lost before I knew him. All my life before I knew him was like being lost on a cold, dark night" (83). His attention, like Stephan's earlier, has literally conjured her into existence. And, again resembling the earlier relationship, Heidler's expectations of Marya shape her sense of self, although, in contrast to Stephan, who images Marya as petted child, desired mistress, and worshipped goddess, Heidler's eyes "confuse and hurt" Marya, and his vision of her is debased:

> He wasn't a good lover, of course. He didn't really like women. She had known that as soon as he touched her. His hands were inexpert, clumsy at caresses; his mouth was hard when he kissed. No, not a lover of women, he could say what he liked.
>
> He despised love. He thought of it grossly, to amuse himself, and then with ferocious contempt. . . .
>
> What mattered was that despising, almost disliking love, he was forcing her to be nothing but the little woman who lived in the Hotel du Bosphore for the express purpose of being made love to. A *petite femme*. It was, of course, part of his mania for classification. But he did it with such conviction that she, miserable weakling that she was, found herself trying to live up to his idea of her.
>
> She lived up to it. (118)

Because Heidler sees her as a "*petite femme,*" as "that sort," Marya sees herself that way and tries to embody his image of her.

Yet Rhys makes clear that Marya psychologically benefits from Heidler's brutality. Before her involvement with him, Marya suffers from "an iron band . . . encircling her head tightly, as though she were sinking slowly down into deep water" (35), an image of suffocation and constriction that Marya identifies as psychic suffering when she visits Stephan in prison: "[H]e was withdrawn from her, enclosed in the circle of his own pain, unreachable" (45). The affair with Heidler punctures this kind of self-imprisonment in the manner described by Baumeister, Califia, and Phillips above. Most notably, her involvement with Heidler results in the cessation of thought: near the beginning of their affair, Marya feels "absorbed, happy, without thought for perhaps the first time in her life. No past. No future. Nothing but the present . . . She glanced at the rough texture of Heidler's coat-sleeve and longed to lay her face against it" (85). Later, feeling "it was horrible, the power he had to hurt her" (103), Marya finds that "every vestige of coherence, of reason had fled from her brain" (103). The loss of control, of the very ability to think, is something Marya longs for:

> His eyes were clear, cool and hard, but something in the depths of them flickered and shifted. She thought: "He'd take any advantage he could—fair or unfair. Caddish he is." Then as she stared back at him she felt a great longing to put her head on his knees and shut her eyes. To stop thinking. Stop the little wheels in her head that worked incessantly. To give in and have a little peace. The unutterably sweet peace of giving in. (107)

In Heidler's absence, significantly, Marya suffers from repetitive, obsessive thought patterns that Rhys images as mechanistic and clocklike: "The mechanism of her brain got to work with a painful jerk and began to tick in time with the clock" (117). Other images for her obsessive desire include a torment akin to dying from thirst (117, 145) and a "perpetual aching longing," a "wound that bled persistently and very slowly" (122): "Love was a terrible thing. You poisoned it and stabbed at it and knocked it down into the mud—well down—and it got up and staggered on, bleeding and muddy and awful. Like—like Rasputin" (122–123). Marya here identifies "love"—herself—in the suffering of the tortured monk.[14] The repetitions underscore Marya's obsessive, tormented thought patterns: "Little wheels in her head that turned perpetually. I love him. I want him. I hate her. And he's a swine. He's out to hurt me. What shall I do? I love him. I want him. I hate her. So she would lie for hours, tortured by love and hate" (124).

The structure of the novel reinforces the claustrophobic quality of Marya's feverish and repetitive thinking. After Heidler sets Marya up in a discreet hotel "of unlimited hospitality," she spends countless hours gazing at the wallpaper of her bedroom, which she finds "vaguely erotic—huge and fantastically shaped mauve, green and yellow flowers sprawling on a black ground" (111).[15] The flowers serve as objective corollaries of all the women who have gone before her, "the succession of *petite femmes* who had extended themselves upon [the bed], clad in carefully thought out pink or mauve chemises" (111). Rhys repeatedly evokes this wallpaper, linking its recurrence to the increasing constriction of both Marya's life and her thought patterns: when Marya first tries to turn off her clocklike mind, succeeding in making it blank for ten seconds, she contemplates the flowers "which crawled like spiders over the black walls of her bedroom" (117); later, after an abortive attempt at rapprochement with her husband, she returns to her hotel bedroom, "where green-yellow and dullish mauve flowers crawled over the black walls":

> She undressed, and all the time she was undressing it was as if Heidler were sitting there watching her with his cool eyes that confused and hurt her.
>
> She lay down. For perhaps thirty seconds she was able to keep her mind a blank; then her obsession gripped her, arid, torturing, gigantic, possessing her as utterly as the longing for water possesses someone who is dying of thirst. (145)

The repetition in the passages underscores Marya's intensifying sense of degradation: the flowers at first sprawl like *petite femmes* and then, insectlike, crawl; at the same time, the identical phrasing—the passage appears both at the beginning and at the end of the chapter that charts Marya's sojourn in the hotel as a kept woman—marks the circularity not only in her thoughts but in her attempts to move out of the room and to escape her obsessive desire for Heidler. The finality of her return to the room, the wallpaper, and her clocklike mind recalls the earlier image of her compulsive thinking, an iron band enclosing her head while she drowns, an image of both constriction and suffocation.

Many readers express frustration with Marya's seeming acquiescence to her intensifying degradation. But Heidler's dominance induces the kind of paralysis DuPlessis identifies as characteristic of erotic domination: Marya feels "so languid as to be almost incapable of movement. A profound conviction of the unreality of everything possessed her"; she even wonders if her languor resembles the state of taking opium (83). She also feels "hypnotized" and "impotent" (89). Eventually, moreover, she will feel obliterated: "[I]t seemed to her that she had forgotten the beginnings of the affair, when she had still reacted and he had reconquered her painstakingly. She never reacted now. She was a thing. Quite dead. Not a kick left in her" (123); "You've smashed me up," she tells Heidler, a statement he finds both true and flattering (129). Heidler does not want Marya when she is no longer capable of fighting against his domination of her, for it is her struggle against and eventual submission to his mastery that excites him. As George Bataille notes, when the slave accepts defeat he has "lost the quality without which he is unable to *recognize* the conqueror so as to satisfy him. The slave is unable to give the master the *satisfaction* without which the master can no longer rest" (12). Benjamin observes that the masochist "increasingly feels that she does not exist, that she is without will or desire, that she has no life apart from the other . . . Once the tension between subjugation and resistance dissolves, death or abandonment is the inevitable end of the story" (*Bonds of Love* 65). She adds that for the masochist, abandonment is "the intolerable end" (65). The closing sections of *Quartet* confirm this assessment: after Heidler breaks off the affair, he finds Marya "lying huddled. As if there were a spring broken somewhere" (153).

Voyage in the Dark also portrays the relationship between Anna and Walter as one of erotic domination, although this relationship conforms more closely to the paradigm of romantic thralldom than does the relationship between Marya and Heidler. As a number of critics have pointed out, this relationship takes on the nuances of the mother-child relationship: Anna's "rebirth" as an 18-year-old chorus girl in England points back to the loss of her mother as well as her mother country; her stepmother, Hester, cold, disapproving, and judgmental, is no substitute either for the lost mother or for the nurturing black servant, Francine.[16] Hester is, in fact, one of Rhys's first portraits of the rejecting mother: she dislikes Anna's "sing-song voice" that sounds "exactly like a nigger" (65); she resents Anna's relationship with the maternal Francine; she hates the island with its strong scents and night sounds; she implies that Anna's mother is black and that Anna is somehow contaminated. Not only is she responsible for selling Anna's property in Dominica and pocketing the money, she brings Anna to England in order to make her a lady and give her "a real chance" (65), thereby cutting her off from the island, her mother's people, and Francine. She continually pronounces Anna to be innately bad: when Anna politely says "My goodness!" to one of Hester's incessant stories about England, Hester responds, "Don't say my goodness . . . My badness, that's what you ought to say" (69). Like Walter, who cannot listen to Anna's stories about Dominica but instead talks to her as if were talking to himself (78), Hester makes disparaging remarks about Anna as if she weren't there, "[i]n that voice as if she were talking to herself" (70).

Rhys represents Hester's emotionally abusive behavior as traumatizing to Anna long before she arrives in England. In an extensive flashback that details Hester's and Anna's interactions, Anna recalls Hester's reaction to Anna's dislike of dogs: "I don't know what'll become of you if you go on like that," Hester said. "Let me tell you that you'll have a very unhappy life if you go on like that. People won't like you. People in England will dislike you very much if you say things like that" (71). Anna's reaction is one of dissociation: "I began to repeat the multiplication-table because I was afraid I was going to cry" (71). In the narrative present of the novel, when Hester begins to rant about her reasons for selling Anna's property and keeping the money, Anna again reacts by dissociating herself from the scene: "I had been expecting something so different that what she was saying didn't seem to make any sense. I was looking out the window. The leaves of the trees in the square were coming out, and there was a pigeon strutting in the street with its neck all green and gold" (62–63). In perhaps the most crucial exchange between them, Hester imposes her own negative sense of menstruation on Anna, thereby poisoning the girl's entrance into womanhood:

> [W]hen I was unwell for the first time it was [Francine] who explained it to me, so that it seemed quite all right and I thought it was all in the day's work like eating or drinking. But then she went off and told Hester, and Hester came and jawed away at me, her eyes wandering all over the place. I kept saying, 'No, rather not. . . . Yes, I see. . . . Oh yes, of course . . . ' But I began to feel awfully miserable, as if everything were shutting up around me and I couldn't breathe. I wanted to die. (68; ellipses in the original)

Anna somatizes her distress, feeling a sense of constriction and suffocation about emotions she is unable to verbalize. Repudiating Hester and separated by race and class from Francine, Anna feels "more alone than anybody had ever been in the world before" (73). She stands in the sun, hoping to contract a fever and die, but although the "pain was like knives" and she does fall seriously ill, she survives.

Anna's repudiation of Hester suggests that one of the reasons Anna allows herself to become involved with Walter is her desire to differentiate herself from the rejecting mother, who, after all, differentiates herself from the (step) daughter by claiming the latter to be dirty and contaminated. Anna images this repudiation in more general terms in her flashback to her fever and Francine's nurturing care of her: "I wanted to be black, I always wanted to be black . . . Being black is warm and gay, being white is cold and sad" (31). Given that the racial discourse of the time sexualized black women—the chorus girls' nickname for Anna is "Hottentot" (13)—Anna's desire to be black suggests her embrace of a degraded and degrading sexuality. Again, Anna's somatic responses chart these inarticulate feelings: coldness comes to mean sadness and respectability, and Anna projects onto the landscape the constriction and sense of suffocation she felt with Hester. At the beginning of the novel, for example, Anna states that "in my heart I was always sad, with the same sort of hurt that the cold gave me in my chest" (15); she describes London as a place with "streets like smooth shut-in ravines and the dark houses frowning down" (17). Walter's respectable house, where Anna always has to leave before morning, feels "quiet and watching and not friendly" (36). When the landlady asks her to leave, telling her, "I don't want no tarts in my house, so now you know" (30), Anna's response is autonomic—"I didn't answer. My heart was beating like hell" (30)—and she remembers a story "about the walls of a room getting smaller and smaller until they crush you to death" (30). In her initial phases of romantic fantasy, Anna pushes away from her conscious mind the kind of relationship Walter really wants with her, but when he brings up the subject of virginity—her claim to respectability—she goes cold: "Then he started talking about my being a virgin and it all went—the feeling of being on fire—and I was cold" (36).

What Anna wants from Walter is, of course, the parental protection she fails to receive from Hester; Rhys explicitly portrays this desire as regressive and infantile. Hence when Walter comes to care for Anna during a bout of fever, he takes on the maternal role Francine played in her memories of her fever in Dominica: he brings food and a warm blanket and sits down next to her to watch over her. "The room looked different, as if it had grown bigger," Anna observes (34): Walter alleviates her sense of constriction and suffocation. Earlier, the room where Walter first tries to seduce her strikes her as warm, womblike, and safe: it is furnished in red with a red-shaded lamp, red flowers, and a warm fire. When she discovers a second room—a bedroom—behind a curtain, this room also strikes her as secret and safe: "In this room too the lights were shaded in red; and it had a secret feeling—quiet, like a place where you crouch down when you are playing hide-and-seek" (23). Yet while she waits there, Anna realizes that there is a split between the look of the room and its actual effect upon her: "There was a fire but the room was cold," she observes (23); "The fire was like a painted fire; no warmth came from it" (24). She begins to feel dissociated from herself: when she looks in the mirror "[i]t was as if I were looking at somebody else. . . . I felt as if I had gone out of myself, as if I were in a dream" (23; my ellipsis).

Walter eventually succeeds in seducing Anna because he nurtures Anna as if he were a parent instead of a lover. Hence his gift of money for the purchase of new clothes makes possible a more positive "rebirth" than the initial image of exile that opens the novel: "This is a beginning," Anna muses. "Out of this warm room that smells of fur I'll go to all the lovely places I've ever dreamt of. This is the beginning" (28). Warmth also functions as an important element of the seduction, for despite feeling "cold and as if I were dreaming" (37), when she gets into bed with Walter Anna discovers "there was warmth coming from him and I got close to him" (37). This discovery seems to prompt the type of preverbal infantile memory that Christopher Bollas terms the "unthought known": "Of course you've always known, always remembered, and then you forget so utterly, except that you've always known it. Always—how long is always?" (37).[17] Significantly, Rhys does not identify what Anna "knows," although earlier, in her feverish flashback to Francine's care of her, Anna had remembered "the heat pressing down on you as if it were something alive" (31). This buried infantile mood gives way to erotic domination and thralldom, for after this first sexual encounter, Walter pays Anna: "[I]nstead of saying, 'Don't do that,' I said, 'All right, if you like—anything you like, any way you like.' And I kissed his hand" (38).[18] She begins to identify herself with a slave girl whose name she had seen on a slave list in Dominica, "Maillotte Boyd, aged 18, mulatto, house servant. The sins of the fathers Hester said are visited upon the children unto the third and fourth generation" (53): her sexual slavery is a form of retribution as well as a way of trying to be "warm and gay" like the degraded black women of her imagination.

Because he is the idealized other from whom she receives recognition, Anna's loss of Walter becomes bound up with the memories of her traumatic loss of her mother and mother country. Trying to persuade him to take her back and imagining that she will die if he doesn't, Anna suddenly remembers her sense impressions of her mother's funeral: "The candles crying wax tears and the smell of stephanotis and I had to go to the funeral in a white dress and white gloves and a wreath around my head and the wreath in my hands made my gloves wet—they said so young to die . . . " (97; ellipsis in the original). Fittingly, in its evocation of wedding white, this memory serves as a link between sexuality and death, between the loss of the mother and the loss of the lover. It is only in the original version of the novel that the depth of the mother's loss become clear: when Hester criticizes a song Anna is singing ("[T]hat one's very melancholy . . . and the words don't seem to me to make any sense") Anna responds, "[I]t means My beautiful girl is singing to her mother" ("Original Version" 382; my ellipsis). Songs become evocations of the lost island, the lost mother, and then the lost lover: "I looked back from the boat. . . . Adieu sweetheart adieu" ("Original Version" 382; my ellipsis). While the original version makes the equation between the mother and Walter more explicit, the published version retains a connection between music, water, the lost mother, and the abandoning lover. Immediately after Walter breaks off the affair, Anna becomes withdrawn and tired, spending long hours in the bath: "I would put my head under the water and listen to the noise of the tap running. I would pretend it was a waterfall, like the one that falls into the pool where we bathed at Morgan's Rest" (90). This passage picks up on and amplifies an earlier moment in the novel, when Anna had heard a piano, "a tinkling sound like water running. . . . But it got farther and farther away and then I couldn't hear it any more. 'Gone for ever,' I thought. There was a tight feeling in my throat as if I wanted to cry" (10). Now Walter takes his place in this series of losses: "The piano began to play. Never again, never, not ever, never. Through caverns measureless to man down to a sunless sea. . . . " (107; ellipsis in the original). Anna's state of mind is now one where she simply lives until she can die: "It's funny when you feel as if you don't want anything more in your life except to sleep, or else to lie without moving. That's when you can hear time sliding past you, like water running" (113).

From Erotic Domination to the Masochistic Aesthetic

After *Voyage in the Dark* Rhys shifted her emphasis from a focus on portrayals of romantic thralldom and erotic domination to a focus on how narrative itself can function as a site of ideological contestation. It is in *Good Morning, Midnight* that Rhys effects this shift most completely, and she does so by moving from a depiction of masochistic character to developing instead a masochistic aesthetic. In order to understand the subversive nature of Rhys's poetics of dominance and submission in this novel, it may be useful to review recent theoretical work on masochistic subjectivity and its relevance to literary structures. In an important essay that paved the way for much recent work, Gilles Deleuze argues that "the clinical specificities of sadism and masochism are not separable from the literary values peculiar to Sade and Masoch" (14); he goes on to analyze masochism as an aesthetic structure with a number of clearly discernable qualities: "Masochism is neither material nor moral, but essentially formal," he argues. "We need . . . a genuinely formal, almost deductive psychoanalysis which would attend first of all to the formal patterns underlying the processes, viewed as formal elements of fictional art" (74). Among those elements Deleuze includes the following: the "dreamed, dramatized, ritualized" element of fantasy; the "suspense factor," which he defines as the waiting or delay that inhibits sexual excitement and that postpones climax; the exhibitonistic or performative manner in which the masochist draws attention to his or her abasement; the demand for punishment; and the masochistic contract (74–75). Building on his analysis, Gaylyn Studlar has posited that the components of a masochistic narrativity include episodic, repetitive scenes; implausible coincidences; and the elision of main events, all of which occur commonly in *Good Morning, Midnight.*

Repetition is the key element structuring the masochistic aesthetic. As Deleuze points out, "[M]asochistic pain depends entirely on the phenomenon of waiting and on the functions of repetition and reiteration which characterize waiting" (119); he argues that masochism alters the "normal function of repetition in its relation to the pleasure principle":

> [I]nstead of repetition being experienced as a form of behavior related to a pleasure already obtained or anticipated, instead of repetition being governed by the idea of experiencing or reexperiencing pleasure, repetition runs wild and becomes independent of all previous pleasure. It has become an idea or ideal. Pleasure is now a form of behavior related to repetition, accompanying and following repetition, which has itself become an awesome, independent force. (120)

Deleuze's analysis of masochistic repetition has interesting ramifications for the influential model of plot based upon Freud's *Beyond the*

Pleasure Principle that Peter Brooks has developed. For Brooks, repetition works as a "binding of textual energies that allows them to be mastered by putting them into serviceable form, usable 'bundles,' within the energetic economy of the narrative" (101). Brooks comes close to articulating the masochistic potential of such "bindings" when he writes that "these formalizations and the recognitions they provoke may in some sense be painful: they create a delay, a postponement in the discharge of energy, a turning back from immediate pleasure, to ensure that the ultimate pleasurable discharge will be more complete. The most effective or . . . the most challenging texts may be those that are most delayed, most highly bound, most painful" (101–102).[19] Setting aside for the moment Brooks' assumption that all narratives do, in fact, come to an end in an "ultimate pleasurable discharge"—an assumption that the masochistic narrative of Rhys's fiction emphatically contradicts—what Brooks identifies is a rhythmic movement or oscillation of textual repetitions, whereby the desire to know "what happens next" competes with the turn back to what has already happened, what Freud would perhaps call an oscillation between Eros and Thanatos. Freud himself speculates that the paradox of finding pleasure in pain may be related to this sort of rhythmic oscillation: "Perhaps it is the rhythm, the temporal sequence of changes, rises and falls in the quantity of stimulus; we do not know," he muses ("The Economic Problem of Masochism" *Standard Edition* 19: 160).[20] Freud's comment resonates with D. W. Winnicott's analysis of environmental failures in which the infant repeatedly experiences intrusions from the caretaker; Winnicott argues that such an individual becomes an adult for whom "environmental impingement must continue . . . and must have a pattern of its own, else chaos reigns since the individual cannot develop a personal pattern" (212). Drawing upon this passage, Emmanuel Ghent argues that masochistic desire may have its source in the need for a "patterned impingement" (118, 124). By extension, in masochistic narrativity textual repetitions function as forms of "patterned impingement."

Such patterned impingements pervade *Good Morning, Midnight.* In particular repetitions cluster in those passages in which Sasha voices the tension between her desire to deaden herself (adhering to a mechanistic "programme," making herself "blank") and her competing desire to attend the "Exhibition" (this tension also recalls Freud's distinction between Thanatos and Eros). The Exhibition is a case in point. This governing metaphor initially appears as a nightmare in the novel's opening pages. Trapped in a London tube with people standing before and behind her, Sasha sees everywhere placards reading "This Way to the Exhibition, This Way to the Exhibition": "But I don't want the way to the Exhibition," Sasha says, "I want the way out. . . . The steel finger points along a long stone passage. This Way—This Way—This Way to the Exhibition" (13; my ellipsis). But as the novel continues, the word "exhibition" appears in multiple contexts, and its meaning shifts accordingly. Hence it functions in a figurative sense for a mode of existence in a specular economy—"He isn't trying to size me up, as they usually do," Sasha says of the gigolo Rene, "he is exhibiting himself, his own person" (72)—and it also functions as a literal place, the Exhibition Sasha visits near the novel's close.[21] This blurring of figurative and literal speaks to the blurring of fantasy and reality that Deleuze identifies as a hallmark of the masochistic aesthetic.[22] At the same time, the Exhibition underscores the performative nature of identity, another key element in the masochistic aesthetic. The performative aspects of the exhibition emerge particularly clearly in Sasha's ambivalent reaction to the Russian painter's portraits of grotesques and social outcasts—misshapen dwarves, old prostitutes, a red-nosed Jewish banjo player. "[T]he four-breasted woman is exhibited," Sasha says; she sees the pictures as animate, resisting specularization: "The canvases resist. They curl up; they don't want to go into the frames" (99).

Like these canvases, Sasha too resists; she doesn't want to go into the frame. But while she eventually acquiesces to the demands of the "transformation act"—buying a new hat and dress and dyeing her hair—her sardonic interior monologue operates as a site of opposition that makes clear how, in Judith Butler's words, "gender identity is a performative accomplishment compelled by social sanction and taboo": "If gender identity is the stylized repetition of acts through time . . . then the possibilities of gender transformation are to be found in the arbitrary relation between such acts, in the possibility of a different sort of repeating, in the breaking or subversive repetition of that style" (402). Thus Sasha's understanding of gender performance as repetitive, ritualized, and performative aligns the masquerade of femininity with the masquerade of the masochist, while her commentary voicing her acquiescence functions as subversive mimicry. It is here that Butler's analysis overlaps suggestively with that of Deleuze. As the latter argues, the theatrical aspect of the masochistic aesthetic is a form of exaggeration or mimicry that exposes, and demonstrates contempt for, the laws that govern its structuring. Deleuze is eloquent on the ironic humor involved in the masochistic aesthetic: "The element of contempt in the submission of the masochist has often been emphasized: his apparent obedience conceals a criticism and a provocation. He simply attacks the law on another flank. . . . The masochist is "insolent in his obsequiousness, rebellious in his submission . . . a humorist, a logician of consequences" (89).[23]

This kind of ironic humor typifies Sasha's analysis of feminine masochistic masquerade. "God, it's funny, being a woman!" Sasha observes (104), going on to parade her conformity to the demands of femininity in terms of masochistic submission:

> Please, please, monsieur et madame, mister, missis and miss, I am trying to hard to be like you. I know I don't succeed, but look how hard I try. Three hours to choose a hat; every morning an hour and a half trying to make myself look like everybody else. Every word I say has chains around its ankles; every thought I think is weighted with heavy weights. Since I was born, hasn't every word I've said, every thought I've thought, everything I've done, been tied up, weighted, chained? (106)

Women would be better off as the "damned dolls" in the reception area of the fashion house: "[W]hat a success they would have made of their lives if they had been women. Satin skin, silk hair, velvet eyes, sawdust heart—all complete," Sasha states enviously (18). But as animate flesh and blood, Sasha must submit to the "extraordinary rituals" of the "transformation act." Her mocking monologue on dyeing her hair "ash blonde," in which Sasha mimics the voice of a hairdresser, marks her ironic distance from this assumption of a feminine uniform:

> Shall I have it blond cendré? But blond cendré, madame, is the most difficult of colours. It is very, very rarely, madame, that hair can be successfully dyed blond cendré. It's even harder on the hair than dyeing it platinum blonde. First it must be bleached, that is to say, its own colour must be taken out of it—and then it must be dyed, that is to say, another colour must be imposed on it. (Educated hair. . . . And then, what?) (52; ellipsis in the original)

Sasha here defines feminine "education" as the relinquishing of what is natural and the full acceptance of something artificial and externally imposed: feminine education involves submission to discipline. At the same time, Sasha's choice of the hair color—"ash blonde" or "blond cendré"—ironically undercuts her submission to feminine "education," for in French the word "Cinderella" is

"Cendrillon": whereas Cinderella's "transformation act" wins her a reprieve from servitude, Sasha's transformation act, undertaken to stave off the inevitable process of aging, offers no such reprieve.

If appearance functions as one form of disciplinary control, so, too, do language and conversation. Sasha exclaims that "everything in their whole bloody world is a cliché. Everything is born out of a cliché, rests on a cliché, survives by a cliché. And they believe in the clichés—there's no hope" (42). But she keeps this rebellious critique to herself and instead adheres to the rituals of social control. When two men approach Sasha in a park and ask her why she is so sad, for example, she thinks to herself, "Yes, I am sad, sad as a circus-lioness, sad as an eagle without wings, sad as a violin with only one string and that string broken, sad as a woman who is growing old. Sad, sad, sad. . . . Or perhaps if I just said 'merde' it would do as well" (45; ellipsis in the original). Sasha here elaborates a series of figures, comparing herself to creatures and objects that have lost the most essential aspect of their beings: the lioness her freedom, the eagle its ability to fly, the violin its capacity for music.[24] In a world in which women are valued only for youth and beauty, she has no chance of succeeding with her "transformation act." The almost shocking insertion of "merde" at the end of this series of images signals Sasha's negation of the whole enterprise.[25] Sasha nonetheless responds to the men with polite banalities that conceal her pain—"But I'm not sad. Why should you think I am sad?"—while internally she rages, "Is it a ritual? Am I bound to answer the same question in the same words?" (45–46).

This doubled movement of acquiescence and rebellion emerges explicitly in a series of images and anecdotes that connect female servitude and revolution. Sasha's very name—homage to a Russian fad and the repudiation of the English "Sophia"—anticipates her description of the "the Russian princess who was shut up in the prison of Peter and Paul to be eaten by rats, because she was a revolutionary" (138). To be a female revolutionary, then, is to risk incarceration and murder. Sasha links herself to revolution elsewhere through her description of a girl in a "tabac" who does all the washing up: "Bare sturdy legs, felt slippers, a black dress, a filthy apron, thick, curly, untidy hair. I know her. This is the girl who does all the dirty work and gets paid very little for it. Salut!"[26] She then asks rhetorically, "[D]on't her strong hands sing the Marseillaise? And when the revolution comes, won't those be the hands to be kissed? Well, so Monsieur Rimbaud says, doesn't he?" (105); the allusion to Rimbaud's poem, "Les Mains de Jeanne-Marie," which celebrates the working-class women revolutionaries in the Paris Commune of 1871, underscores the connection between women's subordination and the threat of revolution. Later, in an image or memory generated by her "film-mind," Sasha describes a masochistic episode in which she, too, wears slippers and a black dress and serves a man both sexually and domestically:

> I am in a little white room. The sun is hot outside. A man is standing with his back to me, whistling that tune and cleaning his shoes. I am wearing a black dress, very short, and heel-less slippers. My legs are bare. I am watching for the expression on the man's face when he turns round. Now he ill-treats me, now he betrays me. He often brings home other women and I have to wait on them, and I don't like that. But as long as he is alive and near me I am not unhappy. If he were to die I should kill myself. (176)

Mary Lou Emery comments that the image of the "film-mind" refers to Sasha's ability to "reel out memories on the same plane with the present, to juxtapose scenes rather than construct them through the linear logic of chronological time or to distinguish between imagined and actual incidents" (162). This blurring of the real and the imaginary is consistent with the masochistic aesthetic: the import of the passage lies not in whether it refers to "actual" events in Sasha's life but rather in the way it dramatizes her preoccupation with submission and servitude. As Baumeister observes, masochism involves "more fiction and illusion than nearly any other pattern of human behavior" (12); "[M]asochists *fictionalize* pain," he argues (14).

This scene from Sasha's "film-mind" opens the novel's last, controversial, ambiguous section. Sasha, lost in her masochistic reverie, opens the door to her room, only to find the gigolo René waiting for her. After a violent struggle, he leaves; Sasha then begins, apparently, to attempt to will him back: she sets the door of her room ajar and strips off her clothes in preparation. The novel ends with a jolt of dislocation, however, as Sasha welcomes into her bed, not René, but the repulsive *commis voyageur*, a man she has described as frightening and uncanny: skeletal, often clad in a white dressing gown, he strikes her as the "ghost of the landing" or the "priest of some obscene, half-understood religion" (14, 35). In another dislocating narrative jolt, Sasha states that she has been expecting the *commis* all along. Images of both rebirth and death coincide, as Sasha, lying "as still as if I were dead," nonetheless pulls the *commis* down onto the bed; the novel ends with her repeated "Yes—yes—yes . . . " (190; ellipsis in the original), an affirmation that circles back to the first line of the novel and the room's query: "Quite like old times . . . Yes? No?" (9; my ellipsis).

This conjunction of rebirth and death, of affirmation and negation, plays out the dissolving of binary categories that is the climactic moment of the masochistic encounter. In fact, the novel's conclusion enacts and dramatizes the terms of the Emily Dickinson poem from which it draws its title: the speaker says farewell to day and greets her new lover, midnight, itself a liminal marker between day and night, a witching hour when ghosts are believed to reanimate and walk. The series of returns in the novel's conclusion similarly breaks down the dichotomy between life and death, happiness and sadness, pleasure and pain. For in opening the door and waiting for the *commis,* Sasha literalizes a moment of fantasy earlier in the novel, when her viewing of Serge's portraits of human misery enabled both a release from self-imprisonment—"Now the room expands and the iron band around my heart loosens. The miracle has happened. I am happy" (99)—and a vague dream of an empty room, "[N]othing in it but the bed, the stove and the looking glass and outside Paris. And the dreams that you have, alone in an empty room, waiting for the door that will open, the thing that is bound to happen" (100).

Good Morning, Midnight does not conclude but rather postpones conclusion; it does not end but rather suspends an ending. Dressed in a white dressing gown and evoking in Sasha a "nightmare feeling" (35), the *commis voyageur* brings the novel full circle, back to the wounded, murdered father in Sasha's nightmare of the Exhibition, a father similarly clad in a white nightshirt. Deeply disturbing, this figure of the incestuous and murderous/murdered father doubles for the figure of Death in the allegory of Death and the Maiden that Sandra M. Gilbert has called an "uncanny merging of death and sexuality, Thanatos and Eros. . . . in which Death, embodied in a grisly corpse or a leering skeleton, accosts a shapely, scantily clad or entirely nude young woman" ("Supple Suitor" 249). As in Gilbert's analysis of the erotics of female suicide, Sasha longs to give herself to a lover who promises voluptuous, orgasmic release from suffering; she longs to give herself to easeful death and cease upon the midnight with no pain. In another instance of return, Sasha's embrace of the skeletal, eerie *commis* recalls the lyrics of the song Sasha hears in the novel's opening pages, the hauntingly lovely "Gloomy Sunday," a song that brings her to tears and evokes a painful memory that she cannot articulate. This song, notoriously known in the 1930s as the "Hungarian Suicide Song," links sexuality and death, for the singer yearns to join her lover in a deathly embrace: "Death is no dream, for in death I'm caressing you," the singer croons, as she waits for "the black coach of sorrow" to stop for her.[27]

In its breaking down of binary categories, its dislocating narrative jolts, and its use of repetition to circle back to the novel's opening, *Good Morning, Midnight* embodies the masochistic aesthetic in which readerly pleasure inheres in the painful binding of textual energies. It also subsumes and in turn becomes the final statement of all the aesthetic objects with which Sasha interacts during the course of the novel: "Gloomy Sunday," Serge's paintings of grotesques and outcasts, the Heinrich Heine poem whose line—"Aus meinen grossen Schmerzen mach ich die kleinen Lieder" ("Out of my great sorrow I make the little songs")—Sasha clings to in the face of a dehumanizing and humiliating employer.[28] Song, poem, and painting, even the fantasy elaborated by Sasha's "film-mind," suggest that for Sasha, as for the reader of this novel, aesthetic pleasure develops out of the formal containment of pain. In the closing pages of the novel, Sasha oscillates between silencing the "little songs" of the oppressed and exiled—telling the banjo player in Serge's painting, "I know the words to the tune you're playing. I know the words to every tune you've ever played on your bloody banjo. Well, I mustn't sing any more—there you are. Finie la chanson. The song is ended. Finished" (185)—and singing instead the demonic music of the inhuman automatons—"[T]he arms wave to an accompaniment of music and of song . . . And I know the music; I can sing the song" (187). She doesn't need to sing it: *Good Morning, Midnight* sings it for her.

Like all of Rhys's novels, *Good Morning, Midnight* problematizes the possibility of rebirth or redemption. Anna is ready to "start all over again" in a cycle that seems more horrific than death from a botched abortion; Antoinette is poised to immolate herself in a conclusion we know is inevitable from its fulfillment in *Jane Eyre; After Leaving Mr. Mackenzie* ends in a liminal space, "the hour between dog and wolf" (191). Such endings radically refuse closure even as they gesture toward the final closure of psychic, if not physical, death. Hence Rhys both accepts and undercuts the strictures of narrative and social convention. Recalling the original ending of *Voyage in the Dark,* Rhys wrote that she had hoped for specific narrative effects, "time and place abolished, past and present the same" (*LJR* 233). Only her publishers' insistence that "she give the girl a chance" made her revise the ending, albeit by providing a chance that seems no chance at all. In closing her novels with scenes of suspension, Rhys forces us to grapple with her own bleak and uncompromising aesthetic, in which so-called "happy endings" are a form of "slow death, the bloodless killing that leaves no stain on your conscience" (*GMM* 23): the only limit to her characters' sufferings is the limit we choose to imagine.

EPILOGUE

"The One Dependable Thing in a World of Strife, Ruin, Chaos": Writing Trauma, Writing Self

Both Woolf and Rhys produced, late in life, unfinished autobiographical accounts of the genesis and uses of writing in their lives. Significantly, both foregrounded the trauma of maternal absence in shaping their approach both to reading and to writing. Hence it is possible to see in their work the ways in which the relationship to the mother helped fashion what psychoanalyst Christopher Bollas terms an "aesthetics of being." Even more importantly, it is possible to chart the ways in which that aesthetics of being impact not only choices about plot, but representational form and pattern: Woolf accords her mother a principle of order and control that became key to her aesthetic of the "interrupted moment," to use Lucio Ruotolo's phrase; Rhys found her mother rejecting, dangerous, and punitive—a source of emotional pain so deep that it arguably haunted her for her entire life. Rhys's extraordinary emphasis on style and form serves as a kind of "anodyne"—her favorite word, she repeatedly said—a way to dull the pain and make what might otherwise be unbearable bearable, to make the "unlovely stuff" "lovely" through work on the material. Form, in other words, becomes crucial in ordering and patterning the "unlovely" content.[1]

Aesthetic form and its relation to the mother has been explored in detail by Christopher Bollas, the most important contemporary writer on object relations and aesthetics. Bollas writes that the mother's actual mode of handling her child is an "idiom" or "logic" of care: "The baby takes in not only the contents of the mother's communications but the form of her utterances, and since in the beginning of life handling of the infant is the primary mode of communicating, I maintain that the internalization of the mother's form (her aesthetic) is prior to the internalization of her verbal messages" ("The Aesthetic Moment" 42). Thus "we learn the grammar of our being before we grasp the rules of our language" (44):

> The mother's idiom of care and the infant's experience of this handling is the first human aesthetic. It is the most profound occasion where the content of the self is formed and transformed by the environment. . . . This first human aesthetic informs the development of personal character (the utterance of self through the manner of being rather than the representations of the mind) . . . The transformational object promises to the beseeching subject an experience where the unintegrations of self find integration through the form provided by the transformational object . . . the mother is the first transformational object, and her style of mothering the paradigm of transformation for her child. (40)[2]

Language then becomes the second human aesthetic: "When the transformational object passes from the mother to the mother's tongue (the word), the first human aesthetic, self to mother, passes toward the second human aesthetic: the finding of the word to speak the self" (43). But the "absolute core of one's being" remains "a wordless, imageless solitude," Bollas remarks (cited in Scalia, xvi); one's idiom makes itself known, elaborates itself through interactions with objects: "Each individual is unique, and the true self is an idiom of organization that seeks its personal world through the use of an object . . . the fashioning of life is something like an aesthetic: a form revealed through one's way of being" (*Forces* 110). Elsewhere he notes:

> To be a character . . . is to abandon the "it" of one's idiom to its precise choosings, an unraveling and dissemination of personality: a bearer of an intelligent form that seeks objects to express its structure. The idiom that gives form to any human character is not a latent content of meaning, but an aesthetic of personality, seeking not to print out unconscious meaning but to discover objects that conjugate into meaning-laden experience. (*Being a Character* 64–65)

Woolf's unfinished "A Sketch of the Past" and Rhys's *Smile Please* trace the ways in which the two women turned to writing as a way of "expressing the structure" of their fractured experiences; in deliberately "fashioning a life" and imposing a pattern retrospectively on their life events, Woolf and Rhys identify the "form" of their experiences.

One significant point of comparison between these two memoirs is their divergent depictions of early childhood and the centrality of the mother. In *Cracking Up: The Work of Unconscious Experience*, Bollas argues that a form of "generative innocence" is an essential aspect of healthy development:

> Generative innocence is essential to the life of every developing person. It is important that one can carry within oneself a belief in a "golden era," a time when all was well; this idealization of the past often takes the form of retrospectively bequeathing upon childhood a simplicity and goodness that do not hold up on closer scrutiny. But this innocence forms the basis for an illusion of absolute safety that is essential to life, even if we know it is a psychically artistic device. (*Cracking Up* 200)

Such "golden eras" recur throughout Woolf's texts: Clarissa Dalloway remembers her girlhood at Bourton; Lily Briscoe, Cam, and James remember to differing degrees the lost world of Mrs. Ramsay; the characters in *The Waves* all remember crucial moments from their childhood (indeed, Woolf characterizes those moments as constitutive of the characters' distinct personalities). Many of Woolf's books serve as memorials for her lost family members, *To the Lighthouse* perhaps the most paradigmatically. For Rhys, on the other hand, no such "generative innocence" exists: in her memoir she represents her childhood as one riven by violence, hatred, repudiation, and punishment, and she almost never represents childhood in her fiction, with the important exceptions of *Wide Sargasso Sea* and some late short stories. A white Creole familiar with the black tradition of carnival, Rhys draws upon the concept of the mask quite often in her work; her use of the mask recalls Winnicott's concept of "false self disorder," whereby the infant adapts and becomes compliant to the mother.[3] Such a person, as an adult, feels compelled to adapt to the environment, to comply and to imitate. Rhys's characters similarly feel compelled to develop such masks as forms of protection from a hostile, alien, and rejecting environment that is often gendered as feminine.

If we turn now to the unfinished "A Sketch of the Past," it is clear that Woolf paints her childhood as a golden era akin to that outlined by Bollas, a golden era made possible by the mother who was "central":

> What a jumble of things I can remember, if I let my mind run, about my mother; but they are all of her in company: of her surrounded; of her generalised; dispersed, omnipresent, of her as the creator of the crowded merry world which spun so gaily in the centre of my

> childhood. . . . there it always was, the common life of the family, very merry, very stirring, crowded with people; and she was the centre; it was herself. This was proved on May 5th 1895. For after that day there was nothing left of it. . . . everything had come to an end. (S 84)

Crucial to Woolf's aesthetic is the sudden rupture and fragmentation of that golden era. Woolf evokes here the "globed compacted thing," the artistic moment that she consistently likens to a kind of preoedipal synaesthesia. Indeed, Woolf writes that her mother's death "unveiled and intensified; made me suddenly develop perceptions, as if a burning glass had been laid over what was shaded and dormant" (S 103). Hermione Lee remarks that "the shock of the death precipitated a peculiarly creative state of mind. Her memories of this period are dramatically lit and shaded. . . . she uses [this] image of the burning glass as a metaphor for the sudden moments of revelation. . . . She often uses images of incandescence and transparency as a way of describing how the mind works at its moments of greatest concentration" (132).

In Woolf's account, her mother's death ruptured this world of completion and wholeness: "With mother's death the merry, various family life which she had held in being shut forever" (S 93). In point of fact, however, Woolf goes on to connect the shock of her mother's death to the death of her half-sister Stella just at the moment that the latter seemed poised to offer a reconstruction of the first "golden era." This second death, only two years after her mother's, shatters Woolf's world again but its psychic effects are amplified. Characterizing herself as feeling the way "a butterfly or moth feels when it pushes out of the chrysalis and emerges and sits quivering beside the broken case for a moment; its wings still creased; its eyes dazzled, incapable of flight" (S 124), Woolf reflects that her mother's death had made her unnaturally apprehensive and hence unnaturally responsive to the promise that Stella's happiness held out:

> [B]eneath the surface of this particular mind and body lay sunk the other death . . . once more unbelievably—incredibly—as if one had been violently cheated of some promise; more than that, brutally to be told not to be such a fool as to hope for things . . . the blow, the second blow of death, struck on me; tremulous, filmy eyed as I was, with my wings still creased, sitting there on the edge of my broken chrysalis. (S 124)

The broken chrysalis recalls the earlier rupture of the merry globed world spun around her mother. And, as Woolf explains in an earlier section of the "Sketch," the "shock-receiving capacity" is what impels her to write. "[A] shock is at once in my case followed by the desire to explain it," she observes:

> [I]t is or will become a revelation of some order; it is a token of some real thing behind appearances; and I make it real by putting it into words. It is only by putting it into words that I make it whole; this wholeness means it has lost its power to hurt me; it gives me, perhaps because by doing so I take away the pain, a great delight to put the severed parts together. Perhaps this is the strongest pleasure known to me. It is the rapture I get when in writing I seem be to discovering what belongs to what; making a scene come right; making a character come together. (S 72)

This Kleinian notion of restoring the shattered and fragmented whole returns Woolf to the experience of rapture she had felt as a young child, although her piercing together of the severed parts serves more as a process of mourning than as Kleinian reparation. Woolf's description of how writing serves her as a psychic and emotional tool recalls Bollas's concept of how the aesthetic moment serves as the transformational object: Bollas writes that "the subject is seeking the transformational object and aspiring to be matched in symbiotic harmony within an aesthetic frame that promises to metamorphose the self" ("The Aesthetic Moment" 46). Similarly, Woolf writes,

> If I were painting myself I should have to find some—rod, shall I say—something that would stand for the conception. It proves that one's life is not confined to one's body and what one says and does; one is living all the time in relation to certain background rods or conceptions. Mine is that there is a pattern hid behind the cotton wool. And this conception affects me every day. I prove this, now, by spending the morning writing. . . . I feel that by writing I am doing what is far more necessary than anything else. (S 72–73)

The need to find the pattern that can connect the severed pieces and restore the work of art to its state as a "globed, compacted thing" develops out of Woolf's experience of the dialectic between wholeness and rupture. Writing becomes the vehicle for the "unthought known," the potential locked within the unconscious. Within this artistic matrix, moreover, the mother figures as central: "She was one of those invisible presences who after all play so important a part in every life," Woolf remarks (S 80).

What Lucio P. Ruotolo calls the pattern of the "interrupted moment" is hence inextricable from Woolf's vision of her childhood and her sense of the traumatic deaths that came in rapid succession between 1895 and 1906—her mother in 1895; Stella in 1897; her father in 1904; her favorite brother, Thoby, in 1906. Indeed, Woolf's obsessive reworking and retelling of the loss of her golden era and her family members constitutes a lifelong memorial to those "invisible presences." As Panthea Reid, Hermione Lee, and Katherine Dalsimer have recently shown, Woolf's very emergence as a writer was shaped in relationship to these losses. Her early writing attempts—the diaries she kept in adolescence and her tentative first essays and reviews—were taken up following the deaths of her parents and severe breakdowns on Woolf's part: she turned to writing first as a way to stabilize her shaky hold on reality, then as a reliable source of pleasure, consolation, and solace. Even in her first journal, begun in the aftermath of her mother's death and witness to Stella's deterioration and death, "[t]here is always a tone of pleasure surrounding the *act of writing* itself," Dalsimer notes. "The very implements of writing are endowed with spirit and animation" (54; italics in the original). Like Lily Briscoe, Woolf discovered in artistry "the one dependable thing in a world of strife, ruin, chaos": writing was not merely work, an economic necessity; it became for Woolf a psychic necessity, "the most reliable way she had to deaden sorrow" (78). The acts of reading and writing were ways of maintaining relationships with both parents, moreover: as "Sketch" demonstrates, Woolf felt more akin to her father than to her mother early on, and he for his part encouraged her reading and writing, seeing in her real talent as a historian. Similarly, gaining her mother's attention—something that Woolf represents as extremely rare, given her mother's busy schedule and preference for sons—was accomplished through writing: "How excited I used to be when the 'Hyde Park Gate News' was laid on her plate on Monday morning, and she liked something I had written!" Woolf recalls. "Never shall I forget my extremity of pleasure—it was like being a violin and being played upon—when I found that she had sent a story of mine to Madge Symonds; it was so imaginative, she said" (S 95).

When we turn from Woolf to Rhys, we discover a different trajectory of the development of writing and traumatic aesthetics. As noted above, Bollas argues that healthy development depends upon the belief of a "golden era" in childhood. For Rhys, no such golden era existed: born as a "replacement child" to a mother who was apparently still depressed and in mourning for her dead sister, Rhys became the family outcast at a very early age, a status heightened for her when a sister born five years later became her mother's favorite. Her biographer Carole Angier observes that "a child with a mourning mother . . . can be left with a lifelong sense of loss and emptiness, of being wanted by no one and belonging nowhere; of being nothing, not really existing at all" (Angier 11). Rhys's account of standing up to her mother and ending her mother's whippings powerfully illustrates the failure of recognition: "She said I've done my best its no use. You'll never be like other people. 'You'll never learn to behave like other people' . . . I saw the long road of isolation & loneliness stretching in front of me as far as the eye could see & further. I collapsed cried heartbroken as my worst enemy could wish" (cited in Angier 24). Angier describes the relationship between the two "a failure of the relation between mother and child. The child's needs are not met; from the start, therefore, it feels what Jean felt: hostility from the world, and deep, unassuageable rage towards it" (658).Angier connects this failure of rapport to Rhys's "voracious, insatiable need for dependence—and then suddenly . . . a fear of being taken over": "It must go back to her mother, who mourned her dead sister and preferred the living one to her. She said it herself, in *Wide Sargasso Sea;* and in the one absolutely clear thing she said about her childhood: that she loved her father, but hated her mother. So she *was* fated, as she felt. From the beginning she was unhealable, a stranger on the face of the earth, and full of rage" (658). A number of other factors intensified Rhys's feelings of alienation and estrangement—her vexed relationship to her black nanny Meta, who taught her a "world of fear and distrust"; her early apprehension of racial tensions and class distinctions in Dominica; her move to England and subsequent permanent loss of her country of origin; the traumatic love affair which encapsulated and repeated her early experience of maternal repudiation—but in her unpublished version of her life history her mother's repudiation takes central place.

Like Woolf, Rhys opens her published memoir with a number of competing memories of her mother. In the first paragraph, Rhys narrates an account of posing for a photograph and then disobeying and thereby invoking her mother's disapproval:

> "Smile Please," the man said. "Not quite so serious."
> . . . .
> "Now," the man said.
> "Keep still," my mother said.
> I tried but my arm shot up of its own accord.
> "Oh what a pity, she moved."
> "You must keep still," my mother said, frowning. (*SP* 13)

Rhys had earlier used a portion of this material in *Voyage in the Dark*, where it forms part of Anna's delirium as she lies bleeding to death from a botched abortion, in effect linking the mother's disapproval to a kind of self-inflicted abortion on the daughter's part. Here, this passage highlights the mother's insistence on a quiescent, compliant, obedient daughter and the daughter's almost compulsive defiance. Her description of this photograph highlights Rhys's ongoing fascination with developing an armor or surface mask that does not reflect time, change, development, or emotion. Some years later, she comes down the stairs and realizes "with dismay" that she no longer resembles her (earlier) self: "The eyes were a stranger's eyes. The forefinger of her right hand was raised as if in warning. She had moved after all. Why I didn't know; she wasn't me any longer. It was the first time I was aware of time, change and the longing for the past. I was nine years old" (*SP* 13–14). Rhys's splitting of her current self from her past self, her current "I" from the third-person "she," speaks to the discontinuity of self that is the hallmark of Rhys's fictional protagonists. This passage underscores, furthermore, Rhys's sense of estrangement from what is essentially her mirror image. She continues, "Catching sight of myself in the long looking glass, I felt despair . . . why was I singled out to be the only fair one, to be called Gwendolen, which means white in Welsh I was told? . . . I hated myself" (*SP* 14). In the first page and a half of her memoir, Rhys moves from the schism between mother and daughter—initiated by the daughter's inability to turn herself into the proper image—to self-loathing at her own image in the mirror, as if the daughter has internalized the mother's disapproval. Heather Ingman has demonstrated the applicability of D. W. Winnicott's work on the mirror-stage in emotional development to Rhys's work. Winnicott writes, "In individual development *the precursor of the mirror is the mother's face*. . . . What does the baby see when he or she looks at the mother's face?. . . . himself or herself. In other words the mother is looking at the baby and *what she looks like is related to what she sees there*" ("Mirror-Role," 111–112). If the mother is unable to confer a sense of coherence on the infant, the infant experiences what Winnicott terms "chaos." Ingman adds to Winnicott's formulation a passage from Roland Barthes which she finds resonant with the former: "[T]he gratifying Mother shows me the Mirror, the Image, and says to me: 'That's you.' But the silent Mother does not tell me what I am: I am no longer established, I drift painfully, without existence" (cited by Ingman, 108). Ingman comments, "As we shall see, this is a state suffered by many of Rhys's heroines."

The word "drift" is, in fact, often evoked by Rhys when she discusses the mother-daughter relationship, either her own or that of her characters (it is also the word she invokes later in *Wide Sargasso Sea*, when Antoinette sadly notes that, when Rochester renames her, "I saw Antoinette drifting out of the window with her scents, her pretty clothes, and her looking-glass" [*WSS* 180]). In a fascinating juxtaposition to the opening anecdote about her alienation from her own photograph, Rhys remembers her similarly ambivalent reaction to a photograph of her mother: "I once came on a photograph of my mother on horseback which must have been taken before she was married. Young, slim and pretty. I hated it." Rhys recalls:

> I don't know whether I was jealous or whether I resented knowing that she had once been very different from the plump, dark and only sometimes comfortable woman I knew. . . . Even after the new baby was born there must have been an interval before she seemed to find me a nuisance and I grew to dread her. Another interval and she was middle-aged and plump and uninterested in me.
>
> Yes, she drifted away from me and when I tried to interest her, she was indifferent. (*SP* 33)

Rhys concludes this short section entitled "My Mother" thus: "Gradually I came to wonder about my mother less and less until at last she was almost a stranger and I stopped imagining what she felt or what she thought" (*SP* 36). These sections of memoir closely resemble a more emotional account of the mother's drift away from the daughter that Rhys penned in *After Leaving Mr. Mackenzie*, where the protagonist Julia remembers her mother as "the warm centre of the world" (*ALMM* 106):

> You loved to watch her brushing her long hair; and when you missed the caresses and the warmth you groped for them. . . . And then her mother—entirely wrapped up in the new baby—had said things like, "Don't be a cry-baby. You're too old to go on like that. You're a great big girl of six." And from being the warm centre of the world her mother had gradually become a dark, austere, rather plump woman, who, because she was worried, slapped you for no reason that you knew. So that there were times when you were afraid of her; other times when you disliked her.
>
> Then you stopped being afraid or disliking. You simply became indifferent . . . (106–107)

What Rhys represents as "indifference" on the daughter's part suggests a numbing of pain. Significantly, Rhys's descriptions of

Dominica suggest that as a child she had transferred her mother's repudiation of her to the "elusive" beauty of the island:

> It's strange growing up in a very beautiful place and seeing that it is beautiful. It was alive, I was sure of it. Behind the bright colours the softness, the hills like clouds and the clouds like fantastic hills. There was something austere, sad, lost, all these things. I wanted to identify myself with it, to lose myself in it. (But it turned its head away, indifferent, and that broke my heart.) (*SP* 66)

Rhys drew this passage of *Smile Please* from the Black Exercise Book, where she links her intolerable feelings of longing and sadness to her discovery that writing provided a release; writing poems, Rhys found, helped her work off the worst of her moods and made her happier. Her favorite words—words such as pain, shame, sleep, sea, and silence—hint at wordless depths of emotional pain and the desire to assuage that pain by deadening affect. Rhys writes in a later portion of the Black Exercise Book that she once showed these poems, written when she was 11 or 12, to a Frenchman, who was genuinely shocked, finding them the work of someone who was doomed.

It is tempting to believe that the Frenchman to whom Rhys shows these childhood poems is the same she describes in *Smile Please*. There, however, Rhys describes the Frenchman in a passage that chronologically follows the end of her traumatic first love affair and the illegal abortion her lover paid for. Significantly, these two passages about the Frenchman link the repudiating mother to the abandoning lover. In the second passage, Rhys does not describe writing as a reaction to the pain of repudiation; rather, she describes a dissociative capacity that she will later incorporate into her distinctive manipulation of chronology and memory in her narratives: "Years later, speaking to a Frenchman in Paris, I said, 'I can abstract myself from my body.' He looked so shocked that I asked if I was speaking bad French. He said, '*Oh non, mais . . . c'est horrible.*' And yet for so long that is exactly what I did" (*SP* 95). Indeed, Rhys insists in *Smile Please* on her ability to forget painful incidents, but in a manner that paradoxically preserves them. In the section entitled "Facts of Life," for example, Rhys includes an enigmatic exchange between her mother and herself over the sexual behavior of her dog: "After this I shut away at the back of my mind any sexual experiences, for of course some occurred, not knowing that this would cause me to remember them in detail all the rest of my life. I became very good at blotting things out, refusing to think about them" (*SP* 50). After her lover ends the love affair but sends her a Christmas tree anyway, Rhys writes, "Here comes a complete blank. The next thing I remember clearly is being back in my room. The tree was gone and there was a full, unopened bottle of gin on the table" (*SP* 100). Angier has commented on Rhys's insistence that she had the ability to blot things out completely: "This capacity to hide and forget was at the heart of her nature. It allowed her to survive as a woman; and it gave her her task as a writer, which was to stop hiding and remember" (Angier 29).

Accounts of writing in the Black Exercise Book frame the "mental seduction": just as that seduction seems to have solidified an association between love and servitude, dependence, and degradation; so writing becomes a masochistic exercise to which Rhys must give herself up to as much as she had had to give herself to the imaginary lover in Mr. Howard's story. In fact, writing becomes a privileged mode of exploring "the motif of pain" that Rhys has found impossible to evade. Pondering her relationship to writing, Rhys finds she does it "Not for hope of heaven not for fear of hell but for love. Was that what I've been always meant to learn? Then I think that after all I've done it   I've given myself up to something which is greater than I am I have tried to be a good instrument.   Then Im not unhappy.   I am even rather happy perhaps" (cited in Angier 374). At the end of *Smile Please,* Rhys includes a portion of a diary she dates back to 1947; in it she puts herself on trial and answers questions about why she writes. Again she presents it as a form of bondage: "The trouble is I have plenty to say. Not only that but I am bound to say it. . . . I must write. If I stop writing my life will have been an abject failure. . . . I will not have earned death. . . . all I can force myself to do is to write, to write. I must trust that out of that will come the pattern, the clue that can be followed" (*SP* 133). This last line echoes Woolf's sense of writing as the shaping force of her life: "[O]ne is living all the time in relation to certain background rods or conceptions. Mine is that there is a pattern hid behind the cotton wool . . . I feel that by writing I am doing what is far more necessary than anything else" (S 72–73).

In her public accounts of becoming a writer, Rhys identifies writing as a compulsion to purge herself of the failure of her first love affair and the death of romantic illusions, a version of events that has been widely disseminated in Rhys criticism.[4] Yet it is clear that this love affair evoked and endorsed not only the "mental seduction" of her childhood, but the earlier experience of her mother's criticism that Rhys would never be like other people. For when the abandoning lover sends her a Christmas tree, Rhys's sense of exile from the human race is worded in the same language as her mother's sentence of exile:

> I stared at the tree and tried to imagine myself at a party with a lot of people laughing and talking and happy. But it was no use, I knew in myself it would never happen. I would never be part of anything. I would never really belong anywhere, and I knew it, and all my life would be the same, trying to belong, and failing. Always something would go wrong. I am a stranger and I always will be, and after all I didn't care. . . . I don't know what I want. And if I did I couldn't say it, for I don't speak their language and I never will. (*SP* 99–100)

Unable to speak the language of the world and its representative, her mother; immersed in a sense of herself as a failure and a stranger, Rhys succumbs to suicidal urges. At the last moment she is saved by an unexpected visit from an acquaintance, a chorus girl who finds Rhys a new flat in Fulham, where, Rhys notes grimly, "'World's End' was on the buses" (*SP* 103). Rhys labels this section of her memoir "World's End and a Beginning," however, for it is here, impelled by a desire to brighten up her drab flat, that Rhys purchases the black exercise notebooks and pens in primary colors that mark her rebirth of herself as a writer: "It was after supper . . . that it happened. My fingers tingled, and the palms of my hands. I pulled a chair up to the table, opened an exercise book, and wrote. . . . I remembered everything that had happened to me in the last year and a half. I remembered what he'd said, what I felt" (*SP* 104). This combination of black notebook and bright primary-colored pens becomes a motif of self-recognition in Rhys's fiction, as when Sasha covets "a black dress with wide sleeves embroidered in vivid colours—red, green, blue, purple" because "I had seen myself in it" (*GMM* 28).[5] Like Rhys's own fiction, Sasha sees herself as the black background that shows up the bright colors.

By juxtaposing "A Sketch of the Past" and *Smile Please,* it is possible to identify the ways in which writing served these two women in very different ways. For Woolf, the artistic impulse is one that strives to create a sense of wholeness that exists only momentarily and always in tension with the forces of destruction and rupture. For Rhys, the formal structure is necessary to contain "the sound and fury" of rage and pain, the way the glassy surface of the sea conceals the destructive forces that inhabit the deep (*Wide Sargasso Sea* is, after all, the title of Rhys's final novel).[6] For both, writing is a way of managing pain and sorrow, and for both later traumatic experiences are mapped onto the mother-daughter matrix: the maternal idiom informs the narrative aesthetic. "Before I could read, almost a baby, I imagined that God, this strange thing or person I had heard about, was a book," Rhys recalls in *Smile Please:*

> Sometimes it was a large book standing upright and half open and I could see the print inside but it made no sense to me. Other times the book was smaller and inside were sharp flashing things. The smaller book was, I am sure now, my mother's needle book, and the sharp flashing things were her needles with the sun on them. (*SP* 20)

These needles, as Deborah Kelly Kloepfer points out, evoke the opening of the fairy tale "Snow White," a moment when the kind mother vanishes, leaving Snow White "in the care of an enraged step-mother" (172); Anne B. Simpson reads them as evocative of the mother's "sharp, flashing look, the critical, wounding gaze that is trained on an unloved child" (3). If Rhys's first images of reading mark the moment of mother-daughter discord, Woolf's are tellingly more generative:

> I see her hands . . . with the very individual square-tipped fingers, each finger with a waist to it, and the nail broadening out. (My own are the same size all the way, so that I can slip a ring over my thumb.) She had three rings; a diamond ring, an emerald ring, and an opal ring. My eyes used to fix themselves upon the lights in the opal as it moved across the page of the lesson book when she taught us, and I was glad that she left it to me . . . (S 82)

Here Woolf oscillates between like and unlike (her mother's curvaceous, womanly, square-tipped fingers juxtaposed with Woolf's straight up-and-down ones); the mother, ringed like royalty, teaches the daughter how to read; and the light of her presence remains in the talismanic opal which is, fittingly, her legacy to her daughter. For Rhys, the legacy is at once more literal and more frightening, resulting in banishment from society:

> I preferred the Catholic catechism . . . "Who made you" it asked and my chief memory of the catechism was a little girl who persisted obstinately in saying, "My mother!"
>
> "No, dear, that's not the answer. Now think—who made you?"
>
> "My mother," the stolid girl replied. At last the nun, exasperated, banished her from the class. (*SP* 64)

Notes

Chapter 1

1. I am much indebted to Estella Lauter's analysis of Lorde's essays in "Revisioning Creativity: Audre Lorde's Refiguration of Eros as the Black Mother Within," esp. 398–400.
2. According to recent research in the field of cognitive science, traumatic memory may be stored in the more primitive amygdala instead of the more highly organized hippocampus. The way in which the brain stores memories is the subject of much recent cognitive science and informs the work of trauma theorists. In addition to van der Kolk, see Antonio Damasio, *The Feeling of What Happens: Body and Emotion in the Making of Consciousness;* Joseph LeDoux, *The Emotional Brain: The Mysterious Underpinnings of Emotional Life;* and Daniel Schacter, *Searching for Memory: The Brain, the Mind, and the Past.* The psychologist Jennifer J. Freyd has drawn on such work to argue the case for traumatic "forgetting"; see *Betrayal Trauma,* esp. chapter 5, as well as the interdisciplinary collection edited by Freyd and Anne P. Deprince, *Trauma and Cognitive Science.*

   Ruth Leys has critiqued the work of van der Kolk and the literary theorist Cathy Caruth for its focus on "the literal nature of traumatic dreams, 'flashbacks,' and other traumatic repetitions, and their literal, belated return" (*Trauma: A Genealogy,* 231). She draws attention to van der Kolk's argument that traumatic memories may resemble "implicit" or "non-declarative" memories, stored in "subsystems thought to be associated with particular areas of the brain" (239). Admitting that he and his associates "are careful to state their views in conditional terms" (239), Leys goes on to blame van der Kolk for the ready adoption of his work by other researchers such as Melvin R. Lansky and Judith Lewis Herman. She does not take into account work by Antonio Damasio, Joseph LeDoux, and Daniel Schacter, which, independently and working from different theoretical models, accords with that of van der Kolk. My own interest here is not in whether traumatic memories are literal or not, but in the literary forms Woolf and Rhys develop to represent traumatic sexual experiences.
3. Several critics have read *Mrs. Dalloway* in relation to trauma theory. See, for example, Marlene Briggs, "Veterans and Civilians: Traumatic Knowledge and Cultural Appropriation in *Mrs. Dalloway*" and Karen DeMeester, "Trauma and Recovery in *Mrs. Dalloway.*"

4. Two important inaugural studies of Woolf in relation to sexual abuse are Louise DeSalvo's *Virginia Woolf: The Impact of Childhood Sexual Abuse on Her Life and Work* (1989) and Toni H. McNaron's "The Uneasy Solace of Art: The Effect of Sexual Abuse on Virginia Woolf's Aesthetic" (1992). Two important studies of "A Sketch of the Past" discuss Woolf's description of molestation in terms of autobiographical memory: these are Shari Benstock's "Authorizing the Autobiographical" and Sidonie Smith's chapter on "Sketch" in her *Subjectivity, Identity, and the Body: Women's Autobiographical Practices in the Twentieth Century*, 83–102, esp. 88–92.
5. The tendency to see the protagonists of Rhys's novels as the trajectory of a composite woman began with the first book-length treatment of Rhys, Thomas Staley's 1979 *Jean Rhys: A Critical Study.* Staley writes,

    > *Quartet* . . . introduces the paradigmatic Rhys heroine, a figure who with only slight transmutation will appear in all her fiction of the 1930s . . . [A]ll exhibit at various stages of development the general characteristics and attitudes of the heroine in *Quartet.* Although each is a fully drawn and well-defined character in her own right, collectively they form a stark portrait of the feminine condition in the modern world. . . . The heroine of *Quartet* is the first figure who goes into the make-up of this sad and woeful portrait of denigration and abuse. (36)

    Even Heather Ingman's chapter on Rhys in her 1998 *Women's Fiction Between the Wars: Mothers, Daughters, and Writing* adopts this framework. She writes that "we will be moving between the novels for there is a quality of interchangeability between Rhys's heroines which invites us to deal with her novels as a continuum rather than treating them as separate works; indeed it can be argued that Rhys's heroines represent different stages in the life of the same woman" (108).
6. Several psychoanalytic studies anticipate this approach: Elizabeth Abel's essay "Women and Schizophrenia: The Fiction of Jean Rhys"; and Rachel Bowlby's chapter on *Good Morning, Midnight* in her *Still Crazy After All These Years: Women, Writing, and Psychoanalysis* (34–58). Commenting that Rhys's "sparse and repetitive narratives are variations on the themes of failure and rejection," Abel notes that Rhys's protagonists manifest the symptoms of schizophrenia, including "impoverished affect, apathy, obsessive thought and behavior . . . a sense of the unreality of both the world and the self, and a feeling of detachment from the body" (156); Abel connects their malaise to women's oppression in patriarchal culture (169). Two recent studies of Rhys read her characters' malaise through the lens of object relations theory, arguing that the failed mother-daughter relationship is at the heart of the characters' estrangement in the world. See Ingman, 107–124; and Anne B. Simpson, *Territories of the Psyche: The Fiction of Jean Rhys.*

7. Although I made a detailed transcription of Rhys's Black Exercise Book on two trips to the McFarlin Library at the University of Tulsa, I was unable to secure permission to quote directly from the material. Hence I have had to rely on passages cited by those scholars fortunate enough to have worked with the Jean Rhys Collection at an earlier date, when permissions were easier to secure.
8. I take the term "romantic thralldom" from Rachel Blau DuPlessis's *Writing Beyond the Ending: Narrative Strategies of Twentieth-Century Women Writers,* esp. 66–67; the concept of "erotic domination" has been developed by Jessica Benjamin in *The Bonds of Love: Psychoanalysis, Feminism, and the Problem of Domination.* I explore the similarities and differences of these terms in my analysis of Rhys's fiction in chapter 6.
9. A discussion of the 1990s' "memory wars" lies outside the scope of this study. For some evenhanded accounts of the controversy, see Daniel Schacter, *Searching for Memory: The Brain, the Mind, and the Past,* esp. chapter 9; Janice Haaken, *Pillar of Salt: Gender, Memory, and the Perils of Looking Back;* and Kali Tal, *Worlds of Hurt: Reading the Literatures of Trauma.* Janice Doane and Devon Hodges have discussed some of the key paradigms and texts of the controversy in *Telling Incest: Narratives of Dangerous Remembering from Stein to Sapphire;* see in particular chapters 4 and 5.
10. Suzanne Nalbantian draws interesting parallels between contemporary research on the science of memory and the work of a number of writers, including Woolf; in particular, she analyzes Lily Briscoe's painting in *To the Lighthouse* in terms of memory retrieval. See *Memory in Literature: From Rousseau to Neuroscience,* esp. 77–85.
11. In *Beyond Feminist Aesthetics: Feminist Literature and Social Change,* Rita Felski argues "against feminist aesthetics," faulting many influential feminist theorists such as Sandra M. Gilbert, Susan Gubar, and Julia Kristeva for assuming a simplistic one-to-one correspondence between gender and textuality: "[T]he political meanings of women's writing cannot be theorized in an a priori fashion, by appealing to an inherent relationship between gender and a specific linguistic form, but can be addressed only by relating the diverse forms of women's writing to the cultural and ideological processes shaping the effects and potential limits of literary production at historically specific contexts," she writes (48). Yet the kinds of questions Felski posits as productive lines of inquiry—"What kinds of genres are characteristic of contemporary feminist fiction? What do such structures reveal about the status and influence of feminism as an oppositional ideology in relation to changing narrative representations of women's lives?" (49)—are precisely the sorts of questions that feminist critics such as Shari Benstock, Rachel Blau DuPlessis, Susan Stanford Friedman, and Bonnie Kime Scott have addressed in their studies of modernist female aesthetics. Felski does not mention these critics; indeed, many of the critics she cites—such as Susan Koppelman

Cornillon, Josephine Donovan, and Patricia Meyer Spacks—were writing in the early to mid-1970s, at the very earliest stages of the development of feminist literary criticism.

12. For the most comprehensive assessment of these three writers' theoretical contributions to women's narrative experimentation see Ellen G. Friedman and Miriam Fuchs, "Contexts and Continuities: An Introduction to Women's Experimental Fiction in English," in *Breaking the Sequence: Women's Experimental Fiction*, ed. Friedman and Fuchs; see esp. 11–17.
13. Numerous studies devoted solely to Woolf highlight the way her formal innovations function as textual politics. For some representative examples, see Elizabeth Abel, "Narrative Structure(s) and Female Development: The Case of *Mrs. Dalloway*"; Edward Bishop, "The Essays: The Subversive Process of Metaphor": Melba Cuddy-Keane, "The Rhetoric of Feminist Conversation: Virginia Woolf and the Trope of the Twist"; Rachel Bowlby, *Virginia Woolf: Feminist Destinations;* Pamela Caughie, *Virginia Woolf and Post-modernism: Literature in Quest and Question of Itself;* Graham Good, "Virginia Woolf: Angles of Vision"; Jane Marcus, *Virginia Woolf and the Languages of Patriarchy;* and Makiko Minow-Pinkney, *Virginia Woolf and the Problem of the Subject.* This list is by no means exhaustive. For more general studies on female aesthetics and modernism which also include discussions of Woolf, see Shari Benstock, *Textualizing the Feminine: On the Limits of Genre;* Rachel Blau DuPlessis, *Writing Beyond the Ending: Narrative Strategies of Twentieth-Century Women Writers;* Marianne DeKoven, *Rich and Strange: Gender, History, Modernism;* Sandra M. Gilbert and Susan Gubar, *No Man's Land: The Place of the Woman Writer in the Twentieth Century;* and Bonnie Kime Scott, *Refiguring Modernism.*
14. For a description of how Melanie Klein theorizes artistry as a form of reparation to the mother, see "Infantile Anxiety Situations Reflected in a Work of Art and in the Creative Impulse," in *The Selected Melanie Klein,* ed. Juliet Mitchell. Several recent biographies of Woolf—those by Katherine Dalsimer, Hermione Lee, and Panthea Reid—show how Woolf's emergence as a writer was shaped in relation to loss and mourning.
15. Like Joplin, Jane Marcus also critiques Geoffrey Hartman for attempting to universalize the story of Procne and Philomela instead of seeing its female specificity. See "Liberty, Sorority, Misogyny" in *Virginia Woolf and the Languages of Patriarchy,* 75–95.
16. A major exception to this neglect is Rishona Zimring's "The Make-Up of Jean Rhys's Fiction." Zimring reads Rhys's work "in relation to the rise of the cosmetics industry to call attention to a feminist aesthetics within modernism" (215). Mary Lou Emery's chapter on *Good Morning, Midnight* focuses on "the paradox of style": "The paradox of style that troubles Sasha—its power to effect new discoveries in the midst of crisis and the threat it presents of empty but controlling mechanical form—is inscribed in the formal strategies of the text" (*Jean Rhys at "World's End": Novels of Colonial and Sexual Exile,* 163).

17. Given Rhys's familiarity with Emily Dickinson, it is possible that her understanding of "anodyne" owes something to the latter's poem #536: Poetry The Heart asks Pleasure—first—/ And then—Excuse from Pain—/ And then—those little Anodynes/ That deaden suffering—/ And then—to go to sleep—/ And then—if it should be/ The will of its Inquisitor/ The privilege to die. (*Complete Poems of Emily Dickinson* 262)/Poetry Significantly, the passage in which Rhys likens the cinema to a form of anodyne occurs in a fantasy of being put on trial to see if she has earned death (*SP* 129–133).
18. In "Masochism, Submission, Surrender," Emmanuel Ghent writes that "masochism is the result of a distortion or perversion of a deep longing for surrender, a yearning to be known, recognized, 'penetrated,' and often represents the miscarriage of a wish to dismantle false self" (134). In light of Rhys's development of a masochistic aesthetic, it is interesting that Ghent speaks of the ritual scenes of masochism as "pointing to the need for patterned impingement" (118). See also Jessica Benjamin, *The Bonds of Love: Psychoanalysis, Feminism, and the Problem of Domination,* 51–84, esp. 72.

Chapter 2

1. Laura Doan and Lucy Bland have edited an interesting collection of essays that study the influence of sexology on literature and culture during Woolf's lifetime. See *Sexology in Culture: Labelling Bodies and Desires,* as well as their edited collection of primary documents, *Sexology Uncensored: The Documents of Sexual Science.*
2. I am indebted to two discussions of Woolf's itinerary: S. P. Rosenbaum's extremely detailed account in his introduction to *Women and Fiction: The Manuscript Versions of* A Room of One's Own; and the editors' notes about the talks in Woolf's diaries (*D*3 199; see also 200n4).
3. I am repeating this history, most of which exists as Appendix 3 in the second volume of Woolf's diary, to show how sexological the origins of *A Room of One's Own* were. For other discussions, see Alice Fox, "Literary Allusion As Feminist Criticism in *A Room of One's Own*" and discussions by Rosenbaum, and Rosenman.
4. Woolf's anxiety about the "fluency" of her style was to plague her throughout the production of *A Room of One's Own*. On June 23, 1929, she notes, "I must learn to write more succinctly . . . . I am horrified by my own looseness. This is partly that I dont think things out first; partly that I stretch my style to take in crumbs of meaning. But the result is a wobble & diffusity & breathlessness which I detest. One must correct A room of one's own very carefully before printing it (*D*3 235).
5. Jane Marcus has located another source for "Shakespeare's sister" in William Black's 1883 novel *Judith Shakespeare,* although the eponymous heroine of the latter is Shakespeare's daughter, not his sister (*Virginia Woolf and the Languages of Patriarchy* 75–95, 87).

6. In *Virginia Woolf and the Real World,* Alex Zwerdling notes that "in Woolf's own time, a sympathetic woman writer, Clemence Dane, suggests that the absence of great female artists ('There has never been a woman Shakespeare! There has never been a woman Michael Angelo!') has become *the* trump card in the argument against women's equality. The question of women's artistic achievement was thus seen in Woolf's time as a sort of last frontier in the exploration of their powers" (224). Zwerdling goes on to speculate that Woolf created the story of Judith Shakespeare "[a]s though she were writing in direct response to Dane's quotations, as well as the taunts of a Bennett or the doubts of a Mill" (224). He does not examine sexological literature or the biological figures I examine here.
7. To read this passage as a metaphorical rebuttal of sexological claims about women's "anemic" and "watery" style is not incompatible with Woolf's actual source for this information in Janet Vaughn's early scientific work in producing England's first liver extract by borrowing all her friends' "mincing-machines" (in Joan Russell Noble, ed. *Recollections of Virginia Woolf by Her Contemporaries,* 96). Vaughn became for Woolf a type of pioneering woman, professional, liberated from the patriarchal home in defiance of her father, who, Vaughn reported, "washed his hands of me. I think this was why Virginia so much disliked my father . . . this was a link . . . and also the fact that I was a woman who was doing a real job in the world . . . she did like a woman to do things, and to do them with moderate success. . . . I had made a job for myself in the world and this was, to her, satisfying" (98).
8. As Lisa Rado demonstrates, Woolf's portrait of the androgyne in *A Room of One's Own* also develops out of contemporaneous sexologists' agreement that artistry and creativity manifested themselves in androgynous people: Rado argues that Woolf used the androgyne "in order to generate the creative inspiration and artistic authority she felt she lacked" (150). Rado goes on to add, however, that the problem with this strategy is that "the empowerment it is designed to produce is predicated on the repression of [Woolf's] own female identity, her own female body" (150). Rado echoes here Elaine Showalter's earlier critique of Woolf's portrait of the "androgynous" writer (*A Literature of Their Own* 285–289), although Rado's account evidences much more understanding of the reasons behind Woolf's repression of femininity than does Showalter's. As I show here, Woolf does not repress the feminine so much as she subordinates the female to the male in her images of the androgyne.
9. Showalter is much more emphatic in her reading of this passage: Woolf "has made the writer male" (*A Literature of Their Own* 288).
10. Arnold Bennett also seems to have relished his bouts with Woolf. After Woolf published "Mr. Bennett and Mrs. Brown," Bennett met her at a dinner party at H. G. Wells' home in 1926: "I really wanted to have a scrap with Virginia Woolf; but got no chance" ("Mr. Bennett and Mrs.

Woolf" 29); later, at a gathering at the hostess' Ethel Sands' home in 1930, Bennett reports he "had a great pow-wow with Virginia Woolf. (Other guests held their breath to listen to us.) Virginia is all right" (29).

11. Jane Marcus has written extensively on Smyth's influence on Woolf in *Virginia Woolf and the Languages of Patriarchy;* see especially the chapters, "*The Years* as Götterdämmerung, Greek Play, and Domestic Novel," 36–56, esp. 51–52; and "Virginia Woolf and Her Violin: Mothering, Madness, and Music," 96–114, esp. 111–113. See also Suzanne Raitt, "'The Tide of Ethel': Femininity as Narrative in the Friendship of Ethel Smyth and Virginia Woolf."

Chapter 3

1. Jane Marcus also notes the way in which Woolf's description of Smyth as a "burning bush" anticipates the plates in *The Dinner Party* in *Virginia Woolf and the Languages of Patriarchy* (113). O'Keeffe's renderings of flowers in the 1920s (e.g., the 1922 "Canna—Red and Orange") attracted much interest from art critics newly familiar with Freud (and perhaps, like Woolf's circle, also familiar with sexologists like Havelock Ellis and Otto Weininger). "Georgia O'Keeffe has had her feet scorched in the laval effusiveness of terrible experience . . . With Georgia O'Keeffe one . . . sees the world of a woman turned inside out," wrote one. Another critic, Paul Rosenfeld, writing in 1922, found that O'Keeffe painted "through the terms of a woman's body. For, there is no stroke laid by her brush, whatever it is she may paint, that is not curiously, arrestingly female in quality." Some paintings, indeed, "appeared licked on with the point of the tongue, so vibrant and lyrical are they . . . [The] essence of very womanhood permeates her pictures."
2. In most versions of Sleeping Beauty, the successful prince differs from his predecessors not because he is more aggressive but because he has better timing: in contrast to the "many kings' sons . . . [who] sought to pass the thorn-hedge," only to be "caught and pierced by the thorns, and [die] a miserable death," the prince arrives when the hundred years are coming to an end, and the hedge opens of its own volition: "When the prince drew near the hedge of thorns, it was changed into a hedge of beautiful large flowers, which parted and bent aside to let him pass, and then closed behind him in a thick hedge" (*Grimm's Fairy Tales,* 206). That Woolf's memory of the story is somewhat inaccurate is interesting, for in other allusions to Sleeping Beauty she also focuses on a moment of violent rupture: in the letter to Smyth that precedes this one, for example, Woolf writes, "[A]lready I am spun over with doubts and impaled with thorns. Would you and Vanessa know how to burst through, free and unscathed? I suppose so . . . (a joke—if I had any red ink, I would write my jokes in it, so that even certain musicians—ahem!)" (*L4* 168). Woolf may have seen the 1921 Diaghilev production of *The Sleeping Beauty* (retitled as *The Sleeping Princess*), for she attended other Diaghilev ballets and was close

friends with Maynard Keynes, whose future wife, Lydia Lopokova, appeared in the production as the Lilac Fairy: in the second act of the ballet, a hedge of thorns was supposed to rise up and conceal the castle (although, in fact, the special effects failed). For a discussion of Woolf's relationship to the Ballet Russes, see Evelyn Haller, "Her Quill Drawn from the Firebird: Virginia Woolf and the Russian Dancers," in *The Multiple Muses of Virginia Woolf,* ed. Diane F. Gillespie, 180–226. For discussions of Diaghilev's ballet, see George Balanchine, *Balanchine's Complete Stories of the Ballets,* ed. Francis Mason; Cyril W. Beaumont, *The Diaghilev Ballet in London: A Personal Record;* and Milo Keynes, ed., *Lydia Lopokova.*

The story of Sigfried or Sigmund and Brunnhilde appears in *The Volsung Saga,* but Woolf was probably most familiar with Wagner's version in *The Ring.* For a reading of Smyth's Wagnerian influence upon Woolf, see Jane Marcus, "*The Years* as Götterdämmerung, Greek Play, and Domestic Novel," in *Virginia Woolf and the Languages of Patriarchy,* esp. 51–54. Marcus notes Woolf's allusions to the story of Sigfried and Brunnhilde in "Virginia Woolf and Her Violin," but reads it in a literal rather than metaphoric sense: "Virginia retreated like the 'cowardly' narrator of 'An Unwritten Novel,' from rescuing her Brunnhilde from the ring of fire" (113).

3. For example, in *A Room of One's Own,* the male poet of Woolf's description relies upon female domestic creativity to "fertilise" his literary vision: "He would open the door of drawing-room or nursery . . . and find her among her children perhaps, or with a piece of embroidery on her knee . . . the centre of some different order and system of life" (*R* 90). As late as 1941, Woolf describes her mother Julia Stephen as similarly central ("Sketch" 83).
4. I take the term "women-for-men" from Margaret Whitford's concise and provocative summary of Irigaray's work, "Irigaray's Body Symbolic," 98. I am deeply indebted to Whitford's work on Irigaray. In addition to this article, see *Luce Irigaray: Philosophy in the Feminine; The Irigaray Reader,* which Whitford edited and for which she provides a number of useful introductory essays; and the collection Whitford edited with Carolyn Burke and Naomi Schor, *Engaging with Irigaray.*
5. Cited by Whitford, "Irigaray's Body Symbolic," 103. I am much indebted to Whitford's clear analysis of the import of this image in Irigaray's recent work. See also Gail M. Schwab, "Mother's Body, Father's Tongue," in *Engaging with Irigaray* 351–378, esp. 367.
6. Teresa de Lauretis, "The Practice of Sexual Difference and Feminist Thought in Italy: An Introductory Essay," in The Milan Women's Bookstore Collective, *Sexual Difference: A Theory of Social-Symbolic Practice,* trans. Patricia Cicogna and Teresa de Lauretis, 8–9. Woolf's relationship with Vita Sackville-West is often cited as an example of entrustment by this collective (e.g., 31–32).

7. I agree with Marcus that Smyth's "formative influence on Virginia Woolf in the thirties was . . . of decisive importance aesthetically" ("*The Years* as Götterdämmerung, Greek Play, and Domestic Novel" 51), although Marcus reads that influence in *The Years* as primarily musical and Wagnerian. My own emphasis is on the metaphorical shift that Smyth enabled. I am much indebted to Marcus's eloquent and moving discussions of Smyth's role and influence upon Woolf. See "Virginia Woolf and Her Violin" (111–113) as well as "*The Years* as Götterdämmerung, Greek Play, and Domestic Novel" 51–54, and "Thinking Back Through Our Mothers," in *New Feminist Essays on Virginia Woolf*, ed. Jane Marcus (1–30).

   Suzanne Raitt's "'The tide of Ethel': Femininity as Narrative in the Friendship of Ethel Smyth and Virginia Woolf" (3–21) discusses the way in which this ten-year friendship became "an exploration for both women of the involvement of friendship, and of femininity, with narratives of the self" (3); she similarly notes Ethel's maternal role in the friendship and Woolf's fascination with Ethel's frankness, which she argues "perhaps held in their bravado the key to a more authentic feminine honesty" (8). She does not focus on the specific metaphorical reappropriation I explore here.

8. As the editors of Woolf's letters note,

   > [G]radually under pressure, [Woolf] yielded, and wrote to Ethel about matters she had scarcely mentioned to anyone, her madness, her feeling about sex, the inspiration for her books, and even her thoughts of suicide. For Ethel she was living her entire life, because Ethel's curiosity was compulsive, and because Virginia became eager to explain herself to a woman who seemed suddenly the most sympathetic person she had ever known. (*L4* xvii)

9. In a letter filled with misgivings about what she terms her "egotistic loquacity," for example, Woolf luxuriates in Smyth's interest in her:

   > I can assure you I dont romanticise quite so freely about myself as a rule—It was only that you pressed some nerve, and then up started in profusion the usual chaos of pictures of myself . . . I ought not to have been so profuse. Next time it shall be the other story—yours. But in your benignity and perspicacity . . . you can penetrate my stumbling and fitful ways: my childish chatter. Yes—for that reason, that you see through, yet kindly, for you are, I believe, one of the kindest of women, one of the best balanced, with that maternal quality which of all others I need and adore—what was I saying?—for that reason I chatter faster and freer to you than to other people. But I wont next time. And you won't think the worse of me, will you? . . . going home . . . I thought, My God what an egoist I am; and that was the only twangling wire in the whole composition. (*L4* 188)

10. See, for example, *L4* 329. Woolf's images for Smyth's artistic courage are almost always strikingly male: Smyth is a "game old cock" (*L4* 277), "the hedgehog" (*L4* 354), and in one passage a savage boar: "I realise why I am so essential to you—precisely my quality of scratching post, what the granite pillar in the Cornish field gives the rough-haired, burr-tangled Cornish pig—that's you. An uncastrated pig into the bargain; a wild boar, a savage sow, and my fate in life is to stand there, a granite pillar, and be scraped by Ethel's hoary hide . . . we may meet . . . one scrape more, one more grind of your infuriated hide and rasping tusks . . . like rending a rib open with a knife" (*L4* 348–349). Woolf's emphasis throughout is on Smyth's aura of *presence:* she is hairy, tusked, testicled, and Woolf is clearly exhilarated by Smyth's aggressive self-assertion. During a period of illness and seclusion, Woolf wrote, "[W]rite me a friendly letter and dont be a sleek tabby but my old uncastrated wild cat . . . I'd like to read one of Ethels most violent, disruptive, abruptive, fuliginous, catastrophic, panoramic, I cant think of any other adjectives—effusions" (*L5* 89–90).
11. See Susan Stanford Friedman, "The Return of the Repressed in Women's Narrative," esp. 141. I find Friedman's analysis of H.D.'s work—and her explanations of the operation of censorship in women's literature in general—exciting and persuasive. In contrast to Friedman, however, who sees drafts as the "textual unconscious" of the final, published version (145), a reading that argues for an author's deliberate occlusions, Woolf's gradual movement from a symptomatic female aesthetic to overt contestation seems to follow a more classic Freudian path of remembrance and working through. As I show in a later portion of the essay, Woolf's revisions of *A Room of One's Own* become unconscious occlusions of her anxiety that female authorship equals a loss of chastity. In this sense, I am using Freud's model in a more traditional sense than does Friedman.
12. Freud's first remarks on the phenomenon of transference occur in "Fragment of an Analysis of a Case of Hysteria" ("Dora"), in *Dora: An Analysis of a Case of Hysteria,* ed. Philip Rieff, esp. 138. Further remarks on transference as the patient's typical perception of the analyst as a parent substitute occur in "The Dynamics of the Transference," in *Therapy and Technique,* ed. Philip Rieff, 105–115, esp. 107. Freud's clearest discussion of repetition occurs in "Further Recommendations in the Technique of Psychoanalysis: Recollection, Repetition, and Working Through," also in *Therapy and Technique* (157–166). In the symptomatic stage of a compulsive behavior, Freud writes, "The patient *remembers* nothing of what is forgotten and repressed, but . . . he expresses it in *action.* He reproduces it not in his memory but in his behavior; he *repeats* it without of course knowing that he is repeating it" (160).
13. "Recollection, Repetition, and Working Through," 164.

14. Smyth believed that art inevitably betrayed its human origins. In an incident Woolf related to both Vita Sackville-West and Vanessa Bell, Smyth took Woolf to a concert at the Austrian embassy and shocked all the diplomats by announcing "Isn't this slow movement sublime—natural and heavy and irresistible like the movement of one's own bowels" (*L4* 244; *L4* 240).
15. Louise DeSalvo, *Virginia Woolf: The Impact of Childhood Sexual Abuse on Her Life and Work,* 119. Whether or not DeSalvo is correct in deducing from this passage that Woolf's half-brother ruptured her hymen is irrelevant to my argument: what this passage demonstrates unmistakably is Woolf's linking of writing with hymenal rupture. My focus is on the textuality the hymen assumes for Woolf.
16. It may well be the case that, as Susan Stanford Friedman has argued, these texts taken together constitute a serial narrative whereby a traumatic memory is recovered through the process of repeatedly writing about it, a process Friedman likens to the process of "'working through' the 'repetition compulsion' to 'remembering.'" If so, Woolf's images of hymenal rupture represent a stellar instance of Friedman's claims that modernist women's writing often evidences the "return of the repressed" by becoming an "insistent record—a trace, a web, a palimpsest, a rune, a disguise—of what has not or cannot be spoken directly because of the external and internalized censors of patriarchal social order" (142). At the same time, my own process of reading the drafts of *Room* differs from Friedman's model. I perceive the published version as the version most subject to "secondary revision," a process Freud describes in *The Interpretation of Dreams* as an ordering one: like the waking thought which it resembles, the "secondary revision" "establish[es] order in the material . . . set[s] up relations in it . . . and . . . make[s] it conform to our expectations of an intelligible whole" (537). Freud describes how the dream's "weak spot" can be ascertained by having the patient repeat the dream: "In doing so he rarely uses the same words. But the parts of the dream which he describes in different terms are by that fact revealed to me as the weak spot in the dream's disguise . . . My request to the patient to repeat his account of the dream has warned him that I was proposing to take special pains in solving it; under pressure of the resistance, therefore, he hastily covers the weak spots in the dream's disguise by replacing any expressions that threaten to betray its meaning by other less revealing ones. In this way he draws my attention to the expression which he has dropped out" (553–554). The manuscript drafts similarly serve as repetitions which expose the points of resistance and conflict.
17. I first identified this anxiety in *Word of Mouth: Body Language in Katherine Mansfield and Virginia Woolf* (74–76). At that time, I had not realized the symptomatic nature of *Room's* hymenal imagery, nor had I understood completely the way Woolf works through this anxiety in her

letters to Ethel Smyth. My reading of these passages from *Room* and *Three Guineas* hence differs from the interpretations offered there.

18. Virginia Woolf, *Women & Fiction: The Manuscript Versions of A Room of One's Own,* transcribed and edited by S. P. Rosenbaum, 65. The phrases in square brackets appear thus in the typescripts.
19. During her composition of *Three Guineas,* Woolf mentions reading the Christian historian Ernest Renan's *St Paul* and the Acts of the Apostles, and she records as well her plans to buy the Old Testament: "At last I am illuminating that dark spot in my reading," she notes (*D*4 271).
20. Given Woolf's interest in women's history and the history of women's writing and speech, she may have learned that Quakers were well-known for encouraging the full participation of women, and were horribly persecuted by other religious and social bodies for violating St. Paul's dictum that "woman must not speak in the church." A 1907 history of Quaker belief in England reports the numerous public beatings women endured for preaching in public (most germane to Woolf, perhaps, would be women whipped for preaching outside the gates of Oxford and Cambridge). See *First Publishers of Truth,* ed. Norman Penney. Woolf's favorite aunt, Caroline Emelia Stephen, was a well-known Quaker mystic who published a number of books on Quaker history and belief, and Woolf stayed with her often in the early years of the century. The later sections of *Three Guineas* suggest Woolf's familiarity with the traditions of female mysticism; Woolf argues that women writers occupy the same position culturally as early female prophets, for, Woolf writes, "[T]there can be no doubt that in those early days there were prophetesses—women upon whom the divine gift had descended" (*TG* 122). She goes on, "[T]he profession of religion seems to have been originally much what the profession of literature is now. It was originally open to anyone who had received the gift of prophecy. No training was needed; the professional requirements were simple in the extreme—a voice and a marketplace, a pen and paper" (*TG* 123). Woolf embeds this proscription on female speech in a long discussion of the history of chastity; she concludes that the nineteenth-century woman who longed for independence first had "to kill the lady" and then faced the more difficult task of "kill[ing] the woman" (*TG* 134). Significantly, Woolf's examples here are the woman writers Elizabeth Barrett Browning and Charlotte Brontë; of the latter Woolf notes "[I]f she earned money in the one profession that was open to her, the oldest profession of all, she unsexed herself" (*TG* 135). The "oldest profession" is, of course, stereotypically prostitution, not writing; Woolf's wording here suggests that Brontë's "unsexing" of herself is the "fall" of writing, that is, the loss of chastity. For other discussions of Woolf's relationship to her aunt, see Jane Marcus, "The Niece of a Nun: Virginia Woolf, Caroline Stephen, and the Cloistered Imagination," in *Virginia Woolf and the Languages of Patriarchy* (115–135); and Catherine F. Smith, "*Three Guineas:* Virginia Woolf's Prophecy," in Marcus, ed. *Virginia Woolf and Bloomsbury: A Centenary*

Collection, 228–230: Smith considers Caroline Stephen's impact upon the "political mysticism" of *Three Guineas* and the connections between female prophecy and writing. For a discussion of Quaker women and the persecution they faced, see Elaine C. Huber, "'A Woman Must Not Speak': Quaker Women in the English Left Wing," in Rosemary Ruether and Eleanor McLaughlin, eds. *Women of Spirit: Female Leadership in the Jewish and Christian Traditions*, 155–181. Although I have found no evidence of Quaker material in lists of Woolf's reading, she may have known of the publication and general arguments of her aunt's and other books on Quaker thought; in addition to *First Publishers of Truth* (1907), these would include John P. Fry, *The Advent of Quakerism* (1908), George Fox's *Journal*, revised by Norman Penney (1924), and two volumes authored by Dorothy Richardson, *The Quakers Past and Present* (1914), and *Gleanings from the Works of George Fox* (nd).

21. Woolf draws the connections between veiling and chastity and modesty with more clarity in the 1928 *Orlando:* describing how Purity, Chastity, and Modesty have given up their attempts to cover Orlando's naked body, the narrator wonders, "Is nothing, then, going to happen this pale March morning to mitigate, to veil, to conceal, to shroud this undeniable event whatever it may be?" (191). The undeniable event—the birth of Orlando's son—blurs the distinctions between literal and literary birth much as *Room* does; significantly, the language of rending and tearing attendant on that birth is deeply ambiguous, suggestive of a memory of hymenal rupture: "[H]ail not those dreams . . . which splinter the whole and tear us asunder and wound us and split us apart in the night when we would sleep" (193).
22. Clive Bell and Roger Fry argued for form in art, and Woolf may have had Fry's remarks on Cezanne in mind while writing about the structure of female fiction. Fry wrote that Cezanne "saw always, however dimly, behind this veil [of color] an architecture and a logic" (*Cezanne*, 37–38). Woolf seems to fear that behind the veil of anonymity women's fictional structures inevitably contain disfiguring wholes.
23. See *Word of Mouth*, 122, for a different reading of these passages: here I am interested in the way repetitive images of deformity and disfiguration betray Woolf's anxiety that the woman writer "unsexes" herself.
24. Woolf's published texts during her last decade mute her critique of middle-class female socialization and its disastrous effects upon women's powers of self-expression. Yet while it is true that Woolf edits out much of her overt analysis, enough remains for readers to detect a marked shift in emphasis, from the anxiety about female self-expression that characterizes *A Room of One's Own* to anger directed at cultural insistence upon female self-silencing. As I show in the next chapter, moreover, it is possible to read silence and censorship as narrative strategies in the later works.
25. See, for example, Woolf's description of the Duchess of Newcastle, whose untutored talent and rage poured out "in torrents . . . which stand

congealed in quartos and folios that nobody ever reads" (*R* 64–65); the word "congealed" suggests properties of blood. Woolf goes on to compare the Duchess's mind to "some giant cucumber [that] had spread itself over all the roses and carnations in the garden and choked them to death" (*R* 65), an image of a watery and tasteless vegetable run amok over the more distilled, feminine flowers. See my more detailed analysis of these passages in chapter 2.

26. Woolf articulates this philosophy most completely in "A Sketch of the Past." Considering why she believes her "shock-receiving capacity" has made her a writer, Woolf muses that "a blow . . . is a token of some real thing behind appearances; and I make it real by putting it into words. It is only by putting it into words that I make it whole; this wholeness means that it has lost its power to hurt me; it gives me, perhaps because by doing so I take away the pain, a great delight to put the severed parts together" (S 72). Yet although Woolf continues to espouse "completion," many of her plots in the 1930s foreground disjunction and fragmentation (e.g., *The Pargiters, The Years, Between the Acts*).
27. Woolf's sense of this division is particularly evident in this passage from "A Sketch of the Past": "[W]hat reality can remain real of a person who died forty-four years ago at the age of forty-nine, without leaving a book, or a picture, or any piece of work—apart from the three children who now survive and the memory of her that remains in their minds?" (S 85).
28. Marie Stopes describes the practice then known as "preparation for marriage": "In their surgeries [physicians] stretch the hymen or lance it, and then fit the bride before marriage with some contraceptive device" (*Marriage in My Time,*80–81). Although Stopes did not recommend the practice, others, such as E. F. Griffith (*Modern Marriage and Birth Control*) did. I am indebted to Christina Hauck for locating this information.
29. Woolf's description of Smyth as an intricate thorn-hedge (see above) resonates with her description of maternal inaccessibility in terms of an intricate and tangled hedge in *To the Lighthouse;* Mr. Ramsay, Cam, and Lily all have complicated relationships to that hedge. Lily's only means of accessing maternal presence is through representing Mrs. Ramsay's "centrality" in her painting, a painting that orders "the relations of those lines cutting across, slicing down, and in the mass of the hedge with its green cave of blues and browns" (*TTL* 157). Woolf explicitly discusses the "intricacy" and "darkness" of the hedge's tangle in relation to Mrs. Ramsay throughout the first section of the novel (e.g., 35, 64).

Chapter 4

1. Christine Froula's *Virginia Woolf and the Bloomsbury Avant-Garde: War, Civilization, Modernity* appeared while this book was in press. Froula similarly studies the process by which Woolf edited out her accounts of sexual trauma as she moved from *The Pargiters* to *The Years.* Froula

writes, "As the novel-essay becomes modernist-realist narrative, gender as loss recedes into a sealed-off past, mourning into unconscious sadness, grief into a vision of society . . . As talk gives way to hystericized silence, symptoms, allegory, *The Years* overwrites the Speech's visionary artist and audience with a realist portrait of a society whose painful truths remain choked in somatic speech" (240). Froula does not identify the encryption of trauma I discuss here.

2. Marlene Briggs, Karen DeMeester, and Toni McNaron have also discussed Woolf's work in relation to trauma theory; Briggs and, DeMeester focus on war trauma in *Mrs. Dalloway.* McNaron studies more generally the effect of Woolf's traumatic experiences upon her narrative aesthetic.
3. Radin draws this connection in her work on *The Years* (xii); here, I wish to extend her argument to the specific issue of female sexuality.
4. For a typescript of Woolf's speech to the London National Society for Women's Service on January 21, 1931, see *The Pargiters,* xxvii–xliv. Woolf's speech apparently followed Smyth's; for a contemporaneous review of it see Vera Brittain's column in the *Nation* of January 31 (p. 571). Woolf would eventually revise her speech into "Professions for Women."
5. I refer not to Woolf's experiences with George, which she discussed much earlier, but to the experience with Gerald, which she does not discuss until 1939.
6. That language is inadequate in conveying the nature of traumatic experience is a hallmark of trauma literature. Many theorists of trauma discuss this aspect at length (e.g., Felman and Laub, Herman, Tal, and van der Kolk and van der Hart).
7. Contemporary cognitive science offers a number of complex models that explain how certain types of memories may undergo a form of amnesia and then become available for retrieval at a later date. See, for example, Joseph LeDoux, *The Emotional Brain,* esp. 138–225; and Daniel Schacter, *Searching for Memory.* Schacter's account is especially useful in that he juxtaposes his understanding of memory loss and retrieval with a balanced overview of the contemporary "memory wars" over what has come to be called "Recovered Memory Syndrome." The latter refers to the wave of recovered memories of sexual abuse that arose in the 1980s and 1990s. Such memories typically arose in a therapeutic setting or with the help of self-help manuals, contexts that may have encouraged the development of false memories. For some analyses of "Recovered Memory Syndrome," see, in addition to Schacter, Janice Haaken, *Pillar of Salt* and Marita Sturken, "Narratives of Recovery: Repressed Memory as Cultural Memory," in *Acts of Memory,* eds. Bal, Mieke, Crewe, and Spitzer.
8. Woolf's model strongly resembles the cognitive model of memory and identity that Antonio Damasio develops in *The Feeling of What Happens.* Damasio posits a "core consciousness," a self-awareness of the here and now, and an "extended consciousness," which provides the person with

"an elaborate sense of self" (16). These two kinds of consciousness correspond to two versions of selfhood:

> The sense of self which emerges in core consciousness is the *core self,* a transient entity, ceaselessly re-created for each and every object with which the brain interacts. Our traditional notion of self, however, is linked to the idea of identity and corresponds to a nontransient collection of unique facts and ways of being which characterize a person. My term for that entity is the *autobiographical self.* The autobiographical self depends on systematized memories of situations in which core consciousness was involved in the knowing of the most invariant characteristics of an organism's life . . . I use the term *autobiographical memory* to denote the organized record of the main aspects of an organism's biography (17–18).

Damasio's model provides a means for understanding why members of a family, who share some invariant characteristics (common homes, parents, relatives, and so forth), may nonetheless develop different autobiographical narratives which seemingly contradict one another, as in fact occurs in the Pargiter family.

For an overview of contemporary cognitive science and models of memory and the emotions, see Suzanne Nalbantian, *Memory in Literature,* esp. 135–152. Nalbantian also provides an overview of turn-of-the-century models of memory and assesses a number of Woolf's texts in relation to these models; Nalbantian concludes that Woolf's method is one of associative memory. I believe, however, that Woolf provides different models of memory throughout her work. It is telling that Nalbantian limits her discussion to *Mrs. Dalloway, To the Lighthouse,* and "A Sketch of the Past," but says very little about *The Waves, The Years,* or *Between the Acts,* which all develop concepts of collective memory and different kinds of personal memory. See Nalbantian, 77–85.

9. See "Introduction: States of Shame," in *L'Esprit Createur.*
10. An important exception is J. Brooks Bouson's recent analysis of the intersections of shame, trauma, and race in Toni Morrison's work in *Quiet As It's Kept.*
11. I take this passage from Martin's January 10, 2001, call for MLA papers for a panel "Theorizing Shame Affect and Trauma Interdependency."

Chapter 5

1. I made my own transcriptions of Rhys's Black Exercise Book during my visits there in 1995 and 2002, but I was unable to secure permissions from the current literary executors of Rhys's estate. Any quoted material is limited to passages already cited in other studies.
2. "Recovered memory" and "false memory syndrome" are the two poles of debate in the so-called "memory wars" of the 1990s. "False memory syndrome," a term invented by the False Memory Syndrome Foundation,

refers to false memories implanted through therapeutic suggestion during psychotherapy. For discussions that try to summarize each side objectively, see Janice Doane and Devon Hodges, *Telling Incest;* Janice Haaken, *Pillar of Salt;* and Daniel Schacter, *Searching for Memory.*

3. The DSM IV defines a "dissociative fugue" as "sudden, unexpected travel away from home or one's customary place of daily activities, with inability to recall some or all of one's past. . . . During a fugue, individuals may appear to be without psychopathology and generally do not attract attention. . . . Once the individual returns to the prefugue state, there may be no memory for the events that occurred during the fugue" (523–524). Such mental states may indicate the existence of "a Mood Disorder, Posttraumatic Stress Disorder, or a Substance-Related Disorder" (524).
4. Of the seven factors Freyd lists as predictors of traumatic amnesia, six are implicated in Rhys's account. The seven factors are "1. abuse by caregiver; 2. explicit threats demanding silence; 3. alternative realities in environment (abuse context different from nonabuse context); 4. isolation during abuse; 5. young at age of abuse; 6. alternative reality-defining statements by caregiver; 7. lack of discussion of abuse" (*Betrayal Trauma* 140). Rhys's account shows evidence of all factors except two and five; she does, however, describe implicit threats that impel her to remain silent.
5. Frank W. Putnum calls self-hypnosis and numbing forms of "analgesia": "many victims of repetitive trauma report being able to activate analgesia in response to environmental cues or by using trance-inducing strategies . . . chronic analgesia may become maladaptive contributing to feelings of depersonalization or . . . other self-destructive behavior" (121).
6. Steven Marcus was the first critic to draw attention to the literariness of Freud's case history of Dora and the first to compare it to modernist fiction in "Freud and Dora: Story, History, Case History" in *Representations: Essays on Literature and Society,* 247–310. Marcus writes that "[t]he general form . . . of what Freud has written bears certain suggestive resemblances to a modern experimental novel" (263); he goes on to detail the formal characteristics that suggest this resemblance and compares the case history to "a play by Ibsen, or more precisely . . . a series of plays by Ibsen" (264). Both Philip Rieff and Neil Hertz compare the Dora case history to Henry James's *What Maisie Knew* in, respectively, *Fellow Teachers,* 85; and "Dora's Secrets, Freud's Techniques," in *In Dora's Case: Freud-Hysteria-Feminism,* eds. Charles Bernheimer and Claire Kahane (221–242, esp. 221–226). Freud himself famously compared his case histories of hysteria to short stories and characterized himself as a detective.
7. As Judith Herman notes in *Trauma and Recovery,* "Traumatic events, by definition, thwart initiative and overwhelm individual competence. . . . Guilt may be understood as an attempt to draw some useful lesson from disaster and to regain some sense of power and control. To imagine that

one could have done better may be more tolerable than to face the reality of utter helplessness" (54).

8. As Sue Thomas has shown, Rhys was probably looking at Freud's essay "On the History of the Psychoanalytic Movement," wherein Freud describes his renunciation of the seduction theory thus:

   > [O]ne was readily inclined to accept as true and aetiologically significant the statements made by patients in which they ascribed their symptoms to passive sexual experiences in early childhood—broadly speaking, to seduction. . . . Analysis had led by the right paths back to these sexual traumas, and yet they were not true. . . . At last came the reflection that, after all, one has no right to despair because one has been deceived in one's expectations; one must revise them. If hysterics trace their symptoms to fictitious traumas, this new fact signifies that they create such scenes in phantasy, and psychical reality requires to be taken into account alongside actual reality. (51–52)

9. Sue Thomas argues that this question may mean that Mr. Howard was aware of laws concerning adolescent girls' legal age of consent.
10. Sue Thomas notes that the prose in the notebook is "not polished." I believe this is only partially true. As I note above, the notebook contains many rewritten passages and marginal comments that gloss the main text. While the notebook is not "tortured into the shape of a novel," it is not completely unshaped either. Rhys is by this time an accomplished practitioner of modernist prose, and the many repetitions are reminiscent of the way in which she deploys repetition in *Good Morning, Midnight,* close to completion at the time of her writing this account. Furthermore, Rhys went on to rework a number of passages almost verbatim into published works such as the short story "Good-bye Marcus, Good-bye Rose," the novel *Wide Sargasso Sea,* and her autobiography *Smile Please.* To read the narrative as completely without craft is, I think, a mistake.
11. I am, of course, well aware of the fact that victims of childhood sexual abuse believe that the abuse confirms them as "bad," particularly if they enjoy the attention or feel sexual arousal. See Herman (104). Thomas elaborates upon the implications of this passage in relationship to Rhys (42–43).
12. This oversight or dismissal of the mother's culpability suggests that the mainly feminist critics who have worked on Rhys may be uneasy with the idea of maternal child abuse and prefer to focus on the more familiar figure of the male predator. Angier's dismissal is particularly interesting, since she identifies Rhys as suffering from Borderline Personality Disorder (657–658), a syndrome typically seen in child abuse victims (Herman 126–128).
13. I have no way of establishing that the mother's punishment was in fact abusive. What I show here is that Rhys's reactions are consistent with what we know about abused children. According to Angier, to the end of her life Rhys hated her mother: "It must go back to her mother, who

mourned her dead sister and preferred the living one to her. She said it . . . in the one absolutely clear thing she said about her childhood: that she loved her father, but hated her mother. So she *was* fated, as she felt. From the beginning she was unhealable, a stranger on the face of the earth, and full of rage" (658).

14. This progression from extreme reaction to withdrawal and seeming death recalls Emily Dickinson's sense that "After great pain, a formal feeling comes" (#341). Dickinson, like Rhys, depicts the way in which automatic, mechanistic responses and increasingly death-like paralysis overtake the sufferer of great pain; Dickinson's concluding stanza finds that "This is the Hour of Lead—/Remembered, if outlived,/ As Freezing persons, recollect the Snow—/First—Chill—then Stupor—then the letting go" (*The Complete Poems of Emily Dickinson,* 162). Dickinson's progression of chill, stupor, and letting go closely resembles Rhys's progression of pain, shame, sleep, sea, and silence. Interestingly, Dickinson, like Rhys, connects the experience of pain to the desire for form, as if aesthetic desire develops in part as a response to an experience of the unnameable "flooding" of emotion that is pain. I am indebted to Joanne Feit Diehl (as always!) for drawing my attention to this poem.
15. See also Ferenczi, "Confusion of Tongues"; and Shengold, *Soul Murder.*
16. The phrase "Would you like to belong to me?" suggests the common parental ploy of asking a young child "Are you Daddy's [or Mommy's] baby?"
17. Sue Thomas, Veronica Marie Gregg, and Judith L. Raiskin have analyzed extensively the development of Rhys's Creole subjectivity in relation to this history; although my own interest lies in the way in which forms of erotic domination became familiar to Rhys, I am much indebted to their meticulous historical analyses.
18. This story bears a curious resemblance to the poet H.D.'s account of a snake biting her mouth in *The Gift:* "He has bitten the side of my mouth. I will never get well, I will die soon of the poison of this horrible snake . . . She looks at the scar on my mouth. How ugly my mouth is with a scar, and the side of my face seems stung to death" (113). Susan Stanford Friedman observes that this nightmare is a reenactment of the primal scene: in the dream H.D. observes her parents in bed, and the snakes have obvious phallic overtones. The snake that bites her mouth enacts a symbolic castration, "the wound which leaves an ugly scar that can never be healed. Female genitals and mouth conflate in a scene of 'castration'—the theft of both erotic pleasure and speech—which is the destiny of both mother and daughter in the primal scene and its repetition" (*Penelope's Web* 338).
19. See Gregg's *Jean Rhys's Historical Imagination* for an extended analysis of Rhys's relationship to blacks in life and in fiction; as Gregg writes, in *Smile Please,* "[T]he black Other occupies a wide range of discursive locations contingent upon the desires or the positions from which the narrated self speaks" (65). My own interest here is in understanding the way

in which Mr. Howard's "mental seduction" brings together a set of scenarios of domination and submission, crystallizing in Rhys an interest in masochistic plots.

20. A number of recent critics have analyzed the racial and colonial issues involved in Meta's dislike of Rhys's reading. See, for example, analyses by Helen Tiffin, Sue Thomas, Veronica Marie Gregg, and Judith Raiskin.
21. The 14 stations are (1) Jesus is condemned to death; (2) Jesus accepts His Cross; (3) Jesus falls under the Cross; (4) Jesus meets His Mother; (5) Simon helps Jesus with the Cross; (6) Veronica wipes the Face of Jesus; (7) Jesus falls again; (8) Jesus speaks to the holy women; (9) Jesus falls a third time; (10) Jesus is stripped of His clothes; (11) Jesus is nailed to the Cross; (12) Jesus dies on the Cross; (13) Our Lady receives the Body of Jesus; (14) Our Lady watches Her Son being buried (*The New Saint Joseph Baltimore Catechism* [New York: Catholic Book Publishing Company, 1969], 252–253.
22. For those familiar with the Hollywood version of *Quo Vadis*—the1950s epic version with Robert Taylor as Marcus Vinicius, Deborah Kerr as Ligia, and Peter Ustinov (!) as Nero—it may come as something of a surprise that this novel won Sienkiewicz the Nobel Prize and that it remains the best-selling European novel of all time. My thanks to the employee at Cody's Books in Berkeley for sharing with me his extensive knowledge of *Quo Vadis.*
23. It is an interesting parallel that Ligia, a hostage princess, is in thrall to the Roman patrician; such social subordination resembles the relationship of the white Creole girl to the distinguished English gentleman and landowner.
24. Here is a representative passage, taken from a point where the tortures have been devised as enactments of Roman mythology:

    > The violent deaths of young girls, after being raped by gladiators costumed as wild beasts, delighted the rabble. They watched animal rites. . . . the fate of Dirce, punished for her cruelties by being tied under a wild ox and raped until dead; and the passions of Pasiphae, in love with a bull, who later gave birth to the Minotaur. They saw young girls, barely out of childhood, torn apart by mustangs. (490)

    There are innumerable such descriptions in the novel.
25. Petronius debates the question of whether women have souls in the first chapter of *Quo Vadis.*
26. The resemblance between the names Petronius and Petronella suggest other parallels: Petronella is an outside in the story, an observer; Petronius is similarly an arbiter of taste, someone who serves as a detached observer of the vices and follies of Nero's court.
27. Sue Thomas also notes this shift in reading habits: "These experiences . . . produce Rhys's transformation from disgusted reader of the childbirth section of one of her father's medical books to avid reader of books about prostitutes in the Carnegie Library in Roseau" (43). Thomas does

not consider the fusion of the figures of Mr. Howard and the mother, nor does she consider the implications of this shift, i.e., the repudiation of maternity and the shift to narratives of prostitution.

28. Researchers have recently established the existence of inhibitory processes that seem to corroborate Freud's original theory of repression. In addition to Jennifer J. Freyd, *Betrayal Trauma*, see Michael C. Anderson, "Active Forgetting: Evidence for Functional Inhibition as a Source of Memory Failure"; Michael C. Anderson and Collin Green, "Suppressing unwanted memories by executive control"; and Martin A. Conway, "Repression Revisited." In essence, Conway found that "if a memory . . . associated with something that is familiar . . . is actively avoided every time that familiar object is seen, then the memory becomes repressed and the avoided item is later difficult to remember . . . The results therefore further demonstrate the ubiquity of inhibitory processes in human memory" (319). Conway's interest in memory developed out of his work with abused children; hence his work on inhibitory processes is especially compelling for this study: "Children abused by a trusted caregiver are more likely eventually to forget the abuse than those maltreated by strangers. This led to the insight that a trusted caregiver might represent an unavoidable cue for memory retrieval. The only way to prevent persistent recall of damaging memories would be to adapt internally and to deliberately avoid thinking of such memories—in Freud's terms, to push them away from consciousness" (319). Such splitting would be, of course, consistent with the account of splitting Herman identifies in abused children. These studies do not address the cognitive processes by which such repressed memories return to consciousness. Janice Haaken's *Pillar of Salt* is a compelling overview of competing theories of memory; hers is an evenhanded analysis of the issues involved in the recovered memory controversy, and the implicit as well as explicit agendas structuring contemporary models of treating trauma victims. See also Kali Tal, *Worlds of Hurt: Reading the Literatures of Trauma*, for a discussion of the popular and cultural issues involved in contemporary trauma writing.
29. Sue Thomas argues that Rhys's sense that the memory went out of her "like a stone" "links ingestion of the story and lived experience with urinary tract calculus (kidney, ureter or bladder stone" and that "[t]he somatic metaphor suggests the pain attendant on repressing the memory, attendant on her silence" (57). My reading of this phrase is very different: to me the image of a memory passing out of consciousness like a stone suggests an image of the psyche as stream or pool of water, much as Woolf describes her mind in "A Sketch of the Past."

Chapter 6

1. The suggestion that Anna experiences her first sexual encounter with Walter as a rape does not emerge clearly in the published version of the

book, but does in the novel's original ending, conveniently reprinted in *The Gender of Modernism,* ed. Bonnie Kime Scott. Rhys always resented the fact that she had to change the ending in order to get the book published; in a letter to her friend Evelyn Scott she complained, "I supposed I shall have to give in and cut the book and I'm afraid it will make it meaningless. The worst is that it is precisely the last part which I am most certain of that will have to be mutilated. . . . I *know* the ending is the only possible ending" (*LJR* 25; emphasis in the original). Rhys's biographer, Carole Angier, believes that Rhys would have reinstated the original ending when the novel was reprinted if she had really believed the original ending was better. Rhys, however, always felt that once a novel was published it had a life of its own; her refusal to tamper with the published version seems consistent with this attitude. It is one shared by other writers: e.g., Djuna Barnes never reinstated the sections omitted from *Ryder,* even though they were omitted in order to get the novel published in the censorious 1920s. When the novel was reprinted in the 1970s, Barnes simply marked the excisions with asterisks.

2. To be sure, most critics mention the passivity, dependence, and self-destruction of the protagonists, but they usually go on to explain how such behavior results from social, cultural, colonial, or patriarchal structures. A significant exception is Mary Lou Emery's chapter on masochism and *Quartet* in *Jean Rhys at "World's End": Novels of Colonial and Sexual Exile,* 105–121. Emery argues *against* reading *Quartet* as a study of masochism; rather, she reads Marya as victimized by "the social relations and institutions that involve her" (194n1). She also provides a brief overview of contemporaneous debates concerning female masochism, in the main adopting Karen Horney's critique to situate and to analyze Marya's victimization at the hands of the Heidlers. She does not consider masochism as a pervasive motif recurring throughout Rhys's work, nor does she consider its psychological uses for Rhys's protagonists, as I do here.

   A number of writers do, of course, point to masochism in *Quartet,* but they read it as deriving simply from desire without exploring what psychological needs might be involved; indeed, Peter Wolfe simply observes Marya's "readiness to subjugate herself" and incredibly goes on to state that "Jean Rhys does not study the dynamics of dominance and dependence" (25, 28–29).

3. Robert McClure Smith has eloquently made the case for how women writers' representations of masochism can function as a form of oppositional discourse. See, for example, "'A Recent Martyr': The Masochistic Aesthetic of Valerie Martin," "Dickinson and the Masochistic Aesthetic," and "'I Don't Dream about it Any More': The Textual Unconscious in Jean Rhys's *Wide Sargasso Sea.*" Kaja Silverman also discusses the problems associated with conceptualizing a female masochism that is potentially disruptive in "Masochism and Male Subjectivity." Marianne Noble (in *The Masochistic Pleasures of Sentimental Literature*) and Sandra Lee

Bartky (in *Femininity and Domination: Studies in the Phenomenology of Oppression*) have defended women's rights to, in Bartky's words, "a politically incorrect sexuality."

4. See the collection of essays *Sacred Possessions: Vodou, Santeria, Obeah, and the Caribbean*, eds. Margarite Fernandez Olmos and Lizabeth Paravisini-Gebert, for numerous discussions of zombies, soucriants, and obeah. Elaine Savory's essay in this collection, "'Another Poor Devil of a Human Being . . . ': Jean Rhys and the Novel as Obeah," analyzes these practices specifically in relation to Rhys. She writes that "[o]ne important form of the isolated self in Rhys's texts is the ghost": "Being present and yet not seen is the essence of ghostly occupation of a given space. . . . Related to ghostliness is the sensation of being in a dream" (226–227).
5. This line from a canonical male English poet in the mind of a disenfranchised West Indian Creole underscores the way in which British culture has been imposed upon and internalized by Anna, "drowning" her ability to recapture, even imaginatively, her place of origin.
6. In addition to Susan J. Brison and Roberta Culbertson, see Russell Meares, "Episodic Memory, Trauma, and the Narrative of Self," and Michele L. Crossley, "Narrative Psychology, Trauma and the Study of Self/Identity."
7. Their response to her underscores Sasha's inability to find empathic witnessing: the woman scolds her, and Sasha retreats to the bathroom. When she returns, they have gone. She then repeats to the waiter what she had said to them, "It was something I remembered," but he only stares at her "blankly" (11).
8. According to a website devoted to "Gloomy Sunday," the song was first released in 1936, in several English recordings and at least one French recording (with the title "Sombre Dimanche"). Known as the "Hungarian Suicide Song," the song was banned by the BBC and other radio playcasts because so many suicides either left the song with their suicide notes or were found with a copy of the song's lyrics on their bodies. For a copy of the song's lyrics and details about recordings, see "Gloomy Sunday" http://www.phespirit.info/gloomysunday). It is worth noting that the song's lyrics describe a death wish in which the writer longs for the "black coach of sorrow" to convey him to a deathly realm: "Death is no dream for in death I'm caressing you," he writes.
9. In letters Rhys repeatedly emphasized her efforts to create an altered time sense for both Anna and Sasha. Of *Voyage in the Dark*'s original ending Rhys wrote that the "big idea" was "Something to do with time being an illusion I think. I mean that the past exists—side by side with the present, not behind it; that what was—is" (*LJR* 24). Writing of her attempts to portray madness in *Wide Sargasso Sea*, Rhys recalled the forced changes to *Voyage in the Dark*'s ending that she made to accommodate her publishers: "I remembered the last part of 'Voyage in the Dark' written like that—time and place abolished, past and present the same—and I had been almost satisfied. Then everybody said it was

'confused and confusing—impossible to understand etc.' and I had to cut and rewrite it (I still think I was right, and they were wrong, tho' it was long ago)" (*LJR* 233). Rhys similarly described the ending of *Good Morning, Midnight* in terms of altered time sense: "I wanted Sasha to enter the No time region there. 'Everything is on the same plane'" (138).

10. Anna pinpoints the geographical location of her island: "Lying between 15° 10' and 15° 40' N. and 61° 14' and 61° 30' West" (17), which is in fact Dominica. See Erica L. Johnson's chapters on *Voyage in the Dark* in *Home, Maison, Casa* for a discussion of Anna's geographic exile.
11. Blau DuPlessis notes in passing that Rhys's novels, particularly *Wide Sargasso Sea,* critique "romantic thralldom and marital power—internalized and external institutions that support gender inequality": "Antoinette's childhood history of isolation and rejection has contributed to a blank vulnerability (typical of other Rhys heroines), which brings her, devoid of a center, to a marriage without marriage contract, settlement, or legal protection" (46).
12. See Robert J. Stoller, *Pain and Pleasure* and *Sexual Excitement;* Jessica Benjamin, *The Bonds of Love: Psychoanalysis, Feminism, and the Problem of Domination* as well as her essay, "The Alienation of Desire: Women's Masochism and Ideal Love"; and Janice Haaken, *Pillar of Salt: Gender, Memory, and the Perils of Looking Back.*
13. Mary Lou Emery writes that "the fair suggests excitement, possibly sexual excitement associated with its working-class origins and traditional license, but the images . . . render the fair a harsh and possibly false scene of joy" (108); taken in conjunction with the passage of the little girl, Emery notes that "[b]oth passages . . . draw upon carnival scenes to express the ambiguity of the streets for Marya" (108). Emery does not see these passages as latently sadomasochistic, although she does see Lois's remark as signifying a shift whereby the carnival images no longer promise an inversion of joy and pain but rather have solidified into images of cruelty (111). Further on, however, Emery notes that the Montmartre scenes exemplify Bakhtin's notion of official feasts, that "sanctioned the existing pattern of things and reinforced it" (113). I would argue that the merry-go-rounds are congruent with this latter sense of "official" street life.
14. This cross-gender identification supports the insights of Adela Pinch, Eve Kosofsky Sedgwick, and Gaylyn Studlar that masochistic fantasy permits precisely this mobility of gender positions. Studlar writes, following Deleuze, that because masochism is situated in the pregenital stage and in relation to the oral mother, sexual difference may be "unimportant to the perversion's basic dynamics" (16). Similarly, Pinch writes that "'Masochism' is the name for a structure that involves not only an identification with suffering . . . but also an identification across gender boundaries" (115).

15. I have found no evidence that Rhys knew Charlotte Perkins Gilman's "The Yellow Wallpaper," but it is interesting that she uses the wallpaper to chart Marya's growing obsessiveness in the same way that Gilman uses wallpaper to trace her protagonist's increasing madness/clarity about her predicament. In both works, the wallpaper signals confinement—physical and psychic.
16. See especially Anne B. Simpson, *Territories of the Psyche: The Fiction of Jean Rhys;* Heather Ingman's chapter on Rhys in *Women's Fiction Between the Wars: Mothers, Daughters, and Writing,* esp. 110–115; and Deborah Kelly Kloepfer's chapter on *Voyage in the Dark* in *The Unspeakable Mother: Forbidden Discourse in Jean Rhys and H.D.,* 63–78. Ingman does not acknowledge Kloepfer's work, although much of her own reading is anticipated there. Other accounts of the "lost mother"—although they concern *Wide Sargasso Sea*—include Ronnie Scharfman's "Mirroring and Mothering in Simone Schwarz-Bart's *Pluie et Vent sur Telumée Miracle* and Jean Rhys's *Wide Sargasso Sea*" and Maggie Humm's "Jean Rhys: Race, Gender and History"; Humm writes that the lost mother is "Rhys's organising motif" (48).
17. See Christopher Bollas, *The Shadow of the Object: Psychoanalysis of the Unthought Known.* The "unthought known" refers to an "aesthetic of being" created by the mother's care of the infant; these infantile memories are lost to the process of primary repression and return only as moods or states of being.
18. In her unfinished autobiography Rhys elaborates on the connections she draws between money and sex thus: "It seems to me that the whole business of money and sex is mixed up with something very primitive and deep. When you take money directly from someone you love it becomes not money but a symbol. The bond is now there. The bond has been established. I am sure the woman's deep-down feeling is 'I belong to this man, I want to belong to him completely.' It is at once humiliating and exciting" (*SP* 97). The bonds of love indeed!
19. Robert McClure Smith also draws upon Peter Brooks in articulating the characteristics of masochistic narrative, although his focus is slightly different. See "'*A Recent Martyr*': The Masochistic Aesthetic of Valerie Martin," esp. 403–404.
20. As Robert McClure Smith writes, "If a specific masochistic pleasure is to be found in rhythm, in the rise and fall in the quantity of stimulus, in the temporal sequence of changes, then it is not unlike a reader's cognitive reactions and responses to the dislocations and delays of a repetitive narrative" ("*A Recent Martyr*" 403). Adela Pinch argues that poetic meter functions as a way of managing pain in her analysis of those of Wordsworth's poems that represent feminine suffering; she relates this passage in Freud specifically to meter ("Female Chatter" 842–843). Eve Kosofsky Sedgwick similarly relates poetic meter to masochism and spanking in her autobiographical "A Poem is Being Written."

21. Mary Lou Emery has identified this Exhibition as the 1937 Exhibition Internationale des Arts et des Techniques Appliqués à la Vie Moderne (*Jean Rhys at "World's End": Novels of Colonial and Sexual Exile* 144).
22. The word "blank" similarly shifts in meaning, from a figurative description of keeping one's mind or face "blank" to the name of a former employer of Sasha's, "Mr. Blank."
23. Theodore Reik anticipates this analysis when he writes that the masochist achieves pleasure "by another road, by a detour": he "submits voluntarily to punishment, suffering and humiliation, and thus has defiantly purchased the right to enjoy the gratification denied before" (428).
24. I am indebted to Valerie Kaussen for pointing out the significance of this passage.
25. In light of what Maggie Humm calls the "organizing motif of the lost mother" in Rhys's work (48), the French word "merde"—with its close resemblance to the French word for mother, "mere"—may mark an(other) site of maternal absence.
26. For a different reading of Sasha's similarity to the girl in the tabac, see Sue Thomas, *The Worlding of Jean Rhys*, 135.
27. For a detailed account of the song's impact on suicide rates in the 1930s, as well as a comprehensive list of recordings, see "Gloomy Sunday: The Suicide Song" (http://www.phespirit.info/gloomysunday).
28. Mary Lou Emery remarks that "the allusion to Heine's poem connects Sasha's isolated thoughts to those of a poet whom sociologists have named a 'marginal man.' Like the Jewish Heine, Sasha faces homelessness and persecution . . . Through the line . . . Sasha breaks through the enclosed privacy of the isolated self and joins the world of public, literary discourse" (31).

Epilogue

1. I take this formulation from Marion Milner's "The Role of Illusion in Symbol Formation." Reprinted in *Transitional Objects and Potential Spaces: Literary Uses of D. W. Winnicott*, ed. Peter L. Rudnytsky (13–39).
2. Bollas builds here not only on Winnicott's concept of the "facilitating environment"; he builds on a number of previous object relations theorists who focus on how the individual mother's care provides the infant with a sense of pattern and order. Winnicott, for example, describes how the infant goes from an "unintegrated state" to a structured integration thus: "Associated with this attainment is the infant's psychosomatic existence, which begins to take on a personal pattern; I have referred to this as the psyche indwelling in the soma . . . In this way meaning comes to the function of intake and output; moreover, it gradually becomes meaningful to postulate a personal or inner psychic reality for the infant" (*Maturational Processes* 124). Similarly, in his

1950s paper "On the Therapeutic Action of Psycho-Analysis," Hans Loewald locates the primary sense of self in the mother's care in a description that very much anticipates Bollas's: "[T]he manner in which a child is fed, touched, cleaned . . . looked at, talked to, called by name, recognized and re-recognized . . . communicat[es] to him his identity, sameness, unity, and individuality, shape[s] and mold[s] him so that he can begin to identify himself, to feel and recognize himself as one and as separate from others yet with others. The child begins to experience himself as a centered unity by being centered upon" (cited in Juhasz 10).

3. Both Heather Ingman and Anne B. Simpson analyze the relevance of D. W. Winnicott to Rhys: see Ingman 108–109 and Simpson, esp. 19–20.
4. In his introduction to Rhys's letters, for example, Rhys's close friend and literary executor Francis Wyndham writes,

> [M]ysteriously, ever since the end of her first love affair she had also been cursed by a kind of spiritual sickness—a feeling of belonging nowhere, of being ill at ease and out of place in her surroundings wherever these happened to be, a stranger in an indifferent, even hostile, world. She may have wanted to think that this crippling sense of alienation was merely that of a native West Indian exiled in a cold, foreign land, but in fact she believed that the whole earth had become inhospitable to her after the shock of that humdrum betrayal. All that had happened was that a kind, rather fatherly businessman, who had picked up a pretty chorus girl with a disconcertingly vague manner, decided after a year or so to pension her off. ("Introduction" 10–11)

5. Rhys exaggerates when she designates this compulsive writing as her first such attempt. It is true, nonetheless, that this manuscript, "Triple Sec"—the foundation for *Voyage in the Dark*—represented for Rhys a turning point in her life: a choice in her mind of writing over a life of respectability. It also marked her commitment to plots of erotic domination, plots that reiterate the pattern identified by Jessica Benjamin: without a sense of recognition and a confirmation of her own desire and agency, the girl comes to idealize a powerful man through whom she can vicariously experience power and desire. In Rhys's fiction, that man seems to promise the recognition that the mother has withheld; hence the eventual loss of that man reinvokes the primary loss, the primary trauma. As Heather Ingman perceptively notes, "All her life Rhys wrote and rewrote the story of a woman rejected by her mother and then by her lovers and haunted by memories of the lost maternal bond" (*Women's Fiction* 121).
6. Rhys never gives a completely clear rationale for titling her last novel *Wide Sargasso Sea*. One wonders if she knew Ezra Pound's 1912 poem

"Portrait d'une Femme," that opens with the line, "Your mind and you are our Sargasso Sea." As a note to that poem explains, the Sargasso Sea "is choked with seaweed; it was widely believed, though eventually disproved, that many ships had been inextricably tangled in the weeds" (*The Norton Anthology of Modern Poetry.* 2nd ed. Ed. Richard Ellman and Robert O'Clair [New York and London: W. W. Norton, 1988], 378).

Bibliography

Jean Rhys—Primary Texts

The Jean Rhys Papers and the David Plante Papers are held by the Department of Special Collections, McFarlin Library, University of Tulsa, Oklahoma.

Rhys, Jean. *After Leaving Mr. Mackenzie.* 1930. New York: Carroll & Graf, 1990.

———. Black Exercise Book. Jean Rhys Papers.

———. *The Collected Short Stories.* New York and London: W. W. Norton, 1987.

———. *Good Morning, Midnight.* 1939. New York and London: W. W. Norton, 1986.

———. *The Letters of Jean Rhys, 1931-66.* Ed. Francis Wyndham and Diana Melly. New York: Viking, 1984.

———. *Quartet.* 1928. New York: Vintage Books, 1974.

———. *Smile Please: An Unfinished Autobiography.* Berkeley, CA: Creative Arts Book Company, 1983.

———. *Voyage in the Dark.* 1934. New York and London: W. W. Norton, 1982.

———. "Voyage in the Dark: Part IV (Original Version)." Jean Rhys Papers. Reprinted in Scott 381–389.

———. *Wide Sargasso Sea.* 1966. Ed. Judith L. Raiskin. New York and London: W. W. Norton, 1999.

Virginia Woolf—Primary Texts

Woolf, Virginia. *Between the Acts.* New York: Harcourt Brace Jovanovich, 1941.

———. *The Captain's Death Bed and Other Essays.* New York: Harcourt Brace Jovanovich, 1950.

———. *The Collected Essays of Virginia Woolf.* Ed. Andrew McNeillie. New York: Harcourt Brace Jovanovich. 1, 1904–1912 (1986); 2, 1912–1918 (1987); 3, 1919–1924 (1988).

———. *The Diary of Virginia Woolf.* Ed. Anne Olivier Bell. New York: Harcourt Brace Jovanovich. 1, 1915–1919 (1977); 2, 1920–1924 (1978); 3, 1925–1930 (1980); 4, 1931–1935 (1982); 5, 1936–1941 (1984).

———. Letter to the editor. "The Intellectual Status of Women." *New Statesman*, October 9, 1920: 16–17.

———. Letter to the editor. "The Intellectual Status of Women." *New Statesman*, October 16, 1920: 45–46.

———. *The Letters of Virginia Woolf.* Ed. Nigel Nicolson and Joanne Trautmann. New York: Harcourt Brace Jovanovich. 1, 1888–1912 (1975); 2, 1912–1922 (1976); 3, 1923–1928 (1977); 4, 1929–1931 (1978); 5, 1933–1935 (1979); 6, 1936–1941 (1980).

———. *Moments of Being.* 2nd ed. Ed. Jeanne Schulkind. New York: Harcourt, 1985.

———. *Mrs. Dalloway.* New York: Harcourt Brace Jovanovich, 1925.

———. *Orlando.* 1928. New York: Signet, 1960.

———. *The Pargiters: The Novel-Essay Portion of* The Years. Ed. and with an introduction by Mitchell A. Leaska. New York and London: Harcourt Brace Jovanovich, 1977.

———. *A Room of One's Own.* New York: Harcourt Brace Jovanovich, 1929.

———. *Three Guineas.* New York: Harcourt Brace Jovanovich, 1938.

———. *To the Lighthouse.* New York: Harcourt Brace Jovanovich, 1927.

———. *The Voyage Out.* 1915. New York: Harcourt Brace Jovanovich, 1920.

———. *The Waves.* New York: Harcourt Brace Jovanovich, 1931.

———. *Women and Fiction: The Manuscript Versions of* A Room of One's Own. Transcribed and edited by S. P. Rosenbaum. Oxford: Blackwell Publishers, 1992.

———. *Women and Writing.* Ed. Michele A. Barrett. New York: Harcourt Brace Jovanovich, 1979.

———. *The Years.* New York: Harcourt Brace Jovanovich, 1937.

Secondary References

Abel, Elizabeth. "Women and Schizophrenia: The Fiction of Jean Rhys." *Contemporary Literature* 20 (Spring 1979): 155–177.

Abraham, Nicolas and Maria Torok. *The Shell and the Kernel: Renewals of Psychoanalysis.* Vol 1. Ed., trans., and with an introduction by Nicholas T. Rand. Chicago and London: University of Chicago Press, 1994.

Adamson, Joseph and Hilary Clark, eds. *Scenes of Shame: Psychoanalysis, Shame, and Writing.* Albany, NY: State University of New York Press, 1999.

Allison, Dorothy. *Skin: Talking About Sex, Class and Literature.* Ithaca, NY: Firebrand Books, 1994.

Anderson, Michael C. "Active Forgetting: Evidence for Functional Inhibition as a Source of Memory Failure." In Freyd and DePrince, 185–210.

——— and Collin Green. "Suppressing Unwanted Memories by Executive Control." *Nature* 410 (March 15, 2001): 366–370.

Angier, Carole. *Jean Rhys: Life and Work.* London: Andre Deutsch, 1990.

Athill, Diana. "Foreword." *Smile Please: An Unfinished Autobiography.* Berkeley, CA: Creative Arts Book Company, 1983. 3–9.

———. "Introduction." *The Collected Short Stories of Jean Rhys.* New York and London: W. W. Norton, 1987. vii–x.

Attwater, Donald and Catherine Rachel John, eds. *The Penguin Dictionary of Saints.* 3rd ed. Harmondsworth, UK: Penguin Books, 1993.

Bal, Mieke, Jonathan Crewe, and Leo Spitzer, eds. *Acts of Memory: Cultural Recall in the Present.* Hanover and London: University Press of New England, 1999.

Balanchine, George. *Balanchine's Complete Stories of the Ballets.* Ed. Francis Mason. New York: Doubleday, 1954.

Barrett, Eileen. "Unmasking Lesbian Passion: The Inverted World of *Mrs. Dalloway.*" In Barrett and Cramer, *Virginia Woolf: Lesbian Readings* 146–164.

——— and Patricia Cramer, eds. *Re: Reading, Re: Writing, Re: Teaching Virginia Woolf: Selected Papers from the Fourth Annual Conference on Virginia Woolf.* New York: Pace University Press, 1995.

——— and Patricia Cramer, ed. *Virginia Woolf: Lesbian Readings.* New York and London: New York University Press, 1997.

Bartky, Sandra Lee. *Femininity and Domination: Studies in the Phenomenology of Oppression.* New York and London: Routledge, 1990.

Bataille, George. "Hemingway in the Light of Hegel." *Semiotext(e)* 2, no. 2 (1976): 12–22.

Battersby, Christine. *Gender and Genius: Towards a Feminist Aesthetics.* London: Women's Press, 1989.

Baumeister, Roy E. *Masochism and the Self.* Hillsdale, NJ, and Hove and London: Lawrence Erlbaum, 1989.

Beaumont, Cyril W. *The Diaghilev Ballet in London: A Personal Record.* 3rd ed. London: Adam and Charles Black, 1951.

Bell, Quentin. *Virginia Woolf: A Biography.* New York: Harcourt Brace Jovanovich, 1972.

Benjamin, Jessica. "The Alienation of Desire: Women's Masochism and Ideal Love." In Judith Alpert, *The Bonds of Love: Psychoanalysis, Feminism, and the Problem of Domination.* New York: Pantheon Books, 1988.

———. *Like Subjects, Love Objects: Essays on Recognition and Sexual Difference.* New Haven and London: Yale University Press, 1995.

———. "Master and Slave: The Fantasy of Erotic Domination." In Snitow et al., 280–299.

———. ed. *Psychoanalysis and Women: Contemporary Reappraisals.* Hillsdale, NJ: Analytic Press, 1986.

Benjamin, Walter. "The Image of Proust." *Illuminations.* Ed. and with an introduction by Hannah Arendt. New York: Harcourt Brace Jovonavich, 1968.

Bennett, Arnold. "Mr. Bennett and Mrs. Woolf." In Stape, 29–30.

Benstock, Shari. "Authorizing the Autobiographical." In *The Private Self: Theory and Practice in Women's Autobiographical Practice.* Ed. Shari Benstock. Durham: University of North Carolina Press, 1988. 10–33.

———. *Textualizing the Feminine: On the Limits of Genre.* Norman and London: University of Oklahoma Press, 1991.

———. *Women of the Left Bank: Paris, 1900-1940.* Austin: University of Texas Press, 1986.

Berliner, Bernhard. "Libido and Reality in Masochism." *Psychoanalytic Quarterly* 9 (1940): 322–333.

———. "On Some Psychodynamics of Masochism." *Psychoanalytic Quarterly* 16 (1947): 459–471.

Bernheimer, Charles and Claire Kahane, eds. *In Dora's Case: Freud—Hysteria—Feminism.* New York: Columbia University Press, 1985.

Bishop, Edward. "The Essays: The Subversive Process of Metaphor." *Virginia Woolf.* Macmillan Modern Novelists. Basingstoke: Macmillan, 1991. 67–78.

Bland, Lucy and Laura Doan, eds. *Sexology in Culture: Labelling Bodies and Desires.* Chicago: University of Chicago Press, 1998.

———, eds. *Sexology Uncensored: The Documents of Sexual Science.* Cambridge, UK: Polity Press, 1998.

Blau DuPlessis, Rachel. *Writing Beyond the Ending: Narrative Strategies of Twentieth-Century Women Writers.* Bloomington: Indiana University Press, 1985.

Bollas, Christopher. "The Aesthetic Moment and the Search for Transformation." In Rudnytsky, 40–49.

———. *Being a Character: Psychoanalysis and Self Experience.* London and New York: Routledge,1992.

———. *Cracking Up: The Work of Unconscious Experience.* New York: Hill and Wang, 1995.

———. *Forces of Destiny.* London: Free Association Books, 1989.

———. *The Shadow of the Object: Psychoanalysis of the Unthought Known.* New York: Columbia University Press, 1987.

Bouson, J. Brooks. *Quiet As It's Kept: Shame, Trauma, and Race in the Novels of Toni Morrison.* Albany: State University of New York Press, 2000.

Bowen, Stella. *Drawn from Life.* 1941. London: Virago Press, 1984.

Bowlby, Rachel. "The Impasse: Jean Rhys's *Good Morning, Midnight.*" *Still Crazy After All These Years: Women, Writing and Psychoanalysis.* London and New York: Routledge, 1992. 34–58.

———, ed. *Virginia Woolf.* Longman Critical Readers. New York and London: Longman, 1992.

Brandmark, Wendy. "The Power of the Victim: A Study of *Quartet, After Leaving Mr. Mackenzie* and *Voyage in the Dark* by Jean Rhys." *Kunapipi* 8, no. 2 (1986): 21–29.

Brathwaite, Edward Kamau. "English in the Caribbean: Notes on Nation, Language, and Poetry." In *English Literature: Opening Up the Canon.* Ed. Leslie Fiedler and Houston A. Baker. Selected Papers from the English Institute 4 (1979). Baltimore: Johns Hopkins University Press, 1981. 15–53.

Briggs, Marlene. "Veterans and Civilians: Traumatic Knowledge and Cultural Appropriation in *Mrs. Dalloway.*" In McVickers and Davis, 43–50.

Brison, Susan J. "Trauma Narratives and the Remaking of the Self." In Bal, Crewe, and Spitzer, 39–54.

Broe, Mary Lynn. "My Art Belongs to Daddy: Incest as Exile, The Textual Economics of Hayford Hall." In Broe and Ingram, 41–86.

———, ed. *Silence and Power: A Reevaluation of Djuna Barnes.* Carbondale: Southern Illinois University Press, 1991.

——— and Angela Ingram, eds. *Women Writing in Exile.* Chapel Hill: University of North Carolina Press, 1989.

Brooks, Peter. *Reading for the Plot: Design and Intention in Narrative.* New York: Vintage Books, 1985.

Buckley, Jerome Hamilton. *The Victorian Temper: A Study in Literary Culture.* New York: Vintage Books, 1951.

Burke, Carolyn, Naomi Schor, and Margaret Whitford, eds. *Engaging with Irigaray.* New York: Columbia University Press, 1994.

Butler, Judith. "Performative Acts and Gender Constitution: An Essay in Phenomenology and Feminist Theory." In *Writing on the Body: Female Embodiment and Feminist Theory.* Ed. Katie Conboy, Nadia Medina, and Sarah Stanbury. New York: Columbia University Press, 1997. 401–417.

Califia, Pat. "A Secret Side of Lesbian Sexuality." In Weinberg and Kamal, 129–136.

Campbell, Beatrix. "A Feminist Sexual Politics: Now You See It, Now You Don't." In *Sexuality: A Reader*, ed. Feminist Review. London: Virago Press, 1987. 19–39.

Campbell, Elaine. "Reflections of Obeah in Jean Rhys's Fiction." *Kunapipi* 4, no. 2 (1982): 42–50.

Carr, Helen. *Jean Rhys.* Plymouth: Northcote House in assoc. with the British Council, 1996.

Carter, Angela. *The Sadeian Woman and the Ideology of Pornography.* Harmondsworth, UK: Penguin Books, 1979.

Caruth, Cathy, ed. *Trauma: Explorations in Memory.* Baltimore and London: Johns Hopkins University Press, 1995.

Casey, Nancy. "Study in the Alienation of a Creole Woman: Jean Rhys's *Voyage in the Dark.*" *Caribbean Quarterly* 19 (September 1973): 95–102.

Chasseguet-Smirgel, Janine. "Freud and Female Sexuality: The Consideration of Some Blind Spots in the Exploration of the 'Dark Continent." *International Journal of Psychoanalysis* 57 (1976): 275–286.

Chodorow, Nancy. *The Reproduction of Mothering.* Berkeley: University of California Press, 1978.

Constable, Liz. "Introduction: States of Shame." *L'Esprit Createur.* Special issue "States of Shame," ed. Liz Constable. 39, no. 4 (Winter 1999): 3–12.

Conway, Martin A. "Repression Revisited." *Nature* 410 (March 2001): 319.

Crossley, Michele L. "Narrative Psychology, Trauma and the Study of Self/Identity." *Theory and Psychology* 10, no. 4 (2000): 528–546.

Culbertson, Roberta. "Embodied Memory, Transcendence, and Telling: Recounting Trauma, Re-establishing the Self." *New Literary History* 26 (1995): 169–195.

Dalsimer, Katherine. *Virginia Woolf: Becoming a Writer.* New Haven and London: Yale University Press, 2001.

Damasio, Antonio. *The Feeling of What Happens: Body and Emotion in the Making of Consciousness.* San Diego, New York, and London: Harcourt, 1999.

Davidson, Arnold E. *Jean Rhys.* New York: Fredrick Ungar, 1985.

Davidson, H. R. Ellis. *Gods and Myths of Northern Europe.* Middlesex, England: Penguin, 1964.

De Lauretis, Teresa. "The Practice of Sexual Difference and Feminist Thought in Italy: An Introductory Essay." In The Milan Women's Bookstore Collective, *Sexual Difference: A Theory of Social-Symbolic Practice.* Trans. Patricia Cicogna and Teresa de Lauretis. Bloomington and Indianapolis: Indiana University Press, 1990.

Decker, Hannah S. *Freud, Dora, and Vienna 1900.* New York: Free Press, 1991.

Deleuze, Gilles. "Coldness and Cruelty." *Masochism.* New York: Zone Books, 1991. 9–138.

DeKoven, Marianne. *Rich and Strange: Gender, History, Modernism.* Princeton: Princeton University Press, 1991.

DeMeester, Karen. "Trauma and Recovery in Virginia Woolf's *Mrs. Dalloway.*" *Modern Fiction Studies* 44, no. 3 (Fall 1998): 649–673.

DeSalvo, Louise. "'To Make Her Mutton at Sixteen': Rape, Incest, and Child Abuse in *The Antiphon.*" In Broe, *Silence and Power.* 300–315.

———. *Virginia Woolf: The Impact of Childhood Sexual Abuse on Her Life and Work.* Boston: Beacon Press, 1989.

DSM IV. *Diagnostic and Statistical Manual of Mental Disorders.* 4th ed. Washington, D.C.: American Psychiatric Association, 1994.

Dickinson, Emily. *The Complete Poems of Emily Dickinson.* Ed. Thomas H. Johnson. Boston and Toronto: Little, Brown, 1960.

Doane, Janice and Devon Hodges. *Telling Incest: Narratives of Dangerous Remembering from Stein to Sapphire.* Ann Arbor: University of Michigan Press, 2001.

Duncan-Jones, E. E. "Mrs. Woolf Comes to Dine." In Philips, 174–175.

Duncan-Jones, E. E. and U. K. N. Stevenson. "Mrs. Woolf Comes to Dinner." In Stape, 14–15.

Ellis, Havelock. *Man and Woman: A Study of Human Secondary Characteristics.* 5th ed. 1894. New York: Scribner, 1914.

———. "Studies in the Psychology of Sex." In Weinberg and Kamal, 33–35.

Emery, Mary Lou. *Jean Rhys at "World's End": Novels of Colonial and Sexual Exile.* Austin: University of Texas Press, 1990.

Ezell, Margaret J. M. "The Myth of Judith Shakespeare: Creating the Canon of Women's Literature." *New Literary History* 21 (1990): 579–592.

Fassler, Barbara. "Theories of Homosexuality as Sources of Bloomsbury's Androgyny." *Signs: Journal of Women in Culture and Society* 5, no. 2 (1979): 237–251.

Felman, Shoshana, and Dori Laub, eds. *Testimony: Crises of Witnessing in Literature, Psychoanalysis, and History.* New York: Routledge, 1991.

Felski, Rita. *Beyond Feminist Aesthetics: Feminist Literature and Social Change.* Cambridge, MA: Harvard University Press, 1989.

Feminist Review, eds. *Sexuality: A Reader.* London: Virago, 1987.

Fenichel, Otto. *Psychoanalytic Theory of Neurosis.* New York: Norton, 1945.

Ferenczi, Sandor. "Confusion of Tongues between Adults and the Child." Trans. Jeffrey M. Masson and Marianne Loring. In Masson, 291–303.

Finke, Michael C. and Carl Niekerk. *One Hundred Years of Masochism: Literary Texts, Social and Cultural Contexts.* Psychoanalysis and Culture 10. Amsterdam and Atlanta, GA: Rodopi, 2000.

Folkenflik, Robert, ed. *The Culture of Autobiography: Constructions of Self-Representations.* Stanford: Stanford University Press, 1993.

Folsom, Marcia McClintock. "Gallant Red Brick and Plain China: Teaching *A Room of One's Own.*" *College English* 45 (1983): 254–262.

Fowler, Rowena. "Virginia Woolf and Katharine Furse: An Unpublished Correspondence." *Tulsa Studies in Women's Literature* 9, no. 2 (1990): 201–227.

Fox, Alice. "Literary Allusion as Feminist Criticism in *A Room of One's Own.*" *Philological Quarterly* 63 (1984): 145–161.

Fox, George. *Journal.* Rev. Norman Penney. New York: Dutton, 1924.

Freud, Sigmund. "A Child is Being Beaten." In *Sexuality and the Psychology of Love.* Ed. Philip Rieff. New York: Macmillan/Collier Books, 1963. 107–132.

———. "The Dynamics of the Transference." In *Therapy and Technique,* 105–115.

———. "The Economic Problem of Masochism." *General Psychological Theory: Papers on Metapsychology.* Ed. Philip Rieff. New York: Macmillan/Collier Books, 1963. 193–201.

———. "Fragment of an Analysis of a Case of Hysteria." In *Dora: An Analysis of a Case of Hysteria.* Ed. Philip Rieff. New York: Macmillan/Collier Books, 1963. 21–144.

———. "Further Recommendations in the Technique of Psychoanalysis: Recollection, Repetition, and Working Through." In *Therapy and Technique,* 157–166.

———. *The Interpretation of Dreams.* Trans. and ed. James Strachey. 1900. New York: Avon Books, 1965.

———. "Instincts and Their Vicissitudes." *General Psychological Theory: Papers on Metapsychology.* Ed. Philip Rieff. New York: Macmillan/Collier Books, 1963. 83–103.

———. *The Origins of Psychoanalysis: Letters to Wilhelm Fleiss, Drafts and Notes: 1887–1902.* Ed. Marie Bonaparte, Anna Freud, and Ernst Kris. New York: Basic Books, 1954.

———. *The Standard Edition of the Complete Psychological Works of Sigmund Freud*. 3rd ed. Trans. and ed. James Strachey. 23 vols. London: Hogarth Press, 1953–1966. (Hereafter cited as *SE*).

———. *Therapy and Technique*. Ed. Philip Rieff. New York: Collier Books, 1963.

———. "Three Essays on the Theory of Sexuality." In *SE*. Vol. 7: 133–243.

Freyd, Jennifer J. *Betrayal Trauma: The Logic of Forgetting Childhood Abuse*. Cambridge, MA: Harvard University Press, 1996.

——— and Anne P. Deprince, eds. *Trauma and Cognitive Science: A Meeting of Minds, Science, and Human Experience*. Binghamton, NY: Haworth Press, 2001.

Frickey, Pierrette. Introduction. *Critical Perspectives on Jean Rhys*. Ed. Pierette Frickey. Washington, D.C.: Three Continents Press, 1990. 1–16.

Friedman, Ellen G. and Miriam Fuchs, eds. *Breaking the Sequence: Women's Experimental Fiction*. Princeton, NJ: Princeton University Press, 1989.

Friedman, Susan Stanford. "Hysteria, Dreams, and Modernity: A Reading of the Origins of Psychoanalysis in Freud's Early Corpus." *Rereading the New: A Backward Glance at Modernism*. Ed. Kevin J. H. Dettmar. Ann Arbor: University of Michigan Press, 1992.

———. *Penelope's Web: Gender, Modernity, H.D.'s Fiction*. Cambridge: Cambridge University Press, 1990.

———. "The Return of the Repressed in Women's Narrative." *Journal of Narrative Technique* 19, no. 1 (Winter 1989): 141–156.

Froula, Christine. *Virginia Woolf and the Bloomsbury Avant-Garde: War, Civilization, Modernity*. New York: Columbia University Press, 2004.

Fry, John P. *The Advent of Quakerism*. London: Forsaith, 1908.

Fry, Roger. *Cezanne*. New York: Macmillan, 1927.

Fuchs, Miriam. *The Text is Myself: Women's Life Writing and Catastrophe*. Madison: University of Wisconsin Press, 2004.

Gardiner, Judith Kegan. "The Exhilaration of Exile: Rhys, Stead, and Lessing." *Women's Writing in Exile*. Ed. Mary Lynn Broe and Angela Ingram. Chapel Hill: University of North Carolina Press, 1989. 133–150.

———. "Good Morning, Midnight; Good Night, Modernism." *Boundary 2* 11, nos. 1–2 (Fall/Winter 1982–1983): 233–251.

———. *Rhys, Stead, Lessing and the Politics of Empathy*. Bloomington: Indiana University Press, 1989.

Gebhard, Paul. "Sadomasochism." In Weinberg and Kamal, 36–39.

Ghent, Emmanuel. "Masochism, Submission, Surrender." *Contemporary Psychoanalysis* 26, no. 1 (1990): 108–136.

Gilbert, Sandra M. "The Supple Suitor: Death, Women, Feminism and (Assisted or Unassisted Suicide." *Tulsa Studies in Women's Literature* 24, no. 2 (Fall 2005): 247–255.

Gilbert, Sandra M. and Susan Gubar. *No Man's Land: The Place of the Woman Writer in the Twentieth Century*. Vol. 1: *The War of the Words*. New Haven, CT: Yale University Press, 1988.

———. *No Man's Land: The Place of the Woman Writer in the Twentieth Century*. Vol. 2. *Sexchanges*. New Haven, CT: Yale University Press, 1989.

———. *No Man's Land: The Place of the Woman Writer in the Twentieth Century*. Vol. 3. *Letters from the Front*. New Haven, CT: Yale University Press, 1994.

Gilman, Sander L. *Difference and Pathology: Stereotypes of Sexuality, Race, and Madness*. Ithaca, NY: Cornell University Press, 1985.

Good, Graham. "Virginia Woolf: Angles of Vision." *The Observing Self: Rediscovering the Essay*. London: Routledge, 1988. 112–134.

Gregg, Veronica Marie. *Jean Rhys's Historical Imagination: Reading and Writing the Creole*. Chapel Hill and London: University of North Carolina Press, 1995.

Griffith, E. F. *Modern Marriage and Birth Control*. London: V. Gollancz, 1937.

Grimm, J. L. C. and W. C. *Grimm's Fairy Tales*. Hertfordshire, UK: Wordsworth Editions, 1993.

Grosz, Elizabeth. *Sexual Subversions: Three French Feminists*. Sydney: Allen & Unwin, 1989.

Haaken, Janice. *Pillar of Salt: Gender, Memory, and the Perils of Looking Back*. New Brunswick, New Jersey, and London: Rutgers University Press, 1998.

Haller, Evelyn. "Her Quill Drawn from the Firebird: Virginia Woolf and the Russian Dancers." In *The Multiple Muses of Virginia Woolf*. Ed. Diane F. Gillespie. Columbia: University of Missouri Press, 1993. 180–226.

Harris, Wilson. "Carnival of Psyche: Jean Rhys's *Wide Sargasso Sea*." *Kunapipi* 2, no. 2 (1980): 142–150.

Harrison, Nancy R. *Jean Rhys and the Novel as Women's Text*. Chapel Hill: University of North Carolina Press, 1988.

Hartmann, Heinz, Ernst Kris, and R. M. Loewenstein. "Comments on the Formation of Psychoanalytic Structure." *The Psychoanalytic Study of the Child* 2 (1946): 11–38.

———. "Notes on the Theory of Aggression." *The Psychoanalytic Study of the Child* 3–4 (1949): 9–39.

H.D. *The Gift: The Complete Text*. Ed. and annotated by Jane Augustine. Gainesville: University Press of Florida, 1998.

Henke, Suzette A. *Shattered Subjects: Trauma and Testimony in Women's Life-Writing*. New York: St. Martin's Press, 1998.

Herman, Judith Lewis. *Father-Daughter Incest*. Cambridge, MA: Harvard University Press, 1981.

———. *Trauma and Recovery: The Aftermath of Violence–From Domestic Abuse to Political Terror*. New York: Basic Books, 1992.

Hertz, Neil. "Dora's Secrets, Freud's Techniques." In Bernheimer and Kahane, 221–242.

Hite, Molly. "Writing in the Margins: Jean Rhys." *The Other Side of the Story: Structures and Strategies of Contemporary Feminist Narrative*. Ithaca, NY: Cornell University Press, 1989. 19–54.

Hoffmann, Charles G. "Virginia Woolf's Manuscript Revision of *The Years*." *PMLA* 84 (January 1969): 79–86.

Hollibaugh, Amber and Cherrie Moraga. "What We're Rollin Around in Bed With: Sexual Silences in Feminism." In Snitow et al., 394–405.

Horney, Karen. *Feminine Psychology*. Ed. and with an introduction by Harold Kelman. New York: Norton, 1967.

Horowitz, Mardi J., ed. *Essential Papers on Posttraumatic Stress Disorder.* New York: New York University Press, 1999.

Howells, Coral Ann. *Jean Rhys*. New York: St. Martin's Press, 1991.

Huber, Elaine C. "'A Woman Must Not Speak': Quaker Women in the English Left Wing." In *Women of Spirit: Female Leadership in the Jewish and Christian Traditions*. Ed. Rosemary Ruether and Eleanor McLaughlin. New York: Simon and Schuster, 1979. 155–181.

Humm, Maggie. "Jean Rhys: Race, Gender and History." In Wisker, 44–79.

Ingman, Heather. *Women's Fiction Between the Wars: Mothers, Daughters, and Writing*. New York: St. Martin's Press, 1998.

Irigaray, Luce. "Body against Body: In Relation to the Mother." *Sexes et parentes*. Paris: Minuit, 1987. *Sexes and Genealogies*. Trans. Gillian C. Gill. New York: Columbia University Press, 1993. 9–21.

———. *Ethique de la difference sexuelle*. Paris: Minuit, 1984. *An Ethics of Sexual Difference*. Trans. Carolyn Burke and Gillian C. Gill. Ithaca, NY: Cornell University Press, 1993.

———. *This Sex Which Is Not One*. Trans. Catherine Porter and Carolyn Burke. Ithaca, NY: Cornell University Press, 1985.

———. "Women's Exile." *Ideology and Consciousness*. (1978). Reprinted in *The Feminist Critique of Language: A Reader.* Ed. Deborah Cameron. London and New York: Routledge, 1990. 80–96.

Janoff-Bulman, Ronnie. *Shattered Assumptions: Towards a New Psychology of Trauma*. New York: Free Press, 1992.

Johnson, Erica L. *Home, Maison, Casa: The Politics of Location in Jean Rhys, Marguerite Duras, and Erminia Dell'Oro*. New Jersey: Farleigh Dickinson University Press, 2002.

Jones, Suzanne W. *Writing the Woman Artist: Essays on Poetics, Politics, and Portraiture*. Philadelphia: University of Pennsylvania Press, 1991.

Joplin, Patricia Klindienst. "The Voice of the Shuttle Is Ours." *Stanford Literature Review* 1, no. 1 (Spring 1984): 25–53.

Juhasz, Suzanne. *A Desire for Women: Relational Psychoanalysis, Writing, and Relationships between Women*. New Brunswick and London: Rutgers University Press, 2003.

Kacandes, Irene. "Narrative Witnessing as Memory Work: Reading Gertrud Kolmar's *A Jewish Mother.*" In Bal, Crewe, and Spitzer, 55–71.

Kamal, G. W. Levi. "Toward a Sexology of Sadomasochism." In Weinberg and Kamal, 197–203.

Kamuf, Peggy. "Penelope at Work: Interruptions in *A Room of One's Own*." Reprinted in *Virginia Woolf*. Ed. Rachel Bowlby. London and New York: Longman, 1992. 180–195.

Kaufman, Gershem. *The Psychology of Shame: Theory and Treatment of Shame-Based Syndromes*. New York: Springer, 1989.

Kaussen, Valerie. "Reflections on Aging: Identity and the Maternal in the Fiction of Jean Rhys." Master's thesis. University of California, Davis, 1990.
Kelley, Bennet, ed. *The New Saint Joseph Baltimore Catechism*. New York: Catholic Book Publishing Company, 1969.
Keynes, Milo, ed. *Lydia Lopokova*. London: Weidenfeld and Nicolson, 1983.
Khan, Masud. *Alienation in Perversions*. New York: International Universities Press, 1979.
Kilborne, Benjamin. "The Disappearing Who: Kierkegaard, Shame, and the Self." In Adamson and Clark, 35–51.
Klein, Melanie. *The Selected Melanie Klein*. Ed. Juliet Mitchell. New York: Free Press, 1986.
Kloepfer, Deborah Kelly. *The Unspeakable Mother: Forbidden Discourse in Jean Rhys and H.D.* Ithaca, NY: Cornell University Press, 1989.
Krafft-Ebing, Richard von. "Pschopathia Sexualis." In Weinberg and Kamal, 25–29.
Kris, Ernst. "Introduction." In Bonaparte, Freud, and Kris, 3–47.
Laplanche, Jean. *Life and Death in Psychoanalysis*. Trans. Jeffrey Mehlman. Baltimore: Johns Hopkins University Press, 1976.
——— and J.B. Pontalis. *The Language of Psychoanalysis*. Trans. Donald Nicholson-Smith. New York and London: W. W. Norton, 1973.
Lauter, Estella. "Re-visioning Creativity: Audre Lorde's Refiguration of Eros as the Black Mother Within." In Jones, 398–418.
Lawrence, Patricia Ondek. *The Reading of Silence: Virginia Woolf in the English Tradition*. Stanford, CA: Stanford University Press, 1991.
LeDoux, Joseph. *The Emotional Brain: The Mysterious Underpinning of Emotional Life*. New York: Simon & Schuster, 1996.
Lee, Hermione. *Virginia Woolf*. New York: Knopf, 1997.
Lee, Thomas. "Patterns of the Zombie in Jean Rhys's *Wide Sargasso Sea*." *World Literature Written in English* 31 no. 1 (1991): 34–42.
Leigh, Nancy J. "Mirror, Mirror: The Development of Female Identity in Jean Rhys's Fiction." *World Literature Written in English* 25 no. 2 (1985): 270–285.
Lewis, Helen Block. "Introduction: Shame—The 'Sleeper' in Psychopathology." In *The Role of Shame in Symptom Formation*. Ed. Helen Block Lewis. 1–28.
———, ed. *The Role of Shame in Symptom Formation*. Hillsdale, NJ: Lawrence Erlbaum, 1987.
———. *Shame and Guilt in Neurosis*. New York: International Universities Press, 1971.
———. "Shame and the Narcissistic Personality." In Nathanson, 93–132.
Leys, Ruth. *Trauma: A Genealogy*. Chicago and London: University of Chicago Press, 2000.
Loewald, Hans. "On the Therapeutic Action of Psychoanalysis." *International Journal of Psychoanalysis* 58 (1960): 463–472.
Look Lai, Wally. "The Road to Thornfield Hall." *New World Quarterly* 4 (1968): 17–27.

Lorde, Audre. "Poetry is Not a Luxury." In *Sister Outsider,* 36–39.
———. *Sister Outsider.* Freedom, CA: Freedom Crossing Press, 1984.
———. "Uses of the Erotic: The Erotic as Power." In *Sister Outsider,* 53–59.
MacCarthy, Desmond. Rev. of *Our Women* by Arnold Bennett. "Books in General." *New Statesman,* October 2, 1920: 704.
———. "The Bubble Reputation." *Life and Letters,* September 1931.
———. Response to Virginia Woolf's letter. "The Intellectual Status of Women." *New Statesman,* October 9, 1920: 15–16.
———. Response to Virginia Woolf's letter. "The Intellectual Status of Women." *New Statesman,* October 16, 1920: 46.
Mansfield, Nick. *Masochism: The Art of Power.* Westport, CT, and London: Praeger, 1997.
Marcus, Jane. "Thinking Back through Our Mothers." *New Feminist Essays on Virginia Woolf.* Ed. Jane Marcus. Lincoln: University of Nebraska Press, 1981. 1–30.
———, ed. *Virginia Woolf and Bloomsbury: A Centenary Collection.* Bloomington: Indiana University Press, 1987.
———. *Virginia Woolf and the Languages of Patriarchy.* Bloomington: Indiana University Press, 1987.
Marcus, Steven. *Representations: Essays on Literature and Society.* New York: Columbia University Press, 1975.
Masse, Michelle A. *In the Name of Love: Women, Masochism, and the Gothic.* Ithaca, NY and London: Cornell University Press, 1992.
Masson, Jeffrey Moussaieff. *The Assault on Truth: Freud's Suppression of the Seduction Theory.* 1984. New York and London: Pocket Books, 1998.
———, ed. *The Complete Letters of Sigmund Freud to Wilhelm Fleiss, 1887–1904.* Trans. Jeffrey Moussaieff Masson. Cambridge, MA, and London: Harvard University Press, 1985.
Maudsley, Henry. "Sex in Mind and Education." *Fortnightly Review* 15 (1874): 466–483.
McNaron, Toni H. "The Uneasy Solace of Art: The Effect of Sexual Abuse on Virginia Woolf's Aesthetic." *Women's Studies: An International Forum.* 15, no. 2 (1992): 251–266.
McVickers, Jeanette, and Laura Davis. *Virginia Woolf and Communities: Proceedings from the Eighth Annual Virginia Woolf Conference.* New York: Pace University Press, 1999.
Meares, Russell. "Episodic Memory, Trauma, and the Narrative of Self." *Contemporary Psychoanalysis* 31, no. 4 (October 1995): 541–556.
Meyers, Diana T. "The Politics of Self-Respect: A Feminist Perspective." *Hypatia* 1, no. 1 (1986): 83–100.
Mezei, Kathy, ed. *Ambiguous Discourse: Feminist Narratology and British Women Writers.* Chapel Hill and London: University of North Carolina Press, 1996.
———."'And It Kept Its Secret': Narration, Memory, and Madness in Jean Rhys' *Wide Sargasso Sea.*" *Critique: Studies in Contemporary Literature* 28 (1987): 195–209.

Miller, Nancy K. *Subject to Change: Reading Feminist Writing*. New York: Columbia University Press, 1988.

Milner, Marion. "The Role of Illusion in Symptom Formation." In *New Directions in Psychoanalysis*. Ed. Melanie Klein, Paula Heimann, and Robert E. Money-Kyrle. New York: Basic Books, 1965. Reprinted in Rudnytsky, 13–39.

Moran, Patricia. "'The Cat Is out of the Bag and It Is a Tom': Desmond MacCarthy and the Writing of *A Room of One's Own*." In *Essays on Transgressive Reading: Reading Over the Lines*. Ed. Georgia Johnston. Lewiston, Queenston, and Lampeter: Edwin Mellen Press, 1997.

———. "Cock-a-doodle-dum: Sexology and the Writing of *A Room of One's Own*." *Women's Studies: An Interdisciplinary Journal* 30 (2001): 477–498.

———. "The Flaw in the Centre: Writing as Hymenal Rupture in Virginia Woolf's Work." *Tulsa Studies in Women's Literature* 17, no. 1 (Spring 1998): 101–121.

———. "Gunpowder Plots: Narrative and Sexual Trauma in Virginia Woolf's Work." In *Virginia Woolf Out of Bounds*. Ed. Jessica Berman. New York: Pace University Press, 2002.

———. *Word of Mouth: Body/Language in Katherine Mansfield and Virginia Woolf*. Charlottesville and London: University of Virginia Press, 1996.

Morrison, Andrew P. *The Culture of Shame*. New York: Ballantine, 1996.

———. "The Eye Turned Inward: Shame and the Self." In Nathanson, 271–291.

———. "Shame, the Ideal Self, and Narcissism." *Contemporary Psychoanalysis* 19, no. 2 (1983): 295–318.

———. *Shame: The Underside of Narcissism*. Hillsdale, NJ: Analytic Press, 1989.

Morrison, Toni. *Playing in the Dark: Whiteness and the Literary Imagination*. Cambridge: Harvard University Press, 1992.

Mudge, Bernard. "Burning Down the House: Sara Coleridge, Virginia Woolf, and the Politics of Literary Revision." *Tulsa Studies in Women's Literature* 5 (1986): 229–250.

Nalbantian, Suzanne. *Memory in Literature: From Rousseau to Neuroscience*. New York: Palgrave Macmillan, 2003.

Nasta, Susheila, ed. *Motherlands: Black Women's Writing from Africa, the Caribbean and South Asia*. London: Women's Press, 1991.

Nathanson, Donald L., ed. *The Many Faces of Shame*. New York and London: Guilford Press, 1987.

———. "The Shame/Pride Axis." In Lewis, 183–205.

———. *Shame and Pride: Affect, Sex, and the Birth of the Self*. New York: Norton, 1992.

———. "A Timetable for Shame." In Nathanson, 1–63.

Nebeker, Helen. *Jean Rhys: Woman in Passage*. Montreal: Eden, 1981.

Noble, Joan Russell, ed. *Recollections of Virginia Woolf by her Contemporaries*. 1972. Great Britain: Sphere Books, 1989.

Noble, Marianne. *The Masochistic Pleasures of Sentimental Literature.* Princeton, NJ: Princeton University Press, 2000.

Noyes, John K. *The Mastery of Submission: Inventions of Masochism.* Ithaca, NY, and London: Cornell University Press, 1997.

Nunez-Harrell, Elizabeth. "The Paradoxes of Belonging: The White West Indian Woman in Fiction." *Modern Fiction Studies* 31, no. 2 (Summer 1985): 281–293.

O'Connor, Teresa F. *Jean Rhys: The West Indian Novels.* New York: New York University Press, 1986.

Olmos, Margarite Fernandez and Lizabeth Paravisini-Gebert, eds. *Sacred Possessions: Vodou, Santeria, Obeah, and the Caribbean.* New Brunswick, New Jersey, and London: Rutgers University Press, 1999.

Paravisini-Gebert, Lizabeth. "Women Possessed: Eroticism and Exoticism in the Representation of Woman as Zombie." In Olmos and Paravisini-Gebert, 37–58.

Pennebaker, James W. *Opening Up: The Healing Powers of Confiding in Others.* New York: William Morrow, 1990.

Penney, Norman, ed. *First Publishers of Truth.* London: Headley Brothers, 1907.

Person, Ethel Specter. "Sexuality as the Mainstay of Identity: Psychoanalytic Perspectives." *Signs* 5, no. 4 (Summer 1980): 605–630.

Philips, Ann, ed. *A Newnham Anthology.* Cambridge: Cambridge University Press, 1979.

Phillips, Anita. *A Defence of Masochism.* London: Faber and Faber, 1998.

Pierpont, Claudia Roth. *Passionate Minds: Women Rewriting the World.* New York: Vintage Books, 2000.

Pinch, Adela. "Female Chatter: Meter, Masochism, and the *Lyrical Ballads.*" *ELH* 55 (1988): 835–852.

Putnum, Frank W. "Pierre Janet and Modern Views of Dissociation." In Horowitz, 116–135.

Radin, Grace. *Virginia Woolf's* The Years: *The Evolution of a Novel.* Knoxville: University of Tennessee Press, 1981.

Rado, Lisa. "Would the Real Virginia Woolf Please Stand Up? Feminist Criticism, the Androgyny Debates, and *Orlando.*" *Women's Studies* 26 (1997): 147–169.

Raine, Kathleen. *The Land Unknown.* London: Hamish Hamilton, 1975.

Raiskin, Judith L. *Snow on the Cane Fields: Women's Writing and Creole Subjectivity.* Minneapolis and London: University of Minnesota Press, 1996.

Raitt, Suzanne. "'The Tide of Ethel': Femininity as Narrative in the Friendship of Ethel Smyth and Virginia Woolf." *Critical Quarterly* 30, no. 4 (1988): 3–21.

Ramchand, Kenneth. "Introduction." *Tales of the Wide Caribbean: Stories by Jean Rhys.* London: Heinemann, 1985. 1–21.

Rashkin, Esther. *Family Secrets and the Psychoanalysis of Narrative.* Princeton, NJ: Princeton University Press, 1992.

Reik, Theodore. *Masochism in Modern Man*. Trans. Margaret H. Beigel and Gertrud M. Kruth. New York: Farrar, Straus, 1941.

Restuccia, Frances L. "Molly in Furs." *Novel* (Winter 1985): 101–116.

Richardson, Alan. "Romantic Voodoo: Obeah and British Culture, 1797-1807." In Olmos and Paravisini-Gebert, 171–194.

Richardson, Dorothy. *Gleanings from the Works of George Fox*. London: Headley Brothers, nd.

———. *The Quakers Past and Present*. New York: Dodge Publishing Company, 1914.

Rieff, Philip. *Fellow Teachers*. New York: Harper and Row, 1973.

Roe, Sue. "'The Shadow of Light': The Symbolic Underworld of Jean Rhys." *Women Reading Women Writers*. Ed. Sue Roe. Brighton: Harvester, 1987. 229–264.

Rosenbaum, S. P., ed. *Women & Fiction: The Manuscript Versions of* A Room of One's Own." By Virginia Woolf. Oxford: Blackwell, 1992.

Rosenman, Ellen Bayuk. A Room of One's Own. *Women Writers and the Politics of Creativity*. New York: Twayne [Masterworks Studies], 1995.

Rudnytsky, Peter L., ed. *Transitional Objects and Potential Spaces: Literary Uses of D. W. Winnicott*. New York: Columbia University Press, 1993.

Ruotolo, Lucio P. *The Interrupted Moment: A View of Virginia Woolf's Novels*. Stanford, CA: Stanford University Press, 1986.

Rylands, George. "George Rylands." In Noble, 168–175.

Savory, Elaine. "'Another Poor Devil of a Human Being...': Jean Rhys and the Novel as Obeah." In Olmos and Paravisini-Gebert, 216–230.

Scalia, Joseph, ed. *The Vitality of Objects: Exploring the Work of Christopher Bollas*. Middletown, CT: Wesleyan University Press, 2002.

Schacter, Daniel. *Searching for Memory: The Brain, the Mind, and the Past*. New York: Basic Books, 1996.

Schafer, Roy. "Problems in Freud's Psychology of Women." *Journal of the American Psychoanalytic Association* 22 (1974): 463–477.

Scharfman, Ronnie. "Mirroring and Mothering in Simone Schwarz-Bart's *Pluie et Vent sur Telumée Miracle* and Jean Rhys's *Wide Sargasso Sea*." *Yale French Studies* 62 (1981): 88–106.

Schwab, Gail M. "Mother's Body, Father's Tongue." In Burke, Schor, and Whitford, 351–378.

Scott, Bonnie Kime, ed. *The Gender of Modernism: A Critical Anthology*. Bloomington and Indiana Polis: Indiana University Press, 1990.

———. *Refiguring Modernism*. Vol. 1: *The Women of 1928*. Bloomington and Indianapolis: Illinois University Press, 1995.

———. *Refiguring Modernism*. Vol. 2: *Postmodern Feminist Readings of Woolf, West, and Barnes*. Bloomington and Indianapolis: Illinois University Press, 1995.

Sedgwick, Eve Kosofsky. "A Poem is Being Written." *Representations* 17 (1987): 110–143.

Sedgwick, Eve Kosofsky, and Adam Frank, eds. *Shame and Its Sisters: A Silvan Tompkins Reader.* Durham, NC: Duke University Press, 1995.

Shengold, Leonard. *Soul Murder: The Effects of Childhood Abuse and Deprivation.* New York: Fawcett Columbine, 1989.

Showalter, Elaine. *The Female Malady: Women, Madness, and English Culture, 1830-1980.* New York: Pantheon Books, 1985.

———. *A Literature of Their Own: British Women Novelists from Bronte to Lessing.* Princeton: Princeton University Press, 1977.

Sienkiewicz, Henryk. *Quo Vadis.* Trans. W. S. Kuniczak. 1896. New York: Hippocrene Books, 1993.

Silverman, Kaja. "Masochism and Male Subjectivity." *Camera Obscura: A Journal of Feminism and Film Theory* 17 (1988): 31–66.

Simpson, Anne B. *Territories of the Psyche: The Fiction of Jean Rhys.* New York and Houndmills, Basingstoke, Hampshire, UK: Palgrave Macmillan, 2005.

Smilowitz, Erika. "Childlike Women and Paternal Men: Colonialism in Jean Rhys's Fiction." *Ariel* 17, no. 4 (October 1986): 93–103.

Smirnoff, V. "The Masochistic Contract." *International Journal of Psychoanalysis* 50 (1969): 665–671.

Smith, Robert McClure. "Dickinson and the Masochistic Aesthetic." *The Emily Dickinson Journal.* 7, no. 2 (1998): 1–21.

———. "'I Don't Dream About It Anymore': The Textual Unconscious of Jean Rhys's *Wide Sargasso Sea.*" *The Journal of Narrative Technique* 26, no. 2 (1996): 113–136.

———. "'A Recent Martyr': The Masochistic Aesthetic of Valerie Martin." *Contemporary Literature* 37 (Fall 1996): 391–415.

———. "The Strange Case of Valerie Martin and Mary Reilly." *Narrative* 1 (Fall 1993): 244–264.

Smith, Sidonie. *Subjectivity, Identity, and the Body: Women's Autobiographical Practices in the Twentieth Century.* Bloomington and Indianapolis: Indiana University Press, 1993.

Smith, Sidonie, and Julia Watson, eds. *Getting A Life: Everyday Uses of Autobiography.* Minneapolis: University of Minnesota Press, 1996.

Snitow, Ann, Christine Stansell, and Sharon Thompson. *Powers of Desire: The Politics of Sexuality.* New York: Monthly Review Press, 1983.

Spiegel, David, Thurman Hunt, and Harvey E. Dondershine. "Dissociation and Hypnotizability in Posttraumatic Stress Disorder." In Horowitz, 243–252.

Staley, Thomas. *Jean Rhys: A Critical Study.* Austin: University of Texas Press, 1979.

Stape, J. H. *Virginia Woolf: Interviews and Recollections.* Iowa City: University of Iowa Press, 1995.

Stekel, Wilhelm. *Frigidity in Woman in Relation to Her Love Life.* 2 vols. Trans. James S. van Teslaar. New York: Boni and Liveright, 1926.

Stevenson, U. K. N. "A Room of One's Own." In Philips, 174–175.

Stoller, Robert J. *Observing the Erotic Imagination.* New Haven and London: Yale University Press, 1985.

———. *Pain and Pleasure: A Psychoanalyst Explores the World of S & M.* New York and London: Plenum Press, 1991.
———. *Perversion: The Erotic Form of Hatred.* New York: Pantheon Books, 1975.
———. *Sexual Excitement: Dynamics of Erotic Life.* New York: Pantheon Books, 1979.
Stopes, Marie. *Marriage in My Time.* London: Rich & Cowan, 1935.
Streip, Katharine. "'Just a Cerebrale': Jean Rhys, Women's Humor, and Ressentiment." *Representations* 45 (Winter 1994): 117–144.
Studlar, Gaylyn. *In the Realm of Pleasure: Von Sternberg, Dietrich, and the Masochistic Aesthetic.* Urbana and Chicago: University of Illinois Press, 1988.
Sturken, Marita. "Narratives of Recovery: Repressed Memory as Cultural Memory." In Bal, Crewe, and Spitzer, 231–248.
Sturluson, Snorri. "The Deluding of Gylfi." *The Prose Edda of Snorri Sturluson: Tales from Norse Mythology.* Selected and translated by Jean I. Young. Berkeley: University of California Press, 1954.
Tal, Kali. *Worlds of Hurt: Reading the Literatures of Trauma.* Cambridge Studies in American Literature and Culture. Cambridge: Cambridge University Press, 1996.
Terr, Lenore C. "Childhood Traumas: An Outline and Overview." In Horowitz, 61–81.
Thomas, Sue. *The Worlding of Jean Rhys.* Westport, CT, and London: Greenwood Press, 1999.
Thurman, Judith. "The Mistress and the Mask." *Ms.* 4, no. 2 (January 1976): 50–53.
Tiffin, Helen. "Mirror and Mask: Colonial Motifs in the Novels of Jean Rhys." *World Literature Written in English* 17, no. 1 (April 1978): 328–341.
Tomkins, Silvan. "Shame." In Nathanson, 133–161.
Van Alphen, Ernst. "Symptoms of Discursivity: Experience, Memory, and Trauma." In Bal, Crewe, and Spitzer, 24–38.
van der Kolk, Bessel A., and van der Hart, Onno. "The Intrusive Past: The Flexibility of Memory and the Engraving of Trauma." In Caruth, 158–182.
Vance, Carole, ed. *Pleasure and Danger: Exploring Female Sexuality.* Boston, London, Melbourne, and Henley: Routledge, 1984.
———. "Pleasure and Danger: Toward a Politics of Sexuality." In Vance, 1–27.
Vaughn, Janet. "Janet Vaughn." In Noble, 96–101.
Walker, Barbara G. *The Woman's Encyclopedia of Myths and Secrets.* San Francisco and New York: Harper and Row, 1983.
Warhol, Robyn R. and Diane Price Herndl. *Feminisms: An Anthology of Literary Theory and Criticism.* Rutgers, NJ: Rutgers University Press, 1991.
Weinberg, Thomas S. "Sadism and Masochism: Sociological Perspectives." In Weinberg and Kamal, 99–112.

Weinberg, Thomas S. and Gerhard Falk. "The Social Organization of Sadism and Masochism." In Weinberg and Kamal, 149–161.

Weinberg, Thomas S. and G. W. Levi Kamal, eds. *S and M: Studies in Sadomasochism*. Buffalo, NY: Prometheus Books, 1983.

Weininger, Otto. *Sex and Character*. 1903. Translated from the 6th ed., 1906. New York: G. P. Putnam, 1906.

Whitford, Margaret. "Irigaray's Body Symbolic." *Hypatia* 6, no. 3 (Fall 1991): 97–110.

———, ed. *The Irigaray Reader*. Oxford and Cambridge, MA: Basil Blackwell, 1991.

———. *Luce Irigaray: Philosophy in the Feminine*. London and New York: Routledge, 1991.

Wiesel, Elie. "Why I Write." *Confronting the Holocaust: The Impact of Elie Wiesel*. Ed. Alvin Rosenfield and Greenburg. Bloomington: Indiana University Press, 1978.

Williams, Linda Meyer. "Recall of Childhood Trauma: A Prospective Study of Women's Memories of Child Sexual Abuse." *Journal of Consulting and Clinical Psychology*. 62, no. 6 (1994): 1167–1176.

———. "Recovered Memories of Abuse in Women with Documented Child Sexual Victimization Histories." *Journal of Traumatic Stress*. 8, no. 4 (1995): 649–673.

Wilson, Lucy. "'Women Must Have Spunks': Jean Rhys's West Indian Outcasts." *Modern Fiction Studies* 32, no. 3 (Autumn 1986): 439–448.

Winnicott, D. W. *The Maturational Processes and the Facilitating Environment: Studies in the Theory of Emotional Development*. New York: International Universities Press, 1965.

———. *From Paediatrics to Psycho-Analysis*. New York: Basic Books, 1975.

———. "Mirror-role of Mother and Family in Child Development." In Winnicott, *Playing and Reality*, 111–118.

———. *Playing and Reality*. London: Tavistock Publications, 1971.

Wisker, Gina, ed. *It's My Party: Reading Twentieth-Century Women's Writing*. London and Boulder, CO: Pluto Press, 1994.

Wolfe, Peter. *Jean Rhys*. Boston: Twayne, 1980.

Wurmser, Leon. *The Mask of Shame*. Baltimore: Johns Hopkins University Press, 1981.

———. *The Power of the Inner Judge: Psychodynamic Treatment of the Severe Neuroses*. Northvale, NJ, and London: Jason Aronson, 2000.

———. "Shame: The Veiled Companion of Narcissism." In Nathanson, 64–92.

Zimring, Rishona. "The Make-up of Jean Rhys's Fiction." *Novel: A Forum on Fiction* 33, no. 2 (Spring 2000): 212–234.

Zwerdling, Alex. *Virginia Woolf and the Real World*. Berkeley: University of California Press, 1986.

Index